Dear Reader,

I'm often asked how I got started as a writer. People are sometimes surprised to find out that I began my career writing romances for Bantam's Loveswept line. Romantic comedy may seem like a far cry from the hard-boiled suspense novels I write now, but they're really not that far apart.

For me, there are two essential components at the core of every good story: characters that a reader can fall in love with and root for, and a mystery—whether it's the mystery of an unsolved crime or the mystery of that most complex and complicated of human emotions, love. Even the most intricate murder plot pales in comparison to the labyrinthine maze of the human heart.

In this special edition, you'll read two of my early romance novels. In *Tempestuous,* Alexandra Gianni is trying to start over with her infant daughter by rebuilding her life and the ramshackle farm she's purchased with the last of her money. Alex's goal of independence may be upset when she meets handsome, aristocratic Christian Atherton, who could lead her dangerously astray. . . . In *The Restless Heart,* you'll meet Danielle Hamilton, a world-renowned, globe-trotting photographer who didn't think she'd ever survive six weeks babysitting her sister's five small children in New Orleans. But then she meets the nanny . . . tall, dark, and Cajun Remy Doucet, who doesn't accept Danielle's claim that true love isn't in the cards for her.

I enjoyed writing these novels years ago, and I hope that you'll be entertained by the journeys of these heroines and heroes.

All my best,

Tami Hoag

Tami Hoag

## BANTAM BOOKS BY TAMI HOAG

THE ALIBI MAN
PRIOR BAD ACTS
KILL THE MESSENGER
DARK HORSE
DUST TO DUST
ASHES TO ASHES
A THIN DARK LINE
GUILTY AS SIN
NIGHT SINS
DARK PARADISE
CRY WOLF
STILL WATERS
LUCKY'S LADY
THE LAST WHITE KNIGHT
STRAIGHT FROM THE HEART

TAMI HOAG

# *Tempestuous*

# *The Restless Heart*

BANTAM BOOKS

TEMPESTUOUS / THE RESTLESS HEART
A Bantam Book / August 2007

Published by Bantam Dell
A Division of Random House, Inc.
New York, New York

These are works of fiction. Names, characters, places, and incidents either are the product of the author's imagination or are used fictitiously. Any resemblance to actual persons, living or dead, events, or locales is entirely coincidental.



ISBN 978-0-553-38520-5

These titles were originally published individually by Bantam Books.

Printed in the United States of America
Published simultaneously in Canada

www.bantamdell.com

10 9 8 7 6 5 4 3 2 1
OPM

# *Tempestuous*

To all the readers who wrote me
and asked for Christian's story.

This one's for you.

# one

**"GOOD LORD, SHE'S LOVELY!" CHRISTIAN** Atherton murmured, his accent carrying the undiluted, polished tones of a British public-school student. As he came to attention his shoulders pulled back beneath the fine wool of his navy jacket. His square chin came up a notch above his neatly knotted maroon tie, emphasizing the classic lines of his lean face. In response to the tensing of his muscles his horse shifted restively beneath him.

His attention was locked on the young woman riding into the show ring to collect a blue ribbon. He'd been a connoisseur of women for nearly twenty-two years, ever since the summer he'd turned thirteen and the gardener's daughter had suddenly developed breasts. The lady he had his eye on now was well worth a long look.

"Who is she?"

"Where have you been? Living in a cave?" drawled Robert Braddock, his voice as rich and Southern as pecan pie. His wide mouth cut upward in a sharp, handsome smile. He leaned lazily against the pommel of his saddle, showing none of the form that had made him one of the top hunter-jumper trainers in Virginia at the tender age of twenty-seven.

"Close," Christian said dryly. "I've just spent three weeks in

England at the family mausoleum, better known as Westerleigh Manor. Uncle Richard passed away."

Braddock's manners asserted themselves, and he straightened in his saddle out of respect for the dead. "I'm sorry, Chris."

"Don't be." Christian grinned at his friend and rival, a brilliant square white smile that made him look exactly what he was—handsome, aristocratic, and a bit of a rake. "Uncle Dicky was ninety-seven. He drank like a fish, drove like a maniac, and died—er—in the saddle, so to speak. He had a wonderful life and a pleasant passing. We should all be so lucky."

His neon-blue eyes took on a slightly wistful expression, and the glittering good humor that usually resided there faded momentarily as he sighed. Uncle Dicky was dead. The stuffy Athertons were down to one black sheep—him.

"Alexandra Gianni," Braddock said, answering Christian's original question. "Cold as a pump handle on a January morning," he added in ill-disguised disgust.

"Turned you down, did she?" Christian said dryly, arching a brow.

"She's been here three weeks and has managed to say one word to every fella who's asked her out—no."

"Well, that just shows she has good taste and sound judgment."

"I suppose you think you can do better?"

"Please," Christian drawled disdainfully. "Of course I could do better. Admit it, Braddock, you've won your share of dimwitted stable girls, but you're simply not in my league."

"You pompous ass," Braddock said with a good-natured grin. "I'll bet you don't get anywhere with her either. You might be the Casanova of the show-jumping world, but this lady would give the iceberg that sank the *Titanic* a run for its money."

Christian's speculative gaze settled again on Alexandra Gianni. She didn't look the ice-maiden type to him. With her olive complexion and dark eyes, her unruly short black hair and lush mouth, she looked more like the hot, feisty type. Tempestuous. The type to stand toe-to-toe with a man in a fight and rake her nails down his back in bed.

Braddock turned and grinned at him suddenly. "How much do you want to bet?"

"I beg your pardon?"

"Put your money where your mouth is, Romeo," he challenged. "I'll bet you a hundred dollars you can't get her to go with you to Hayden Hill's big bash before the Green Hills Jumper Classic."

Christian barked a laugh of surprise that startled his horse. The thoroughbred danced beneath him, and he quieted the gelding with a hand on the horse's neck, never taking his eyes off Braddock. "That's more than a month away! Have you developed a sudden yearning for poverty?"

"You forget, my friend," Braddock said slyly. "I've spoken with the lady. I have firsthand experience and the frostbite to prove it. A hundred says she won't go with you."

Christian considered the outrageous wager for a moment. It appealed to the reckless rogue in him, the quality that made his stiff-necked family shake their heads in disappointment. He thought of what Uncle Dicky would have done, and grinned. "Make it a thousand and it's a deal."

Braddock's dark eyes glowed with delight and greed. "You've got yourself a bet, my friend."

# two

**"GOOD JOB, HONEY," TULLY HASKELL SAID** in parting.

Alex murmured a thank-you and turned toward the stalls she had rented for the day. She jumped and gasped when the man patted her fanny, but when she wheeled to glare at him, he was calmly walking away as if what he'd done hadn't been the least bit out of line.

Alex stood in the aisle, fuming for a moment, then turned to stare pensively at the stalls of her two star performers, both owned by Haskell. A Touch of Dutch, the sweet-tempered mare she'd just won on, and Terminator, an arrogant, ill-mannered lout—not unlike his owner. That was the world in a nutshell. Females were meek and malleable, and males took what they wanted.

Everything inside Alex tightened against the memory that tried to surface. Squeezing her eyes shut, she fought it with every scrap of willpower she had, succeeding only in fighting back the images themselves, not the feelings they evoked. Her muscles tensed until she was trembling.

When a large male hand settled on her shoulder, she didn't think, didn't question, didn't turn to confront. She simply reacted as she had been trained to react. A second later Christian Atherton lay sprawled on the cobbled floor at her feet.

Alex stared, wide-eyed, aghast at what she'd just done. She had just heaved the three-time American Grand Prix Association Rider of the Year over her shoulder. She had just slammed to the floor one of the most highly regarded people in her profession.

"Oh, no..." Her groan mingled with his. She slapped a hand to her forehead and cursed herself in rapid Italian.

Christian sat up gingerly, wincing at the stinging pain in his shoulders and back. He'd been thrown from horses with less force. Shaking his head to clear it, he looked up at Alexandra Gianni with a stunned expression. Petite, dainty Alexandra Gianni, who stood no more than five feet five.

"I say, are you a former commando or something?"

"I'm sorry," Alex whispered, too mortified to speak any louder. She bit her lip and squeezed her eyes shut again, wishing the scene would disappear by the time she opened them.

This was no way to build a favorable reputation in Virginia, she scolded herself. Flinging influential people around was not going to win her friends or respect. She had learned to live without the first, but the second was essential.

She put a hand over her eyes and peeked cautiously through her fingers. Christian was still sitting on the stable floor. He had taken up a relaxed pose, with one knee drawn up and an arm draped across it. He stared down the corridor at the half-dozen people staring back at him, a look of annoyance drawing his brows together and twisting his handsome mouth. His champagne blond hair fell rakishly across his forehead. All in all, he looked damned sexy.

Alex imagined he looked that way regardless. Her heart was pounding, and she knew it had little to do with the exertion of throwing him over her shoulder. She could have told herself it was because he had startled her. She could have told herself it had nothing to do with the fact that Christian Atherton was even better looking in person than he was on the glossy pages of the horse magazines. She could have told herself those things, but they would have been lies.

"I'm really so sorry," she mumbled in an agony of embarrassment.

"So you said. Do you always go about throwing chaps to the ground, or was I singled out?" he questioned, his cultured tone martini dry.

"You snuck up on me!" Alex said accusingly, tossing her hands up, then grabbing them back against her as if she were trying to recapture and subdue her emotional outburst. She looked more guilty for having openly reacted than for hurling Christian to the cobblestones. Taking a calming breath, she composed herself and said, "You shouldn't have snuck up on me."

"I see." Christian's brows rose and fell. There was a whole passel of odd mysteries to decipher just in her action and reaction. He shook his head again. "Well, I've always known better than to approach a horse from behind. I guess I should add women to that rule of thumb as well."

"I'm really very sorry," Alex said, contrite again, holding out a hand to help him up.

Christian eyed her hand dubiously. "I'm not sure I should accept that," he said dryly. "Do you promise not to twist my arm behind my back and slam me face first into a post?"

Alex couldn't help but laugh in both relief and humor. He was taking it better than most men would have. She had humiliated him in front of his peers, and he was looking up at her with twinkling blue eyes and a wry, self-deprecating smile.

Her own smile faded as she realized how easily he had breached her mental defenses with that infamous grin of his. Professionally, he would be a very good man to befriend. Personally, he would be a very dangerous man for her to be around.

"I'll be on my best behavior," she promised soberly.

"That may not be saying very much," Christian teased, taking hold of her small hand. "But I guess I'll have to trust you."

He rose gracefully to his feet, somehow managing not to look rumpled in the least. Not even his maroon necktie was out of place, Alex marveled as she gazed up at him, unable to keep from admiring his appearance.

He wasn't overly tall, perhaps an inch or so shy of six feet, but his physique was athletic and elegant. His shoulders filled his custom-tailored coat to perfection. His hips were narrow, his thighs the thighs of dancers and horsemen—powerful with long, solid muscles that were blatantly displayed by the tight knit of his expensive buff breeches. The black boots that rose to his knees were impeccably polished.

While Alex looked him over, Christian returned the favor, though his perusal was much slower, much more openly appreciative than her surreptitious glances. His gaze poured down over her with all the slow heat of sun-warmed honey, taking in her petite frame as if she were much taller, infinitely more voluptuous, and clad in something far sexier than riding togs.

Alex almost looked down to make certain her jacket and breeches hadn't somehow been miraculously transformed into a diaphanous negligee. She felt stripped naked by his blue eyes, and as a flush spread under her skin, she hooked a finger beneath the choker of her blouse and tugged at it in an attempt to breathe easier.

Christian smiled to himself, well aware of her reaction to his slow assessment of her, and well aware of his own body's response. He liked what he saw.

Her hair shone blue black under the soft light of the stable. It was cut severely short on the sides and in back, but was longer on top, thick and wild with a tendency to spill across her forehead. The boyishness of the cut did nothing to detract from the almost pixielike femininity of her features. In fact, the simplicity of the style drew the eye to appreciate the delicate lines of her oval face—the high, well-defined cheekbones, the slim straight nose, the lush pouty mouth. Christian groaned inwardly, desire stirring deep in his belly. Very kissable, that mouth.

Continuing on with the visual tour he realized there was a slightly defiant tilt to her chin. Sassy. And her eyes were not the dark brown he had thought them to be, but a dark translucent shade of amber set with flecks of gold: Beautiful, intense, and . . . what? . . . wary? How odd.

Alex shifted uncomfortably and tried to extricate her hand from his grasp. He held it firmly but gently. There was nothing punishing or aggressive in his grasp. He merely let her know with a slight tightening of his fingers that he wasn't quite ready to let go of her. No wonder his horses were so good, she thought. With hands like his there would be no fighting the bit; he would simply guide, quietly insist, and get his way every time—just as he was getting his way now.

"Let's pretend you didn't try to permanently disable me, and we'll begin this conversation again," he suggested, his dazzling smile still in place.

"I suppose I can't pass up an offer like that," Alex said, doing her best to ignore the warm sliding sensation in her stomach. She couldn't afford to let Christian Atherton affect her in that way. They were simply fellow professional riders. The fact that he was charmingly, deliciously male, and she was susceptibly female, couldn't enter into it.

Christian resisted the urge to grind his teeth at her less-than-enthusiastic reply. She didn't have to sound so bloody resigned about it. Didn't she realize there were plenty of women who would have fought her tooth and nail for the chance to hold his hand? And she would likely knock them all flat, he thought, unable to suppress his amusement.

"Christian Atherton," he said, giving her a smile.

Television didn't do him justice, Alex thought. On television

Christian Atherton was merely handsome. In person, he was dazzling. He had the air of a prince—self-assured, confident of his own brilliant qualities and the responses those qualities would elicit from the mere mortals around him.

It almost made Alex laugh to think he had introduced himself. As if there weren't a girl or woman interested in horses who didn't know him on sight! Christian Atherton was the golden boy of the show-jumping world. His career accomplishments included wins at every major show in America and abroad. He also had a notorious reputation for being a playboy. By all accounts he had garnered as many feminine hearts as he had blue ribbons over the years. It wasn't difficult to imagine why.

No, Alex thought wryly, it wasn't difficult to imagine why this man had women falling at his booted feet. The difficult thing was keeping her own feminine reaction to his aristocratic looks to herself. Fortunately—or unfortunately—she had had plenty of practice at hiding her emotions over the past couple of years. Her expression remained carefully blank, giving away none of her inner turmoil.

"I'm Alex Gianni. What can I do for you, Mr. Atherton?" Alex asked neutrally. This time when she pulled back her hand, he let her go.

"Call me Christian, for starters," he said smoothly. "I'm afraid I had the frightfully bad manners to be abroad when you moved into the neighborhood. I haven't had a chance to welcome you to Briarwood, Ms. Gianni. I insist on making it up to you. What do you say to lunch tomorrow and a little motor tour of the area?"

Oh, no, Alex thought, groaning inwardly as her heart jumped and sank. Another one. What was it about her that attracted so much male attention? She really couldn't figure it out. She didn't think herself particularly beautiful. She didn't have the kind of figure to turn male heads. She wasn't the least bit flirtatious or even encouraging. She had, in fact, done everything she could think of to *avoid* attracting attention of any kind. Still, in the three weeks since she and her baby daughter Isabella had settled on the little farm outside of Briarwood, she'd had no less than a half-dozen offers for dates.

And now Christian Atherton, the man whose poster adorned the bedrooms of every horse-crazy girl in the Western world, had set his sights on her. It was too ironic. At some point in her past she would have been flattered at having him merely speak to her, let alone ask her out. She would have been bubbling over with excitement. But those days were past. Now she was simply rattled and vaguely disappointed.

"I'm sorry, Mr. Atherton," she said with deceptive calm. "I'm afraid I don't have much time for that kind of thing. Thank you for offering, though."

"Come now," Christian insisted. "We should get to know each other, don't you think?"

The glow in his laser blue eyes made his suggestion seem much more intimate than neighborly. He stood half a step closer than was strictly necessary—close enough to make Alex uncomfortably aware of him, and yet not so close that she had a good excuse to move away. The man was a master and he knew it. The teasing lights in his eyes told Alex he knew exactly what he was doing to her and that he knew she knew. It was all a marvelous game to him, charming women into joining the ranks of his conquests. Everyone was aware up front what the rules and the stakes were—fun, nothing serious; no harm, no foul.

Alex felt herself relaxing and realized it was dangerous. Christian Atherton may not have been threatening, but he was a threat—one she had to nip in the bud. She acknowledged the truth with a frighteningly strong sense of regret. It might have been fun. . . .

"I know all about you," she said, a wry smile lifting one corner of her wide mouth.

"My reputation has preceded me?" He quirked a brow and

looked immensely pleased with himself. It was an expression that changed quickly to a comical scowl when she answered.

"Sure. My mother warned me about men like you when I turned thirteen."

"Surely you didn't listen," Christian chided, his eyes sparkling with good humor.

No, Alex thought, glancing away, her own teasing expression melting into sudden pensiveness, she hadn't listened. Maybe if she had listened, she would still have been married, would still have been in California, would still have the unqualified, untried support of her family. But she hadn't listened, and now all of those things were lost to her.

"I prefer the smile," Christian murmured gently, leaning closer. He didn't know where she'd gone in those few seconds, but it wasn't a happy place. She looked haunted and regretful, and he felt a strong desire to put his arms around her in a show of comfort, but he doubted she would have appreciated the gesture. Instead, he reached out and brushed her wild black curls back from her forehead, leaning closer so that when he spoke his voice was just above a whisper, smooth and velvety. "The gold flecks in your eyes light up when you smile."

For a moment Alex merely stared at him, mesmerized by his gaze, his voice, the gentle concern in his eyes. It felt strange to be so close to him, to be enveloped by the awesome power of his personality. In a way it felt as intimate as anything she had ever encountered, and yet they weren't even touching. It was intoxicating . . . and dangerous.

Finally she shook herself out of her brooding reverie and looked up at him, suddenly all business, self-preservation uppermost in her mind. "I might as well tell you straight out to save your charm, Mr. Atherton. It's wasted on me."

"Charm is never wasted on a beautiful woman," Christian argued, lifting his chin up a notch. He planted one hand on the stall door beside her and leaned a millimeter closer.

He'd played this hard-to-get game before. It required determination, but it was always worth the extra effort. There was fire beneath Alexandra Gianni's ice. He could see it in her amber eyes, in the stubborn set of her chin, in the line of that lush, lush mouth. He wanted to be the one to melt the ice and bring that fire out. He wanted to be the one to feel those flames lick over him and consume him.

It had nothing to do with the wager. He didn't need the money, nor did his ego need the boost. It had to do with challenge. It had to do with feelings that dated back to the first man and woman, feelings that were a little more primitive than what he was used to feeling. They intrigued him. Alex intrigued him.

"Thank you for the compliment," Alex murmured, pressing back against the post between her stalls in an unconscious effort to escape not only the man but the force of his personality as well.

Her resolve wavered as she took in the frankly appreciative look Christian was giving her. That warm sliding sensation stirred her insides again as her own gaze settled on his mouth. It was wide and mobile with firm, well-cut lips and a seemingly endless repertoire of sexy smiles.

She couldn't help but wonder what it would be like to have him kiss her. The thought was unwanted, unwelcome, but it managed to get past her considerable will just the same. It had been so long since she'd had a man kiss her with the kind of tenderness and passion she instinctively knew this one was capable of. She'd been so alone for so long....

He read the message in her eyes unerringly and lowered his head a fraction of an inch in invitation, his lips hovering just a breath above hers. But before she could take him up on his offer, her defenses reasserted themselves and she ducked away, kneeling to dig her gloves out of her gear bag.

What was the matter with her, she wondered angrily. Her hands were shaking as she fussed unnecessarily with the big red duffel bag that held all her personal paraphernalia. She knew exactly what Christian Atherton was. He was a rake and a womanizer, and she didn't have the time or the desire to play his kind of game. Nor would he want to play with her once they had gotten to know each other. Lord knew he would probably set a new sprint record getting away from her once he discovered who she really was.

"Merely stating fact," Christian drawled, leaning lazily against the narrow post. "If a woman is beautiful, she deserves to be told."

"And if she's not?"

He grinned. "Then I tell her anyway."

He was by nature a flatterer. It was a skill he had perfected as a child. Even at the tender age of four he had known the fairer sex enjoyed praise. He'd filled his piggy bank time and again with the quarters his aunts and his mother's friends had rewarded him with for his astute observations.

In Alex's case it was entirely justified. She was very lovely in a sophisticated way. The longer he looked at her, the more he liked what he saw. Hers was a beauty that was at once subtle and exotic, and he realized with a start that she wasn't wearing a scrap of makeup, not even mascara, nothing to emphasize or draw the eye. He also realized that she wasn't entirely comfortable with his compliment or his scrutiny. He got the distinct impression she would rather he had not noticed her at all.

He watched with a mixture of confusion and amusement as she busied herself taking items out of her bag and putting them back in. She was rattled, and she clearly didn't like being rattled. Information worth filing away for future reference, he noted.

"You're extremely tidy," he said pleasantly, bending over to peer into her gear bag. When he turned his head toward her, he was again within kissing distance. He smiled lazily. "A quality nearly as priceless as your looks."

Alex flushed, suddenly hot beneath her proper white cotton

blouse and charcoal jacket. "Care to look at my teeth while you're at it?" she asked dryly.

"I have," he admitted. "They're adorable. I like the way the front two on top overlap slightly. Gives you a certain innocent quality."

"Complimenting women is a hobby of yours." She said it as if he would be put off by her knowing that about him.

Christian chuckled. "More like a calling, actually."

"You do it very well," Alex said, the corners of her mouth cutting upwards as that dangerous relaxation stole through her again. She couldn't seem to resist the urge to like him. His irreverently charming manner made it difficult to think he could ever be a danger to her.

"Thank you," he said, straightening only to lean indolently against a stall door once again, as if he found it necessary to reserve his strength for more important things than standing around.

"But you're wasting your time on me if you think anything will come of it," Alex warned, struggling once more to resurrect her cool reserve. She pushed herself to her feet and tugged on her thin black leather gloves. "I've got a stable to run and a daughter to raise. I'm afraid my schedule doesn't allow for flirtations."

His brows lifted in a show of mock surprise and shock. "Doesn't allow?" He shook his head and sighed dramatically. "My dear girl, flirtations are an essential part of life—like good horses and really fine wine."

Alex looked up at him, frustrated. She was trying to be serious, trying to set things straight between them right off. She couldn't afford another misunderstanding; the last one had cost her too much. She didn't want there to be any question in Christian Atherton's mind about her intentions. And he had the gall to stand there and tease her, looking impossibly handsome and terribly British and damned sexy.

He shot her an infectious, lopsided grin that easily cracked all her barriers as if they had been constructed of eggshells. She shook her head in amazement and managed a weary laugh. "You don't give up easily, do you?"

"I never give up," Christian declared, the unmistakable steely glint of determination brightening his eyes and threading through his smooth, pleasant voice. "I am on rare occasions beaten, but I *never* give up."

"You're doomed to defeat this time. I feel it only fair to warn you."

He clearly didn't believe her. Of course, she couldn't have expected him to. Men like Christian Atherton had a boundless belief in their own appeal to women. Most of them came across as arrogant. This one came across as endearing. Alex would have preferred the arrogance; it was much easier to resist.

"We'll see," he said absently. "You have a daughter. Can I assume you're divorced? I'd hate to discover I've set my sights on a married lady. That is my one absolutely unbreakable rule—no married ladies."

"It's nice to know you have at least one scruple," Alex reflected dryly. "Yes, I'm divorced."

There didn't seem to be any harm in revealing that much about her background. The alternative—letting people believe Isabella had been born out of wedlock—went too strongly against her grain. Her daughter had in fact been born after her divorce from Michael DeGrazia, but she had been conceived in love, regardless of what Michael chose to think. It wasn't Isabella's fault her parents' marriage hadn't been able to withstand the pressure inflicted on it by forces both from the outside and from within.

"Recently divorced?"

She gave Christian an apologetic look and moved to the door of Terminator's stall. "I'd love to stand around here and play *This Is Your Life*, but I have a competition to get ready for."

"After then? Over dinner?" he said with another of his smiles. "There's an excellent Italian restaurant in Briarwood. The owner is a friend of mine."

"Then maybe she'll eat with you," Alex suggested sweetly. "I have chores to do and a baby to take care of."

"All right," Christian said on a good-humored sigh. He bowed slightly. "I concede round one to you, Ms. Gianni. What competition are you getting ready for?"

"Open Jumper."

She swung the stall door open and let Christian get his first good look at her mount. His eyes widened in horror.

"Oh my Lord, it can't be," he muttered, staring. But there was no mistaking the big, rawboned, washy chestnut gelding with the distinctive crooked white stripe running down his face. "I thought they'd shot him."

"Not yet," Alex said through her teeth. It was one thing for her to think nasty things of the horses she trained—and she had plenty about this one—but having a fellow trainer express those same thoughts aloud was another thing altogether. It rankled.

Christian turned away from the horse and gave her an incredulous look as a riot of unfamiliar feelings tore loose inside him. There was a strangely urgent note in his voice when he said, "You can't be serious about riding this beast."

"It's what I get paid to do," she said stiffly, shoving her helmet down on her head and buckling the chin strap.

"There isn't enough money in the commonwealth of Virginia to make it worth your while."

Your opinion, Alex thought darkly. It would be easy for him to refuse horses like Terminator. Quaid Farm, the stable Christian rode for, had paddocks full of top-quality, beautifully bred, beautifully behaved animals. Christian also reportedly had enough money of his own to make riding strictly a hobby. She, on the other hand, had to charge bargain rates, beg for mounts, and be grateful even for evil-tempered jugheads like Terminator.

"I'm serious, Alex," Christian said, and indeed he was. The corners of his handsome mouth were turning down. A line of disapproval etched itself between his eyebrows. He looked as serious as a banker. "I've never had the misfortune of riding Terminator myself, but I am well aware of the horse's reputation. It actually frightens me to think of you climbing up on that animal's back. You can't weigh much more than seven stone, and you don't look particularly strong. That beast is as big as a freight train with a mouth like granite and a disturbed, diabolical mind."

As if to illustrate the point Terminator struck out at him with a front foot as he was led from the stall, and Christian had to jump back out of the way or lose a kneecap. Eyes flashing, ears pinned, the gelding danced restlessly in the aisle while Alex snugged up the girth on her saddle.

"You're new around here," Christian said, planting his hands on his slim hips. "That's the only way anyone ever gets on this brute. I saw him in a point-to-point race at Oatlands before he began his show career. He went berserk at the ninth fence and ran himself into a tree. Pity he wasn't killed," he muttered, shaking his head. "That was when it was decided that he would be better off confined to jumping in an arena." He eyed the gelding with open dislike. "He's changed hands more times than a bad used car. Who owns him now?"

"Tully Haskell."

"Bloody hell."

It was on the tip of his tongue to give Alex his undiluted opinion of the man she was riding for, but she had her hands full trying to get Terminator out of the barn without incident. Muttering under his breath about men who take advantage of innocent women, Christian nudged Alex aside, took the recalcitrant animal by the bridle, and coerced him out into the bright April sunshine.

Alex slapped her crop against her boot and fumed, her ready

temper rising to the surface. Who did he think he was, telling her what horeses she should or should not ride, what owners she should or should not do business with? Who did he think he was, charming her off her feet one minute, then belittling her judgment and her ability the next?

"I'll take my horse now, Mr. Atherton," she said, deftly avoiding Terminator's teeth as she reached for his reins.

Christian refused to let go of the horse's head. He gave Alex a grave look that would have done his stuffier relatives proud. "If you have any sense, you'll send both this rogue and his owner packing. They're nothing but trouble, the pair of them."

"Thank you for sharing your opinion with me," she said with a sneer. Leaving the reins to him, she went to the horse's side and vaulted quickly into the saddle. Terminator danced, shaking his head violently against Christian's hold. Alex gathered up the reins and settled her feet firmly in the irons. She looked down at Christian with golden fire snapping in her eyes. "I don't have the luxury of picking and choosing my clients, Mr. Atherton. This horse can jump, and I can ride him. It's not always fun, but it's what I get paid to do, and since I don't have a family fortune to fall back on, I do it without complaint."

Christian winced at the dressing-down. He'd obviously struck a nerve. Dammit, it wasn't like him to go spouting off that way, telling other people what to do. His brothers had made careers of it, but he had always adhered to a strict laissez-faire policy. It was none of his business what other people did with their lives. Why he had suddenly deviated from that philosophy, he didn't know. It was clear, however, that Alex hadn't appreciated it.

"Alex, I'm sorry—" he started.

"Tell someone who cares," she said, her concentration on her horse. Terminator's muscles were bunched and trembling beneath her. It was like sitting on a volcano that was ready to blow. Already there were dark stains of sweat on his neck and foam edging his mouth.

She shot Christian a glance, the genuine apology and concern in his eyes going straight to her heart. She gave him a lopsided smile. "You can wish me luck."

"Yes." He nodded, letting go of the bridle and waving her off.

The big gelding bounded away, struggling furiously for control of the bit for five strides before giving in and settling into a strong, ground-eating canter.

Christian sighed and shifted his weight from foot to foot, physically uncomfortable with his sudden overwhelming concern for another person. He thought of himself as the consummate bachelor, concerned with only his own needs, responsible for no one but himself. That was the way he had lived his entire life.

As the fourth son of the Earl of Westly, he was far down the line when it came to looking after the family business. His stiff-necked older brothers had taken up those reins of responsibility, leaving him to take up reins of another kind.

He had signed on as trainer at Quaid Farm because he hadn't wanted the responsibility of running his own place. He had remained single because he had never wanted the responsibility of a wife. And now he stood watching Alexandra Gianni fighting with that devil of a horse, feeling responsible because he hadn't convinced her to stay off the ruddy beast!

Gads. What would Uncle Dicky have said?

"Losing your touch, your lordship?" a sardonic voice drawled from beside him.

Christian dragged his attention away from Alex, who had taken Terminator across the field to work off his initial burst of hatefulness, and turned toward the source of the amused drawl. Robert Braddock stood beside him, idly paging through the catalog of a pricey tack shop. Braddock was just his equal in height, but stockier and swarthy. In another era he could have been a pirate or a Gypsy. The beginnings of laughter twitched the corners of his lips and sent lines fanning out beside his dark eyes.

"What do you want?" Christian asked irritably. He had no doubt Robert had ferreted out every detail of the undignified greeting he'd received from Alex in the alleyway of the stable. It wouldn't have surprised him had Braddock somehow managed to produce a videotape of his humiliation. Robert took great pride in being the first on the show circuit to know everything about anything that was going on. It was a trait Christian had always found irksome; he generally considered gossip beneath his dignity. He narrowed his eyes now and tried to think of the most conspicuous, frivolous, insulting way he could spend his friend's money once he won the bet.

"What's this? Bad manners from my British buddy?" Robert teased mercilessly, his dark eyes dancing. "My, my, what would the queen say?"

"She'd say you were an obnoxious pig. Do go away."

"Ah, well, I've got better things to think about, like how I'm gonna spend my thousand bucks. Think I'll start with a new pair of custom-made boots."

"I'll feed you the ones you're wearing in a minute," Christian said, his ego smarting just a little too much to have his pal pour salt on the wound.

"Tsk, tsk, Christian," Braddock said, shaking his head. "Your frostbite is showing."

"Shove off."

Robert sighed happily and turned a page in his catalog. "I'm just thinking I might buy myself a new jacket to go with the boots. Think I'd look good in pinstripes?"

Christian raised a disdainful brow. "Considering where you normally shop, I should think you could replace your entire wardrobe twice over for a thousand dollars, but that's irrelevant. You shan't have the money."

"Oh, really? I think that little tumble you took over Ms. Gianni's shoulder rattled your brains, friend. Too bad you weren't wearing your helmet. There're some good ones in this catalog," he said slyly, fanning the pages in Christian's face. "Maybe I'll be nice and buy you one with your own money."

Christian gave him a long, cool look, then smiled like a crocodile. "I am going to take great delight in humiliating you with your cash, Robert. I wonder what billboards cost these days."

"You'll never need to know." Braddock folded the catalog and tucked it beneath one arm. "Just to make things clear up front—you do realize this has to be an honest-to-gosh date you get with her. You have to escort her to the party, eat with her, dance with her, and kiss her in full view of everybody."

"Really, Robert," Christian said with distaste, "you can be absolutely adolescent."

"Those are the terms," Braddock said, unruffled. "Agreed?"

Christian rolled his eyes. "Agreed."

He could, after all, be just as adolescent as the next man. There was no reason for him not to be. He had no one to answer to. There was no harm in a little wager between gentlemen. It wasn't as if the lady in question would be hurt in any way. They would both enjoy a nice night out, Christian would be a thousand dollars richer, and Robert would be a poorer but wiser man. It seemed a good deal all around.

They turned their attention to Alex and Terminator as she worked him in circles in their own private corner of the field, staying well away from the other horses and riders.

"What do you know about her?" Christian asked.

"Not much more than I already told you. She's renting that place down the hill from you, taking on horses to train and show. Got some girls taking lessons from her. But as far as where she came from and how she got here—that's a mystery."

"Hmmm..." Christian mused, his curiosity more than piqued by Alex Gianni. "I do love a good mystery."

"Well, pal, you'd better hit the bookstore then and stock up, because that little lady isn't interested in playing Sherlock and Dr. Watson with anybody."

"We'll see."

"Look at the way she sits that old boy," Braddock said in admiration. "Deep in the saddle, solid as a rock. She's good."

"Yes, quite," Christian agreed. "Too good to be getting herself killed on the likes of that ill-bred nag. Tully Haskell has sunk to a new low, foisting Terminator off on an unsuspecting young woman. If she gets hurt..." The threat trailed off as he realized what he was saying.

A shudder snaked through his lean body. Where had this sudden virtuous streak come from? It wasn't any of his business what went on between Alex Gianni and Tully Haskell. It certainly wasn't his place to act as either guardian or avenging angel. Good Lord, he wasn't now, nor did he ever want to be, responsible for Alex Gianni or anyone else!

"You all right?" Robert asked, concerned. "You're looking a mite pale."

"I'm fine," Christian muttered. "Just the leftover bits of something I picked up in England."

"Speaking of things you picked up in England," Braddock drawled sardonically as his gaze homed in on the slim young woman striding toward them in fashionably tattered jeans and a black-leather motorcycle jacket.

Christian groaned from the bottom of his heart.

"Blimey, gov, I heard you flipped for some bird in the stables!" the woman exclaimed, her cockney accent ringing out as loudly as the bells of Saint Mary's Church. She stopped several feet away from them, doubling over as she dissolved into a fit of laughter. "Flipped! Crikey, I'd 'a' killed to see that! His nibs sprawled out on the cobblestones, tossed over by a lady!"

"Charlotte, must you always use a tone of voice loud enough to drown out aircraft engines?" Christian hissed between his teeth.

The girl's outburst had drawn amused stares from all around them. Snickers went through the little knots of people like ripples moving outward from one loud splash in a pond. There was no hope of keeping the little incident with Alex a secret, of course, but he would have preferred to have had the gossip spread by someone other than one of his own grooms.

She laughed, waving a hand at him. "Oh, go on! Ain't nobody here what hasn't heard the tale half a dozen times already!" she exclaimed, dropping all the *H*s off her words in typical East End fashion.

Braddock rubbed a hand across his jaw to discreetly cover his grin. Christian turned a dull red and spoke through clenched teeth. "Charlotte, you are the bane of my existence."

"Oh, go on!" She laughed and batted his arm, not contrite in the least.

Charlotte "Charlie" Simmonds was eighteen, a petite cockney firecracker with an accent as thick as London fog, and burgundy hair, which she wore combed straight up. It was shorn off on the top and looked as thick and flat as the yew hedges in Windsor Great Park. Christian suspected she got it to stay up that way through sheer stubbornness. Her face was still slightly round with baby fat and striking due to an overabundance of eye makeup and dark lipstick. A cluster of earrings dangled from her right lobe. The left one held a single garnet stud.

She was the niece of Old Ned, head stable lad at Westerleigh Manor. "A bright, precocious girl," Ned had called her. "Needs to see a bit o' the world, is all," he'd said. "Her dad run off and her mum drinks a bit, and there's no proper jobs about for a girl her age."

There had been a kind of desperation in his eyes at the time, and Christian could only wonder now why he hadn't taken heed of the signs. Ned had fairly begged him to take the girl back to Virginia with him. He had yet to figure out why he had said yes.

"You might be slipping, luv," Charlie said, digging him in the ribs with her bony elbow. "The ladies are supposed to fall at your feet, not the other way round!"

Christian bit back half a dozen different remarks, all along the lines of "mind your betters." He cursed a royal blue streak under his breath. Each and every one of those remarks were things his brothers might have said to the servants. One couldn't say those sorts of things in America. According to ideology no one had any "betters" here. It was one of the reasons he had moved to the States—to get away from the blue blooded, stuffy class system he'd grown up in. And here he was, ready to revert to type at a little needling from an impudent teenager. Maybe he *was* slipping.

"What's the matter, ducky?" Charlie asked, squinting so that her eyes became tiny bright spots of brown in her pixie face. "Can't take a little ribbing? Stuffy, stuffy," she scolded in a singsong voice, shaking a finger at him.

"Oh, don't be so tedious," Christian grumbled, scowling at her. "I ought to give you the sack for lack of proper respect."

He grimaced the instant the words were out of his mouth. Uncle Dicky would have been rolling in his grave if they hadn't cremated him and scattered him over Cheltenham racecourse.

"Right. Right. Go on. Go ahead and fire me," Charlie said lightly, shrugging without concern. She turned her young womanly wiles in Robert's direction and batted her spiky lashes at him. "I hear they're looking for help at Green Hills, and the trainer's a real dishy guy. Ain't that right, Bobby?"

Braddock wheeled toward his friend with stark panic in his eyes, but Christian took no pity on him. He was too wrapped up in his own worries.

"I'm going to watch the next competition," he mumbled, and wandered off in the direction of the show ring.

It was all that time he'd spent with his family, he thought morosely. They'd rubbed off on him. Three weeks with the Athertons was enough to give anybody a stiff neck. He rubbed the back of his now as he leaned against a light pole and stared, unseeing, at the horse and rider negotiating the jumper course in the arena.

The effect would wear off, he was certain. He would loosen up again. All he needed was a bit of fun with any one of a number of ladies whose names would have rated gold stars in his address book had he been gauche enough to use such a system. He preferred to appreciate every woman for her own unique qualities and leave rating systems to men with no class.

There was Hillary Collins, he reflected. She was always pleasant company. And then there was Regina Worth, who had two *really* outstanding qualities, he thought with a lazy grin. And Louisa Thomas . . .

But each name that came to mind faded quickly away. The truth of the matter was, he didn't feel like seeing any of them. The only woman he was interested in seeing was the one who had turned him down. The one with the flashing amber eyes and sexy, sexy mouth. The one with the mysterious past. The one who had sent him sprawling with the ruthless efficiency of a Ninja warrior. The only woman he was interested in was at that very moment riding into the arena on a horse he wouldn't have wished on his worst enemy.

So maybe it wasn't going to be quite so simple to win this bet, Christian thought as he watched the unflappable Ms. Gianni cast an imperious glance at the course she was about to negotiate, but then he had all the time in the world. It had never taken Christian Atherton a month to get a date with a woman in his life. Alexandra Gianni was not going to be the exception to that rule.

# three

**TERMINATOR REARED AS THE ARENA GATE** swung closed behind him. Alex calmly forced him forward, driving him with her legs. She had learned very quickly that it did no good to punish him for his bad manners. He tended to take reprimands as a challenge and exacted his revenge with even more outlandish behavior. She had decided the only hope she had for redeeming him was to ignore his little fits and do her best to help him keep his mind on his business.

The horse could jump like a champion. His talent over fences was the only thing that had saved his miserable hide from being made into so many baseballs. If she could get him to concentrate on his job and forget the shenanigans, she might prolong his career and put off his trip to the butcher's for another few years.

With that in mind she urged him into a canter and glanced over the course as she circled him near the gate. Because this was just a schooling show, and most of the horses participating were either young, unseasoned, or simply not good enough to make it on the A circuit, the fences were not terribly high—nothing over four feet. And though the course itself was more complicated than those of the hunter classes that had preceded it, it was still well beneath Terminator's capabilities. He had already been shown at higher levels of competition, but Alex had chosen to restart him and bring him up gradually to the tougher levels as they got to know each other, and as she gained more control over his unbalanced mind.

When she noticed Christian standing outside the ring, his gaze riveted on her, she caught herself straightening in the saddle, bringing her chin up, making half a dozen little adjustments that might impress him. Dammit, she scolded herself as she pointed her horse toward his first fence, there was no room for Christian Atherton in her life, and there was certainly no room for him in her head now. She was going to need every scrap of concentration she possessed to get through this round unscathed.

It took Terminator exactly two fences to decide that the course bored him. He lugged on the bit, doing his best to pull Alex's arms out of their sockets while charging toward each low fence and launching himself flatly over them like a steeplechaser. The battle for control waged throughout their round, and Alex was glad jumpers weren't scored on style and manners, as hunters were. All that mattered was that they get themselves over the fences without knocking anything down, and despite everything, Terminator managed to accomplish his task. They would be coming back for the jump-off and competing this time not only against the other horses that had jumped clean first rounds, but against the clock as well. The horse with the best time and least faults would win.

Christian watched her exit the ring. He was impressed with her riding if not her horse. Beyond being proper in her leg position and seat, she had savvy and style. There was something in that style, in the way she held her head, in the way she brought her horse to the fence and moved him away from it, that prodded at his memory. He wanted to think he'd seen her ride before, and yet he hadn't. Odd. Her name didn't ring a bell, and there had been nothing in their conversation—a conversation held in delightfully close quarters—that had sparked further recognition.

Finally he dismissed the whole idea from his head. He had never met Alex Gianni. A grin spread slowly across his face. He had never met her before, but he was definitely going to get to know her.

"Looks damn fine on a horse, don't she?"

The graveled voice had much the same effect on Christian as fingernails on a chalkboard. He turned and treated Tully Haskell to the trick he'd learned as a schoolboy at Winchester—looking down his nose at someone who was taller than he.

Haskell was a big man in his forties with an upper body made solid from years of physical work, and a paunch that was the result of a more recent sedentary lifestyle and too much fried food. He had taken up a stance beside Christian, planting himself like an oak tree, and was lighting up a long cigar with a gaudy ruby-studded gold lighter.

Christian eyed the blue ribbon pinned to the pocket of his western-cut shirt with sardonic disdain. "Giving out prizes for obnoxious qualities, are they?" he questioned dryly. "You're destined to be a champion, Tully."

"You're a regular laugh riot, Atherton," Haskell said with a sneer, his fleshy face coloring red from the neck up, as if his shirt collar had suddenly gone too tight on him. He shook his cigar at Christian. "We'll see how hard you laugh when Alex and Terminator start mopping up at the big shows."

"You can't be serious, meaning to send that unhinged animal up against a grand prix course?" Christian shuddered at the thought. The grand prix was the most demanding and most prestigious of all the jumper classes, usually held amidst considerable pomp and pageantry and for big purses. The fences and courses were formidable. It took both a sound mind and a sound body for a horse to take the stress. "What are you trying do, get Alexandra killed?"

"Hardly." A reptilian smile curved Haskell's mouth. "This is just the beginning of a long and mutually advantageous relationship between Alex and me."

Christian gave him a sharp look, his brows drawing together above intense blue eyes.

"Yes, Lordy, she do sit a horse nice," the man drawled, his gaze roaming over Alex as she jogged his horse some distance away. He took a long drag on his cigar and exhaled on a sigh that rang unmistakably in Christian's ears as the first stirrings of desire.

Tully turned back toward him with a maliciously smug gleam in his eyes. "I hear she gave you what-for in the stable. About time you got put in your place."

"Oh, I know my place, Tully," Christian said coolly. "On top."

He stared at the arena where the grounds crew was raising several fences and taking others down in preparation for the jump-off. "Alexandra and I had a bit of a misunderstanding. Rest assured, we'll work it out."

Haskell turned and jabbed Christian hard on the shoulder with a blunt-tipped forefinger. "You stay the hell away from my trainer, you pompous British prig. She's got better things to do than have you pantin' after her. I know your game, Atherton. Charm them into your bed, and they won't try so hard to beat you in the ring. Well, you can just forget it this time."

Christian coldly eyed the finger pressed to his jacket. Using every bit of his inborn self-control, he reined in his temper, rerouting its energy to the force of his personality so that icy contempt rolled off him in a frigid blast. Haskell, sensing he had crossed a line, took an involuntary step backward, and Christian calmly brushed off the shoulder of his coat.

"Regarding Ms. Gianni," he said formally, his blue eyes blazing as he stared into Tully's florid, fleshy face. "You're not her owner and you're not her father, which, in case you haven't noticed, you are more than old enough to be. You pay her to ride your horses. What she does on her own time is none of your damned business."

Glaring at him, and growing redder by the second, Haskell chewed back a retort. The ring announcer called for the first horse of the jump-off. Tully turned abruptly on his booted heel and stalked off in a cloud of smoke.

"Ill-mannered, ill-bred swine," Christian muttered, scowling after him.

"The horse or the owner?" Robert queried, taking up Haskell's place.

"Both. They deserve each other. Would you believe he actually had the nerve to warn me off?" Christian fumed. "The unmitigated gall!"

Braddock arched a dark brow. "Tully's got his eye on the Italian Iceberg too? Well, I'll be damned. That old tub o' lard!" He laughed in disbelief and tucked his hands into the pockets of the green windbreaker he'd thrown on over his riding coat. Grinning, he nudged his friend with an elbow. "Bet she can't throw *him* over her shoulder."

Christian didn't so much as pretend to smile. "Pray to God for his sake she never has to try."

The words came out in nothing short of a growl, making Braddock's eyebrows climb his forehead again. Christian shuddered and rubbed a hand across his eyes. Maybe he was coming down with something after all: terminal respectability. Defending the honor of young women! Gads.

He cleared his throat and changed the subject. "Hard luck on that vertical, old boy."

"Yeah," Robert said on a sigh of resignation. He stared at the fence in question, a barrier of green-and-white poles placed one above the other to make the jump the highest on the course. His horse had been one of many to bring it down in the first round of the class. Now it had been raised for the jump-off and the approach made more difficult. "I don't think that mare's ready to leave the hunter division," he said reflectively. "The distances throw her. She's always trying to add a stride at the last second."

"She's worried," Christian said with a shrug. "She doesn't trust you because you're letting her try to set herself right, and she's not quite ready to do that. Take her in hand a bit, reassure her."

"You always know how to handle a lady," Braddock drawled, teasing lights sparkling in his dark eyes. "What are you supposed to do when she throws you?"

"Oh, shut up," Christian said with good humor.

They turned their attention back to the ring, where yet another competitor had brought down the green-and-white vertical jump. Christian's gaze slid to the far end of the arena, where Alex was waiting on Terminator.

What did one do after being thrown? One got up and tried again. He had every intention of trying again with Alex, and the sooner the better. There was a wager to be won, a jackass to be shown up, and a lady he wanted to know more about.

Terminator pinned his ears and tried to bite the horse that was leaving the ring. Alex jerked his head aside and scolded him in rapid Italian. The strongly accented words floated to Christian on the gentle spring breeze, and he chuckled. Italian was one of the few useful things he'd learned at Cambridge before being asked to leave after scuttling a professor's punt with the professor still in it.

"What'd she say?" Braddock asked.

"Commenting on the members of his family tree."

"Oh, well, he's obviously Tully's. He bears a striking family resemblance from behind."

They broke into laughter and were immediately caught for posterity on film.

"Carter, what are you doing with that camera?" Robert asked.

Carter Hill glanced up from the array of knobs and switches on his camera and raked back a strand of auburn hair. He was thirty-three, tall and slender, as were all the Hills. He smiled pleasantly, somehow still managing to look like a lawyer even without his pinstripes.

"First show in the new arena and all," he said. "Dad wants plenty of pictures. Too bad we won't get you in the winner's circle this time around, Robert."

Braddock shrugged. "Breaks of the game."

Alex rode into the ring then, and Christian's attention focused on her and on the game men and women had been playing since the days of Adam and Eve. He had a feeling he was going to have to make his own breaks, but as far as he was concerned, both he and Alex would come out winners when all was said and done.

Alex sucked in a deep breath and let it out slowly, nudging her horse into a canter as her body relaxed. She pointed Terminator toward the first fence and cursed herself as a lone thought intruded on her concentration. *This is your chance to show Christian Atherton what you're made of.*

Terminator pricked his ears and launched himself over the fence, realizing belatedly that it was higher than before and required more effort on his part. Alex nearly lost her seat at the unexpectedly high jump he made. By the time they landed, she had her position back and her mind on the matter at hand.

They won it at the green vertical. While the other horses had had trouble managing the sharp turn and sudden acceleration needed to clear it cleanly, diving in on corners and charging fences were Terminator's forte. He left the fence intact and kicked up his heels as he dashed away from it.

Alex laughed and slapped him on the neck. It felt good to win. She'd lost so much in the past couple of years, every small victory was another brick for rebuilding the wall of her self-esteem.

Outside the ring she slid off her horse and handed him to her teenage helpers, the two Heathers—Heather Connelly and Heather Montrose, riding students who were trading work for lessons. She gave the girls instructions for them to cool Terminator down and keep him away from other horses. She wouldn't have charged one girl with the task, but between the two of them they would have no trouble. They threw a bright red woolen cooler over the gelding and led him away.

Congratulations floated to her from passing riders, and Alex smiled her thanks as she pulled her helmet off and shook her hair free.

"What'd I tell you, sweetheart?" Tully Haskell said with a grin. He spread his arms expansively, as if expecting Alex to rush into them.

She couldn't quite keep from frowning at his greeting as heads turned in their direction. "Please call me Alex, Mr. Haskell," she said quietly, her stomach churning.

He shrugged, smile in place on his mouth but not in his eyes. "Whatever you say, sweet—a—Alex." He jerked a thumb toward the arena. "Let's go get our picture taken."

He offered her his arm, but Alex busied herself with her helmet and crop and walked into the ring beside him, thinking this was really unnecessary. It wasn't as if they'd just won the World Cup. Owners—even overbearing ones like Tully Haskell—didn't get their pictures taken with their riders for winning at schooling shows.

*Relax, Alex. Just get it over with, and you can go home to Isabella.*

"Where's the trophy?" Carter Hill asked, camera in hand as he looked toward the judge's stand where some sort of commotion was taking place among the half-dozen people gathered there.

Suddenly Christian Atherton emerged from the mob with a triumphant look on his face and a small gold cup in his hands.

His steady gaze zoomed in on Alex, magnetism turned up full beam. She froze, mesmerized, amazed. It seemed inconceivable that he could elicit such a response from her with so little effort. That he could excite her, and the excitement made her afraid.

"I've been given the great honor of presenting you with your prize, Ms. Gianni," he said smoothly, wedging himself neatly between her and Haskell. The truth of the matter was he had wrested the trophy away from a nine-year-old girl and then consoled her with a bribe of a dollar. Low but effective.

"That's mine, Atherton," Tully said with all the sulky impudence of a spoiled child. He reached for the cup with greedy hands.

Christian grinned brilliantly as Carter Hill shot a picture. "Then here you are, Mr. Haskell." *And may you choke on it*, he silently added.

He turned his smile back toward Alex. "Congratulations."

"Thank you," she said, quelling the juvenile urge to thumb her nose at him. "I guess Terminator and I get along well enough."

"Yes," Christian said, his own teasing temper responding to the fiery lights in her amber eyes as well as to the challenging tilt of her chin. Gads but she was lovely! That inner flame he had caught glimpses of in the stables burned bright now. She was too caught up in the heady sense of victory to try to suppress it as she had before. He flicked a finger down the short slope of her nose and watched the golden sparks shoot off in her eyes. "Perhaps you can have him ready for the fall steeplechase season."

"Plenty of time for us to win a grand prix or two before then," Alex replied tartly, surprised to realize that she enjoyed sparring with Christian. Her blood was racing in much the same way it did when she was soaring over fences on a fast, powerful horse.

Haskell grunted and hugged his cup to his belly. "See there, hotshot. She'll give you a run for your money."

Christian went on staring down into Alex's amber eyes, reading a rich mix of emotions in their sparkling depths, and he felt his blood heat in answer. His gaze slid to the pouty curve of her lower lip, and a lazy smile curled one corner of his mouth as desire curled low and tight in his groin. "I dare say she will," he murmured silkily.

"Just one more picture, folks?" Carter Hill said, raising his camera.

Tully lifted his trophy and bared his teeth. Alex looked up at Christian, unable to look away. And Christian leaned down and kissed her just as the shutter clicked.

A languid warmth flowed through Alex, swirling first through her head then downward, washing all physical strength with it. It wasn't much of an effort as far as kisses went. It wasn't aggressive or even intimate. It was merely a taste, a brushing of his firm lips over hers. And still it made her weak and dizzy.

Alex told herself it was the shock. She hadn't been kissed in a long time. She hadn't allowed a man near enough to accomplish the task. Christian hadn't asked permission. He'd simply seized the moment and kissed her as if he had every right to.

He didn't have the right. His presumptuousness triggered an old flame of anger, and her own guilt at having enjoyed the kiss for an instant poured gasoline on the fire. She pulled back and slapped him, spewing out a stream of violent blistering Italian while Carter Hill snapped pictures.

Christian laughed, perversely delighted by her temper. She had wanted to melt against him—he was too experienced not to know that. Instead she had given him what he no doubt deserved. His cheek was stinging, but it was nothing compared to the lingering sensation of her lips beneath his. Wonderful. Delicious. Instantly addictive.

"My apologies, Ms. Gianni," he said smoothly, capturing her wildly gesticulating hands with his. "I'm afraid I lost my head."

Still speaking Italian, Alex muttered that his head wasn't the only thing he should worry about losing if he tried to kiss her again.

"I'll bear that in mind," Christian said, blue eyes dancing. "I'm rather attached to that particular part of my anatomy."

Alex blushed furiously at the sudden realization that he had understood every word she'd said. Irrational anger burned through her because he hadn't had the grace to tell her he spoke Italian.

"Just don't let it happen again, Mr. Atherton," she said. Tilting her nose up to a haughty angle, she whirled and stormed out of the ring.

"Oh, I can't promise that, Ms. Gianni," Christian murmured, watching her go, admiring the sway of her slim hips. "I can't promise that at all."

Alex stormed around her stall area, flinging things into her gear bag, cursing the day God created man. He should have skipped the first effort, made woman, and called it a day. She was sure everything that was wrong with the world—certainly everything that was wrong with *her* world—could be directly attributed to men. They weren't good for anything except opening jars and reaching things on high shelves . . . and kissing.

She swore long and colorfully as that thought intruded on her tantrum. Her lips were still buzzing from contact with Christian's mouth. She dropped the gloves she was holding and pressed her fingers to her lips, swaying slightly as a strong current of residual desire wafted through her. She could still taste him, warm and fresh and too, too tempting.

The sigh that slid from her lungs was heavy with despair.

She couldn't afford to be attracted to Christian Atherton. Nor could she afford to have him make a public spectacle of her, she thought, her anger stirring again, rising to the top of the emotional whirlpool.

Damn him for kissing her that way! Who did he think he was? Royalty?

Actually, he was, if memory served. Alex frowned. There was another reason she couldn't go getting tangled up with him. She would be a fool to think her future might include the wealthy son of an earl, and she was not a fool. She'd stopped being a fool the day Michael DeGrazia had walked out on her. She had a life to rebuild and a daughter to raise. She seriously doubted Christian Atherton would be interested in any of that. Men of his ilk were concerned with little beyond their own immediate needs and desires. That was just another fact of life she had learned to accept.

Putting the whole subject from her mind, Alex let herself into Terminator's stall to remove his cooler. She double-checked the gelding's cross-ties and left the stall, never turning her back on the horse. He glared at her and tossed his head threateningly.

She didn't like the washy chestnut any better than she liked his owner, but beggars couldn't be choosers. She had come to Virginia with no reputation. She couldn't expect to attract a better class of owners until she had made a name for herself among the affluent hunter-jumper crowd.

That would come with time. She had no doubts about her abilities to compete with the likes of Christian Atherton or Robert Braddock or even the legendary Rodney Jenkins. All she needed was time and a chance to prove herself. That she would have to prove herself on horses like Terminator was not the most pleasant prospect, but that was the way it was.

Latching the bottom door of the box she allowed herself a brief, envious glance at her surroundings. The stables at Green Hills Farm spoke of old money and good taste. The oak stalls were light and roomy. The aisle was wide with a polished cobbled floor. There wasn't a cobweb in sight, and the air smelled of sweet hay and pine shavings and horses that had been groomed to perfection.

The stalls she was renting for the day were in the original barn, but Alex knew the Hills had recently expanded their facilities, building an additional barn with a large indoor arena. After years in the legal profession Hayden Hill had retired and decided to make show horses his full-time hobby. He'd spared no expense, up to and including luring Robert Braddock away from SpruceTree to train for him.

Money. While it may well have been the root of all evil, it was also at the bottom of every successful operation.

Alex had sunk every nickel Michael had given her into setting up her own business on the little farm she'd rented outside of Briarwood. The place was run-down, to put it nicely. None of the buildings had seen a coat of paint in twenty years, and the fences were in a sorry state. Even in its best days it hadn't been able to compete with the likes of Green Hills or Quaid Farm, which was located a hill or two beyond her place.

A shiver of awareness went through her at the thought that Christian Atherton was living just a few fields away from her. A very short distance, but light-years away in terms of status. He would probably turn up his aristocratic nose at the sight of her little ramshackle farm.

"I admit it's not much, but it's a start," she murmured, hugging herself. A fresh start in a place where she had no past. A clean slate.

"We did all right today, didn't we, sweetheart?"

Alex jumped but composed herself so quickly, she was certain Tully hadn't noticed. She tugged at the hem of the baggy black sweatshirt she had put on over her white blouse, trying to push aside the feeling that Haskell's eyes lingered longer than was necessary on the skintight pale gray breeches that encased her thighs.

"Yes, very well, Mr. Haskell," she said, all business. "I was especially pleased with the mare. I have no doubts about her going on to A shows."

"She sure as hell outclassed this bunch, didn't she, sugar?" Haskell patted Alex's shoulder and laughed a laugh that managed to sound more smug than good-natured. Of course, that was Tully Haskell all over. He was a man who had, by hook or by crook, pulled himself up from poverty to prosperity and never failed to remind people of the fact. He seemed to believe it made him superior in some way. Survival-of-the-fittest mentality, Alex supposed.

She shrugged off his touch as casually as she could and watched him lean negligently against the bottom door of the mare's stall. Had he been a horse, Alex would have rejected him as a prospect on the basis of his eyes alone. They were small and cold, hinting at a temperament to match. He wore the blue ribbon his mare had won pinned to his shirt for all the world to see, as if her accomplishments somehow reflected favorably on him.

"Well, this is just a schooling show," Alex reminded him. "Still, I think she'll hold her own in fancier company. She's a very nice mare."

That was an understatement. A Touch of Dutch was world-class. Alex couldn't stop thanking God for sending her this one wonderful horse to work with. If she could have just one like Duchess, she would ride a dozen Terminators and deal with a dozen Tully Haskells and not complain. The sorrel mare was sweet tempered, beautiful, talented, and worth a small fortune. What a man like Tully Haskell was doing with her, Alex couldn't imagine. It was like trying to picture the man with Princess Di on his arm. Completely incongruous.

"Yeah," Tully drawled, extracting a long cigar from the

breast pocket of his shirt and rolling it between his fingers in defiance of the many No Smoking signs posted around the barn, "she's a mighty fine mare. And her rider's not too damn shabby, either." Haskell shot her a wink and clamped the cigar between his teeth.

Alex swallowed down the instantaneous rush of revulsion and told herself her employer meant nothing by the remark—he was merely complimenting her on her riding.

The hell he was, she fumed, anger bubbling up inside her. He was flirting with her the way he always flirted with her. She never responded in kind, but that hadn't deterred him yet.

"Thank you, Mr. Haskell," she said coolly, staring down at the toes of her boots. How long was it going to take this cretin to get the message?

"Tully," he scolded in a too-familiar voice. "You just call me Tully, sweetheart, and we'll get on like peas in a pod."

The idea of being a pea in a pod with Tully Haskell was hardly an appealing one. Although he made no move to come closer to her, Alex couldn't quite quell the urge to bolt away from him. Where the hell was Heather—either one of them—she wondered crossly as she unlatched Terminator's door and slipped into the stall, preferring the company of the horse to that of his owner.

Keeping a watchful eye on the chestnut she picked up a brush and applied it briskly to his coat.

"Here's that soda you asked for, Mr. Haskell."

"Thanks, Heather, honey, 'preciate it."

The brush stilled on Terminator's back as Alex looked out of the stall, her straight, dark brows drawing together in suspicion. Haskell accepted the can of soda, looking neither contrite nor annoyed. Heather C. set about her work cleaning tack without giving the man another glance.

You've got to stop being so paranoid, Alex told herself. It was ridiculous to think Haskell had sent the girl on an errand for the sole purpose of getting her alone. Besides, there was virtually no chance of being alone in the barn, what with competitors going in and out continually. She was just wasting energy being nervous, and in view of the amount of work she had to do, energy was the last thing she could afford to waste.

Terminator took advantage of his trainer's lapse in attention, taking a swipe at her arm. Alex jumped out of her trance and scolded herself for being so careless. If the cross ties had been any looser, people could have started calling her Lefty. Where would she and Isabella have been then?

"He's got a lot of fire," Tully observed, perversely pleased by the gelding's nasty attitude.

Alex bit back her opinion as she let herself out of the stall and began packing her equipment in her tack trunk. Terminator would have better served the world as a bag of kibble and a bottle of glue, but owners didn't like to hear that kind of thing from trainers.

"Let me help you with that, honey," Haskell said, reaching for the saddle on the rack at the same time Alex did.

His arms brushed her sides as he reached around her. His paunch bumped against her back. Alex grabbed the saddle and twisted out of his embrace, making sure he got a good poke in the ribs with a stirrup iron as she did so.

"I can get it, Mr. Haskell," she said, struggling to curb her reaction and form a polite smile. "Thank you anyway."

Rubbing his side absently, he gave her a brief scowl, then shrugged as if to say it was her loss. "Well, I've got to be taking off. I'll stop by the farm one day next week."

Choking back the urge to tell him not to bother, Alex managed a nod, then breathed a sigh of relief as Tully swaggered off. She went about her work cursing herself under her breath in Italian all the while and throwing in a couple of colorful words for the odious Mr. Haskell. She had overreacted. She was a ninny. She was a coward. She was a fool.

Tully Haskell was a man. That seemed enough of a curse to heap on his balding head. He didn't mean anything by his flirtation. He was just testing the waters, seeing what kind of reception he would get. Any man would have done the same—curse them all. When the fact finally penetrated his tiny brain that he wasn't going to get any encouragement from her, he would back off.

It was simple, she told herself. She was sending out the right signals. As soon as she had ceased to be a novelty, and as soon as the male population of her professional circle figured out she wasn't interested in fun and games, life would settle down to the kind of quiet routine she wanted for herself and her daughter.

She finished her packing, still muttering to herself in the language she had grown up with. Her grandparents, who had emigrated from Italy to California after the Second World War, had insisted the Gianni offspring speak their native tongue while in their home. Alex still spoke it out of habit around the house and in the stable, much to the delight of her teenage students, who thought it very chic to pick up a word or two themselves.

"I'm finished here, Alex," Heather said, brushing her blond braid back over her shoulder. "Is it okay if I go watch?"

Alex absently waved her away. *"Si, si."*

*"Mille grazie!"* The girl grinned and bounded for the stable door calling, *"Ciao!"*

Alex smiled and shook her head.

*"Bon giorno, Signorina Gianni."*

The smooth male voice immediately sent her senses on red alert. Red-hot alert. Responses she'd forgotten she possessed rushed through her—heat and tingling and a strange, giddy pleasure. Alex throttled them guiltily, strangling them into control before she looked up to see Christian standing across the aisle from her, lounging against a stall. He had changed out of his riding clothes to trim, faded jeans, a T-shirt that matched his eyes, and a gold suede jacket that looked butter soft and infinitely touchable.

He looked comfortable and sexy, and that blasted come-hither grin of his invited her to come be comfortable and sexy with him. The worst of it was, a part of her wanted to—badly.

She scolded at him as he sauntered toward her, moving with a lazy, subtle grace that spoke volumes about both his athleticism and his background. His eyes caught hers in their powerful tractor beam, and he let his slow, I-know-how-good-we'd-be-in-bed smile ease across his face.

*"Mi fa molto piacere veder la,"* he said, his pronunciation smooth and perfectly accented. The words rolled over Alex like the caress of silk.

"Well, I'm not delighted to see you," she replied tartly, stiffening her resolve.

He gave her a sad-hurt look that made her stomach somersault, and lifted his hands in question. *"Perche?"*

"Why? Why!" Alex fumed, taking a step toward him. She lifted an accusatory finger under his nose. "I'll tell you why—" She caught herself just before planting that forefinger on his chest. Control, Alex. Calm, control. No wild emotional outbursts, no show of temper, no show of passion. She pulled her hand back, then flung it downward as she stepped away from him, trying to dodge his magnetic field. "No, no, just go away. *Va al diavolo! Mi lasci in pace, per favore!*"

Christian listened to her order to leave her alone but didn't heed it. He was already far too curious about who this lady was. He wanted to know why she kept yanking back her emotions every time they threatened to melt the ice that surrounded her. He wanted to know why she was so anxious to escape when the spark between them was so obvious and so compelling.

He stepped closer and felt the level of heat between them rise. "Don't be angry with me," he said sincerely, his eyebrows lifting in an endearing look of penitence.

Alex sniffed indignantly, determined not be swayed by his handsome contrition. "I'll be angry if I want. You're not sorry for what you did. You're sorry I slapped you."

"A—well, I expect you're right about that," he admitted with a brilliant grin that invited her to grin back. She didn't. Gads, she was a tough one! That was his best bloody smile! He'd melted more resolves with that grin than he could remember. Sobering, he cleared his throat and apologized in earnest. "Look here, Alex, I'm sorry if I embarrassed you. I didn't mean any harm."

"That doesn't make it all right," Alex muttered, thinking of another wealthy, privileged man who had thought he could get away with anything, too, then make it all better with an apology.

"Then let me make it up to you . . . over dinner? Nick does an excellent *pollo del padrone*."

"I'll have to try it sometime."

"But not tonight . . ." he said slowly. "And not with me."

"No."

He sighed heavily, as if he were finding this whole thing tiring in the extreme. Fine, thought Alex, let him get bored and lose interest. That was, after all, the plan, she reminded herself while trying to ignore the stirring of disappointment inside her.

"I have to ask myself why," Christian said, his eyes narrowing in speculation as he leaned closer. Alex tried to back away, but once again he had managed to corner her.

"There's the obvious reason," she said, sticking her chin out defiantly. "Maybe I don't like you."

One corner of his mouth hooked upward. "That's not what your kiss told me, darling."

"What did my slap tell you?"

"That you're tempestuous."

"You've got an answer for everything, don't you?"

"No," he murmured. "I haven't a clue about who you really are, Alexandra Gianni. But I mean to find out."

The fear that flashed through her eyes was instantaneous. Alex couldn't stop Christian from seeing it. Damn him! Why couldn't he just accept her rejection and walk away like the half-dozen others who had gone before him?

The predatory gleam in his eyes softened to something warm and curious as he took in the tension in Alex's expression. What a pretty little puzzle she was—fire and ice, arrogance and uncertainty. Without even trying, she was weaving a spell around him, and he had no doubt that she would not have been happy to hear it.

"I'll take a rain check on the dinner," he murmured.

Unable to resist, he bent his head and brushed his lips across hers, again tasting the sweet yearning, the longing to respond, then the abrupt retreat of her emotions. He stepped back quickly and caught the hand she lifted to slap him. Though she resisted, he raised it easily to his lips and kissed her knuckles.

"Until we meet again, darling," he said with a grin, backing gracefully away from her. "*Arrivederci*, Alexandra!"

# four

**"POMPOUS, PRESUMPTUOUS, ARROGANT . . .** *man*!" Alex spat the last word as if it were the vilest of curses.

The rigid tension in her muscles was telegraphed to her horse. Terminator's head came up, and his haunches bunched beneath him as he hopped forward nervously. He snorted and jogged sideways as a rabbit rustled the budding leaves of a low bush along the trail.

Alex spoke to him in a gentle voice, mentally scolding herself for letting her mind wander. When she was on this one's back, there could be no room in her head for thoughts of anything but surviving the excursion. As she had been telling herself for the better part of a day, there should never be any room for thoughts of Christian Atherton, and yet her brain stubbornly persisted in conjuring up his image every five minutes. She chased the apparition away with manufactured anger, wasting another five minutes of time and energy. Damn him anyway.

She wanted only peace, a place to raise her daughter, a chance to establish herself in her profession. It made no sense that men insisted on pursuing her when she made no effort to lead them on. It made no sense that a man like Christian Atherton would look her way twice, let alone steal a kiss from her.

She bit her lip and sighed with no small amount of despair when the tingling sensation of his lips against hers came back to her as real as if it had just happened. She could still taste him, warm and sweet. She could still feel the temptation to lean into him.

Damn him for making her want again! Damn him for awakening needs she would sooner have left behind.

Perhaps the most frustrating thing about this business of attracting men was the fact that she had gone to considerable trouble to make herself *less* noticeable. The waist-long wild mane of black ringlets Michael had delighted in had been shorn off. She no longer wore makeup. The bottles of fragrance she so loved stood unused on her dresser. With the necessary exception of her riding breeches, her clothes were baggy and mannish, enhancing no part of her feminine anatomy. She had made a concerted effort to subdue her naturally outgoing personality, to speak quietly, coolly, evenly, to show little of the hot Italian temper and volatile emotions that ran beneath her surface. She had even shortened her name to its least feminine form.

In short, she was sure she had done nothing to attract or encourage Christian Atherton, and still he had made it clear he intended to pursue her.

Sensing her lack of concentration, Terminator bolted suddenly beneath her. Only lightning reflexes and an excellent sense of balance kept her from being unhorsed. Sawing gently on the reins, Alex rose in the saddle and let the big horse move into a ground-eating canter. She had discovered that Terminator quickly soured on arena work and so had chosen to take him for a gallop in the woods that ran up the hill behind her farmstead. He had earned a day away from fences, and Alex herself had had a longing to escape. That she could never really escape her thoughts or her memories was a reality she didn't care to accept.

With an effort she focused on her horse. He moved with unwavering strength and grace up the old logging trail. The forest they swept through was still half-naked, drab with the dead leaves of last season, but brightening with the new leaves of this one. The air was heavy and sweet with the promise of rain and new growth. Alex breathed deeply of it, letting it fill her lungs and clear her mind . . . and still she thought of Christian Atherton.

Christian eased his horse along the trail. His position was perfect—head up, heels down, back straight—but his mind was elsewhere. On the far side of the hill, to be precise. He didn't have a plan as yet, but he hoped something brilliant would come to him by the time he reached Alex's stable. He had yet to be at a loss for either words or actions around a lovely, intriguing woman.

The taste of her was still lingering on his lips. The memory of that instant when her body had swayed ever so slightly into his was still fresh. So was the memory of her flashing amber eyes, her hot tongue, and the stinging slap she had delivered along with her words. A grin curved his mouth at the thought. The lady had a temper. He suspected the lady had a lot of other equally strong feelings as well, but she seemed determined to keep them on a short rein.

He frowned as he recalled her spontaneous bursts of emotion and the way she had instantly throttled each one. His frown deepened as he thought of the bright smiles that had lit up her face only to be extinguished, doused by the wariness in her eyes.

"Secrets, secrets, Alexandra," he murmured, a strong, undefinable emotion of his own surging through him. "I'm going to learn them all, whether you like it or not."

The two riders broke through the trees at the same time. Christian grinned as he recognized the rider in the scarlet jockey cap and black sweater, then scowled as he recognized the horse. He turned his gray to the right to avoid a collision. Alex and

Terminator turned in the same direction, and the pair of them cantered up the slight incline of the high meadow.

The horses drifted toward each other. Terminator pinned his ears and surged against the bit. Alex hauled back on the reins and cursed under her breath when she got no response for her actions except an increase in speed. Ahead of them lay a mile-long stretch of open field, and Terminator was determined to reach the end of it ahead of the horse running beside him.

"Dammit, Christian, pull up!" Alex shouted. "He thinks it's a race!"

Christian eased the gray back half a length, then a length, but Terminator surged on, faster still, out of control. Rising in his irons, he kicked his gelding ahead, urging him with hands and legs. The gray responded with a burst of speed that brought the two horses even once again.

Alex was leaning back, sawing on the reins with every ounce of strength and determination she had and making no impression on her animal whatsoever. Taking his own reins in his right hand, Christian stretched his left arm out, his fingers grasping for Alex's rein, then curling around it.

"Let him go!" Alex ordered as Christian sat back, his movement pulling the two horses closer together.

Alex frantically tried to pull Terminator the other way, but the chestnut had already changed his course and his mind. He was no longer bent on winning the race but on beating the daylights out of his opponent. Ears flattened, he willingly turned his head in Christian's direction and lunged at the gray.

Christian's startled mount bolted sideways to escape his adversary's teeth, stumbled, and went down, sending Christian sprawling. Alex overbalanced to the right, and Terminator neatly dodged left, ducking out from under her. She hit the ground with a teeth-jarring thud and slowly pushed herself to a sitting position just in time to see Terminator disappearing down the trail for home.

"Damn!" she said, tearing up a clump of grass with her gloved fist and throwing it away.

Christian's mount had righted himself and stood near the edge of the clearing, alternately grazing and staring at his fallen master with wide eyes. Alex's heart went to her throat as her own gaze fell on Christian. He seemed ominously still.

"Christian?" she called, her voice trembling as she scrambled over to him. She unbuckled the chin strap of her jockey's helmet, which suddenly seemed to be strangling her, and still couldn't get a decent breath.

Christian lay like a mannequin in the grass, unnaturally still. What if he were unconscious? He wasn't wearing a helmet—he might have hit his head or been kicked. What if he were—Alex swallowed hard and refused to finish the thought. On her knees she bent over him looking for blood and bruises. "Christian?"

He opened his eyes and smiled weakly. "I do love how you say my name, darling."

Relief washed through Alex like the waters of a burst dam. And in their aftermath came a tide of anger. She pushed herself to her feet and swore at him in Italian. "You're not hurt at all!"

"Try not to sound so disappointed," he said dryly. He sat up gingerly, mentally assessing the damage. A few aches, no major pains, all extremities attached and working.

*"Madre di Dio!"* Alex flung her hands at him, amber eyes flashing. "I thought you'd been killed!"

"Is that a goal of yours or something?" he questioned suspiciously, rubbing an aching shoulder through his dark leather jacket. "This is the second time I've found myself on the ground because of you. Of course, I wouldn't mind if you were down here with me," he added with a roguish grin.

Alex just growled at him and paced, crossing her arms tightly over her chest.

"I say, you won't be able to talk with your hands tucked up against you."

His teasing earned him a baleful glare. He chuckled. The lady didn't want him to know how badly rattled she'd been at the prospect of his death. It was a start.

"You could thank me for saving your beautiful neck," he suggested, fighting back the grin that threatened when her cat's eyes flashed at him again.

"Saving me? You got me thrown!"

"Yes, well, it appeared that beast of yours was going to run all the way to Maryland. I saved you a long trip home."

"At least I would have had a ride," Alex muttered, staring at the woods and the path that eventually led back to her farm. She had a good mile hike ahead of her.

"You can ride my horse. I'll walk. We'll go to your place, since it's nearer," Christian said as he started to get up. Planting his right foot, he winced, sucked in a breath through his teeth, and sank back down to the ground. There was a definite strain in his voice when he said, "Check that. I'm afraid I won't be able to play the gallant after all."

Alex's heart leapt into her throat again as she hurried over to him, forgetting all about cool restraint and suppressing her emotions. "What is it? Is something broken?"

"Ankle," he barked between held breaths. Gradually the pain subsided to a vicious throb, and the rest of his body relaxed. "I must have twisted it in the fall."

Guilt and anger warred inside Alex. He had been trying to save her from a possible disaster, but he wouldn't have gotten hurt if he had stayed out of her life altogether. Blast it, she hadn't asked for him to take an interest in her. Nor had she asked for the tender feelings and the longing to comfort that blossomed within her now.

"Be a love and help me get the boot off before the swelling makes it impossible," he said.

"Are you sure?" she asked, hesitantly taking his foot in her hands. "It'll hurt."

"Not as bad as having to cut it off. These are my favorite boots."

Not to mention expensive, Alex thought, eyeing the softly polished black leather. She could have paid a month's feed bill with what these boots cost, and they were just his everyday pair.

"Hang on," she said, biting her lip for his pain as she tried to pull the boot off. He paled visibly as he strained backward. Sweat filmed his forehead. The knee-high boot didn't budge.

"Hold it. Hold it," he said, gasping. "I need to brace against something. Turn around."

Alex gave him a skeptical look, but turned her back to him, leaned over, and took hold of his foot again, holding it between her slightly spread legs.

"That's it," Christian said. "If nothing else, the view is exceedingly fine."

"On three," Alex muttered, not liking the leap in her pulse at his comment about her derriere. "One . . . two . . ."

He planted his other foot on the seat of her breeches, sucked in a deep breath, and pushed hard as she called three and pulled at the reluctant boot. Pain exploded in his ankle and shot up his leg like an electric current, but the boot came free. The easing of the pressure and the cool spring air immediately soothed the injury.

Christian leaned back on his elbows, panting, his hair falling rakishly across his forehead. Relief allowed him to smile up at Alex.

"Was it as good for you?" he asked breathlessly.

Alex scowled at the sexy, tempting picture he presented, tossed his boot at him, and knelt down. She peeled his sock off and gingerly examined the ankle that had already begun to puff up. With gentle hands she felt for any sign of a broken bone and found none.

"Please feel free to do that to any other part of me," Christian said, his voice a low sensual purr. Pain or no, he was enjoying the feel of her small capable hands on his flesh. He groaned a little under his breath as her ministrations called to mind the particularly erotic dream he'd had about her the night before.

"I ought to leave you for dead," Alex grumbled, trying to ignore the heat in her cheeks and the sudden sensitivity in her nipples.

"If you do that, then you won't be able to go to dinner with me this evening."

"I'm not going to dinner with you regardless," she said firmly, looking him straight in the eye. "I'm not getting involved with you."

Christian looked hurt. "How can you say that after you've fondled my foot? What kind of fellow do you take me for?"

"You don't want to know."

"Sure I do." Leaning forward he caught her wrist as she tried to move away. She stiffened immediately, her dark eyes going wide with an instinctive fear reaction she couldn't mask. Her involuntary response tugged at his curiosity and his heart. "I want to know all about you, Alex," he said gently, his fingers rubbing soothingly against the fragile skin of her wrist, feeling the pulse that raced there.

Alex stared at him, her heart pounding. She felt like a rabbit caught in a snare. Christian was watching her with his steady blue gaze. He was far too close. She could feel the magnetic power of him, luring her, tempting her to close the distance between them. Her mouth tingled at the memory of his kiss. Unconsciously she ran her tongue across her full lower lip. Finally his words penetrated. *I want to know all about you*.

"No," she whispered, pulling away from him. "No, you don't."

Confused and upset, she rose unsteadily to her feet and went to catch the gray gelding. The horse came to her willingly, trustingly, obediently, and she spared a singularly nasty thought for the bag of dog chow that had left her stranded. Faithlessness was just another of Terminator's long list of unattractive traits.

Christian managed to mount with some difficulty. After he'd settled himself in the saddle, he sat for a long minute with his eyes squeezed shut, fighting off the screaming pain in his ankle. When it subsided, he managed a tepid version of his rogue's smile for Alex and patted the limited space in front of him on the jumping saddle.

"You can ride with me," he invited, knowing she would refuse him.

Just the idea of being that close to him gave Alex a hot flash. She could too vividly imagine the feel of his strong arms around her, of her breast flattening against the solid wall of his chest, and her hip pressing intimately against his groin as she sat sideways in front of him. Angry with herself and her traitorous hormones, she merely shot him a scowl and set off on foot down the path toward her farm.

Christian watched her stride off with his boot in her arms, and he couldn't help but think she was running away. But from what? He meant to find out. Sooner or later, one way or another, he would find out.

"Lord, Alex, you had me scared out of my wits!" Pearl Washington exclaimed as Alex trudged into the yard.

Pearl's dark round face was lined with worry over the natural creases of sixty-eight years of living. Balancing Isabella on one plump hip, she pressed her free hand to her ample bosom and heaved a sigh of relief. "That devil came galloping back here all by himself. I could only think the worst. This poor child left motherless. Lord have mercy." She shook her head for emphasis.

"You've got cause to worry when she goes out on that one,

Pearl," Christian said, sliding carefully off his horse. Alex scowled at him and hit him in the stomach with his boot as she handed it to him. His breath left him with an "oof."

"It was just a minor crash. Christian twisted his ankle, but I'm fine," Alex said. Terminator stood some distance away, near the barn. She glared at him, then turned with a smile to take her daughter.

"Mama," Isabella said, grinning, attaching herself to her mother's side like a limpet. Her attention was immediately snared by the swinging strap of Alex's helmet. She wrapped a chubby hand around it and stuck the end in her mouth. Alex fondly tousled her daughter's black curls and kissed her cheek.

When she had moved to Virginia, she had feared she would have to put Isabella in day care. Both the idea of the cost and the thought of separation had upset her. But it seemed fate had been smiling down on her for a change. She had found Pearl Washington. Or more accurately, they had found each other.

Pearl, a recent widow, had been looking for a renter and some new meaning in her life. She had retired from her job as an elementary-school secretary, planning to spend her time with her husband. Then Rube had died suddenly, leaving her bereft. Alex had needed a stable and care for her ten-month-old daughter. Pearl had gladly rented her the place and had simply stayed on in the house, filling her days with caring for Isabella. It was the ideal arrangement for both of them.

"Do I get an introduction to this charming young lady?" Christian asked, leaning close so the baby could get a good look at his face.

"This is my daughter, Isabella."

"What a lovely name. Isabella." The baby dropped the chin strap and stared at him. He smiled beguilingly, figuring a female was a female. "Hello, Isabella," he murmured. "What a pretty little girl you are."

"Don't feel bad if she starts to cry," Alex said. "She doesn't like—"

Her daughter didn't give her a chance to finish the sentence. With a little squeal she let go of her mother and launched herself at Christian, who caught her up against his chest.

"—men," Alex said lamely, her dark brows drawing together in confusion.

Isabella seldom went to strangers and *never* to a strange man, perhaps picking up on her mother's sense of caution. But she certainly looked happy in Christian's arms, smiling her cherubic little smile as he whispered in her ear, amusing herself with the zipper of his leather jacket. Alex could only stare in stunned disbelief, as baffled by Christian's ease as she was with her daughter's. He didn't strike her as the daddy type at all. He didn't even strike her as the marrying type. She would have bet the only thing he knew about babies was how to make them.

"Don't look so surprised, darling," Christian said, looking at her from under his lashes. "Women, with the notable exception of yourself, always like me."

Alex pressed her lips into a thin line and reached for the gray's reins. "I'll see to the horses."

Christian watched her walk away, chuckling a little under his breath.

Pearl snorted. "Laugh now, Mr. Atherton. You've got your work cut out with that one. She's not one of your flighty little fillies for chasing around with."

"Yes, ma'am," he said, giving the older lady his best contrite-little-boy look. He watched her stern glower melt into a laugh that lit up her round face.

"And she's got her work cut out for her, I can see that! Lordy!" She reached for the baby. "Get yourself inside the house, boy. I'll see to that ankle and give you a piece of cherry pie if you're good."

"I'm *always* good," Christian said with just enough suggestiveness to make the woman cluck at him and shake her head with reproach that didn't reach her twinkling eyes.

"Poor Miss Alex," she muttered, heading up the cracked walk to the simple old farmhouse.

Christian glanced around the yard as he hobbled toward the house, taking in the general state of the place. The house itself didn't look too decrepit. Daffodils and tulips were pushing themselves up through the ground along the front porch, lending cheer. The rest of the buildings had not fared as well over time. The stable leaned decidedly to one side. What little paint was left on it had long ago turned from white to dingy gray. The board fences around the small paddocks looked no better. More than one board was held to its post by baling twine. Many of the posts tilted drunkenly.

The place was quiet. Nothing marred the stillness but the occasional bang or nicker coming from the stable and the paddocks adjacent to it. Judging by the size of the barn and the number of animals in the pens, he would have guessed Alex was caring for fifteen to twenty horses. By herself. There was no sign of hired help around.

There were no signs of prosperity either. The dull yellow horse van parked near the barn had to be nearly twenty years old. It looked as though someone had taken a chain to it. Even at that, it appeared to be more roadworthy than the blue '77 Impala that was parked nearer the house, next to Pearl's little red Escort. The tires were almost bald. One back window was missing, the opening covered over with clear plastic and duct tape. All in all, it looked as unsafe as Terminator. He shuddered at the thought of Alex driving it on the area's winding roads.

It was clear to him she needed money. She claimed money was the reason she had taken on Tully Haskell and Terminator. But there were simpler, safer answers to her dilemma. She was a top-notch rider. She would have had no trouble getting hired on at any good stable, including Quaid Farm. She had chosen instead to start her own place and run it on the proverbial shoestring. And a worn, frayed shoestring it was. He couldn't help but wonder why.

"Get along in here now," Pearl scolded from the porch. "I can't be keeping this baby out in the breeze. She'll be up all night with an earache, and where will you be? Long gone, that's where."

He watched the woman disappear into the house, and he hobbled after her, thinking that if anyone around Briarwood knew about Alexandra Gianni and her mysterious past, it would have to be Pearl.

An hour later Christian was sitting in the cab of the horse van with a numbing bag of ice on his ankle, heading up the winding road toward Quaid Farm, none the wiser about the petite woman wrestling with the oversize steering wheel of the truck. Pearl had proved to be as reticent as a clam when it came to doling out information about the young woman with whom she was sharing her home. If she knew any of Alex's secrets, she hadn't been willing to pass them along to him. It seemed he was going to have to go to the source.

"Where did you say you came from?" he asked conversationally. "I can't seem to place you by your accent."

"I haven't got an accent," Alex said evasively. "You have an accent."

"Not according to anyone in Wessex."

Ball to Gianni's court. Alex would have shot him a look if she hadn't needed all her concentration on the twisting road that was growing slick with mist.

"What brought you to the States?" she asked, turning the tables on him. "Show jumping is so big in Britain. I'm sure you could have done well there with your own stable."

"Hmmm," Christian said noncommittally. He could have

done well, but he had been interested by neither the responsibility nor the idea of working under the jaundiced eye of those in his family who thought riding was a proper hobby for a gentleman but not at all suitable as a profession.

"It's a long story," he said at length, surprised at the thought that he might just like to share that story with Alex. He ordinarily had no desire to discuss such complex emotions with a woman, preferring to keep things light and fun. But he had a feeling Alex would be sympathetic. He gave her a beguiling, crooked smile. "I might be persuaded to tell it over a nice plate of scampi with red sauce."

Alex couldn't help but laugh. He was charmingly persistent. She actually felt tempted for the first time in a long time. Hunger stirred inside her at the thought of a cozy restaurant, an excellent meal . . . and Christian sitting across the table from her. Warm, sweet yearnings fluttered through her like ribbons in a slow breeze, stirring, tempting . . . dangerous to her. Her hands tightened on the steering wheel as common sense reminded her of her need for caution, her need for independence.

"I don't think I like the way your chin is lifting up," Christian said wryly, tilting his head back against the cracked vinyl seat of the van. "Bodes ill for my dinner plans, I'd say."

Glancing across at him Alex smiled at the comical expression of disappointment he wore. She doubted he lacked for dinner companions or companions of any sort. She was just a challenge to him. "I'm not going to go out with you, Christian."

"I'm not going to stop asking," he said pleasantly, but his sophistication suddenly seemed like a highly polished veneer over a core of raw masculine determination. "Never surrender and all that," he added lightly.

Alex clucked her tongue and shook her head as she turned her attention back to the road. "Just think of all the lovely ladies you could be going out with while you waste your time on me."

"You're the only lady I'm interested in, Alex," he murmured, suddenly serious.

The cab of the horse van seemed to shrink. Alex was acutely aware of the man sitting beside her, of his compelling personality, of the scent of his leather jacket, and the feel of his steady gaze.

"I mean to woo you, Alexandra," he said, managing to call back some of his usual lightheartedness. He crossed his arms over his chest casually and flashed her a roguish grin. "And if I do say so myself, I'm damned good at it."

"I don't doubt that you're the world champion," Alex said sardonically. "But you're going to knock yourself out this time."

"We'll see."

Mercifully the road changed the topic for her. "Is this the turn?"

"Yes."

Alex hit the blinker, slowed the van, and shifted down, grinding the gears horribly as they turned and started up the gravel drive. They drove up and around a thickly wooded hill, finally emerging at the top where pastures rolled before them like an emerald quilt, each square delineated by dark, four-plank oak fencing. The large white sign at the end of the first field read Quaid Farm in simple, elegant royal blue letters.

The pang of envy was automatic. This was what she had always dreamed of—the long, tree-lined drive, the pastures dotted with top-quality stock, the immaculate white buildings. It was what she had left behind. Now it would be a long time before she would be able to drive up a lane like this one and feel as if she were something other than a delivery person.

"Pull up at the first barn," Christian said.

Alex did as instructed, taking in as much of the place as she could while she parked and shut down the van, ignoring the way the engine ran on, knocking and clanking. There were two long stables with the big end doors rolled back, revealing rows of brightly lit box stalls. The first barn was attached to a large indoor arena. Farther away stood a smaller barn with brood mares waiting patiently in the paddocks, and another low white building that was probably the breeding shed. Off to the right, beyond a small yard strewn with toddler's toys, stood the house, a larger, better-maintained version of the one she was renting. It was a typical old-fashioned Virginia farmhouse with a welcoming porch and a shiny tin roof, and windows full of warm light and lace curtains.

The stable yard was bustling with activity as afternoon chores began. Stable hands moved energetically from one building to the next, each of them followed by at least one dog. The dogs were of all sizes and breeds, and they trotted purposefully along, as if they felt their presence was necessary for the men to do a proper job.

Rylan Quaid sauntered to the doorway of the first barn as Alex climbed down out of the cab of her truck. She recognized him from photographs in the horse magazines. His was one of the most ambitious breeding programs in the country as far as jumping horses went. His younger sister Katie had once been one of the top young riders on the circuit, destined for a spot on the Olympic team, when a fall ended her career and nearly ended her life.

Alex looked up at the owner of Quaid Farm and swallowed hard. If he had looked unapproachable in his photographs, he looked downright intimidating in the flesh. He was a huge man, six feet four and built like a bull. His face looked to be carved of granite, an appropriate pinnacle for a mountain of masculinity. His features were rough-hewn and angular. He seemed physically incapable of smiling. Narrow, stormy eyes stared at her from beneath heavy dark brows.

"Alex, this cantankerous-looking person is Rylan Quaid."

Alex jumped at the sound of Christian's voice so near her ear. He had slid across the seat of the van and eased himself to the ground beside her.

"Ry, this is Alexandra Gianni, the trainer I was telling you about."

"It's a pleasure, miss," Ry said, politely touching the bill of his battered blue baseball cap. He swung immediately in Christian's direction, piercing his friend and trainer with a fierce look of annoyance. "Jeepers cripes, Atherton, where the hell have you been? I've got Bobby and Marlin up in the woods looking for your body."

"Metallica and I took a bit of a tumble, I'm afraid," he explained as Alex went around to the back of the van. "Alex rescued me."

Alex led the gray gelding down the ramp of the van and into the aisle of the barn. Scowling, Ry immediately bent to inspect the animal's legs for damage.

"He's fine," Christian said, hobbling into the barn with his boot in one hand and his ice bag in the other. "I didn't fare as well. Thanks for asking."

Ry turned his scowl at him, rising up to his full height and planting his hands at the waistband of his faded jeans. "You're hurt? How the hell can you be hurt? You're like a damn cat—always land on your feet."

Christian lifted his stockinged foot. "Well, I won't be landing on this foot for a while. I've twisted my ankle."

"I think we ought to shoot him, don't you, gov'nor?" Charlie asked, coming to take the horse. "Put him out of his mis'ry like. Right?"

Christian frowned at the girl as he felt his blood pressure shoot up. "You are perpetually insubordinate," he said through his teeth.

Charlie squinted and laughed her carefree laugh, shaking a finger at him. "My, aren't we stuffy today? Stuffy, stuffy."

"I'll give you stuffy," Christian growled, leaning over her aggressively. "Take that horse and groom him till he shines like sterling, or you'll have the devil to pay."

"Go on. Go on. Cuff me one," Charlie challenged teasingly, turning her round, rouged cheek to him for a target. "Box me a good one right here in front of all these nice witnesses. I'll sue your bloody bum off. That nice Mr. Hill is a solicitor, you know. I'll go straight to him."

Ry's face cracked into a smile at the shade of red Christian was flushing. "Go on along now, girl," he said to Charlie. "Get to work before he takes you up on it."

Alex watched the scene through cautious eyes, wondering if Christian was capable of that kind of violence.

"So, hotshot," Ry said. "You need a lift to the hospital?"

"I don't need a doctor," Christian said, watching Alex edge back toward the door of her truck. She was ready to make her getaway, but he wasn't anywhere near ready to see the last of her. "It's just a sprain. I'll be all right to ride"—he broke off and just managed to suppress a grin at his own genius—"in a week or two."

Rylan heaved a strained sigh and rubbed a big hand across the back of his thick neck. "Jeepers cripes. We can't afford to lay off. Diamond Life is just coming into form. Legendary is finally getting it all together. Bobby can school the young horses, but with Greg gone to Germany . . . well, hell."

"I was thinking perhaps we could get Alex to ride for us until I'm fit." Christian turned to her with one of his dazzling smiles. She was looking at him as if he had just pulled the dirtiest of tricks. "She's excellent. I wouldn't have any qualms about having her."

Alex blushed furiously at the double meaning that was obvious in his mischievous gaze as he grinned down at her.

"What do you say, Ms. Gianni?" Ry asked, oblivious to the undercurrents surging between the two trainers. "Chris tells me you're top-notch. We've got a show string needs riding every day if we're gonna have them ready for Devon."

The Quaid Farm show string. A sharp pang of longing went through Alex's chest. He was talking about horses that made most of hers look like an inferior species. But she didn't want to work for someone else, she reminded herself. The last thing she wanted was to have to answer to Christian, who had set his sights on her like a hawk swooping down on a field mouse. Besides, she had horses of her own to ride. She was working twelve-hour days that left her little energy for anything extra.

"I'm afraid I already have a full schedule, Mr. Quaid," she said with a mix of relief and regret.

"If you had a good groom working for you, you'd have sufficient time to ride at least my grand prix horses as well as your own," Christian said.

Alex stuck her chin out and gave him a steady stare. "But I don't have a groom."

"You ought to have," he insisted, that unfamiliar feeling of responsibility rearing its ugly head again. He didn't want Alex working like a dog. She was too small and fragile. "You will have if I loan you Charlie," he said, smiling as he thought of killing two birds with one stroke of genius.

"I couldn't let you do that."

"It's not as big a favor as you think," he said dryly. "She's going to drive me mad. I'd be more than happy to send her to you and pay her room and board as well as her salary."

"I don't need your charity," Alex said stiffly, her obsessive sense of self-reliance asserting itself. She depended on no one. She had leaned on others for support before, and they had stepped away when she'd needed them most, letting her fall on her face. She had been forced to learn to stand on her own two feet. If she let Christian have his way, she doubted she'd be left standing at all.

Ry snorted. "Hell, girl, that ain't charity, it's business. We need a rider. If we have to trade you a groom on the deal, so be it—as long as Charlie agrees."

"But—"

Cutting to what he felt was the heart of the matter, Ry named a figure for a week's work that made Alex's head swim. She'd forgotten what a good stable could afford to pay. Temptation battered her resistance. The chance to ride world-class horses and get paid handsomely for it. Could she really afford to turn the offer down? Did she really want to?

"Well, that's settled then," Christian said cheerfully, his smile brilliant enough to light the darkening day. He wrapped an arm companionably around Alex's slim shoulders, not missing the way she stiffened at his touch. She shot him a warning glance but didn't try to pull away. His voice dropped automatically to a seductive purr. "Alex, let's you and I go discuss the particulars—say, over a nice glass of wine?"

Ry rolled his eyes and muttered, "I should have guessed." Clearing his throat he offered a big callused hand to Alex and said, "Thanks for helping us out, Ms. Gianni. I appreciate it."

"You're welcome," Alex said, surprised at how gentle his grasp was when he was certainly capable of cracking coconuts with it. She noticed then that his hard-looking gray green eyes had softened subtly and his smile was warm. There was no doubt a very nice man under the gruff exterior, she realized.

A skinny tow-headed groom interrupted them, clearing his throat nervously as he came out of the office. "Mr. Quaid, sir? Mrs. Quaid just called and says you're needed up at the house."

Ry instantly turned gray. He bolted out of the barn and across the yard through the thickening mist.

Alex lifted a questioning brow as Christian chuckled.

"His wife is expecting their second child," he explained. "He worries about her incessantly, even though it isn't necessary. Maggie is as healthy as a horse."

"How sweet," Alex murmured. A sense of loss assailed her

as she watched Ry bound up the steps of his porch and charge into the house. Michael had never worried about her or fussed over her during her pregnancy. He had avoided her, watching her from a distance with hurt and guilt and accusation in his dark eyes. And finally he had divorced her, not able to wait it out, giving in to the pressure before he'd even had the chance to see or hold the daughter who ironically looked just like him.

Christian studied her expression, the need to hold and console her stealing upon him again. He didn't curse it quite as strongly as he might have. It seemed only civilized to feel protective toward a woman with such a terrible, haunted look in her eyes. He couldn't begin to imagine what could have happened to put such a look there. All he could think of was doing his best to erase it.

"Let's go have that drink," he said softly.

Why she went with him, Alex couldn't have said. The idea of going into the lion's den to share his hospitality ordinarily would have set off a cacophony of warning bells. Not this time. She told herself it was because Christian was injured. She could outrun him if necessary. Deeper down she suspected it had something to do with the quiet comfort he'd offered in his cultured British voice and warm blue eyes.

Curiosity played a part as well. What rider wouldn't have wanted to see how Christian Atherton lived?

His cottage sat on a well-tended lawn away from the main house and on the opposite side of the drive, a short walk from the stables, though they took Alex's van because of Christian's lack of mobility. As soon as they were in the front door he dropped onto a deep green overstuffed sofa and eased his aching leg up onto the matching footstool.

The room was impeccably decorated in a masculine English

country style with shades of dark red, beige, and hunter green throughout. The floor was old polished pine with a thick beige area rug covering most of the space. Fox-hunting scenes decorated the walls. The furniture looked antique. The overall effect was of expensive tastes and a comfortable lifestyle.

"I'm afraid I'm not going to be much of a host," Christian admitted ruefully.

His ankle was throbbing something fierce, hurting worse than he had thought it would. Damn, he thought darkly, he had Alex in his lair but no strength to take advantage of the situation. Bloody rotten luck. Of course, the silver lining was the thought of having her at the farm every day for a week. He brightened at the prospect.

"There's a bottle of white zinfandel in the fridge, if you don't mind playing hostess."

"I shouldn't have any. I have to drive home. With these roads and the rain . . ."

"And that truck," Christian muttered under his breath. Fighting off the respectable urge to lecture her on safety, he cleared his throat and nodded. "Quite right. Be a love, though, and bring me a glass, would you? It tastes a far sight better than aspirin."

"Sure."

The way to the kitchen was obvious. Alex went through the archway between the living room and dining room, passed an elegant mahogany dining set that looked older than the United States, and went into the kitchen beyond. The wine in the refrigerator was expensive, the glasses in the cherrywood cupboard crystal.

She treated herself to a sip of the blush-colored wine, moaning in appreciation at the crisp, fresh taste. Good wine was something she couldn't afford to indulge in these days.

As she returned to the living room she glanced down a hall

that led presumably to the bedroom. Something basically feminine in her fluttered with curiosity about what she might find in there. Scolding herself for caring, she hurried on.

"Is there anything else I can get you?" she asked, handing him his drink. "I really should be going. I have chores to do yet tonight."

"Sit for a minute," he said, nodding to the empty end of the couch, amazed when she obeyed. He took a drink, closed his eyes, and sighed reverently, then set the glass aside on an antique pine end table. "I haven't thanked you for offering to help."

"I didn't offer," Alex said sardonically. "You railroaded me."

Christian gave an imperious shrug. "A minor detail. I really do appreciate it, Alex. Besides, it seemed only sporting since you're the one who got me thrown in the first place."

He chuckled as her eyes flashed, and she sucked in a breath in prelude to what was undoubtedly a scathing opinion of his version of the accident. She didn't let the words out, though her face went red with the effort to hold them back.

He was fast discovering all the right buttons to push, Christian thought, feeling a bit smug. Very soon Alex was going to have to give up all pretense of hiding her emotions from him. He liked that idea very much.

"I'd better go," she said stiffly.

Trying to ignore the pain in his ankle, he rose and escorted her to the door, hobbling and wincing all the way.

Alex pulled the door open and groaned aloud at the sight of the strong, steady rain that had begun to fall and the expanse of yard she had to run across to get to her truck.

"Don't suppose you'd rather stay till it lets up?" he said dryly. "I can think of any number of ways for us to pass the time."

Alex gave him a look. "I'll bet."

She was amazed that she didn't feel an urgent need to escape him. The need to escape her own awakening desires was another matter altogether, but Christian . . . He was smiling at her—one of his lopsided, I'm-your-best-friend smiles—his fathomless blue eyes twinkling with good humor. How many other men would have been petulant over her constant rebuffs? She could name one in particular, one other wealthy, handsome, privileged son. . . .

The thought drifted away as Christian leaned forward and kissed her. He didn't try to hold her. He hung on to the open door with one hand and braced the other against the jamb. He touched her only with his mouth, and she responded without thought, tilting her head back. He tasted warm and as intoxicating as the wine that lingered on his lips.

Lifting his head, he murmured, "Drive carefully, darling. I'll see you in the morning."

Stunned by her own reaction, Alex said nothing. She just turned and ran from the house to the sanctuary of her decrepit yellow truck. Once inside the cab she sat clutching the steering wheel with white-knuckled hands, listening to the rain pound down on the roof. And she wondered what the hell she'd just gotten herself into.

# five

**THIS HAD TO BE WHAT IT WAS LIKE TO RIDE** Pegasus, Alex thought dreamily as she and Diamond Life soared over an array of red-and-white bars. The young Hanoverian stallion launched himself effortlessly over the fence and practically floated back to earth. Alex's spirit stayed somewhere in the stratosphere. This was what riding jumpers was all about. To glide and sail on the back of a powerful, willing animal.

It was only her first ride on the blood bay that was Quaid Farm's heir to the throne of their great jumper Rough Cut, the horse that had set a bookful of records and then been retired to stand at stud, and already she was thoroughly in love with him. He was talented, obedient, enthusiastic—in short, Diamond Life was everything most of her mounts were not. He shared a sire with Rough Cut and showed every intention of taking his sibling's place in the arena.

Sadly, Rough Cut would never be in a position to challenge the young bay. Upon his retirement he had been stricken with a devastating illness that had left him chronically lame and sterile. Time and extensive, often experimental, treatment had solved the second problem. He seemed perfectly happy in his role as daddy, seemingly not missing the exquisite grace and speed that had won him fame the world over. He was kept comfortable with painkillers and spent his time out of the breeding shed dozing contentedly in a large paddock that faced the Blue Ridge mountains.

Diamond Life was the up-and-coming star of Quaid Farm and the grand prix circuit, and Alex was more than enjoying the experience of schooling him. She took him around the spacious indoor arena, over a series of jumps known as a gymnastic, designed to improve a horse's rhythm and form, then cantered him diagonally across the ring, popping him over a small vertical and then a spread fence. Each one was perfection and joy.

Christian watched from the gate that led into the barn, his admiration plain on his face. He may have been a flatterer by nature, but he never gave false praise to a rider. Flirting was one thing, riding was serious business. One had to earn respect in the show ring, and Alex had his. It was ridiculous how proud that made him feel. Shaking his head a little, he decided he was behaving like an infatuated schoolboy.

"She's good, isn't she?" Maggie Quaid asked.

Christian glanced down at her and smiled warmly. Maggie had stolen his heart four years ago when she'd asked him to help her overcome her fear of horses so she could spend more time with Ry. Sassy and flirtatious, Maggie had a heart of pure gold. She doted on her friends and adored her irascible husband. Rylan worshiped the ground she walked on.

"How are you feeling today, Maggie?"

She patted her well-rounded belly and made a face. "Like a minivan."

"Oh, you're beautiful and glowing, and well you know it."

She tilted her head so her red bob fell at a flattering angle along her jawline and batted her lashes at him. "Why, Mr. Atherton," she said, her voice pure magnolias and honey, "how you do go on."

Christian chuckled and turned back toward the arena. "To answer your question: Yes, she's very good."

"She must be something special to keep your feet on the ground."

"In case you hadn't noticed," he said dryly, leaning back to display his crutches, "I *am* injured."

"Mmm-hmmm," Maggie murmured, unimpressed by his props. "Like you were injured that time a whole herd of yearlings trampled you and you won the Cavalier Classic the next day?"

He scowled at her sweet, brown-eyed smile. "That was entirely different."

"Oh, you're quite right. That time you had three cracked ribs, bruised kidneys, and a mild concussion."

His scowl darkened, the aristocratic lines of his face sharpening.

"And you didn't have a pretty, black-haired little gal to take your place so you could spend time trying to charm her." Maggie put an arm around his lean waist and gave him an affectionate hug. "Don't try to outfox me, sugar. I know every trick in the book."

He considered asking her to share a few with him, but the day hadn't come when Christian Atherton needed to ask advice about wooing a lady. He shored up his pride and held his tongue.

They watched Alex for another moment, chatting companionably as she and Diamond Life worked in the empty end of the ring, moving laterally, cantering in concentric circles that grew smaller and slower, then larger and faster. Finally she slowed the horse to a walk and pulled off her helmet, shaking her hair free in the gesture that seemed hauntingly familiar to Christian.

"Look at all that hair," Maggie murmured. "Think if it were long, how wild it would be."

Christian grew still as he tried to capture the ghost of a memory floating through his mind. A petite young woman with a long mane of untamed black ringlets and a bright red blouse that stood out like fire against her olive complexion. He could just see her tossing her head back in that certain way. But he couldn't quite place the memory, and he couldn't place Alex.

"How was that?" Alex asked as Diamond Life sauntered lazily toward the gate.

"Smashing." Christian grinned. "How do you like him?"

Alex rolled her eyes and offered her highest praise in heartfelt Italian. As a groom came into the ring and took the horse by the bridle, she hopped to the ground and began unfastening the girth.

"I'll see to that, Ms. Gianni."

"Right." Alex nodded sheepishly. The days of riding and walking away, leaving the dirty work to someone else, had all but faded from her memory. It was a nice treat. But she couldn't get used to it, she reminded herself sternly.

"You look wonderful on him," Maggie said as Alex let herself out the gate. "I'm Maggie Quaid."

"I'm pleased to meet you, Maggie, and thanks. But I think Diamond Life could make anybody look good. He's a fabulous animal."

"You've obviously never seen me ride," Maggie said dryly.

There was a sudden commotion in the alleyway, and from around the corner of a stall appeared a sturdy dark-haired little boy of about three leading a big white goat with a length of twine. The goat was protesting loudly. The boy leaned ahead and trudged along as if he were towing a barge, the determined look on his face a miniature version of his father's scowl.

Alex covered her laughter with her hand. Christian tightened his lips against his.

Maggie rolled her eyes. "Buddy, let that goat be. Buddy . . ."

The toddler and the goat faced-off in a tug of war.

"Thomas Randall Quaid," Maggie snapped. "Leave that animal alone."

Buddy Quaid didn't have a chance to disobey his mother's dictate. The goat lunged forward suddenly, knocked him on the seat of his miniature blue jeans, and scampered out into the arena, its tether floating behind it like a ribbon.

"See what happens when you don't listen to your mama?" Maggie said gently, leaning down to help her son up and dust off his britches.

Buddy's face was a study in disappointment. His lower lip jutted forward threateningly. "Darn goat."

"Don't you worry about the goat, young man. You worry about what your daddy's going to say if he catches you trying to ride that creature again. He's told you a hundred times you can't ride goats."

Buddy scuffed the toe of his little cowboy boot against the concrete and looked dejected. Maggie's stern expression melted, and she pressed a kiss to her son's dark head.

"Christian tells me you have a daughter," she said, smiling up at Alex.

Alex nodded and glowed with maternal pride. "Isabella. She's ten months old."

"We'll have to get together some evening. I can warn you all about the terrible twos."

"Splendid idea!" Christian beamed, seizing the opportunity with gusto. "Why don't we do it over dinner? The four of us at Nick's."

Maggie gave him a look. "Maybe when Alex isn't so busy," she said pointedly. "She's going to be exhausted, what with having to do your riding on top of her own."

Christian frowned at her. Loyalty to gender. He should have expected as much. He shifted on his crutches, guilt nipping at him.

Guilt! Gads, he never felt guilt! It wasn't as if Alex was doing his riding for free. And it wasn't as if he weren't really hurt. Besides, Alex needed to become acquainted with the caliber of horse she deserved. She belonged on mounts like Diamond Life and Legendary, not Terminator. He was doing this for her own good. He all but told her as much a few minutes later, after Maggie had said her good-byes and led Buddy away toward the house.

He invited Alex into the dispensary, where the communal coffee pot was kept. Setting his crutches aside so he could use his hands, he poured two cups and offered one to Alex. They leaned back against the counter and discussed the way the stallion had gone and what the training strategy was to have him ready for the upcoming show. Eventually Christian managed to turn the conversation Alex's way.

"You're really very talented, Alex," he said. "And that isn't simple flattery. Any number of top stables would be lucky to have you, and I think you know it."

*Oh, I know it*, Alex thought, glancing away. She also knew that no top stable would hire her without proper references, and her last employer would hardly write a glowing recommendation. By the time the Reidells got through running her down, she'd be lucky to get a job mucking out stalls at a sale barn.

"Why are you doing this, Alex?" Christian asked, bemused. "Why put up with bastards like Haskell and Terminator when you don't have to?"

"I want to be my own boss," she answered truthfully enough, though she still avoided his eyes. "I put up with Tully and Terminator because that's what I have to do if I want to ride A Touch of Dutch. They're a package deal."

"You don't need rides that badly."

She lifted a black brow but kept her temper in check, projecting ice instead of fire. "Who are you to say so?"

Christian slammed his coffee mug down as an irrational burst of responsibility surged through him. "Dammit, Alex, I'll send you some of my own if that's what it takes. I can't stand to see you risking your neck on that rogue."

"It's my neck," she said stubbornly.

Christian heaved a sigh as he watched her chin go up. "There goes the drawbridge," he muttered.

Alex gave him a suspicious look. "What?"

"Nothing." He shook his head wearily, his shoulders slumping. He ran a hand back through his pale hair and sighed again. "You're right, of course, it's none of my business. Forgive me for being indiscriminately concerned. I really don't know what's gotten into me lately."

*Join the club*, Alex thought as she stared pensively into her coffee. She had come to Virginia with a simple outline for her life. Suddenly things were getting complicated beyond belief. She found herself recklessly drawn to a man who had a reputation for collecting hearts like charms for a bracelet. She found herself liking him, wanting to be with him, yearning for another of his kisses.

It was the height of folly. Even if she let herself think there could be something special between her and Christian Atherton, even if she agreed to go out with him, what would ultimately come of it? He would expect things to progress on their natural course. What would Christian think of her when she finally told him about her past, which she would have to do. It wouldn't be fair not to tell him. Would he believe her side of the story when no one else had—including her own family? Why would he, she wondered cynically.

"Where do you go?" Christian asked on a whisper, his eyes as deep and blue as the sea as he leaned nearer. "Where do you go when you drift away?"

"Nowhere," Alex murmured, knowing the lie was plain on her face.

The corner of Christian's mouth tilted up. "You're such a mystery."

"No, I'm not!" she insisted too vehemently, instinctively wary of having him want to solve the puzzle. She suddenly remembered seeing a shelf full of mystery novels in his cottage, and her blood ran cold. She actually felt herself go pale. "There's nothing mysterious about me! I'm just trying to make a life as best I can."

"All right, all right," Christian murmured, calming her with his soothing, mesmerizing voice. He lifted a hand to gently brush her hair out of her eyes. "It's all right."

Alex relaxed by degrees, her breath gradually coming in slower gasps.

"It's all right," Christian whispered again, inching closer.

He stroked her cheek, running his thumb along her jaw and tilting her head back with subtle pressure. Their gazes locked, and for an instant there was a communication flowing between them that defied words, a current of feeling that was strong and undeniable. Then his lashes fluttered down as he slowly lowered his mouth to hers.

Alex drank in his kiss with a sense of desperation as emotions tore loose from their moorings inside her and crashed into one another. She wanted him, she wanted no one. She wanted to feel, she wanted to remain numb. She wanted a life without memories, she could never forget.

Passion won out momentarily as she blocked out the maelstrom of other emotions. For just an instant she let herself respond the way a woman would want to respond with a handsome, charming man kissing her—hungrily.

Christian groaned low in his throat. Gently he pinned Alex against the counter, flanking her legs with his own. He ran a hand over her short hair, down the sleek column of her throat, down to cup her small, full breast through the loose black polo shirt she wore, and groaned again as her nipple budded beneath his thumb.

"Oh, Alex," he said, his voice low and hoarse, tortured and ecstatic.

He wanted her with a fierceness he hadn't experienced since

his youth. Just one touch, one taste, and he was hard and straining against the fly of his jeans. He tilted his hips into hers, letting her feel what she was doing to him, letting her know in no uncertain terms what he wanted. Just the thought of her tight, hot warmth closing around him bumped his pulse up another notch. The idea of having her naked and willing in his arms sent heat flaming through him.

He kissed her again, this time seeking entrance to her mouth and all the warm, honeyed delights he knew he would find there. Alex sagged against him for just a second or two, giving in to what she had forbidden herself—the comfort of being held, the electricity of desire, the building sense of urgency.

Feelings she had denied for so long rushed to the surface with overwhelming force, and panic was not far behind. She pulled away from him quickly, almost frantically.

"No," she said in a tortured whisper as old feelings of guilt and shame swirled with disappointment and despair inside her. She pushed Christian back with her palms splayed across his chest. She couldn't bring herself to look up at him, afraid of what she might see in his eyes. She focused instead on her fingers and the royal blue jersey beneath them.

"Alex?" Christian asked, stunned by her sudden change of heart. She had been responding so sweetly, her body arching into his, her mouth wild and sweet.

"No," she mumbled again, tears choking her as she stumbled for the door. She pulled up in the doorway, fighting her own urge to flee. Chest heaving, she swallowed hard and said, "I . . . have to get back to work."

Christian watched her go, utterly confused and utterly frustrated. He wasn't used to having a lady fight off the pleasant temptation of desire. Why had Alex? She was single, unattached, definitely attracted to him. There was no earthly reason why they shouldn't simply enjoy the mutual magnetism. And yet there had been the unmistakable bleak look of self-recrimination in her expression before she'd turned and run.

He had a strong urge to go after her, but he fought it. She obviously wanted time alone. He would give her the chance to sort out her feelings. Going back to the cupboard, he poured himself another cup of coffee and drank it as he mused about the whirlwind of a woman's emotions.

Ry stomped into the dispensary, grumbling. "Can you believe that Tully Haskell? Called to try to sell me that daughter of Abdullah when he knows damn well she isn't sound. As if I'd ever buy anything from him." He poured himself a cup of coffee and jabbed his friend with a pointed look. "I wouldn't buy a talking dog from Tully Haskell for a nickel, if it sat right up and called me sweetheart. What's the matter with you?"

Nothing Alex Gianni couldn't fix in the course of a long, hot night, Christian thought ruefully. "Nothing," he said. "Just pondering the fact that women are impossible to figure out."

"Well, hell," Ry growled. "I could have told you that."

# SIX

**ALEX LEANED AGAINST THE DUN MARE'S** side, her eyes drifting shut as sleep beckoned. For the fifth day she had risen at five a.m. to see to some of her own chores before leaving to ride Christian's horses. She would be home by noon, grab a quick bite, and play with Isabella for a few minutes. Then it would be back in the saddle, riding her own string of six horses in training. Then came after-school riding lessons for three students, evening chores, supper, Isabella's bath and bedtime, another hour in the barn to tend to the mare's injured foot, book work until she dozed off, a few hours' fitful sleep, and the process would start all over again.

Charlie had been a big help with chores and grooming. She would have been an even bigger help if Alex would have allowed it. But Alex was determined not to become dependent on having a stable hand. It was her place, not Christian Atherton's. The idea of accepting help from him made her uncomfortable. Old instincts died hard. The one that told her men didn't do favors without expecting something in return prodded at her like a stone in her shoe.

She wanted to trust him. He deserved to have her trust him. Experience had bred caution in her, taught her not to give her trust so easily. She had learned to look for subtle signs of a person's trustworthiness—the way his contemporaries related to him, the way his employees regarded him. Christian was widely liked by his peers. The people working for him respected him because he treated them well. There were no sidelong, furtive looks following him down the aisle after an order was given. By all signs large and small he was a good man. A tad too sure of himself and inclined to play the rake, but a good man where it counted.

Sighing, Alex bent to check the temperature of the water the horse was soaking its abscessed hoof in. She added a little from the steaming bucket she had carried down from the house and tossed in another handful of Epsom salts. The mare, a boarder's field hunter, dozed. Alex resumed her casual position against the horse's side and let her mind wander back over the past few days.

She had done her best to avoid Christian the remainder of her first day at Quaid Farm—not because she had been afraid of him, but because she had been ashamed of herself for letting something get started that she couldn't finish. It was best for both of them that they not exceed the bounds of friendship.

Guilt made a return visit now as she recalled how Christian had finally caught up with her as she'd been about to leave.

"Alex, I'm sorry."

"For what?"

The wind riffled that one roguish strand of hair that fell across his forehead, and he shrugged, a gesture that was the embodiment of male confusion. "Obviously, I upset you . . ." He let the words trail off, at a loss for the reason.

Alex shook her head and stared down at the gravel of the drive.

"I'm the one who should apologize," she said. But the explanation didn't come. Like a logjam trying to move through the narrow neck of a river, the words and reasons stuck in her throat and built up until she could feel the pressure of them.

"I get very high marks for listening," he said softly, his cultured voice as warm and comforting as flannel on a damp fall day.

Alex just sighed and shook her head again, slowly, regretfully. It was a story best left untold, for everyone's sake.

She repeated that to herself now as she leaned against the dun mare. It had become a litany in the last few days as Christian had done his best to charm her and she had done her best to resist him. A litany with dwindling conviction behind it. Conviction that ebbed during the course of long, lonely nights.

Her shoulders jumped and fell with her breath as she rested her cheek against the horse's side and closed her eyes. She was so tired. Physically tired. Tired of the sleepless nights. She had been born with emotions that ran high and close to the surface. She was tired from having to suppress them. Tired of altering herself into some pale, unnoticeable, inoffensive imitation of her former self, and afraid that in the end she would become someone even she didn't recognize.

"How are all my stars?"

The bellowing voice jolted Alex from her trance. She jerked awake with a gasp and a start, spooking the mare, who bolted, overturning the bucket. Tepid water sloshed out, soaking Alex's sneakers and washing across the cracked concrete floor of the barn's aisle in a dark stain.

"Didn't mean to startle you there, sweetheart," Tully Haskell said with a rather unconvincing gleam in his cold little eyes. He rolled a fat, inch-long stub of a cigar between his thumb and forefinger.

"Mr. Haskell," Alex said, automatically putting up the shield of cool control. She righted the bucket and set it aside. The dun mare stood at attention, but didn't show any signs of coming unglued. A good attitude to adopt, Alex decided. "What brings you out this way so early in the morning?"

"Does a man need an excuse to call on a pretty gal these days?"

Alex bit back the retort that was burning on her tongue. It seemed enough punishment for Tully that she did not respond to his sexist remark with a becoming blush and batting eyelashes. He frowned briefly, then ducked under the cross tie, coming close enough to make Alex want to step back.

"I'm out this way to check on a project. My company is building a two-hundred-fifty-thousand-dollar house on Valley Road, and I don't trust the lazy bastards on the crew to get it right." He jammed his cigar stub between his teeth, but it had gone out and acted only as an ugly accessory to his fleshy face. "You gotta stay on top of employees."

Gritting her teeth, Alex moved past him to unhook the horse from the cross ties. "I hope you don't mind if I work while we talk. I have to leave in a few minutes."

"You're working too hard for such a little gal. Ought to have a man around here, don't you think?"

She muttered a few words in Italian as she put the mare back in her stall.

"How's that?"

"Nothing," she answered, fairly certain he wouldn't want to hear that she thought his brain resided in a much lower region of his body than his head.

"Anyhow," Tully went on, never terribly concerned with what anyone else was thinking, "I just swung in to check with you about next weekend. You're taking the horses to Front Royal?"

"Yes. I'll be leaving early Saturday morning."

"And you're staying in what motel?"

"I'm . . . staying with an old girlfriend," she lied smoothly, her deep-seated sense of caution asserting itself. She let herself out of the stall and leaned against the door, staring in at the unremarkable mare because she didn't want to look at Tully. She disliked him intensely and wasn't all that sure of her ability to keep it out of her expression.

"Hmmm," Tully mused. "Well, fine." He planted a big hand on her shoulder and shot her a wink and a grin that was meant to bring a teasing quality to his next words. "I'll be there to give you a kiss in the winner's circle."

Alex barely suppressed the urge to gag at the thought. She gave him a pained smile and shot the bolt home in the mare's stall with unnecessary force. "I'll see you in Front Royal then, Mr. Haskell."

"You can count on that," Tully said.

As he moved away from her he let his hand trail down her back. Alex jumped a bit, sure she felt him pinch her bottom, but when she wheeled to glare accusingly at him, he was sauntering away without giving her a backward glance.

Swearing liberally, she snatched up the empty bucket and stormed into the tack room, banging it against the wall as she went in an effort to blow off some of her steam. She cursed herself out of habit and Tully out of simple dislike. Why had she attracted the likes of him? Why couldn't a dotty little old lady own A Touch of Dutch? She'd never been tempted to slap a little old lady. She'd never been nervous around little old ladies either.

And I won't be nervous around Haskell, she told herself, relaxing with an effort. She didn't have anything to worry about. She hadn't encouraged his advances. He wasn't likely to take them beyond the harmless flirtation stage.

Something scuffed the floor behind her, and she whirled with her heart in her throat, eyes wide, adrenaline pumping, instincts on red alert, only to find the source of her panic was the scruffy old barn cat. The bedraggled gray feline looked up at her, a freshly caught mouse drooping from its jaws. Then it turned and ran away, leaving Alex to lean weakly against the saddle rack, trying to put the memory that had shaken loose back into its sealed black box in her mind.

Christian steered his silver Mercedes carefully off the road and up the pitted, rutted stretch of gravel Alex called a driveway. Once in the farmyard he parked near the barn, briefly contemplating ramming Charlie Simmonds's red-and-white motorbike where it leaned against the weathered side of the building. The only thing that saved him from doing it was the respect he had for his own vehicle and the distaste he had for facing Marcel, the Frenchman who serviced the machine at a specialty garage in Alexandria.

Charlie Simmonds was a blight on his life. He cursed the day her parents had met. It was because of Charlie he was feeling so guilty.

"Ought to be ashamed of yourself," she'd said, screwing her face into a scowl that made her little eyes all but disappear. "Working herself to a limp frazzle, poor little miss. And for what? So you can lay around on your ruddy bum and watch. Selfish, selfish. That's you all over. What a bloody crying shame it is. Better than the likes of you, that's what she deserves, all right, poor little miss."

Even now he growled at the thought of the dressing-down Charlie had given him the night before. She'd ridden up to the farm on her motorbike after evening chores for the sole purpose of giving him a tongue-lashing.

As a result he hadn't slept a wink and had instead spent the entire night berating himself for being a devious, selfish, uncaring cad. These were not welcome feelings, but he couldn't shake them. He couldn't even find any comfort in the knowledge that he had never denied being selfish, that what Charlie called devious tendencies he considered clever thinking, that by uncaring she meant self-absorbed, which he had never denied either. He was a confirmed bachelor, for heaven's sake! Those were all perfectly ordinary traits for a confirmed bachelor.

Grumbling under his breath, he climbed out of his sports

car already dressed for riding in black breeches and a khaki polo shirt. His ankle was still sore, but it was nothing he hadn't endured before. He merely ignored it as best he could as he walked into the poorly lit barn, limping slightly.

It wasn't entirely his fault Alex was overworked, he told himself for the millionth time. He'd sent her a groom, hadn't he? For all her cheek Charlie was a good worker. There was no reason Alex couldn't have been making better use of her, no reason Alex should have to get up an hour early to do tasks Charlie could easily handle.

Stubborn, that's what she was. Bloody stubborn. And a damned attractive trait it was. He ground his teeth at the thought. Where were these ludicrous ideas coming from? Full breasts were an attractive trait, not pigheadedness.

He turned in at the open tack-room door, alarm spurring his pulse into overdrive. Alex was bent over a saddle rack, her eyes squeezed tightly shut, her skin as pale as porcelain. He was across the small room in one stride.

"Alex!" He grabbed her upper arms, fearing she was ill or in pain. Certainly she looked weak.

Her eyes flew open, and the stark terror he saw there was like an electric jolt to his heart. In a purely instinctive reaction, she jerked back with enough force to pull him into the opposite side of the saddle rack.

"Alex, it's me!" he said, not realizing his fingers were biting into her flesh. He'd never had a woman look at him with such pure horror. It was a terrible feeling. "For God's sake, calm down!"

She stared at him for a tense moment as if she had no idea who he was. Then everything started to click into place. The fear left her eyes—but the general wariness didn't. Her body relaxed visibly, her shoulders sagging. She started breathing again, slowly and regularly.

"Christian," she said evenly. "You startled me."

"Startled you?" he said, incredulous, still shaken to the core. "Frightened to death is more like it. What's the matter? I came in and saw you bent over this saddle. . . ."

She looked down at the smooth dark leather, feeling she'd made a disastrous slip. He'd seen her with her guard completely down. It made her feel too vulnerable.

"Alex?"

"Nothing. I had a cramp, that's all."

She fully expected him to drop the topic. No man of her acquaintance had ever wanted to hear any of the gory details of a woman's life. It was a topic guaranteed to scare them off. But then, most men weren't Christian Atherton.

"You're lying," he said flatly, too upset to be polite. "Good Lord, Alexandra, you reacted as if you thought I was going to attack you!"

Instantly she dodged his gaze, glancing toward the open door, unwittingly answering a question that was only half-formed in his mind. The sudden knowledge was a worse shock than her response had been.

"Oh, my . . ." His voice trailed off, and his hands fell away from her as a nauseating weakness spread through him. Leaning back against the saddle rack behind him, he ran a hand back through his hair. He thought of every time she'd shied away from him, of the way she'd thrown him that first day when he'd startled her from behind. Finally it all made sense. Terrible sense.

Alex pressed back against the rough wood wall, wishing with all her heart she could melt right through it. The instant Christian had realized the truth, he had taken his hands off her, as if she were unclean, as if he hoped it wasn't too late to save himself from being tainted. But that was exactly what she had expected.

"Alex," he murmured, lifting his gaze to hers, anguish plain in the fathomless blue depths. "I'm so sorry. I had no idea."

What happened now? she wondered. Did they just say their

good-byes and go their separate ways? Why hadn't he just stayed away from the beginning? They would have both been spared the embarrassment of this moment.

"Do you want to tell me what happened?" Christian asked gently. She looked so alone, so uncomfortable, as if she would have crawled right out of her skin had that been an option. Her shoulders were squared, tensed, pressed back against the wall, her hands splayed against the rough pine boards. She looked like someone expecting a firing squad and no blindfold.

Alex supposed she could have escaped. She doubted Christian would come after her. But she was tired of running. It wasn't in her nature. Stand and fight had always been her motto. She had stood her ground and fought before and come away battered and bloody, disillusioned by everyone and everything she had ever believed in. The choice now was simple in her eyes. She had nothing left to lose.

"My last name was DeGrazia then," she began.

"Alexandra DeGrazia," Christian murmured, the puzzle piece falling into place. "I saw you ride in California." He stared down at the saddle in front of him as if he could see the whole scene on it. "A three-day event outside of Napa. I was there looking at a mare who showed promise in the show ring but not cross-country."

"My husband Michael and I were riding for Wide Acre Farm, the Reidells," she prompted.

"Yes," he said, but there was no further dawning of understanding.

He didn't know. How ironic, Alex thought, almost tempted to laugh. She had been so sure her married name would evoke gasps and looks of self-righteous reproach from everyone who heard it. Because she had been the one at the center of the storm, she had been certain every third person in the free world had known about the trial.

Somehow it would have been easier if Christian had known.

He would have absorbed the details from the media and formed the same opinion everyone else had—that she was a liar. Now she would have the chance to tell her side once again. But no one else had ever believed her, so why would she think Christian might? Christian Atherton, of all people. A deep depression settled in her heart at the thought that he would leave her life now.

She sighed, conceding defeat, then told her tale in the flat, emotionless tone of a victim who has somehow managed to distance herself from the incident after being forced to relive it again and again.

"We had been working at Wide Acre about six months. It was going well. We got along well enough with Mr. Reidell. His son Greg was about our age, a little younger. I guess he was twenty-two or twenty-three, and I was twenty-five. We were friends—Greg and Michael, Greg and I. At least, I thought he was my friend. He was always making . . . remarks to me. Personal remarks. I thought he was teasing. I always gave him a sassy answer. One evening when Michael was gone, Greg came to our apartment and told me it was time I made good on all that talk. He raped me."

Christian felt the words like a physical blow. He hurt for Alex, for what she had been through. To force a woman was unthinkable to him, an intolerable act of violence. And the knowledge that Greg Reidell was handsome and educated and well-off made it all the more despicable.

"I pressed charges," Alex went on, condensing what had seemed an unending nightmare to the barest of facts. "But I didn't have any real proof. It was his word against mine, his family's money and power against a little nobody. He claimed I had been having an affair with him for months, that I liked it a little rough, which discounted the doctor's testimony. He claimed he told me he was going to break it off, and that I was just trying to get back at him, humiliate him, that I was angling for a big chunk of hush money since I couldn't sleep my way into the family. Of course, he was too virtuous to pay for something he hadn't done, so he let the case come to trial to reveal me for the lying, conniving slut I was."

"The bastard," Christian muttered, his voice trembling with fury. His hands clenched into fists at his sides, and for the first time in his life he knew what it was to want to kill another human being. "The bloody bastard."

Alex looked up at him with a strange, bemused expression. "You believe me?" she said incredulously.

Christian's brows pulled together, and he frowned at her. "Of course I believe you. Why wouldn't I believe you?"

"Because no one else did," she said simply.

"You mean, no one outside your family."

"I mean no one."

Her family had offered minimal token support. They had taken her in after her marriage had crumbled, but they hadn't been doing her a favor. It had been an obligation. The Gianni men had been inclined to loyalty toward their gender. The Gianni women had been full of reproach about the way she flirted, the way she dressed, the profession she pursued. All of them had been vaguely ashamed. None of them had believed Greg Reidell would have forced a woman. He was too handsome, too wealthy. He didn't fit their idea of a rapist, and they weren't inclined to change their preconceived ideas—because then their neatly ordered world would be in danger of tilting on its axis. If a man like Greg Reidell could be capable of rape, then who were they supposed to trust, what were they supposed to believe in?

Their subtle betrayal hadn't made her angry. Just sad. It had made her see them as ordinary, flawed humans. The idyllic family of her memories had ceased to exist.

"Surely, your husband . . ." Christian said, looking helpless.

Alex smiled sadly. "Michael tried, but he felt betrayed and he felt guilty, and in the end he just couldn't deal with it. He was always the jealous type. Reidell's lies played on that, preyed on his mind."

She sighed and combed a hand back through her bangs. "I was pregnant with Isabella when it happened. Just a month or so along. I hadn't told Michael yet. I was waiting for the right time," she said with an ironic twist to her mouth. "When I did tell him, he wouldn't believe me when I said the baby couldn't be Greg's. I think that was what ultimately ended the marriage. He couldn't bear the thought of raising another man's child."

As her words trailed off into the silence of the tack room, Alex let the last of the tension drain from her muscles. She was so tired, tired of running from who she was, tired of the fear of ridicule, of the speculative looks. She wished Christian would just leave so she could curl up in a corner and shut the world out with sleep.

Christian studied her quietly. He remembered again the laughing, lovely girl he'd seen in California, so full of spirit and youthful innocence, and he mourned her loss. Now he took in the cropped hair, the drab, baggy sweatshirt, the world-weary eyes, and the dark shadows beneath them—the disguise of a woman haunted by her past. And everything inside him ached for her. She'd been so alone. She'd been doubted by the people she had needed most. Now he understood her obsessive self-reliance. Now he understood a lot of things.

Protectiveness, possessiveness, sifted through him. He was so absolutely focused on Alex, though, that he didn't try to escape them this time. For perhaps the first time in his life his own needs had become secondary.

"I'd take it all away if I could," he whispered, stepping forward and gathering her in his arms. He pulled her close and pressed a kiss to her temple.

Alex pressed her cheek to his chest, stunned for an instant. She had become so used to the rejection, the doubts. But there were no doubts from Christian. He was holding her the way she had longed to be held, giving her the human contact she had been denied. The people she had loved had treated her like a leper, and this man she barely knew was holding her and sharing her pain and offering his comfort.

For the first time in forever she allowed the tears to fall. They streamed down her cheeks and soaked into the soft cotton of Christian's knit shirt. All the hurt and the loneliness poured out, leaving her empty and exhausted.

When the river of tears had finally ceased to flow, Christian gallantly handed her a handkerchief dug out of the small zippered pocket of his breeches. Then he bent and swept her up into his arms and started for the door.

"What are you doing?" Alex asked, her voice hoarse from crying. She swiped at the moisture still clinging to her lashes and let out a little yelp as Christian hefted her slight weight in his arms, resettling her. "Put me down," she demanded weakly even as her arms slid willingly around his neck.

"I'm taking you to the house," he said firmly. His expression brooked no disobedience. "You're taking the day off to rest. Look the word up in the dictionary if you need to."

"But I have work to do!"

"I'll ride your horses for you."

"But—"

He gave her a fierce, hawkish look. "No arguments."

"But your ankle—"

"Is well enough. I'll manage."

Alex opened her mouth again but snapped it shut as Christian arched a brow in warning. She felt a ridiculously strong urge to giggle. In fact, she felt euphoric.

They went in the kitchen door just as Charlie was coming out dragging her jacket in one hand. Alex ducked to hide her tearstained face against Christian's neck, breathing in his warm, clean male scent.

"Blimey, Miss Alex, are you hurt?" the girl asked anxiously, dancing around them like a fractious beagle, her earrings clanging together.

"Nnnnn . . ." Alex muttered, shaking her head against Christian's throat.

"She's not injured," Christian insisted, trying to brush past the concerned, curious groom. "I simply wanted to carry her."

"Gosh, gov, that's a bit Stone Age, isn't it?" Charlie teased, dark eyes crinkling as she stepped back.

Christian scowled at her. "Go mousse your hair or something, Simmonds."

Charlie sniffed in mock affront. "Go on. There's work to be done. Something you wouldn't know anything about."

She sauntered off toward the barn, whistling, her rubber chore boots scuffing on the gravel drive.

In the kitchen Christian deposited Alex on an old chrome-and-red vinyl chair and turned to Pearl, who was busy at the stove.

"Pearl, see that Alex eats an enormous breakfast and goes straight to bed."

Pearl stared at him, spatula in hand. "Have you lost your mind or something, Mr. Atherton?"

Or something, Christian thought, looking down at Alex, who now held Isabella in her lap. The first tremors of fear shuddered through him. Alex was staring up at him, her amber eyes still wet with tears. A soft smile curved her lush mouth. Isabella looked up at him as well, her eyes dark brown and sparkling with wonder. They made a lovely picture—a family, minus one.

Christian's throat constricted. A chill raced over him. He backed toward the door.

"I'll check in on you later," he said, then let himself out into the fresh morning air without waiting for a reply of any kind.

"Good Lord," he muttered as he wandered away from the

house. "I feel weak and hot and cold and rather ill in general. And I'm talking to myself." He stopped in his tracks, going pale as his eyes widened in the horror of sudden realization.

He was in love!

In love. Gads! He had never meant to fall in love. Love was serious stuff. Love meant responsibility for another person. In his case it meant taking responsibility not only for a lady with a wealth of hurt in her past but with a baby as well. A baby! The very thought made him shudder clear down to his boots.

He closed his eyes and was immediately confronted with the image of Alex and Isabella gazing up at him. His heart melted like butter in his chest. He was well and truly in love. Christian Atherton, heartthrob of the show-jumping set, playboy extraordinaire, was irretrievably in love with an amber-eyed minx and her darling daughter. How the mighty bachelor had fallen.

The question was: Could he get Alex to fall as well? Would he be able to bridge the hurt others had caused her and win not only her trust but her heart in the bargain?

The determination and competitive nature that had taken him to the top of his profession surged to the forefront, bringing with it strength. He straightened his elegant shoulders and lifted his aristocratic chin.

He'd had princesses eating out of his hand. He'd had some of the most wealthy, powerful women in the world beg for his affection. Could he get Alexandra Gianni to fall in love with him? Bloody well right he could!

# seven

**"HERE COMES ANOTHER ONE, ALEX!" CHARLIE** called from the open end of the barn. She stood with a shoulder braced lazily against the door frame, watching as the blue-and-gray pickup from Quaid Farm bounced its way up the drive. "What do you suppose he's sent this time?"

"I can't imagine." Alex stepped out of the tack room and around her daughter's walker.

"No, no, Mama!" Isabella squealed and stormed down the aisle after her, chubby arms waving, walker wheels chattering on the concrete. She chanted her favorite new words incessantly, making them into a song of sorts. "No, no, no, no, mine! Mine, mine, mine!"

"He sends any more flowers, an' you'll be able to open a bloomin' green 'ouse." Charlie slapped her skinny thigh and laughed at her own joke, her eyes squinting into slits.

Alex smiled and wiped the saddle soap off her hands and onto her breeches. In the two weeks that had passed since she had made her confession to Christian, he had done anything but shrink away from her. He had been even more determined in his courtship. He sent her a present every day—a single rose, a bunch of balloons, a clutch of violets. The ones he delivered in person were accompanied by delicious kisses Alex no longer tried to fend off.

Not above bribing a baby, Christian had brought Isabella little trinkets as well and had already completely won over the littlest Gianni. Isabella had gotten to the point where she brightened into unrestrained excitement every time she saw Christian. A sneaky tactic, Alex thought, but an effective one. The way to a mother's heart was through her baby. The sight of the elegant Mr. Atherton, the galloping playboy, playing with a baby—and thoroughly enjoying it—was downright impossible to resist.

Thanks to Christian's wooing, Alex found her heart cautiously considering coming out of its shell. Christian Atherton was a wonderful man—charming, sweet, fun to be with. He had brightened her days immeasurably. He had shown her there was a lot more to him than an attractive exterior and a rakish reputation.

They had fought tooth and nail over the issue of Charlie staying on, even though Alex was no longer riding at Quaid Farm. After revealing her past, Alex's instinct had been to retreat. As soon as she had recovered from a giddy sense of relief once things were in the open, her old caution had returned. She was determined to make her way, to pay her own bills, to accept favors from no one.

Christian had been unshakable, however. He had insisted Alex keep his cockney charge, claiming that only a fool would turn down free help. Alex had relented, albeit reluctantly. She might have been many things, but she had ceased to be a fool some time ago. Finally, she had given in.

Christian had rewarded her with another of his mind-numbing kisses. Residual heat seeped through her at the memory of it. The man had world-class lips. He hadn't pressed her for a more physical relationship, but he had made it clear that when she was ready, he would be more than willing.

The idea both frightened and excited her. It had been a long time since she'd been with a man. She and Michael had never made love after the rape. He hadn't wanted to, and she hadn't pressed him, because she'd been afraid of how she would react, afraid of the possibility that she might not be able to enjoy it or that she might freeze up. In the end she had never had the chance to find out. Her husband had rejected her, unable to bear the thought that she'd been with another man. But Christian was showing no such prejudices. He didn't blame her for what had happened, nor did he view her as damaged goods.

Maybe it was time to try another relationship. She had come to Virginia to start a new life. There was no reason going out with Christian couldn't be a part of it. He certainly wasn't showing any signs of giving up on the idea, Alex thought with a wry smile as the Quaid Farm groom climbed out of the truck with a large brown cardboard box in his hands.

"Mornin', Ms. Gianni," he drawled with a shy grin. "Got somethin' for you from Mr. Atherton."

"She don't want it if it ain't a fur coat, ducky," Charlie teased, batting her spiky lashes at the gangly young groom. He blushed to the roots of his wheat-colored hair and grinned.

Alex took the box, her mouth dropping open in delighted surprise. "It's not just a fur coat, Charlie. It's five fur coats."

"Blimey!" Charlie exclaimed, abruptly breaking off from her flirting to wheel toward Alex and the box.

Five kittens, each with a blue bow tied around its neck, clambered over one another to get to the edge of the box so they could peer over the side. There was a gray-striped one, an orange-striped one, one that was black and white, one that was black and orange, and one calico. All of them were eager to get out and explore their new home.

Alex put the box down on the concrete, immediately gaining her daughter's wide-eyed attention. "Look, Isabella, kitties."

"Tees!" the baby said, bouncing in the seat of her walker. She banged a fist excitedly against the plastic tray as the kittens bounded out of the box. The little girl hurried down the aisle after them, laughing and jabbering. "No, no, tees!"

Alex watched them go, hugging herself as her heart warmed her from the inside out.

"Ma'am? Mr. Atherton said he'd stop by around dinner time," the groom said.

Alex thanked him, Charlie winked at him and told him to come back anytime. The groom blushed, tipped the brim of his battered baseball cap, and ambled away.

"What do you think of Christian, Charlie?" Alex asked absently, turning back to keep an eye on her daughter.

Charlie snorted and waved a hand with black polished fingernails and too many rings. "He's a stuffy, pompous, bossy bugger." Her mischievous smile spread across her face. "And you'd be barmy if you let him get away, a dishy guy like that."

"Yeah," Alex said on a sigh, her eyes sparkling as she watched Isabella play hide-and-seek with the kittens. "Maybe you're right."

Christian walked into Nick's Restaurant and was greeted immediately by the delicious aroma of simmering tomatoes and herbs. The restaurant didn't officially open for business until eleven a.m., but he had a great deal to do before he could put his plan into motion, and he knew Nick would already be hard at work in the kitchen.

He strolled through the main dining room, admiring the antiques and the masculine decor. Maggie Quaid and Nick's wife Katie—who was also Rylan Quaid's baby sister—had done the decorating, choosing a soothing color scheme of rich dark green and warm beige. The restaurant was housed in a two-hundred-year-old building that had once been a menswear store, and leftover treasures of that time adorned the walls—bowlers and walking sticks and displays of shirt collars. The overall effect was welcoming and comfortable. The restaurant had quickly become one of the most popular in the Briarwood area.

The sight that he saw as he pushed through the kitchen door brought a smile to Christian's lips. Nick Leone had his petite wife in a passionate embrace and was kissing her thoroughly. Neither of them noticed the intrusion, so engrossed were they in expressing their feelings for each other. They looked as if they should have been posing for the cover of a romantic novel. Nick was big and muscular. His black hair tumbled across his forehead. He banded his arms around Katie's slender frame, almost lifting her off the ground. Katie's fall of silky, waist-long chestnut hair flowed behind her.

Christian cleared his throat discreetly.

"We don't open yet," Nick growled in a thick New Jersey accent, his attention still solely on his wife.

Katie, however, turned toward him, her gray eyes glowing, cheeks blooming a becoming shade of pink to match the piping on her Laura Ashley dress. "Hi, Christian. What brings you to town in the middle of the morning?"

"An errand *de amour*," he said, smiling.

"Ah, *amore*!" Nick grinned, the interruption instantly forgotten. "Who's the lucky lady? Anyone we know?"

"I don't think so. She's new to the area. Alexandra Gianni."

Nick was visibly pleased. "A good Italian girl." He nodded sagely. "That's just what you need—a good Italian girl to make an honest man of you." He slapped Christian on the shoulder, his dark eyes gleaming with good humor. "And if she can't do it, her brothers will."

"What if she hasn't any brothers?"

He waved the notion away. "She's Italian. Trust me. She's got brothers, she's got uncles, she's got cousins. At the very least, she's got a godfather."

Christian lifted a blond brow, his mouth twitching with amusement. "Like in the movies?"

Nick laughed and shook a finger at him. "You better hope not."

"Maggie tells me this could be something special," Katie said with feminine relish for all things romantic. "What can we do to help?"

Lifting the wicker basket he'd borrowed from Maggie, Christian grinned engagingly. "Fit me out with your finest picnic lunch for two."

"I can't believe I'm doing this," Alex said half to herself.

She twirled the stem of the tulip-shaped glass between her fingers, watching the sunlight play through the white wine. On the red-and-white checkered cloth beneath her were white china plates strewn with the remnants of a marvelous meal—cold breast of chicken oreganato, tortellini salad, fresh Italian bread with herb butter, two kinds of cheese and grapes. She felt pleasantly stuffed and sleepy as the strengthening spring sun shone down on them.

"I should be working," she murmured with a minimum of conviction, shifting her position so she was lying back on her elbows. She turned her face to the sun and sighed.

"You know what they say about all work," Christian said, regarding her over the rim of his own wineglass.

"Yes. It pays my rent."

"Even you need to break for lunch, darling. We must eat, so why not eat the finest?"

That was Christian's life philosophy in a nutshell, Alex thought with a wry smile. Driving was necessary, so why not own a Mercedes? Clothing was necessary, so why not buy designer labels? He was an aristocrat through and through, but there was something sweet about his inborn snobbishness. It was never too serious or malicious, more of a front than anything, a shield to hide the sensitive inner man.

"Your friend is a wonderful cook."

"Yes, he is, and he insists we join him and his wife for dinner one evening very soon," Christian said, never passing up an opportunity to ask Alex for a date. One of these days she was going to say yes.

Alex stared at him for a long moment, her amber eyes dark with drowsiness and contemplation. At length she nodded slowly and said, "I'd like that."

Christian nearly spilled his wine. "You would?"

"We must eat," she said, mimicking him. "Why not enjoy pleasant company while we do it?"

Christian felt his smile grow to idiotic proportions. "Why not, indeed."

They were passing a critical point in their relationship. He knew Alex was aware of it. He also knew she didn't want to call too much attention to it. She dodged his gaze almost shyly and played some more with her glass.

*Lord, she's pretty*, he thought, his heart swelling with the love he was slowly growing accustomed to. He let his eyes drink in the sight of her—the sophisticated cut of her dark hair, the delicate lines of her face with its perfectly feminine features. She had traded her breeches for an old pair of jeans with holes in the knees, and her boots for a disreputable-looking pair of white canvas sneakers. She had changed out of the baggy black T-shirt she'd worn riding for an equally baggy olive polo shirt, but as she set her glass aside and leaned back on her hands, the outline of her small, full breasts was clearly visible.

There was certainly nothing fancy in the way she looked, he reflected. She wasn't wearing a trace of makeup. No cloud of expensive perfume surrounded her. She was dressed like a stable hand. He had dated women renowned for their striking beauty, women who wore one-of-a-kind gowns and jewelry to make a thief swoon with envy. Women with fortunes and women with power. But he had never felt about any of them the way he felt about Alex Gianni.

It was powerful and wonderful and terrifying. Fear seized him at the thought that she might not return the feelings or that she might return them with regrets. He felt like a right proper fool most of the time. And he wouldn't have traded it for anything.

Gads, I'm sunk, he thought with a rueful smile as he stretched out on his belly, never taking his eyes off Alex. What would Uncle Dicky say?

"This is much nicer than the last time we were here," Alex said.

Christian laughed. "I dare say."

They were in the high meadow where Christian had been injured trying to rescue her. The woods all around them was in full bloom, and wildflowers dotted the grass.

Christian had shown up, picnic basket in tow. He autocratically ordered Charlie to see to Isabella's every need as Pearl was gone for the day and then badgered Alex into eating with him. She was glad that she had come. Now that she'd settled a few things in her heart, it seemed right to spend a lazy spring afternoon with him.

Something warm and wonderful stirred inside her as she looked at him, at his handsome profile, the elegant way his sapphire blue knit shirt clung to his strong shoulders. He wore jeans and sneakers, but even in casual dress he exuded a sense of privilege and breeding. Alex decided it wouldn't have mattered how he dressed. The power of his personality blazed as strong and hot as the sun. It was the inner man, not his outer trappings, that drew her. She knew better than most that privilege and power didn't make a man superior. It was what was in his heart that counted. It was what she hoped was in Christian's heart that mattered to Alex.

She packed their dishes away while he watched her.

"You're very quiet," he commented, sitting up and draping one arm across a drawn-up knee.

"Mmmm . . . just thinking . . ."

"What about?"

Alex swallowed the fist-sized knot in her throat. "Us."

He straightened subtly. His eyes never left her face. "What about us?"

Lips pursed, she gave a little shrug that made her look very Italian. She busied her hands fussing with the picnic basket. "I just wondered . . . where we go from here."

Christian reached out to set the basket beyond her reach, then hooked a finger under her chin and tilted her face up so she had to meet his gaze. The intensity in her tawny eyes brought out the flecks of gold in the iris, dazzling him, but not quite hiding the wariness from him. Again he cursed the man who had put that look there, and again he vowed to do whatever was necessary to erase it. He wanted Alex so badly, he sometimes thought he wouldn't be able to endure the wait. But wait he would. He had no intention of rushing her into anything.

"That's entirely up to you, sweetheart," he murmured. "I'll do whatever you like."

"Will you?" Alex asked softly, afraid at how badly she needed to believe in him. If he let her down . . . If she let him down . . .

"Tell me what you want," he murmured. "I'll give you anything, Alex."

He couldn't give her back her past or her belief in the greater good of humankind, but he could give her a future, and he could give her his love. That was what shone in the blue of his eyes as he stared down at her, holding his breath, waiting for her answer.

Alex lifted a hand to brush her fingertips along the lean line of his cheek, as if she didn't quite believe he was real. "Will you make love to me?" she asked, her voice as soft as the wings of butterflies that skimmed over the green meadow, as soft as the breeze that brought the rich scents of the Virginia countryside.

"No," Christian whispered, taking her hand in his. "But I'll make love *with* you. I'll gladly make love *with* you, Alexandra."

Lifting her hand to his mouth, he pressed a kiss to each of her knuckles, never taking his eyes from hers. She watched him, her own eyes darkening with passion, her lips parting slightly.

"Are you afraid of me, Alex?" he asked.

She shook her head slowly. "No." A tiny smile twitched up one corner of her mouth. "I'm afraid of me."

"I'm not afraid of you."

To prove it he brought both her hands to his chest and abandoned them there in invitation. Alex screwed up her courage and reached back in her mind, past fear of rejection, past the horror of what had happened to her, back to when it had been all right to want and to please. She slid her palms down the solid wall of his chest, across his flat, hard belly to the waist of his jeans, and dragged his shirttail out. Then she reversed the process, letting her fingers explore the smooth contours of his body as she raised the hem of his shirt.

Christian discarded the garment, tossing it aside carelessly. His own gaze still locked on Alex, he let her look her fill as the sun beat down on the well-defined muscles of his shoulders, arms, and back. Years of demanding physical work had toned his sleek body to perfection. Alex caressed every smooth, hard plane, every mark of delineation. When she ceased her exploration, it was only to take Christian's hand and draw it to the hem of her shirt.

He undressed her slowly, checking his own rampant desire in favor of building her own. What he revealed was the embodiment of femininity. She was dainty and delicate, and she brought out every possessive instinct he had buried beneath his layers of sophistication. Her breasts were small but full, fitting perfectly into his hands, with pouting, dusky pink nipples that tightened at the touch of the breeze. Ever so gently he drew the pads of his thumbs across the turgid tips and groaned appreciatively as they rose to attention.

Alex sighed and let her head fall back and her eyes drift shut. It felt so good to be touched, touched with reverence and care and sweet longing. She leaned back and drank in the sensation as Christian's gentle hands cupped her and caressed her. He blocked out the sun as he leaned down to kiss her, but Alex felt filled with golden light. She wrapped her arms around his neck and opened her mouth beneath his, inviting the intimacy she had so long been denied. His tongue slid along hers, velvety warm, stroking and retreating. And heat swirled through her, chasing out all the cold shadows of the past.

Never breaking the kiss, Christian rose slowly to his feet, lifting Alex with him. Simultaneously each found the button on the other's jeans and popped them free. Zippers rasped in a descending duet. Denim dropped to the checked cloth at their feet.

With trembling hands Alex lowered Christian's snug black briefs, freeing his manhood to her touch. He was smooth and hard, hot and ready, and the stunning sense of need that burned inside her as she stroked him filled her with a dizzying sense of relief. She pressed herself against him, kissing his chest, flicking her tongue over his flat male nipples, all the while rubbing and stroking the essence of what made him male.

Christian groaned at the exquisite torture. Desire doubled and tripled its hold on him as Alex's hold tormented him. He dragged her plain cotton panties down, splaying his hands over the soft fullness of her tight, well-rounded buttocks. He lifted her against him again so that she had to wrap her arms around his neck. His mouth took hers hungrily as her body arched into his, the downy thatch of curls at the apex of her thighs brushing sensually against his belly.

Slowly he lowered them both to the ground, settling Alex

on her back and himself on his side next to her. He set off on an exploration of her body with his hands and lips that was meant to be unhurried. It was meant to slowly stoke the fire in both of them, to slowly bring the level of desire to a fever pitch. But Christian was already bordering on delirium. All the smooth, calm, thorough technique he had honed over the years deserted him. With Alex he knew an almost frantic urge to make her his, to purge every other man from her mind and stake his claim in the most basic way he could.

Struggling with the inner battle, he forced himself to slow the pace, knowing he wouldn't be able to stand it much longer, but fearing he would be rushing Alex if he gave in to his own needs. Gently he swept his hand down across her belly to the slick satin heat between her thighs. Kissing her deeply, he parted the delicate petals and eased a finger into the tight pocket of her womanhood, wringing a moan of unmistakable pleasure from her. Her hips pushed off the blanket, urging him, begging him until she was gasping for air.

"Christian, please," she whispered, clutching at his shoulders and trying to pull him onto her. "I need you. Please don't make me wait."

"Anything you ask, darling," he murmured, pulling away from her for the brief instant it took to dig into the hip pocket of his discarded jeans and pull out the familiar foil packet he'd tucked there in hope.

Alex stared up at him as he positioned himself above her, and felt a quick stab of apprehension. She didn't want to disappoint him. She didn't want to be disappointed. She wanted this to end as beautifully as it had progressed so far.

Christian leaned over her with a gentle smile and brushed her hair back. There was only one thing he could think to say that would allay her fears. He'd said it countless hundreds of times to more women than he cared to remember. But this time when he said it, it wasn't casual, and it came straight from his heart.

"I love you, Alex."

She succeeded in pulling him down to her then and lifted her hips to take him inside her. He filled her slowly, carefully, and when he was embedded deep within her, he checked to make sure she was all right, that she wasn't afraid or hurt. She was incredibly hot and tight around him, and his control was slipping through his grasp like a wet rope, but Alex's needs were uppermost in his mind.

"Oh, Christian." She sighed, her mouth curving into the most sensual of smiles beneath his. *"Tante grazie."*

She arched against him, savoring the feel of him inside her, celebrating the joy and the relief that washed through her. There were no dark memories, only pleasure—wondrous, exquisite pleasure. She felt new and whole and powerfully feminine. It was a feeling more intoxicating than the wine they'd shared.

"I only want to please you, Alex," Christian murmured, every word a kiss as he eased back and slowly moved into her again.

His muscles trembled with the effort to hold back. Alex moved beneath him, inviting him, luring him toward the edge of sexual bliss. Her small hands stroked down the arch of his back to his hips to knead his tight buttocks, to pull him even deeper into her heat.

"I want to take you to paradise, darling," he whispered, kissing her earlobe, tracing the shell of her ear with the tip of his tongue. He drove his hips against her again, slowly, strongly, stroking her in a way he knew would wring a startled gasp of pleasure from her.

Moaning, Alex breathed a stream of reverent Italian. Her nails raked down Christian's back as she murmured, "Paradise . . . let's go there together."

They moved in unison, both their bodies betraying a wonderful kind of urgency, until they were straining into each other, panting and smiling and, finally, replete.

Alex was so happy, she never wanted to move from the spot. She thought she could have stayed forever under the warm spring sun with bees buzzing lazily in the distance and Christian in her arms. But she knew there were horses waiting to be ridden, including Terminator, who had won his class the past Sunday, then proceeded to spend the week trying to throw her. He had succeeded once, flinging her headlong into the bars.

After a while she sat up and began to dress, pulling her shirt on over her head and handing Christian's to him. They kissed and giggled like teenagers as they put themselves back together. Alex found the torn foil wrapper and arched a brow.

"Always prepared?"

Christian flashed her his brilliant grin. "A useful motto I picked up in the Boy Scouts."

Alex shoved him playfully. "You liar. You were never a Boy Scout."

"I most certainly was," he insisted, lifting his square chin. "Until that camping incident with the Girl Guides, which got me chucked out."

"You're too much." Alex groaned, rolling her eyes as she reached for her panties.

"That's not what you were saying a moment ago," Christian murmured in a dark velvet voice as he pulled her against him.

The gold in Alex's eyes glittered like pyrite as she snuggled into him. "Wicked."

"Thoroughly."

He leaned down to kiss her, but something on her hip caught his eye, and he pulled back suddenly with a scowl as black as a thundercloud. "What the bloody hell is that?"

Alex's gaze flicked down over her right hip. The bruise was

three days old, just turning a truly putrid shade of green. It was a good five inches across, and while it looked horrible, it marked only a small area of what actually hurt. As bumps and bruises were typical in her line of work, she had ignored it. Nothing was broken, that was all that really mattered.

Christian was standing in front of her with his hands planted at the waist of his jeans, his brows drawn low and tight over his eyes. "How?"

Alex gave her classic little shrug. "I had a fall. It was nothing."

"It was that bastard Terminator, wasn't it?" he demanded. Her stubborn silence was enough of an answer. "Dammit, Alex, get rid of him! He's dangerous. I'll send you horses from the QF string if you need the rides that badly. I'll fix it with Rylan. I'll pay the bloody training fees myself."

"You won't," Alex snapped, her chin going up. The mounts she got, she got on her own.

"You deserve better, Alex!"

*No, I don't*. The thought came instantly, but she didn't put it into words. She turned away from him instead and pulled on her underwear.

Christian heaved a sigh and raked a hand back through his hair, tilting his head down. He was trying to run her life for her, and she was determined to be independent. He could understand her need to make it on her own, but in his heart, where new love was taking fragile root, he was terrified. He wanted to take care of Alex. He wanted to keep her safe. But she wouldn't let him.

Adding to his frustration was the fact that he had never wanted to interfere in anyone's life before. His old bachelor philosophies warred with these new desires, until his head pounded from the struggle.

"Don't let's fight," he said quietly, rubbing his temples. "It's been such a perfect afternoon."

Alex's temper evaporated like so much steam. Fighting was the last thing she wanted to do. She went directly into Christian's arms when he opened them to her.

They kissed, each desperate to reassure the other that all was forgiven. And as they sank back down to the blanket, the fight was forgotten and paradise was revisited.

# eight

**THE DAY BEGAN WITH A HEAT WAVE AND A** dozen red roses. The heat now permeated everything, making a mockery of the efforts of the groaning old fan Alex had stuck in her bedroom window. The roses now stood in their cut-glass vase, elegant and out of place on the old walnut dresser in the tiny beige-walled bedroom.

Next had come the dress. It was now being arranged over her lithe body by her fairy godmothers, Maggie Quaid and Katie Leone, while Alex fidgeted from black-stockinged foot to black-stockinged foot.

Katie and Nick had volunteered to take Isabella for the night, since Pearl had been called away to spend a few days with one of her nieces, who had just had some minor surgery. Katie and Maggie had shown up together just as Alex had been taking the dress out of its protective bag. They had both insisted on seeing her in it before they left.

"It's gorgeous, Alex," Katie murmured, zipping up the low back. "You say Christian just had it delivered?"

Alex nibbled at her lower lip nervously, frowning at her reflection. She stood on the lumpy green-brocade footstool that had been pilfered from the living room so she could see most of herself in the mirror above the dresser. Her bangs spilled over her forehead in a riot of humidity-enhanced curls. Heavy gold hoops hung from her earlobes. She was wearing makeup for the first time in ages and wondered absently if it would all just melt off before she got where she was going.

"I told him I didn't have anything to wear to this party at Green Hills," she said, shrugging expressively. "He said he wasn't going to let me get away with that tired old line. This morning *this* shows up by special delivery," she said, twitching the royal blue flounced skirt.

"How do you like that?" Maggie said dryly, planting her hands on her hips. "He sends you this fabulous dress just for a date. Do y'all know what Rylan gave me for my birthday this year? A garden weasel. You know, one of those hoe things with the spiky teeth on it." She shook her head in woeful resignation. "He's the soul of romance, isn't he?"

She sounded disgusted, but as usual when she talked about her husband, her face lit up with a loving glow.

They all turned their attention back to Alex's reflection in the mirror, including Isabella, who was playing on the bed. Her dark eyes grew round with wonder as she stared at her mother.

"Isn't Mama pretty?" Katie said, sitting on the brown quilted spread and letting Isabella scramble onto her lap. The baby, clad only in a diaper because of the heat, immediately grabbed the end of Katie's long braid and tickled her nose with it.

"Don't you think it's a little too . . ." Alex's hands fluttered helplessly as words failed her. She felt naked. She hadn't worn anything so . . . provocative . . . in a long time. It felt foreign and forbidden.

"Good heavens, sugar." Maggie clucked. "It doesn't even show any cleavage." She sounded vaguely disappointed in Christian's lack of foresight.

"That's because I haven't got any," Alex declared. She skimmed her hands across the black sequins that covered her stomach, her brows pulling together in concern. "Don't you think it's a little . . . snug?"

"It's perfect," Maggie announced with a note of finality as she adjusted the large taffeta bow at Alex's hip. "You're a pretty young lady, going out with a man most women would give their eyeteeth for, Alex. Why not show off a little bit?"

Because she'd spent the past eighteen months trying to hide herself and her femininity, Alex thought. What had begun as a concerted effort had become second nature to her. She would have felt much more at ease in an oversize shirt and a baggy pair of jeans.

She stared at herself and tried to be objective. It *was* lovely. Whisper-thin straps led down over her shoulders to a simple, fitted bodice of shimmering black sequins that hugged her slender body, nipping in at her tiny waist and stretching slightly over her slim hips. The skirt was of royal blue taffeta edged in fine black lace. It was attached in a wrap-around style set at a sassy angle higher on her left hip, where the bow was perched, and lower on her right. There really wasn't anything revealing about it. It was tasteful and chic and obviously expensive.

"Don't you think it might be too fancy?" she asked, determined to find a reason not to wear it. "This is an outdoor party."

"Honey, when Hayden Hill puts on a party, there is no such thing as too fancy," Maggie said. "I heard they set up a tent big enough to hold a three-ring circus, which is probably what it will be. A black-tie, ball-gown circus. If I thought I had a snowball's chance of squeezing myself into that dress, I'd go in your place." She stood back and heaved a sigh up into her damp red bangs. "We were invited, but I couldn't get Rylan there with a twenty-mule hitch." She rolled her dark eyes expressively. "He still thinks Carter Hill has eyes for me. Can y'all believe that?" Shaking her head, she patted her rounded tummy through the madras-plaid cotton maternity jumper she wore.

Alex broke out of her apprehensive mood with a sparkling

laugh as she hopped down from the footstool in a rustle of taffeta. It had been so long since she'd had real friends, she had forgotten what it was like to get together with them and gossip and tease. The wary shyness she had cultivated since the attack hadn't stopped the gregarious Maggie from taking her into her fold of friends. Nor had it deterred sensible, sweet Katie in any way. If either of them suspected she had a dark secret in her past, they didn't mention it, or they respected her right to keep it. They got together to chat as regularly as their various schedules allowed. They had even begun doing things together as couples.

Couples, Alex thought with a little shiver of excitement. She and Christian were a couple. It seemed so strange after she had convinced herself she would be alone indefinitely. He came over nearly every evening to help her or to cajole her into going into Briarwood with him for a cup of cappuccino at Nick's, or a movie or a walk around the small town's historic district, where a number of old homes had been restored and beautiful gardens overflowed with vibrant color and sweet fragrances.

Many nights Isabella accompanied them, but they had managed to get a few evenings all to themselves, and those had been magic. Christian was a wonderful lover. Under his devoted tutelage Alex found herself rediscovering her sexuality and reveling in it. She found herself falling more in love with him every day.

But with the love came a vague, distant sense of apprehension. She was afraid of becoming too dependent on him, too devoted to him. Experience had taught her to rely on no one and nothing, save herself. She couldn't afford to let Christian run her life or her business, because there was no guarantee that he would always be there. To Michael DeGrazia she had pledged her love and trust unto death, but he was now more than two thousand miles away, as far removed from her life as the moon.

"Look at the time," Maggie said, checking her watch. "I have to get out of here before Christian comes. The sight of that man in a tuxedo is enough to make me swoon." She leaned over and gave Alex an affectionate hug, made awkward by her bulk. "Y'all have fun now, honey, and that's an order—as my daddy the admiral always says."

"Thanks, Maggie. Katie, you're sure Isabella won't be an imposition?"

"Don't be silly," Katie said, rising with the baby in her arms. "We'll have a great time with her. Besides, it'll be good practice. Nick and I are on a waiting list to adopt."

That was apparently a bombshell, if the startled look on Maggie's face was anything to go by, but there was no time to discuss it. The screen door banged, and Christian's voice called out.

"Alex?"

With Isabella perched on her slim hip, Katie led the way out of the bedroom, as calm as if she'd just said she and Nick were getting a puppy. Maggie followed, bubbling over with curiosity. Alex trailed behind with a stomach full of butterflies.

Christian looked the part of the consummate gentleman in his pleated white dress shirt and black bow tie. No one would have guessed by looking at him that it was ninety-plus degrees. He looked cool and sophisticated, too well-bred to sweat. His tuxedo was the absolute latest in chic European styles with a double-breasted jacket that enhanced his lean handsomeness. He definitely belonged somewhere more glamorous than her shabby little kitchen with its cracked gray linoleum and outdated appliances, Alex thought.

Her breath fluttered out of her as their gazes locked. Christian smiled, a slow, devastatingly sexy smile. It generated a fire inside Alex that made the hot day seem like a day in Antarctica.

"Exquisite," he murmured, his sapphire eyes glowing with male appreciation as they scanned Alex from head to toe.

"Don't mind us homely stepsisters," Katie said, grabbing up Alex's diaper bag from the Formica tabletop. "We were just leaving. Come on along now, Mary Margaret."

Maggie was swaying on her feet, staring raptly at Christian and fanning herself with a pot holder she'd picked up from the counter.

"Maggie?" Katie called, tugging at the short sleeve of her friend's pink T-shirt. "Oh, Maggie!"

"You'll have to drive, sugar," she mumbled, fishing in her patch pocket for her keys. "I feel positively overcome."

Isabella took the keys and rattled them merrily.

"Say good-bye, Maggie," Katie said, heading for the door.

"Good-bye, Maggie."

"Bye-bye!" Isabella called, shaking the keys.

Tearing herself away from Christian's magnetism, Alex rushed to the door to thank her friends again and to kiss her daughter good-bye. Feeling the return of the jitters, she watched through the screen door as they drove away in Maggie's blue station wagon.

"I hope Isabella is good for Katie and Nick. She hasn't been sleeping well."

"She'll be fine," Christian murmured, slipping his arms around her from behind and bending down to kiss her neck. "And so will you, darling."

Sometimes the man was too darn perceptive for his own good, Alex thought. He knew she was nervous about attending the Hills' party. Everybody who was anybody in show jumping would be there. She was gradually getting over the feeling that everybody in the world knew about her past, but the equestrian community was a relatively small one. There was a very good chance that she would eventually run into someone who knew. She dreaded the thought.

"I am so very anxious to show you off," Christian murmured, taking his arms from around her waist. A few seconds later he was fastening a necklace around her throat.

"Christian!" Alex said in protest as she fingered the beautiful piece. A vee of dark sapphires rested against her skin just above the neckline of her dress. The gold herringbone chain gleamed against her dark skin. "You've given me way too much already!"

Turning her, he took her in his arms again and bent toward her lips. "I haven't given you even half of what's in my heart," he murmured as he settled his mouth over hers and kissed her deeply, with a hunger that never left him.

A low, rapturous sound rumbled deep in his throat as Alex rose up on tiptoe and twined her arms around his neck, tilting her head to give him better access. He trailed the kiss down the slender column of her throat to the spot where it joined her shoulder and nibbled at her smooth skin around the chain of necklace. Passion leapt to life instantly, a flame that would never be extinguished between them, but with it came something sweeter and softer—the glow of love.

There was still a part of him that shuddered at the thought of committing himself to one woman. But the tremors were gradually becoming weaker as his old rakish tendencies gave way to other feelings. With a certain sense of resignation Christian realized that he was becoming positively domestic.

As he held Alex to him, he murmured a little apology to dearly departed Uncle Dicky. The last of the Atherton black sheep was fading into respectability.

The lawn at Green Hills looked like an emerald carpet liberally dotted with the colors of partygoers—men in their formal black and white, women standing out like jewels among them in their richly colored evening wear. There was indeed an enormous green-and-white-striped tent, the sides of which had been rolled up to let through whatever cooling breeze the evening might bring. Under the big top was a lavish buffet with barbecued beef and pork, platters of fresh fruit, and seafood presented on beds of shaved ice. The bar had been set up directly across from the buffet and was doing a lively business, the heat and the conversation drumming up thirsts all around. One end of the shelter held a number of long tables draped in white and adorned with trailing green ivy plants for centerpieces. The remainder of the space beneath the tent was taken up by a portable dance floor. A five-piece combo nestled into one corner, playing contemporary hits, classics, and standards.

The level of energy and opulence about the place was impressive and infectious. The following day the show horses would take center stage. At present it was their owners and trainers who provided the spectacle.

Alex recognized some of the faces from the smaller shows she had been attending. Others she knew on sight from their photographs in the magazines—Katie Prudent and Debbie Shaffner, Greg Best and George Morris and Rodney Jenkins. Hayden Hill's party was a virtual *Who's Who* of show jumping. It was a thrill to rub shoulders with them, and an even bigger thrill to remember that Christian resided at the top of their ranks.

The pair of them turned a lot of heads. It became apparent very quickly to Alex that more than one of the ladies in attendance coveted her date. Feminine gazes followed them with interest and envy, clinging to Christian's elegant person. He either didn't notice or had grown so accustomed to female scrutiny that it no longer fazed him. It certainly fazed Alex. She didn't like the idea of other women homing in on her date. And she felt a horrendous surge of jealousy when she realized that more than one of those ladies probably knew Christian on intimate terms, given his reputation.

*I'm in love with him*, she thought with renewed wonder as

she watched him laugh at something Carter Hill had said. She'd known it for days, of course. If she was honest with herself, she would have to say she'd been in love with him since that day in the meadow, or even before that. She'd been attracted to him from the first. The day he'd held her after she told him about her past had tipped her heart over the edge. How could she not love him when he had given her the kind of unqualified support not even her husband had been able to manage? He hadn't rejected her or blamed her or found her fundamentally flawed in some irreparable way.

He had told her he loved her, but she hadn't quite let herself believe it. Words like love came easily to men like Christian. And a part of Alex just couldn't quite believe her life could include the handsome, wealthy son of an earl. It was just too good. What had she done to deserve him? She kept thinking there had to be a catch, that eventually the other shoe would drop. But what if he really meant it? What if what they had between them was truly something special?

A shiver of hope ran through her, pebbling her skin in spite of the heat of the Virginia evening.

"All set for tomorrow, honey?" Tully Haskell's voice boomed down on her from above.

Alex jolted out of her trance and turned to look up at him. Tully's version of black tie was a black, western-cut suit and a bolo tie snugged up to his flabby throat. The overall effect might have been trendy and stylish on a younger, trimmer man. Tully tainted it toward the vulgar. He clutched a champagne glass and one of his omnipresent cigars in one hand, leaving the other free to pat Alex's bare shoulder.

She moved away from his touch on the pretense of changing position and gave him the most businesslike smile she could scrape together. "I hope so, Mr. Haskell. Duchess will handle everything well. I'm afraid we may be asking Terminator to do too much too soon."

"Nonsense," Tully barked, his mouth tightening, eyes flashing for the briefest instant.

Alex didn't miss the look, though she erased it quickly. Tully didn't like her questioning his authority. He had been determined his horses would perform in the Green Hills show. They were his ticket into the realm of the sport's elite. He didn't care how his decision affected the horses. With Tully the end always justified the means. So went the relationship between owners and trainers. Some were reasonable and understanding. The majority wanted miracles worked at bargain rates.

"Don't you look pretty tonight, Alex," he said, eyeing her appreciatively. "By golly, I believe this is the first time I've seen you dressed up like a woman. Looks damn good on you."

The backhanded compliment couldn't inspire a thank you from Alex. Every doubt she'd had about wearing the dress rushed back to her with a vengeance. Instead of feeling lovely and special, she felt cheap. She was suddenly overcome by the feeling that the makeup she had applied so sparingly was as overdone as a ten-dollar tramp's.

Christian turned toward her to say something, but the words died on his tongue as he took in the look on her face. All he had to do was glance up to find the root cause of her tension.

"I say," he drawled, lifting his nose in disdain. "Aren't they checking the invitations at the gate?"

"Read it and weep, you arrogant limey bastard," Tully growled, plucking his engraved invitation out of the inner pocket of his jacket and waving it tauntingly in Christian's face.

"Really," Christian said, putting on every snobbish air that had been bred into countless generations of Athertons, "the alarming decline of social standards is truly appalling."

Haskell sneered at him, handing his champagne glass to a passing waiter without even glancing at the man. "Yeah? Well, I don't give a rat's rump what you think. Eat that with your tea and crumpets, your lordship, while Alex gives me the pleasure of this next dance."

Alarm slammed Alex's heart against her breastbone like a paddle ball. Dance with Tully Haskell? Let Tully Haskell put his meaty paws all over her? Her throat constricted as she fought the urge to gag. The last thing she wanted to do was let down the trainer/owner barrier she had struggled to maintain, even if it was only long enough for one brief turn around the dance floor. But how could she refuse the man without offending him?

He reached for her wrist, but Christian stopped him, his fingers closing forcefully on Haskell's forearm. All traces of the dandy fell away from Christian like a crumbling shield. He radiated power and authority. The intense dislike he felt for the older man was more than evident in the curl of his lip and the steel in his eyes.

"Not if you value your precious, tenuous standing in this group," he said with deadly quiet.

There was no need for him to raise his voice, Alex thought with awe. The force of his personality was enough to turn the heads of a number of people nearby. Haskell might have been physically larger, but he was no match for Christian in this kind of a fight, and the quick darting of the man's dark little eyes betrayed the fact that he knew it.

Contempt added another facet to Christian's expression as he spoke again. "My connections make yours look like so many knots in a ratty bootlace, Haskell. I wouldn't think twice about getting you chucked out of here for trying to steal my date."

"Why don't you let the lady decide?" Tully said, his eyes sliding to Alex with a mean gleam in them.

It was a classic damned-if-you-do, damned-if-you-don't situation. Alex looked from one man to the other and took the only option that made any sense at all.

"If you gentlemen will excuse me, I have to go powder my nose."

She crossed the lawn with the steady flow of guests going to and from the Hills' red-brick Georgian mansion. Taking her time, she browsed through the entry hall, eventually making her way to the line for the rest room, where she exchanged idle chat with several ladies about the ruinous effects of heat and humidity on hairdos. When she hiked back toward the tent some time later, her heels punching down into the finely manicured lawn, she hoped cooler male heads had prevailed.

Tully had taken root where she'd left him, no doubt awaiting her return. But before he could spot her, Christian intercepted her and steered her in a different direction.

Alex frowned at him, her full lower lip pouting in disapproval. "I wish you wouldn't bait Haskell that way."

Christian made a face. "He's a pompous, over-blown bully—"

"Who pays his training bills on time."

"You know how I feel about that."

"Yes. And you know how I feel about it."

"Then there's no point in discussing it, is there?" He shrugged off his bad mood and treated her to one of his fabulous smiles, complete with twinkling blue eyes. "You can't blame me for wanting you all to myself, can you, darling? You are, by far, the most dazzling beauty here tonight."

"You're a liar," Alex said, sparkling at his compliment, "but I love the way you do it."

"Do you?" The heat in his gaze went up ten degrees as he pulled her closer, one hand settling possessively on the small of her back. "Well, we both have something to look forward to later on then, don't we?" he murmured, the slow curving of his mouth so frankly sensual, it made Alex's pulse rate pick up a beat. He stared at her as if there weren't two hundred other people milling around them talking and laughing, as if he wanted to take her right there and then and make wild, sweet love to her.

Alex's nerve endings hummed with sexual awareness. All it ever took from him was a look, a word, a touch, and she was on fire for him. It was an addiction, an obsession, and she was powerless to stop it, helpless even to fight against it.

"Dance with me," he commanded, taking her hands in his.

Alex glanced toward the band. "But there's no one else dancing."

"Good."

He led her onto the dance floor, not allowing her to bow to her fears of drawing attention to herself. Still holding her hand, he leaned toward the female singer of the group, a woman with Jessica Lange's looks and Bette Midler's voice, and whispered a few words in her ear. When he drew back, the woman was smiling warmly.

"Everyone is staring at us," Alex muttered as Christian drew her reluctant body into his arms. She held herself formally stiff, refusing to snuggle against him the way he wanted her to.

"So they are," he said with an arrogant shrug. "Let them look their fill. What do I care? I only have eyes for you."

Looking up at him Alex nibbled at her lip, destroying her lipstick and not caring. She knew what he was saying, and she loved him for it. He didn't care who saw them or who knew about her past or what they thought about it. Her importance in his life far overshadowed theirs.

The band started the number with the slow, bluesy strains of a piano. And Alex's eyes filled with tears as the singer's voice started in, strong and smoky, singing from her soul. "When a Man Loves a Woman."

Christian began moving, sensually, drawing Alex to him with his body and with the intensity of his gaze. His hands splayed over her hips, guiding her, inviting her.

As the drum and bass joined in, Alex slid her arms up around his neck and began moving with him, without reservation, without a thought to what anyone else might be thinking.

Everyone else had ceased to exist, had faded away into the heat of the night. There were only Christian and herself and the sexy, heartfelt music that surrounded them with its sensual, steady beat. There were only the two of them and the music and the feelings that flowed between them and twined around them. And when the song faded away, she leaned up into his kiss, giving him her thanks without words, giving him her love.

What better time to tell him, she thought as her feet settled onto the floor. Her heart thumped with anticipation as she looked up at him. Her hands twisted themselves into a knot. "Christian, I—"

"Well, by golly, you did it, pal," a slightly inebriated Robert Braddock said as he slapped Christian on the shoulder. "Honest to Pete, I didn't think even you could pull it off, but you did."

"Do what?" Alex asked, a strange kind of foreboding flooding her. She stood a step or two back from Christian, unable to go to him because of Braddock.

"Robert," Christian said in a warning tone. He held himself absolutely still, as if that would somehow make Braddock lose interest and wander away. "Now is not the time."

"The time for what?" Alex's dark brows drew together in confusion and apprehension.

Braddock waved off his friend's suggestion as he took a gulp of champagne. "I'm a gentleman," he said, his voice slurring a bit. "A gentleman always makes good on his bets."

With his free hand he dug a wad of bills out of his pants pocket and stuffed them messily into Christian's breast pocket. "One iceberg properly melted. You have my congratulations."

Suddenly the truth dawned, descending on Alex with a wave of numbing cold. Unfortunately the pain cut through it quickly, and she was besieged by equal blasts of hurt and humiliation. She had been the object of a wager. A challenge. A stray female to be speculated over and made sport of.

The other shoe had dropped with a resounding thud.

She stared at Christian, not wanting to believe the guilt written all over his face. She loved him. He had battered down every defense she had. He had bullied and begged and bribed her into falling in love with him. And it had all been a game to him.

"Alex—" he began, reaching out toward her. The look in her eyes was ominous.

"You bastard!" She spat the word and slapped him across the face as hard as she could.

"Alex, wait!" he called, all too aware of the crowd that was staring and straining hungrily for any tidbit of gossip. Damn them all to perdition. What he had to say was no secret. "Alex, I love you!"

His words wrenched away the last shred of her control, and the tears she had tried so hard to hold at bay spilled over their barriers and streamed down her cheeks as she pushed her way through the crowd. Love. There wasn't any for her here. There wasn't any for her anywhere. She should have known better.

"Damn you, Braddock!" Christian wheeled on his fellow trainer.

Robert's brows rose over slightly unfocused eyes. "What'd I do?"

"Ruined my entire bloody life, that's all!" Christian bellowed. He pulled the prize money out of his pocket and threw it to the floor like so much scrap paper, then stamped on it with his elegant black Italian shoes.

"You mean you really do love her?" Braddock asked in classic bachelor amazement.

"I really do love her, you imbecile!"

"Well, shoot, Chris," he whined. "That's no fun."

Christian's hands lifted, intent on throttling the life out of his friend. He groaned with the effort to hold himself back, torn between sweet revenge and cursed respectability. Then his gaze caught the nearly full champagne glass Braddock held, and his hands changed their course.

With one he snatched the glass from Robert's hand. With the other he hooked the front of the man's trousers. The chilled champagne went down inside Braddock's pants in a freezing golden stream, but Christian didn't waste an extra second to catch the look on Robert's face. He had to find Alex.

# nine

**ALEX ABANDONED HER SHOES AS SOON AS** she had pushed through the party crowd. Barefoot, she ran across the lawn, away from the tent, away from the house. Her first impulse was to run to the stables, but as she caught sight of the lights she remembered that they were full of show horses and dozens of grooms. She veered instead for the row of dark buildings that sat behind the Hill mansion, the plantation dependencies that had been preserved for their historical value. Reaching the second one, which had once been the kitchen, she stopped running and slumped against the end of the brick building. With the moon on the other side she was swallowed up by the shadow the building cast. Enveloped in darkness, hidden from prying eyes, she was free to cry out all the hurt.

Why did this have to happen? She'd tried so hard to avoid being made a spectacle of again. Hadn't she? She couldn't think of a single thing she'd done to attract attention to herself since she'd moved to Briarwood. She hadn't gone asking for men to call on her. She'd done just the opposite, avoiding them, trying to discourage them.

And they had seen her as a challenge.

It *was* her fault.

She turned and pressed herself against the wall, the rough

brick biting into her cheek and palms. And she sobbed, torn by abject, soul-wrenching misery. She sobbed for the things she'd lost, for the heart that lay broken in her breast, for the love she had that never seemed to find a worthy home. And she cried harder because she didn't understand the reasons why. She had never meant for any of it to happen. She tried to be a good person, tried to mind her own business. But why did these things keep happening to her then, if it wasn't something she did or said or thought?

Wiping back one wave of tears she looked down at the dress she wore, barely able to see the outline in the dark of the shadows. A hundred women could have worn it and felt special. She felt tainted, ashamed that she had ever put it on. She pushed her palms down the front of it, cringing as if it disgusted her, as if she could push it away and have her old baggy clothes magically appear in its stead. But the dress remained, tangible evidence for the old recriminations that came flooding back to ring in her ears.

*"You're too flamboyant, Alexa."*

*"You're too sassy, Alexa."*

*"You were asking for it."*

"But I wasn't!" she whispered in tortured anguish, pressing her hands to her face as the tears came fresh and hot.

She sobbed until she had no tears left to shed, until her head was throbbing and her eyes ached. And then she just stood there, exhausted, nothing left of her inner wall of strength but rubble. She sagged against the brick, not caring that it cut into the bare skin of her back, listening to the cicadas sing in the hot, fragrant summer night.

In the distance she could hear the band playing, the sound rising above the murmur of the crowd. The low thrum of the bass, the vibrant wail of the singer's voice, an occasional crash of a cymbal. Closing her eyes, she relived the dance she'd shared with Christian. For five glorious minutes she had been deliriously happy and in love, soaring higher than she ever could on a horse. And an instant later it had all come crashing down. The heart that had been bursting with joy now lay in a cold, crumbled ruin. The love she had been so ready to give was back inside its little locked box, not to be taken out again for a long, long time.

There were no more tears. Only a pure, piercing ache from which she knew there would be no escape.

The sound that came to her from nearby didn't penetrate immediately, not until she heard the low, rough voice of a man swearing under his breath. He'd bumped into something in the dark and was cursing. Alex brought herself to attention, her whole body straining to hear. He was at the first building in the row, the icehouse. She couldn't see him clearly but was able to distinguish his shape as he moved along the back side of the building where the darkness was intensified by a row of tall crape myrtle shrubs.

Her traitorous heart gave a lurch at the thought that it might be Christian coming to find her. She dismissed both the thought and the sentiment as she inched along the wall intending to slip around the front side of the kitchen, where she would be completely out of view to the man who was approaching. Christian wouldn't come skulking up the back of the buildings if he was looking for her. He would come striding up the path like a prince, demanding in that autocratic tone of voice that she come out of hiding. At any rate, he wouldn't come looking for her. His game was up. Anyone else who had a reason for stalking around in the shadows Alex had no desire to meet.

She glanced at the bright moonlight that fell on the path. She would be in plain sight for an instant as she moved around to the other side of the building. Old instincts of flight and self-preservation rose up inside her as the crape myrtle trees rustled just fifteen feet away. She realized with a stroke of chilling fear just how vulnerable she was, far removed from the party and the safety of the crowd. Beyond these unused buildings lay nothing but dense forest. Christian, if he even cared, had probably decided she'd caught a lift home. No one would miss her until morning.

Swallowing down the knot of fear in her throat, Alex took one last glance in the direction of the man and slipped around the edge of the building. As she turned to run she slammed head-on into a wall of masculinity. Gasping, too terrified to scream, she bolted backward only to be caught in his arms and held.

"Alex!" Christian exclaimed, his relief plain in his voice. "Thank God! I've been searching everywhere for you!"

She said nothing but darted a nervous glance in the direction of the icehouse. Whoever had been there was gone. The trees were still. It had probably been one of the gentlemen too impatient to wait in line for the rest room.

"Darling, we've got to talk."

"What's there to say?" Alex asked tiredly. "It seemed pretty self-explanatory to me. I won you a nice wad of money. You should be happy."

"Oh, hang Robert and his stupid bet," Christian said fiercely, unwittingly tightening his grip on her upper arms. "It's got nothing to do with us."

"Oh, really?" Alex arched a brow. Her tone was one of icy sarcasm. "I think it's got quite a lot to do with me. The Italian Iceberg—isn't that what your pals call me?" she asked bitterly. "You'll be quite the hero with them now, won't you? But of course, you're already a legend among their ranks. How many notches on your bedpost are there now that you can count me?"

"Dammit, Alex, stop it!" Christian said, shaking her. "It's not like that!"

She stared up at him as she wrenched herself free of his hold. "Isn't it?"

"I forgot about the bloody bet as soon as I'd met you."

"Sure, you did," she said with a sneer. "That's why you were so insistent about me going out with you. That's why you hounded me until I agreed to come to this stupid party with you." She enumerated his sins, ticking them off one by one on her fingers. A new supply of tears rose as she glanced down at herself. The shimmer of sequins and taffeta was like moonlight reflected on a lake. "Your pride must have really been on the line for you to go to all the trouble of buying this dress. You had to have lost money on the deal."

Christian ground his teeth at her stubborn refusal to listen. It pricked his pride to think how quickly she'd believed the worst of him, how quickly she had discounted everything that had passed between them. "Do you honestly think if I'd remembered the bet, I would have subjected you to that scene on the dance floor?"

"No," she murmured and smiled ruefully at his sigh of relief. "You're much too British for that. You might be a bastard, but your manners are impeccable."

"Alex—"

"Frightfully bad form on Robert's part, though, wasn't it?" she said, mimicking his upper-crust accent.

Christian's broad shrug was a gesture of supplication. "Alex, what do I have to say to make you believe me when I tell you I love you?"

"There isn't anything you can say. I've seen just how much you love me—enough to bet me to win."

She reached behind her to the nape of her neck, unfastened the heavy gold chain of her necklace, and held it out on her upturned palm for Christian to take. The fight draining out of her, she murmured, "I'll send the dress back tomorrow."

Christian looked at the coil of gold and dark stones in her hand but didn't reach out for it. His heart ached abominably. There was a horrid pressure behind his eyes. Gads, this love business stank to high heaven! His life had been so much less complicated before. There was a great deal to be said for being a carefree bachelor. Affairs were light and fun with clean breaks at the end of them. There would be no clean break with Alex. It would be ragged and bloody, and when Alex left, she would be dragging his heart with her by the ties of love that had bound him to her. He'd never felt so desperate in his life.

He stared into her eyes feeling bleak and lost and guilty. Guilty! Blast it, he hadn't known what guilt was until he'd met Alex! She had him feeling it on a regular basis. Why should he want to go on enduring that?

Because he loved her.

He loved her, and she was going to walk away.

She had managed to arrange her face into the cool, emotionless mask he remembered from when they'd first met. Slowly she turned her hand over, and the necklace spilled to the ground in a river of glimmering gold. He watched it fall and felt it in his heart when it hit the grass.

"Alex, don't do this." He whispered because he didn't trust his voice. He kept his head down and his eyes trained on the ground, because he didn't know what would happen to him if he watched her turn and go.

"Just tell me one thing," Alex said, needing to know more than she needed to flee. "Is there something about me . . . something I did . . . ?"

The only thing that could have cut through Christian's own pain was Alex's. His concern for her had overridden his own selfish needs almost from the first. So his head came up at the strain in her voice, the uncertainty, the hurt. Each of those emotions was reflected in the depths of her wide, dark eyes. Her lush mouth trembled with vulnerability.

Good Lord, she was blaming herself for this fiasco! If he ever got his hands on Robert Braddock again, he wouldn't try to keep from throttling the bastard, he'd do the job proper, then dance on his grave.

"Alex, the bet was nothing more than an idiotic challenge between two overgrown adolescents who should have had sense enough to know better. I didn't see the harm in it. I thought we'd get to know each other, go out, have a few laughs. I didn't count on falling in love with you. I've never been in love," he admitted plaintively. "I'd say it's bloody awful right about now, but I do love you, I can't stand the idea of you not believing me!"

She wanted to believe him. In spite of all the pain and all the doubts, Alex knew she wanted to believe in him. It wasn't a comforting thought. He'd made a fool of her. He'd made her doubt herself. He'd crushed her heart.

Memories came back to make a bid on Christian's behalf. He had listened to the story of her ordeal with compassion and sympathy. He'd held her while she'd cried. He had reawakened her to the joys that could be shared by a man and woman. He'd made her feel like someone special again, like a woman, like someone to be cherished and delighted in instead of someone to be ashamed of and embarrassed by. He'd held her in front of everyone in their world and made it more than clear that his feelings ran deep, that he didn't care who knew it or what they thought.

*When a Man Loves a Woman.*

Heaven help her, how badly she wanted that to be true.

She looked up at him with her heart in her eyes, the moonlight catching her full in the face, stark and white, hiding no secrets, hiding no tears. Christian stepped closer, holding her gaze with his. He lifted his hands to cup her face, his thumbs gently brushing along her cheekbones. Moving closer still, he slid his palms slowly down the column of her throat, over her shoulders, and down her bare back. His fingers traced the low vee in the back of her gown and pressed gently, drawing her near.

"I love you, Alex." He murmured the words against her lips, feathered them along her cheek, brushed them across her forehead. He pulled her full against him in an embrace that was both fierce and tender and whispered into the lush, scented mass of curls atop her head. "Believe me. Please, believe me."

Alex pressed her cheek to his chest. Through the warm, damp fabric of his dress shirt she could feel the solid strength of him. She could hear his heart beating a little quickly as he waited for her answer. Wrapping her arms around his lean waist she hugged herself to him. It might have been smarter to walk away. It might have been safer to leave him. But the thought of living without him, of going back to the life she'd had before him, was so cold and lonely. If there was a chance he could love her, she needed to take it.

"Alex?"

He whispered her name so softly, she might have imagined it. "Yes," she answered, just as softly. "I believe you."

The music drifted from speakers that were built into the bookshelves in the bedroom wall. Soft, smoky, sexy, as hot as the night itself, it twined around the couple dancing in the dark, weaving them into the magic, seeping into their souls.

*When a Man Loves a Woman . . .*

Christian had left his coat tossed carelessly in the back seat of the Mercedes along with Alex's panty-hose. His tie was gone, as were the studs from his shirt front. The garment hung open, exposing the smooth, hard planes of his chest. Alex arched herself against him. Her arms were wrapped around his neck, his banded around the small of her back, lifting her into him. Together they swayed to the sensual beat. Thigh brushing thigh, breast to chest, every move was a caress, each caress leading to another, with no sound except the music and the soft rustle of fabric.

The moon spilled its silver light through the sheer curtain at the window. The breeze stirred the curtain to a dance of its own. The sultry heat that hung thick in the air was as much a product of the mood as it was of the sun. It rose from their entwined bodies, from the intensity of their gaze, as Christian looked down into Alex's face, and Alex tilted her head back and stared up into Christian's hot blue eyes. It steamed around them as Christian settled his mouth against hers in a deep kiss.

Tongues dancing, twining, sliding over each other, they tasted and savored the flavor of love, a flavor made sweeter by having nearly lost it. Alex let her hands set off on an exploration of Christian's chest, taking joy in the simple pleasure of touching him. As the angle of the kiss altered, she slid her fingers over the slick hot skin of his belly, dipping inside the opened waistband of his black trousers, teasing.

Trailing his mouth down Alex's jaw to the arched column of her throat, Christian slid the straps of her dress down until they dangled against her arms. With just the tips of his fingers he stroked the satin skin of her shoulders, drawing a sigh from her. The sigh deepened to a moan as his hands slid down over the curve of her back and softened to another sigh as the zipper of her dress whispered its descent. His fingers splayed across her hips as the taffeta skirt rustled to the floor, leaving Alex naked in his arms.

She let her head fall back as he lifted her to him, reveling in the feel of her breasts caressing his chest and the dark delta of curls that protected her femininity rubbing against his belly. He turned with her in his arms and lowered her gently to the cool cotton sheets of the big mahogany four-poster bed. She lay back against the mountain of pillows and watched as he lowered the zipper of his trousers and stepped out of them, then lowered his snug briefs and dropped them to the thick ruby carpet that stretched across the polished pine floor.

He came to her the perfect example of the male animal—sleek, hard muscled, beautifully aroused. His gaze was on her face, reading every nuance of her desire, telegraphing the intense quality of his. His fine, silky hair spilled across his forehead. A bead of sweat trickled down the center of his chest. The bed dipped beneath his weight as he settled one knee on the mattress and slid toward Alex.

Before he even touched her she felt him, felt that awesome power that radiated from him, and a thrill of excitement went through her.

He leaned over her, bracing himself up on his left arm as his right hand glided up her leg. Bending down to kiss her, he caught her sighs with his mouth as he stroked the heated core of her femininity with his thumb. Alex lifted her hips off the mattress, arching into his caress, begging for deeper contact. And she whimpered in frustration when he took his touch away. But then his mouth was on her breast, and her attention focused on the exquisite sensations there—the tingling that came with each tug of his hot, wet mouth on her nipple, the sparks that shot through her as his teeth grazed her flesh. He made her forget everything when he made love to her. She forgot the past, forgot her inhibitions, forgot everything but him and the beautiful, sensuous harmony they created together.

The music rambled on, bluesy and soulful, mingling with the sighs and moans of the dancers and the whisper of skin against sheets. The breeze blew in hot and sultry with the promise of a storm. Thunder rumbled somewhere over the mountains, but they didn't hear it. They were too caught up in the expression of feelings that went soul-deep, too caught up in the music.

*When a Man Loves a Woman . . .*

Christian trailed his mouth down Alex's belly, tasting her skin. His tongue dipped into her navel, skimmed lower, stroked languidly at the sweet, hot flower of her femininity. Alex's chest heaved as she gasped for a breath of the humid air. She tangled a hand in Christian's hair and moaned as she arched up, sliding one bare foot up and down his sweat-slicked back. The pleasure built, taking her higher and higher, but never over the edge.

Pulling away, he rolled her onto her belly and kissed his way up the backs of her thighs, over the swell of her buttocks to the sensitive indentation at the small of her back, where he planted a slow kiss. He slid over her in a full body caress, settling himself intimately between her legs as he bent to nibble at the side of her throat.

"I need you. Alex," he murmured darkly, nuzzling her ear. "I need to be inside you, to feel you around me. I've never needed anything—anyone—the way I need you."

With the admission came a piercing shaft of fear deep inside him. Alex had become a part of him. No other woman had ever gotten so close. No other woman had ever held such power to hurt him. No other woman had ever stirred within him such a savage need to possess and protect. No other woman but this woman.

*When a Man Loves a Woman . . .*

She twisted beneath him, arching up, seeking contact. "I need you too," she whispered, turning her head to brush her lips across his. "Take me, Christian. Take me to paradise again."

They rolled across the bed then, Christian ending up with Alex draped over him, the heat of her pressing against his belly, her hands on either side of his head. Her head was thrown back, her breasts thrust magnificently forward. Christian arched up to take one mauve point into his mouth, and she wrapped her arms around him, holding him there until she finally pulled away, panting.

"I love you, Alex," he said with a growl, easing her down on his shaft.

Alex held her breath as he filled her with his strength, with his essence. Her body stretched and tightened around him, clutching him deep within her where she wanted him most, where she needed him so urgently. She lifted herself and slid down on him, slowly, prolonging the sensation. He kissed her, his mouth hot, avid, slanting hungrily across hers, his tongue plunging into her.

It was indescribable—the wondrous, mysterious, frightening sensation of being locked intimately with the man she loved. They were so close, so in tune. The physical expression of their feelings was so beautiful, it battered down the barriers inside her, reached straight to her heart. And she shivered a little at the thought of what awesome power this man held over her. She did her best to ignore the little voice that tried to tell her she shouldn't have let him so close, that she shouldn't love him so much, that she didn't deserve this kind of happiness. She shut out those dark thoughts that were trying to drift into her mind like smoke. Moving strongly on Christian, she took him deep and hard and gasped as the exquisite explosion of feeling obliterated all else.

Christian's control broke as lightning flashed over the distant hills and Alex's body stroked over his, taut as a bowstring, slick with sweat, trembling with building passion. She was the woman he loved—the only woman he'd ever truly loved with everything that was in his heart, with all that made up the man he was. He had nearly lost her, and the fear of that realization shot through him again as he held her to him.

With a desperate need to make her his, to brand her again with his possession, he rolled her beneath him and drove himself into her, urgent and frightened in a way he had never known before. Love reached past the pleasant surface emotions he'd shared with other women. It cut deeper than the heart, touched his soul, changed him forever in a way he could never begin to understand.

He looked down into Alex's face, no more than a breath away, into the glowing amber of her eyes, and saw his own feelings reflected back. They both groaned together as rapture built to a fever pitch and took them over the crest. Then they held each other, spent and sweating, tangled in the sheets, their sighs trailing off to melt into the music, their feelings hanging thick in the sultry air around them.

*When a man loves a woman.*

And in the still of the night the storm rumbled closer.

# ten

**"BLOODY BEGGAR TRIED TO BITE ME!" CHARLIE** exclaimed indignantly as she dashed out of Terminator's stall and slammed shut the lower half of the door, her hasty actions belying the truculent look on her face. "Tried to take me arm right off, he did, the bleedin' sod!"

She gave the horse her meanest look, narrowing her eyes until they were mere slits between scowling brows and pudgy rouged cheeks. She shook a finger at the wild-eyed gelding. "Next stop's the canning factory, mind you."

"And it can't happen soon enough, as far as I'm concerned," Christian muttered.

He stood in the aisle, dressed for his first competition of the day in buff breeches and a pristine white shirt, which would not remain pristine for long. The storm that had rumbled through during the night had done nothing to alleviate the stifling heat but had managed to add another level of thickness to the humidity. It had also left the top layer of ground just wet enough to make mud—guaranteeing tricky footing in the ring and plenty of work for the grooms and the laundry services.

It was not yet midmorning, and already the temperature had climbed into the high eighties. Tempers had climbed in direct proportion. There were a great many more raised voices in the stables than usual, more horses with pinned ears, more grooms grumbling about menial tasks. Hanging on the grillwork of many stalls were big square electric fans, humming incessantly in an effort to keep the horses cool. There was nothing to be done about the human tempers. They rose and fell as sporadically as the sultry breeze, adding their staccato accents to the sounds of steel-shod hooves on concrete and rock music blasting from a tape player.

"Are you all right?" Christian asked, eyeing the girl.

Charlie flashed him an acrimonious look, the trio of silver earrings on her right ear clanging together like warning bells. She waited to speak until a pair of junior hunters had been led past. As soon as their handlers were out of earshot, she lit into her employer. "A lot you care. Bloody well glad to be rid of me, you are. And using me to do your dirty work without me even knowing." She sneered at him, clearly expressing her opinion of him as a life form lower than pond scum. "You're a right flaming cad, you are. No better than that horse," she said, jerking a thumb over her shoulder at Terminator, who pinned his ears and shook his head. "Worse, even. At least he shows his colors."

Christian scowled. News traveled at the speed of sound through the ranks of the grooms. No doubt the nasty little scene he and Alex and Robert had played out at the party had made its way to every corner of the show grounds by now. It was probably the hot topic over doughnuts at the concession stand. The show secretaries were probably buzzing about it in their little office. It was a wonder the recapped version hadn't come over the PA system with the morning announcements.

He heaved a sigh and planted his fists at his waist. Guilt dug a talon into him at the thought that Charlie was more than half-right that he was using her. Contrite or not, he wasn't going to admit that to her, but he was going to set her straight as far as his relationship with Alex went.

"I know what the rumors are, Charlotte," he said, all traces of the flip, charming rogue gone. He looked as serious as any of his stuffy brothers. "I also know what the facts are. I care very deeply for Alex. Feel free to spread that little bit of news around to all your gossiping friends."

Charlie rubbed a hand across her chin and gave him a long, measuring look. Finally she shrugged one shoulder and tugged up the strap of her orange tank top. "Maybe I will." She dragged the words out grudgingly.

Christian watched her scuff the toe of her sneaker against the concrete as she slid her hands into the pockets of baggy khaki shorts, and realized with a start that he wanted the girl's respect. Gads, he was turning into a bona fide Atherton! Respectability, responsibility, love. He sighed and shrugged, conceding defeat.

"You're looking grim," Alex said cheerfully, tapping him on the seat of his breeches with her crop as she sauntered in from the show office. She was dressed much the same as Christian was in buff breeches and a white blouse. Her blouse was sleeveless, a concession to the heat. Christian's sleeves were rolled neatly to his elbows, displaying strong tan arms and an expensive platinum watch. Her gaze lingered appreciatively on the way his breeches clung to the muscles of his thighs.

"It's this bloody heat," Christian grumbled, leaning down to kiss her lightly. "And the thought of you facing a grand prix course on that rabid animal."

Alex sighed and speared a hand back through her damp hair. "Let's not start on that, please."

Christian ground his teeth and glared at the chestnut. "He just tried to attack Simmonds."

"Are you okay?" Alex asked the groom, taking in the belligerent set of the girl's chin as well as the brief flash of uncertainty in her eyes. Charlie liked to play it tougher than she was. They had a lot in common that way.

"I'm fine. The guv'nor's stretching it a bit," she said evenly, her gaze steady on Christian's face. "The bloody pig tried to bite me, is all. He does that every flippin' day."

At least he had to admire the girl's loyalty to Alex, Christian thought, rubbing at the tension in the back of his neck.

Alex looked into Terminator's stall, pensive as she stared at the horse. He was restless, weaving back and forth in front of his grain box in a habit that had schizophrenic overtones. His washy chestnut coat was already dark with sweat in patches along his neck and flank. The tension rolled off him in waves.

He wasn't ready for a show of this kind. He had earned his way into it, having accumulated a substantial amount of prize money during his checkered career. He had demonstrated to Alex that he could handle the fences, but his temperament had worsened with every increase in competition. A show like this one carried a certain excitement in the air. The grooms were busier, the general bustle in the stable was increased. The show grounds were alive with spectators, all of them excited about the caliber of horses and competition they were there to see. And the riders transmitted a nervous tension of their own. This wasn't some penny-ante schooling show with little fake gold cups for prizes. This was the highest echelon of competition. The horses here were worth tens of thousands and even hundreds of thousands of dollars. The riders were people who had competed internationally, people who had ridden in the Olympics. The prize money for the grand prix was fifty thousand dollars.

No, it wasn't that Terminator couldn't handle the fences. He couldn't handle the pressure. Alex knew it. She also knew that his owner would pack up Terminator and his stable mate and take them to another trainer if she scratched him from the competition.

Her gaze slid to the next stall where A Touch of Dutch stood on the far side, placidly submitting to the ministrations of the two Heathers, dozing as she enjoyed the breeze from the fan that was hooked to the box adjacent to hers.

"I can get you five that are her equal and better," Christian said softly, standing so close behind her, she could feel his body heat. "She's not the issue here, Alex."

No. The issue was her independence, Alex thought. This had to do with paying her dues and working her way up and not relying on anyone else for her livelihood or her success. It had to do with fighting demons and winning. Christian was asking her to lean on him, and she couldn't do it. She loved him, but she couldn't let herself allow him to save her, because she couldn't allow herself to believe he would be there the next time.

"I've got two in the pregreen class in an hour," she murmured, not looking up at him. "I'd better get cracking."

He raised his hands and rubbed at the tension in her shoulders, forcing a long sigh out of his lungs. Let it go, don't push, he told himself, and he smiled ruefully at the thought that it was far easier said than done these days, since this chronic case of responsibility had set in. A turbulent mix of emotions twisted inside him as he turned Alex and gazed down into her amber eyes.

"I love you," he whispered, bending his head down near hers.

"And I love you," Alex whispered back, rising up on the toes of her boots to kiss him. "Just don't try to run my life."

Standing at attention he clicked his heels together and gave her a smart salute and a dazzling smile. "I shall endeavor to do my best."

But the smile faded as he walked away, assailed by doubts.

"Do yourself a favor," Rylan grumbled as Christian reached the new barn and the row of box stalls that were draped in Quaid Farm blue. Christian's brows lifted. Ry shot a dark look at his wife, who stood holding their son's hand near the open door of Diamond Life's stall. "If you're going to get tangled up with a woman, make sure she's got sense enough to mind you."

"Too late for that," Christian muttered wryly.

His employer ignored him, wheeling instead to face his pregnant wife again with a thunderous black scowl. "You shouldn't be out in this heat, Mary Margaret."

"Oh, pooh, sugar." Maggie batted her lashes at him and patted her free hand to the crown of her wide-brimmed straw hat. "I've got my sunhat and my sundress on. I've got enough sunscreen to coat a horse with. Besides, I'm not a piece of wax fruit that's going to melt in the heat."

Christian bent and brushed a kiss to Maggie's expectantly upturned cheek and couldn't help but smile at her. "I think you look very fetching."

"Why, thank you," she said, preening as she let go of her son's hand and turned in a somewhat awkward circle, showing off her yellow dress and her enormous belly.

Ry snorted. "Yeah, we'll see how fetching she looks when we have to scrape her up off the ground after she passes out from the heat."

Maggie sent him a ferocious look.

"I expect Maggie knows her limits," Christian said without much conviction.

"She never has," Ry said flatly. "Why should she start now?"

Christian wasn't inclined to argue the point. He was in no position to. Hadn't he just finished trying to dissuade Alex from something she was bent on doing? He certainly didn't believe she knew her limits. Or maybe she did, he thought, frowning darkly as his suspicion came creeping back to him.

"Buddy Quaid, get out of that stall!" Ry barked, his fierce-eyed stare on his son, who had gone into the stall where the young stallion, Diamond Life, was being readied.

"But I was just gonna help Marlin," the boy said, frowning as his father scooped him up.

"You got to be taller to help Marlin," Ry explained, tucking the boy under his arm like a football.

"But I'm big," Buddy protested, looking at his father upside down. "I'm gonna be a big brother."

"Big brothers help their mamas," Katie Leone said, coming to stand beside her own big brother, who leaned down and kissed her dutifully. She tickled her nephew's chin and chuckled as he squealed and squirmed.

"How did the babysitting go?" Christian asked as he took Isabella from Nick's arms and rubbed noses with her. The baby immediately began regaling him with gibberish, her small hands waving as she spoke.

"Great," Nick said, pulling Katie backward into his embrace. "Isabella is an angel."

"Yes, she is, isn't she," Christian said, feeling ridiculously proud of the dark-eyed little girl, as if he were somehow responsible for her good behavior. As if he were her father. Gads, he thought, swallowing hard.

"Maybe you're the one who shouldn't go out in the heat, sugar," Maggie said, giving him a look that mixed humor and sympathy. "You're looking a mite peaked."

The woman was too perceptive by half. He ignored her remark, turning instead to Katie and Nick. "Alex tells me you two are expecting, so to speak."

"We're on the list," Nick said with glowing brown eyes as he hugged his wife and grinned.

Katie looked more than a little nervous at the idea. "It could be a long wait," she said, fussing with the gathers in her pink gauze skirt.

"Well, congratulations anyway, luv," Christian said sincerely as he handed Isabella to her. "You'll be a wonderful mother."

Katie smiled and glanced away, blinking back sudden tears.

"We should maybe go find Alex, huh?" Nick suggested gently, steering her away. He glanced back over his shoulder at the others apologetically but managed a happy tone as he said,

"Hey, dinner at our place after the show. My mama's special deep-dish pizza and plenty of cold stuff to wash it down."

"Was it something I said?" Christian murmured as he watched them walk away, Nick with his arm around Katie's shoulder and his dark head tilted down toward hers solicitously.

"She's just a little unsure of herself," Maggie said, her eyes full of concern.

Ry scowled as he set his son down. "And we all know whose fault that is."

"Rylan, let it go," Maggie said wearily, leaning against his oaklike frame. "Your mama ran out on you a long time ago. It's best left in the past."

"Yeah," he said reflectively, "but look how often the past comes back to haunt us."

Christian went into the stall to check on his horse, his mind wandering once again to Alex. If his suspicions were correct, it was her past that was driving her to take risks. How long would she allow it to haunt her? More important, could he stop her before she let it destroy her?

Charlie ran a cloth over the sorrel mare's glossy coat, then ran a different one over Alex's boots, removing every speck of mud from horse and rider in preparation for their appearance in the show ring. If they came out looking less than spotless, it would be through no fault of the groom.

"Make sure Heather C. keeps Rugby moving," Alex said, straightening her jacket and wincing at the feel of sweat running between her shoulder blades. "His back will tighten up if she just sits around on him gossiping."

"Don't you worry, miss. I'll crack the whip," Charlie said.

"And I'll want you here with him the instant I finish with Duchess."

"Right."

As she polished the visible edge of stirrup iron, the groom suddenly cast a suspicious glance over her shoulder and stiffened in affront.

"What the bloody hell do you want?" she barked. "A flaming lot of nerve you have, showing your face round here! Who do think you are?"

Alex's gaze was immediately pulled from the ring to the handsome man standing beside her horse wearing dark sunglasses and a sheepish expression. Robert Braddock. If Charlie's reception of the man had been fiery, Alex's was glacial. She stared down at him from her much greater height as if she were the queen of the world and he a filthy, traitorous pockmarked peasant.

He cleared his throat nervously and pulled his sunglasses off, revealing the remnants of a beastly hangover. "I wonder if I could have a word with you, Alex?"

"For what?" Charlie demanded. She cuffed Braddock on the arm and scolded him in a voice a decibel too shrill for his pounding head to stand. "Go on, you ruddy blighter! You've got nothing to say my miss wants to hear! We've all had a bellyful of you, we have. You ought to be ashamed—"

"I am," he admitted, giving her a determined look, his words stopping her arm in midswing as she hauled back to clip him another one.

They both glanced up to Alex for a sign. She nodded Charlie away. The girl took a reluctant step in the direction of the ring, shaking a warning finger at Braddock. "This had better be good, Bobby, mind you, or you'll have me to answer to. Right?"

"Gawd, she's something else," Braddock muttered, rubbing at his throbbing temples. "That girl could sell sass by the gallon and still have a surplus," he said, turning his patented good-ol'-boy grin up toward Alex.

"What did you want to say to me, Mr. Braddock?" Alex

asked, freezing the charming smile right off his square face. The wounds that had been opened the night before were still too tender for her to be readily forgiving. "Please be brief, I have to ride soon."

"I want to apologize for last night," he said smoothly, going for endearing contrition, since charm had been knocked out of the box. He tilted his head and gave her a boyish smile. "I'm really sorry, Alex."

"And that makes it all right?" Alex asked, cold fury building inside her from the leftover ashes of another fight with a handsome, charming man who had believed his looks and his position allowed him to get away with anything. "I don't think so."

Braddock's bloodshot dark eyes flashed a little. His jaw hardened a fraction. His drawl had lost some of its honey when he spoke again. "I didn't mean any harm."

Alex stared at him, unblinking. "You made me the butt of a joke. You thought you could just play with my life for your own amusement."

"I said I was sorry." His patience was wearing thin in big patches now, his expression taking on a hardness Alex doubted he often let other people see. "You know, maybe if you'd been a little friendlier to begin with, none of this would have happened."

His tone and his words struck another raw nerve. "I'm sorry, Mr. Braddock," she said with frigid formality, "but I don't feel obligated to be 'friendly' to men who consider it their due."

With that Alex nudged her horse forward, buckling the strap of her helmet as she headed for the arena. As she cantered her mare in a slow circle she glanced out to see Robert Braddock glare at her, then turn on his booted heel and storm away. She'd made herself an enemy, but there was no time to dwell on it now.

By late afternoon everyone had abandoned their jackets to ride in shirtsleeves with the blessings of the judges. The heat had climbed another sweltering degree toward one hundred, and what little breeze there had been in the morning had died a stagnant death. The air hung damp and hazy over the thickly forested hillsides that rose around Green Hills.

"He's gonna tear 'em up today. Aren't you, big guy?" Tully boomed, slapping his hand against the wire grill of Terminator's stall.

The gelding was tacked up and tied to either side of the stall. He sat back on his haunches, wild-eyed, and lunged forward, jerking at his bonds.

Tully laughed and banged the stall again. "Just look at him. He's rearin' to go!"

"Mr. Haskell, please don't do that," Alex snapped, impulsively grabbing hold of Tully's wrist as he started to hit the grill again.

The big man turned and looked down at her, a curious mix of anger and speculation on his meaty face.

Alex dropped his hand abruptly and stepped back. "We don't want him to leave his game in the locker room, do we?"

"No," Haskell said slowly, pulling out a handkerchief to dab at the sweat on his forehead.

Uncomfortable with his sudden close scrutiny, Alex moved away from him and bent to dig her gloves and crop out of her gear bag. She sincerely wished Tully Haskell would have been too caught up rubbing elbows with the rich and famous to bother checking up on her. Both she and Terminator were nervous enough as it was. The course for the grand prix was being set up. In a few moments the riders would be allowed to walk it, judging the distances, making strategy. Alex wanted no distractions.

"I see you haven't come to your senses yet," Christian said dryly.

She closed her eyes, loath to look up and see whether he was talking to her or Tully. This is all I need, she thought, for the two of them to get into it right here in Hill's stable. Lovely.

"Don't you have stalls to muck out, Atherton?" Tully asked caustically.

Christian gave the man a cool, dismissing look and turned away from him, his focus on Alex. He'd watched her warm up Terminator. The rogue had done his best to run off with her. He'd fought her every step. And now he stood in his stall looking as if he were possessed by demons—rolling his eyes, grinding his teeth, kicking out with his hind legs. The horse looked insane, and the thought of Alex climbing back up on him drove Christian near that very same edge. His earlier promise of noninterference had gone by the wayside, thrown over by the suddenly dominant need to protect the woman he loved.

"Christian, we aren't going to discuss this," Alex said, struggling for an ounce of coolheadedness as she straightened.

"Don't be such a stubborn little fool, Alex!" he said, his temper flaring to rival the heat wave. Grabbing her arm he turned her toward the stall. "Look at him. The poor beast is completely off his head!"

"Butt out, Atherton," Tully said, shoving Christian back a step. "You charmed her into sleeping with you, but you can't charm her into losing to you."

"You bastard!" Christian spat the word, his British reserve evaporating in a haze of fury. He had taken all he intended to from this ill-mannered lout. He wasn't about to stand for Haskell making sleazy gossip of his love for Alex. Acting completely on instinct, he hauled his arm back and bloodied Haskell's nose with one forceful punch.

"Christian, stop it!" Alex shouted.

He dragged his eyes off Tully, who was swearing a muffled blue streak as he held his handkerchief to his nose and dyed it red with his own blood. Reason came seeping back into his brain as he looked down at Alex. She was furious with him. Her eyes blazed with golden light beneath ominously lowered black brows. Her chin had lifted to that foreboding angle he recognized all too well.

"I think you'd better go," she said.

"Alex, please—"

She held her hands up to ward off whatever explanation he had to offer. "Go. Now."

"Fine," he said, pulling himself together, straightening his back, setting his shoulders, lifting his aristocratic nose a fraction. Love had reduced him to a brawlling bully. It had reduced him to begging. Who needed it? "Don't expect sympathy when that rogue throws you through a fence."

There were thirty horses entered in the Green Hills grand prix. Three had been scratched due to heat exhaustion. Terminator was not among them. Christian watched from stop Diamond Life as Alex tried to work the horse in a slow circle. The gelding refused to walk, dancing instead in a series of hops and leaps, his head way up, nostrils flaring. His coat was nearly black with sweat, white lather foaming along his neck and dripping from his mouth. Alex sat on him, her back rigid with the strain of holding the big horse in check, the muscles standing out in her arms. Christian's stomach churned.

"She deserves whatever happens to her, If you ask me," Robert grumbled, circling his gray around Christian's horse.

Christian shot him a dire look. "Nobody asked you."

Braddock swore under his breath. "What's the matter with you? Getting yourself all tied up in knots over a woman. It's not like you."

It might not have been like the Christian Atherton who had cavalierly bet his friend he could win a certain lady's favors, but it was very like the Christian Atherton who had evolved over the past few weeks. He had done a great deal of growing and changing in a short space of time. The pains of that growth were still stinging and aching through him, evident in the set of his square chin and the tension in his shoulders.

Braddock grinned. "Why don't I call us up a couple of first-stringers from my little black book? We'll head into DC tonight and take your mind off that razor-tongued little viper."

Christian gave him a look of utter disdain and moved his horse away. "Grow up, Robert."

He was as disgusted with himself as he was with his friend. He didn't enjoy the turbulent emotions warring inside him. He didn't like dealing with new feelings. He wasn't at all certain he would be any good at respectability. Just look what he'd done defending Alex's honor. Punching her client in the nose! She'd love him for that. Well, bloody hell, she deserved better than Tully Haskell, whether she believed it or not.

Wiping the sweat off his brow with his forearm, he tried to drag his concentration off Alex and back to the matter at hand. He had a jump course to ride.

A grand prix course is designed to challenge both horse and rider. The fences are imposing, the distances between them difficult. This course was no exception, and adding to the difficulty was the gooey top layer of footing in the ring. The heat and humidity would be a factor for horses who lacked stamina. Whoever went home with the lion's share of the prize money was going to have earned it. There would be no easy victories.

Christian set his young stallion to the task with his characteristic determination. He may have been easygoing outside the ring, but in it he was the consummate competitor. He attacked the course with a combination of aggression and finesse and a confidence that was telegraphed to the handsome equine star beneath him. They came away with a clear round.

Others were not so fortunate. Countless rails came down, particularly at a big triple bar with a deceptive curving approach.

Several horses slipped turning corners. Two riders came off. By the time twenty had gone, there were only four clean rounds.

Alex waited her turn near the end gate, a terrible feeling of foreboding boring through her like acid. There was no way in hell Terminator was going to make it through this, and yet she felt she had no alternative but to try him. Driven by something that went way beyond the issue of job security, she rode the chestnut gelding into the ring. She had to prove herself. She had to pay her dues.

Wrestling for control of the bit, she took her horse into the first fence. He put an extra stride in at the last second, jumped badly, and rapped the top rail hard, but it stayed up. The instant his feet touched the ground, the battle was on again. He lunged against the bit, pulling Alex up out of the saddle. This time he left the ground too early, ignoring the signals of his rider, but jumped big and left the second fence intact.

The fight for control raged on. Alex's arms felt like hot lead from trying to hold Terminator to a manageable pace. Pain knifed into her shoulders and fear climbed high in her throat. Because Terminator refused to listen to her, he was out of position coming into nearly every fence, and as a consequence Alex was out of position. The horse made the jumps on sheer physical talent. She clung to him through pure athleticism.

They were coming into the toughest part of the course—a combination of three jumps with one stride between each followed by the curve into the triple bar. As they started for it, Terminator ducked his head again, jerking the reins through Alex's numb hands, which allowed him a burst of dangerous speed. By luck they made the first of the combination in perfect stride, but they hit the second one soundly, bringing down the top rail. Alex was thrown forward on landing, giving Terminator free rein as she struggled to stay aboard. He ducked out on the third fence of the combination and rounded the turn at breakneck pace for the triple bar.

Alex had taken falls before—as a seasoned rider, she expected to take her share of spills. But this wasn't just a tumble, it was a catastrophe. This was the kind of crash that ended careers, even lives.

Terminator galloped for the triple bar out of control, wild, running as if he were being chased by the devil himself. He cut the corner too sharply, saw the fence too late, tried to put on the brakes, and slipped in the mud, then took off in a last-ditch effort to save himself. He went up in the air, twisting as his hind legs slipped out from under him, and then went crashing down.

Alex saw it all happen in slow motion—the jerky takeoff, the sudden terrible change of angle, the red-and-white bars of the fence rushing up at her, then nothing.

When the blackness receded, she was looking up at half a dozen anxious faces. Her fuzzy gaze focused in on one.

"Christian?"

He was on his knees beside her, mud staining his immaculate white breeches, sweat running in rivers down his ashen face. His eyes were bright with an emotion like panic. "Lie still, darling," he said, his voice choked and hoarse. He ran a trembling hand back through her hair. "Just lie still. There's a doctor coming."

"I'm all right," she said, groaning as she struggled to sit up. "All right" was a gross exaggeration. She felt as if she'd been beaten with a club, but none of the pain was the kind associated with broken bones. She looked at him anxiously. "The horse?"

"Damn the horse!" Christian barked, his face flaming a furious shade of red.

The horse! If he'd had a gun, he would have shot the hateful creature there and then. Nothing, *nothing* in his life had ever terrified him the way seeing her fall had—watching Alex lose control, watching the horse go down in a tangle of legs and lumber. It had nearly killed him to see it happen, to fear the worst, to bend over Alex as she lay unconscious for those few terrible seconds. And she was asking about the bloody horse!

"The horse is fine, Ms. Gianni," one of the ring stewards said from somewhere above her.

Alex nodded, wincing at the throbbing that set off in her head. Helmet or no, she'd taken quite a jolt. Still, she was in one piece and saw no reason not to demonstrate that fact to the five hundred people watching. Hanging on to Christian's arm for support, she pushed herself to her feet and was rewarded with a round of applause for her efforts.

An hour later she'd been thoroughly checked over by the doctor on call and pronounced whole and healthy. Half her body was liable to turn black and blue, and she had a nasty cut on her right cheekbone, but it wasn't anything she hadn't endured before.

She was sitting on a trunk in the stall where her tack was stored, holding a bag of ice to her cheek when Christian reappeared. After helping her from the ring to the ambulance and hovering like a mother hen while the doctor checked her for a concussion, he had been called back to the arena to ride in the jump-off.

"How'd it go?" she asked, trying to muster a smile that ended up looking more like a grimace.

"I blew the combination," he said flatly. "We came third."

"Oh."

She watched him pace the small enclosure with his hands on his hips. His head was bent, his pale hair falling onto his forehead. Nervous tension surrounded him like an electrical field. It beamed out of his blue eyes like lasers when he stopped and looked at her from under lowered brows. He was angry, she realized. Furious. The storm was being controlled by his proper British manners, but the manners were clearly in danger of losing their grip.

"You could have been killed," he said, breaking the silence that had become unbearable.

"But I wasn't."

The first explosion broke through his control like a thunderclap. "Dammit, Alex, that isn't the point!"

"We ride, we take risks, Christian," she said, maintaining her calm. "You know that. You take them too."

"Acceptable risks," he stipulated, jabbing the air between them with a slender forefinger. "There's a line there, and you've gone way across it, Alex."

"What are you saying?"

"I'm saying that this reckless disregard for your life has got to stop. You're shipping that horse back to Haskell immediately."

She bristled at his autocratic mind-your-betters tone of voice. "That's not for you to decide, Christian. You don't run my life."

The second rumble of thunder shook the rafters above them. "Well, somebody's got to, because you're bloody well going to kill yourself!"

"I'm just doing my job," Alex said tightly.

Christian shook his head. "This goes well beyond doing your job or hanging on to your damnable independence. You're trying to punish yourself. You think you have to take on the likes of that rogue to make up for all the imagined sins you committed in California, for all the things you lost—"

"That's absurd!" she exclaimed, vaulting off the tack trunk as if it had suddenly turned red-hot.

"It's self-destructive, Alex, and it's stupid—"

"It's a damned lie!" she shouted, her heart pounding wildly.

"Is it?" Christian demanded softly. His fingers closed around her chin and tilted her bruised face upward. "Look me in the eye, Alex. Look me in the eye and tell me you don't blame yourself for what that bastard Reidell did to you."

Tears and defiance rose in her eyes, but denial wouldn't come. She could feel the words stick in her throat like a rock, but she couldn't force them out. She glared at Christian, hating him for doing this to her, for making her feel things she didn't want to feel and face things she didn't want to face. Her own sense of fury built inside her, but all the words stayed bottled up, and the pressure built.

Christian sighed and slid his palm along her uninjured cheek.

"I love you, Alex," he murmured. "But I can't stand by and watch you break your neck in penance for something that wasn't your fault."

"What are you saying?"

"I'm saying that horse goes or I go," Christian said, gritting his teeth. He'd never been one for ultimatums. He'd never been one for manipulating people. But then he'd never been in love. Nor had he ever stood helplessly by while someone he loved risked her life and came close to losing it. He had to do something to save her, to save himself, and this was the only thing he could think of.

"I can't afford—"

"You can't afford not to. Think of Isabella if you can't think of yourself. What would have happened to her if you'd been killed or crippled out there today? And all for nothing, Alex!" he said plaintively. "I know money is a problem, but I can help you if you'll let me. You don't need Haskell." *You need me. Please say you need me.*

"I don't need to be bullied either," Alex said, striking out, old wounds stinging more sharply than the new. "And I don't need you psychoanalyzing me. You're blowing this all out of proportion because you've got some macho obsessive need to control my life. Well, I've got news for you, buster," she said, flinging the ice bag at him. It hit his shoulder and fell to the wooden floor of the stall. She kicked it aside as she moved to stand toe to toe with him. "I'm in control," she declared. "Nobody tells me what to do or who to be or how to dress," she said, her voice rising with each word. *"I'm in control!"*

The shout rang in her own ears, the volume and pitch making it painfully obvious that what she said was not true. She stared at Christian just the same, unwilling to back down. And he stared back, his handsome face carefully blank.

"You know where to find me," he said quietly, using every ounce of strength he had to tamp down the pain ripping through his chest.

"Who says I'll come looking?" Alex was certain her words hurt her more than they hurt Christian. Her heart wrenched as she said them and he walked away, out of her stall and out of her life.

# eleven

**IT HURT TO MOVE. THE SLIGHTEST SHIFT OF** weight set off small explosions of pain throughout the right side of her body. Her shoulder throbbed abominably. The muscles all down her side felt as though they'd been run through a meat grinder. Alex recognized the distinctive kinds of pain from each distinctive injury. She'd been hurt often enough to distinguish one from the next. There was the pain that came from torn muscle fibers. The pain that came from blood pooling beneath the surface of the skin. The pain that lingered from the jolt of a sudden, hard impact.

But the physical pain was a welcomed distraction from the emotional pain that permeated her entire being, so on Monday morning, at the crack of dawn, Alex inched her way out of bed and hobbled down the hall for a therapeutic soak in the tub. Rigid muscles let loose to some degree, at least until she was able to raise her right arm almost to shoulder height by the time she struggled out of the water twenty minutes later.

As she had expected, most of the right side of her body was purpling from the forceful landing on the thick wooden bars of the jump. Anything but the slightest brush of the towel made her wince, and every time she winced, the cut on her cheek tugged at the butterfly patch the doctor had applied. The pain in her cheek made her grit her teeth, and gritting her teeth amplified the pounding in her head.

"Face it, Gianni," she muttered to her battered reflection in the mirror. "You just can't win for losing."

She would have made a good extra for a horror movie. Cheap, too. There would have been no need for a makeup artist to make her look ghastly. In addition to the welts and bruises her fall had raised, she was pasty pale. The dark crescents under her eyes were a testimony to a night spent doing something other than sleeping.

Hurting had taken up the entire night. Hurting from the fall. Hurting worse from Christian's abdication. Hurting from loneliness. Hurting from self-doubt. Hurting from anger. There had seemed to be no escape from it as the night had stretched on, hot and relentless. And morning offered no respite. Every painful thought gave birth to another, creating a never-ending cycle of pain.

Struggling into her peach-colored robe and fumbling awkwardly with the belt, Alex hobbled out of the bathroom and down the hall to see the one person in her life who had yet to pass judgment on her.

Isabella sat in her crib carrying on a conversation with herself as she played with a yellow stuffed pony Christian had given her. Her attention snapped immediately to the door as Alex stepped in, and the baby grinned her father's endearing, crooked grin.

"Mama!"

"Hi, button," Alex whispered, managing to smile on only one side of her face as she crossed the room to lift her daughter out of the crib with her good arm. "Glad you recognized me. I don't think I could have stood it if you'd have started crying at the sight of me."

Isabella was more interested in the bandage on her mother's cheek than on what her mother had to say. Dark eyes intense, she reached out to poke her index finger at it, making Alex suck her breath in through her teeth.

"No-no, sweetie. That hurts Mama."

"No no no no no," Isabella babbled, shaking her head emphatically, her dark curls bouncing.

Alex smiled and rubbed her daughter's nose with the tip of her own. "Hey, you, keep the racket down. You'll wake Pearl. She'll go back to her niece and leave us to fend for ourselves if we don't watch out."

Isabella giggled, delighted by her mother's expression if not her words.

They went through their regular morning routine at the changing table—a fresh diaper, a liberal dusting of powder to combat the sweltering heat, brushing the baby's thick hair and pinning it off her neck and away from her face with half a dozen minuscule barrettes. Alex moved much more slowly and clumsily than usual, but she had no intention of giving up this time with her daughter. Isabella was the one constant thing in her life, the one person who loved her unconditionally. This morning in particular Alex felt the need to take comfort in those basic truths. This morning when she felt so alone.

What a difference a day could make, she thought. Yesterday she had awakened in Christian's arms, the warm magic of his lips drawing her up out of the depths of sleep. They had made love as the sun rose, neither of them saying a word, just watching each other's eyes as their bodies communicated the love that was in their hearts. This morning he was on the other side of the hill, going about his life, and she was there aching, feeling adrift and uncertain and alone, as if she'd been abandoned for a hundred years.

"I miss him," she admitted in a tight whisper.

Her left hand fumbled with Isabella's little duckie hairbrush, and the tears she had managed to hold at bay all night sprang up suddenly to fill her eyes. Saying the words aloud had opened the floodgates she had fought to keep bolted shut. Now the whole complement of marauding emotions rushed to assault her, all of them expressed in one torturous word that seemed to reverberate through her chest—*why*.

Why did he have to be so demanding? Why did she have to be so stubborn? Why did life have to kick her every time she thought she finally had it by the tail? And why did it have to hurt so damn much?

"Alex! What are you doing out of bed?" Pearl demanded, bustling into the room. She was already dressed in spite of the fact that it was not yet seven o'clock. A sensible cotton shift flowed shapelessly over her pudgy frame. Her frizz of steel gray hair was combed. Pearl maintained that she had risen at six-thirty for sixty-some years, and retirement was no reason to break a perfectly good habit.

"I'm better off moving around," Alex said, mentally wincing at the hoarseness in her voice. She kept her back to her housemate, trying to erase discreetly any remnants of the tears that had threatened. "Trust me. I've been through this before. It only hurts when I laugh."

"Doesn't look like you've been doing much of that," the older woman observed sagely as she scooped up Isabella from the changing table and perched her on one plump hip.

*Nor am I likely to*, Alex thought grimly.

"I've got two good ears," Pearl said. "And there ain't nothing they haven't heard at least once already. So if you feel like talking, honey, you just go right on ahead."

Once she would have accepted the offer eagerly, but Alex had since taught herself to keep her own counsel. Too many confidants had been disappointed and disapproving. Still, she appreciated Pearl's offer and mustered a half-smile for it. "Thanks, Pearl, but I'll be all right."

The woman frowned. "Only the good Lord can handle everything by himself, girl, and you're not the Almighty. You'd best remember that." Clucking to herself, she bustled out of the room, bouncing Isabella in her arms as she went.

Alex hobbled to her room to dress. It was already sweltering in the little cubicle. The old fan in the window groaned and rattled, threatening death due to overwork. Alex stripped off her robe and caught what little breeze the thing made, thinking it might be her last chance to do so before it gave out altogether. She stared at the image of herself in the mirror above the dresser, taking in the cropped hair, the gaunt cheeks, the haunted eyes. And she remembered the girl with the long, wild mane and the flashing, tempestuous smile. The woman who stared back at her looked like a prisoner. A prisoner of the past. A prisoner of the ideas that had taken root in her mind during that horrible time after the rape.

*You're too forward, Alexa.*

*You've always been so flirtatious.*

*You were asking for it.*

*It was your own fault.*

And joining in that chorus from the past came Christian's voice. *You're punishing yourself.*

Was she?

Her good hand lifted to her boyish short hair and fingered the ends absently as a strange sense of panic slid through her.

Suddenly she jerked her hand away and put on the mental brakes. No, she wasn't trying to punish herself. She wasn't doing anything destructive. She was just trying to make a living. No one had ever said it should be easy or without risks. She had to pay her dues.

*Pay your dues for what?*

She pressed a hand to her belly as that chilling, sliding sensation dropped through her stomach again. Swearing in Italian, she turned from the mirror and limped to the closet. Refusing to sink any further into depression, she fumbled into a pair of jeans and a loose, sleeveless blue work shirt and made her way down to the barn, where Charlie had already begun morning chores.

"Blimey, miss! You hadn't ought to be down here!" the girl protested as she scooped oats out of the feed cart and dumped them into the box of the roan anxiously awaiting his breakfast. A chorus of nickers sounded down the row from the still hungry. Charlie ignored their pleas and stared indignantly at Alex, as if her being there was somehow insulting.

Alex frowned. "Everyone seems to know what's best for me."

"Well, it's a cinch you don't," Charlie said with typical bluntness. "You couldn't ride a bicycle, the shape you're in, let alone a horse!"

"I'll agree with you there. No reason I can't do the grooming, though, while you muck out the stalls."

"Oh, right," the groom said sarcastically. "No reason a'tall. It's not like you just got yourself chucked off into a fence and half-fallen on by that ugly great moose of an animal."

They both looked across the aisle at Terminator, who was weaving in his stall with his ears pinned, looking angry at the world.

"The work will do me good," Alex said.

"I'm sure," Charlie said with a rude snort. She shook her head in reproach, wiping the sweat from her forehead up into the hedge of burgundy hair that defied even the most wilting humidity. "A right flaming twit, you are."

Alex watched the girl move off down the aisle muttering under her breath and shaking her head in utter disgust. She wondered briefly what she was going to do about Charlie, then wondered miserably what she was going to do without her. She had grown terribly fond of the sassy groom, but she couldn't allow Christian to go on paying Charlie's wages, and she couldn't afford to pay them herself. The van needed repairs, and Terminator had managed to destroy her best saddle in the fall. Those two things were priorities. Hired help was a luxury.

Some people found solace in music, some in gardening, some in prayer. Alex had always found hers in the methodical work of brushing a horse. Her mind was free to contemplate as her hands stroked the various brushes over the coat of the animal, working out the dust and bringing a lustrous shine to the hair. Today she found no real peace. The task itself was painful and difficult, and her mind was bent on dredging up anger and excuses instead of sorting through all that for calmer emotions.

She was sick of people telling her what to do and how to do it. She was sick of people analyzing her at every turn. She had come there to rebuild her life, and that was what she was going to do. So she had gotten hurt in the process—it was a dangerous business. She'd known Terminator wasn't ready for that course. The only mistake she'd made had been in not insisting they pull him from the competition. The horse just needed some time and understanding. He'd come around.

"Get away from me, you son of a dog!" Charlie's voice rang out, fierce and panicked. It was followed by the snort of a horse, the sharp pounding sound of hooves striking wood, and then a cry.

Heart in her throat, Alex dropped her brush and hurried down the aisle, blocking her own injuries from her mind. The wheelbarrow stood by Terminator's door, and she could see the big gelding whirling and lunging in the stall, his ears flat to his head. Her blood ran cold as she realized she couldn't see the groom.

"Charlie!" she yelled, flinging the stall door back.

The girl lay in the straw, huddled into a fetal position with her hands over her head and her back against the wall. Blood ran freely from a cut on one forearm. The horse wheeled and lunged toward her again.

Pain exploding through her own body, Alex grabbed up the pitchfork and swung it like a baseball bat, catching Terminator hard across the chest and startling him into retreat. He stood at the back of the stall, snorting and rearing, his eyes rolling wildly in his head.

Straining to hold the pitchfork up with her right arm, Alex inched her way into the stall and squatted down next to the fallen groom. "Charlie, can you hear me? Are you conscious?"

"Bloody hell," the girl said, sobbing. "I wish I weren't. The bastard broke me arm."

"Can you move? I don't know if I can drag you."

Crying and cursing, Charlie struggled to her knees and crawled out of the stall while Alex fended Terminator off with the fork.

They drove to the emergency room in Briarwood in grim silence, Charlie caught up in trying to ward off the pain, Alex plunged into a black depression that didn't lessen even two hours later when the girl's arm had been set and she had been given permission to leave the hospital.

"It weren't your fault, miss," Charlie mumbled as Alex piloted her old car back toward the farm. Painkillers had dulled her senses. She leaned back against the torn upholstery and gazed down at the pristine plaster cast on her arm. "It weren't your fault a'tall."

Alex said nothing.

When she had Charlie settled in the house, she went back down to the barn and stood in front of Terminator's stall.

It *was* her fault. She'd known all along the horse was dangerous. Why, then, had she kept him? Her gaze drifted to the next stall where Duchess stood quietly munching hay, and she knew that Christian was right. This didn't really have anything to do with the mare. She had told herself it did, because that had been a convenient and viable excuse—but it wasn't the truth.

When she looked deep inside herself, past logic and rationalization, past all the defenses she brandished like a warrior's shield, there lay the fear that she had somehow brought all her troubles down on her own head, that she was to blame and now she had to earn back everything she'd lost.

Maybe Christian was right. Maybe those fears had driven her to take the kind of risks she had with Terminator.

Despite the choking heat Alex shivered at the thought. Why hadn't she seen it? Why hadn't she realized how stupid she was being, how stubborn? Why hadn't she seen what her past had driven her to? It was self-destructive and irresponsible. Now Charlie lay with a broken arm because of her. The girl might have been killed. She thought of the fall she'd taken and all the other injuries this animal had inflicted on her. She might have been killed, and for what? Because she had seen a need to punish herself.

*"Madre di Dio,"* she whispered, pressing a hand across her eyes as misery spread through her.

What had she become? What had she allowed Greg Reidell to turn her into? The rape had destroyed her life, shattered her support network, driven her to an obsessive need for self-reliance and a destructive need to punish herself. And now someone else had been endangered because of it. How long was she going to let Greg Reidell go on raping her life?

"Enough," she whispered as she backed away from the stall. She was all through being a victim.

Feeling old and tired Alex went into the tack room and used the phone there to call Tully Haskell. She left a message on his answering machine asking him to stop by. Then she went back to her grooming and her thinking, letting her mind work on the best way to get Christian back.

Christian sat on the fence of the outdoor arena, staring off at the rolling pastures of Quaid Farm, feeling an odd sort of detachment. This was the only home he had ever known in the States. In many ways it had been more of a home to him than

Westerleigh Manor ever had. But the sense of comfort and contentment he had always known here had drifted away. There was a restlessness inside him, a yearning that had been stirred to life by a tempestuous, amber-eyed minx. He suddenly found himself wanting all the things he had shied away from his whole life—ties, responsibilities, a wife, children.

Poor Uncle Dicky, he thought with a fond, sad smile, the last of the Atherton black sheep has gone respectable.

The storm of emotions that had raged inside him had played itself out. He felt calm, accepting of his fate. The role of bachelor rake could fall on some younger buck's shoulders. Christian Atherton was ready for other, more important things.

The question was: How to convince Alex? In many ways she was as untamable as that horse she rode, fiery and spirited and full of distrust. He smiled at the thought. He was going to have his hands full trying to handle her, but he knew how sweet and loving she could be, how responsive she was to a gentle touch, how tender was her heart.

He ached with missing her. Walking out of that stall had been one of the hardest things he'd ever done. All night long he'd lain awake in his empty bed feeling as if a huge chunk had been snatched out of his life. And he'd known a fear that had chilled him to the bone.

Alex was so bloody stubborn, so full of pride—what if she never gave in? What if his speculation had hit too close to the truth? She might choose to distance herself from him, thinking it too uncomfortable to be around someone who knew all her deepest secrets and vulnerabilities.

He simply couldn't let that happen.

He'd never been so consumed by a woman, so intrigued by all the facets that made up her complex personality. He was going to enjoy her riddles and mysteries for the rest of his life—provided he could make it over that final barrier of Alex's stubborn pride.

Confidence welled inside him as he hopped down from the fence and started across the dusty ring. There hadn't been a fence built that Christian Atherton couldn't jump.

Alex shut the stall door and leaned back against it with a sigh. The grooming was finished. The stalls were going to have to wait until her students came out in the evening. She simply couldn't manage the task herself. She felt as if she didn't have a bone left in her body. They had all melted down into the puddle of dull pain washing through her.

Picking up her bottle of mineral water from the floor, she took a swig, then poured the rest of it down over her head, letting it cool her and wash some of the dirt and sweat away.

"Mighty hot, ain't it?"

Gasping, Alex started back against the stall door. Staring at the open end of the barn, it took her eyes a moment to adjust to the bright sun that backlit the tall, bulky man. Her pulse raced, then slowed again. "Mr. Haskell, you startled me."

"Don't know why," Tully said smoothly, his boot heels clicking on the concrete as he ambled down the aisle. His yellow western shirt was sweat stained in big patches, and his fleshy face was red and shiny from the heat. His big nose looked mushy and swollen from the blow Christian had delivered. As he drew close, his squinting eyes followed the water stain that soaked into Alex's cotton work shirt, plastering it to her chest. "You called me."

"Yes, I did." She straightened away from the stall, plucking the damp fabric from her skin and clutching it in her fist. Dammit, when would she stop being so nervous in this man's company? Probably never, but then she doubted she would be seeing much of him after today.

"I thought you might," he admitted.

"Well, then, you know what I'm going to say."

"Got a pretty good idea," he said, his mouth twisting into a slow smile. "I was there yesterday when you sent Atherton packing. I was wondering how long it'd take for you to get sick of that British prig."

Alex frowned, unease sifting through her. "Mr. Haskell, I don't see what this has to do with my reason for calling you."

"You don't have to be coy with me, Alex. I know all about you."

Those last five words shot ice through her veins. She looked up at Haskell, praying to God she had misunderstood him.

"I know what kind of woman you are," he said, stepping a little closer, his gaze raking over her in a way that made her skin crawl. "I know what you need, what you're after."

"I don't know what you're talking about." The denial came almost as automatically as the need to step away, to put some distance between herself and the man towering over her.

"Sure you do, honey," Haskell insisted, his voice low and too friendly. Unperturbed by her retreat, he turned and followed her as she backed toward the tack room. "Doesn't the name Reidell ring a bell?"

Another bolt of cold electricity jolted through Alex. She took another jerky step backward.

"Ol' Jack and I have some mutual business interests," Tully went on, his smile growing lascivious. "He told me all about you, darlin'."

Alex felt her fear pool in her throat to choke her. She had been almost ready to let her guard down, to believe that no one around there knew or cared about her past. Now Tully Haskell was saying he'd known all along. The idea made her stomach turn. How many times had he looked at her, touched her, thinking heaven knew what?

"I know where Jack made his mistake," he said. "He should have paid you off and kept you at Wide Acre. You'd have done that snotty kid of his some good."

"It wasn't like that," Alex said in one desperate effort to make him understand. But Tully Haskell was no more interested in listening to her than anyone else had been. She could see by the feral gleam in his eyes that Reidell had told him the worst version of the story and he had eagerly believed it.

"Don't worry," he said, backing her up against the wall beside the tack-room door. "I won't make the same mistake. I'll take care of you, honey," he said, his voice dropping as his gaze settled on her mouth, "and you'll take care of me."

"No!" Alex shouted as Haskell lowered his head and tried to kiss her. She dodged his mouth, bringing her knee up hard into his groin.

Tully grunted and staggered back, his face turning burgundy as he clutched himself. "You little bitch!"

Alex turned to run, but he lunged out and caught her, his fingers digging brutally into her injured arm. The pain came in a wave that knocked her to her knees and dimmed her vision. Haskell's hands closed on her shoulders, and he dragged her back toward the tack room.

Alex let her body go limp, and for one blissful second unconsciousness beckoned, but Haskell's voice drew her back.

"Think you're too good for me, don't you? You'll only spread your legs for men like Reidell and Atherton because of their high-and-mighty names. Well, I've got news for you, sweetheart, you'll do it for me, and you'll damn well like it."

Galvanized into action, Alex jerked against his hold, her feet scrambling to make contact with the floor. He loosened his grip for an instant, and she bolted, only to be hauled back against him in a crushing bear hug. The smell of sweat and cigars choked her, and as she gasped for air, he tightened his embrace against her bruised ribs. She couldn't help but cry out, not only at the pain to her already-abused body, but at the injustice. She had done nothing to deserve this. Nothing at all.

Christian turned his car in at the end of Alex's drive, frowning at the sight of Tully Haskell's pickup parked at the end of the barn. The insufferable swine. He hadn't even bothered to come to the ambulance after Alex had fallen with his horse. The man was simply going to have to leave—now and forever. And Christian didn't much care how forceful he had to be in getting that message across. He didn't like the way Tully Haskell looked at Alex. The thought of him getting anywhere near her made him absolutely blind with jealous fury.

The cry that came from the dark interior of the stables as Christian climbed out of the Mercedes went through his heart like a knife. He ran for the barn, skidding to a startled halt at the sight that greeted him—Tully Haskell trying to force Alex into the tack room.

As Haskell turned his head to squint at the intruder, Alex managed to get one arm free. Her hand grabbed the first thing it found—a bridle hanging on a hook beside the door. Twisting around as best she could, she swung her weapon, and the heavy metal bit smashed into the side of Tully's face. Then they all went crashing to the ground as Christian hit Haskell at a run.

Alex rolled to the side and managed to pull herself up along the wall, gasping for air and wincing at the pain racking her body. Half doubled over, she watched as Christian hauled her attacker to his feet and hit him with a solid right to the stomach and a left to the jaw. Tully swayed on his feet. He managed to take one wild swing at Christian's head, but Christian blocked it and bloodied Haskell's nose for the second time in two days. This time the resounding crack of breaking bone went through the stable like a gunshot. Tully went down on his knees, blood running through his fingers as he pressed his hands to his face.

"Get up!" Christian demanded, his fists still curled in front of him. "Get up, you bastard, and let me finish the job!"

He spun around as Alex laid her hand on his arm. The

adrenaline was humming through him. He'd never felt so furious or so primitive or so ready to kill. His cool veneer of sophistication had fallen completely away in the instant he'd realized Haskell's intent.

"I'll call the sheriff," Alex said, her voice trembling so badly, she could manage nothing more than a whisper. She looked up at Christian, at the tautness of his face, the fierce intensity in his eyes, and a shiver went through her. "Let him deal with it."

Christian glanced back down at the man bleeding all over the concrete floor, and disgust coiled inside him like a snake. "Let's wait outside," he said, wrapping an arm around Alex's shoulders and steering her toward the door. "I can't stand the sight of him."

"Are you sure you're all right?" Christian asked again as he parked the Mercedes at the end of the barn.

Haskell's pickup was gone, having been driven into Briarwood by a deputy. They'd made a queer little motorcade winding down out of the hills to the quaint little college town—a sheriff's car, a truck, and a Mercedes, all of them headed for the courthouse. It hadn't been a pleasant experience, walking up the wide steps with the eyes of the curious following them. Nor had what followed been enjoyable. Christian had watched Alex give her statement as calmly as she could. He'd watched her fight back the tears and the fresh memory of what had happened to her, and it had made him thirst for Haskell's blood all over again.

That a man could treat a woman with such contempt, with such violence, sickened him. And to think that Alex had suffered through it all before, that she had suffered through it under the weight of disbelief and suspicion, tore him apart inside. He had never hurt for another person before in quite the same way. He had always considered himself compassionate, but only so far as his selfishness would allow. His own needs had come first. That was no longer the case.

"I'm better than I would have been if you hadn't shown up," Alex said, trying in vain to lighten the mood. She felt on the brink of shattering as she climbed out of the sports car and leaned back against the roof, stiff and trembling as she watched Christian round the front of the car.

"My God, Alex," he whispered, his voice strained.

He pulled her gently into his arms, careful of how he handled her. He needed to hold her, to reassure himself that he had indeed gotten there in time. If he'd had any reservations left about wanting to be responsible for another person, they had vaporized the instant he'd seen Alex struggling to get free of the man who would have raped her. He wanted never to let her out of his sight again, never to let her out of his arms again.

"I could have killed him for putting his hands on you."

"Me too," Alex said, tears fighting their way out of her tightly closed eyes and soaking into Christian's torn blue T-shirt. She let them come for a minute, let some of the pressure release. It seemed all right now that they were away from watchful eyes.

There was a peacefulness about the yard now. The sun had slid past its hottest point. A breeze stirred down through the woods, bringing a breath of fresh air and the lush scent of the forest. The calm of early evening hung around them, and Alex tried to absorb some of it into her, but she felt too dirty and too battered to accomplish it. Her skin crawled at the memory of what had happened and what had nearly happened.

"I hate that he touched me!" She snarled the words through her teeth, angry at the liberty Haskell had taken, at her inability to stop him, at the knowledge that the memory of those moments would stay with her forever.

"He won't touch you again, darling. We'll see to that."

Alex shuddered at the thought of another trial. Memories of

the last one were too fresh in her mind—the humiliation, the futility of fighting on her own, the broken faith of the people she had needed most. She couldn't go through that again.

Christian easily read her mind. "I'll be right there with you, love. I'll be beside you every step of the way." Bending his head down, he pressed a kiss to her temple.

"Ouch."

Christian jerked back and sent her an accusatory look. "You *are* hurt."

"So are you," Alex pointed out, sniffing back the tears.

She raised her good arm and brushed a fingertip against an abrasion on his left cheekbone. He winced. Stepping back, she looked him over for further damage. Both knees had torn out of his faded jeans. There was blood splattered on his blue T-shirt, but it wasn't his. His knuckles were raw where they had connected with Tully Haskell's face.

Her own blouse had torn at one shoulder, and her jeans were dirty. Blood from a scrape on her knee had soaked a stain through the denim. "We should go to the house. Pearl will put some antiseptic on those scrapes for you. She's thinking of turning the place into an infirmary."

"In a minute. We need to talk."

Alex tried to muster a nervous smile. "It can't wait until we're more presentable?"

"It's waited long enough already."

Taking her by the hand, he led her to the simple wooden bench that sat along the end of the barn and motioned for her to sit down. Alex lowered herself gingerly, her eyes on Christian as he paced back and forth in front of her. He looked like a man with a mission. Her heart pounded as she wondered whether that mission was good or bad.

In her mind there was a good chance that he would bow out of her life. Look what she'd embroiled him in! He had come looking for a woman to date, to have a few laughs with, and instead had gotten caught up in the web of her past, a past that showed no signs of fading away.

Finally, Christian stopped and turned to stare down at her, his eyes bluer than the summer sky above them. There was a tension in his chest that made breathing painful. He knew this was probably not the time or the place. He would have preferred a romantic setting. But what they had been through in the last twenty-four hours had shaken him to the core and spurred him now to say what was in his heart.

"I love you, Alex. Everything I said yesterday still holds true, but the fact of the matter is, I can't stand to be away from you. I love you, and I want you to be my wife."

He said it as if he expected her to put up a fight. Alex blinked at him, stunned.

"I want us to get married, buy a place of our own, and have a dozen children."

He stared at her again, waiting for a rebuttal like a disputatious debate-team captain.

"Sounds like you've got it all planned out," Alex said, watching him closely, awestruck by the determination that rolled off him like steam. People said clothes made the man, but even in tattered jeans Christian's powerful personality radiated around him like an aura.

He ran a hand back through his hair and set his jaw at a stubborn angle. "I know you don't want me trying to run your life, but you're wrong, Alex. I do have a right to say whether or not you should take risks. Loving you gives me that right, because it's no longer only your life you're risking, it's mine as well. Our lives are intertwined, now and forever, if I have anything to say about it. You may not like it, but there you have it."

Alex sat for a long minute staring down at the road as cars drove past. She had come to Virginia thinking she would have no one to rely on but herself. The idea of a relationship had seemed remote, nonexistent really. Now this magnificent man was towering over her telling her he wanted her to be his wife. This untamable rake who had collected hearts all over the Western world was asking her to marry him.

"I—I don't know what to say," she murmured, her brows knitting in confusion as emotions swirled inside her like a tempest.

"Say you love me," Christian whispered, his heart in his throat. He dropped to his knees in front of her, gritting his teeth as gravel bit into his scraped skin.

Alex caught her breath at the sudden vulnerability in his expression. How could he doubt she loved him? Her heart ached from loving him. "I do love you."

"Then say you'll marry me." He hung on her silence, dying a little bit with every second that passed.

"I—I'm scared, Christian," Alex said at last, the words tumbling out as the realization struck her.

Too many good things had gone bad on her. Too many dreams had ended in disappointment. Christian knelt before her, golden and tempting, too good to be true. She trembled from the desire to embrace him and from the fear that he would somehow vanish from her grasp as so many other things dear to her had.

"I'm scared."

Christian took her hands in his. "Don't be afraid to reach out for happiness, Alex. You deserve it. You deserve to be loved and cherished. Don't deny yourself any longer because of the past. We have a future ahead of us."

He was right. She'd let her past wield too much power over her. She'd paid penance for it and suffered and cried. It was time to let go, to put it all behind her and look to the future, a future with a man she loved, a man who believed in her.

Christian watched as a slow smile curved Alex's lush mouth, and her eyes lit up with gold. He could actually feel his heart warm and expand in response. Leaning forward, he captured her smile with a tender kiss.

"Let's go see Dr. Pearl," he said, rising and drawing Alex up with him.

He draped an arm around her and held her close as they started toward the old farmhouse, toward their new life.

And in his heart of hearts he said, *Good-bye, Uncle Dicky, wherever you are.*

# *The Restless Heart*

# one

**"AUNTIE DANIELLE, JEREMY SPIT ON MY** dessert!"

Danielle Hamilton quickly wiped a grimace of distaste from her face, lest Jeremy see it and catalog it away for future reference in his diabolical nine-year-old brain. Almost too exhausted to think, she leaned heavily against the white framed archway that led into the family room.

"Well, spit on his, Dahlia," she suggested. What did she know about kids? Nothing. She'd had an easier time of it dealing with the Bushmen of Kenya. The Tibetan nomads had been less of a mystery to her. Even as a child, she had known nothing about kids; she'd been raised in a world of adults.

"I did spit on his," declared eleven-year-old Dahlia Beauvais. "He ate it anyway."

"Gross," Danielle muttered as the doorbell rang. With a tremendous effort she pushed herself away from the door frame, sidestepping the carnage a plastic fighter jet had wreaked on a field of miniature soldiers.

"Hey, look out!" Tinks Beauvais shouted indignantly. The seven-year-old tomboy crouched behind a wing chair, poised to send a spaceship into the fray. "You're in a war zone!"

"Tell me about it," Danielle grumbled dryly.

*North and South* revisited. And this time the South was winning. One world-renowned photographer from New Hampshire didn't stand a chance against this quintet of seasoned veterans in the kids-versus-adults power-struggle game. She was seriously outnumbered. They also had an age advantage she didn't care to dwell on. Their energy reserves were amazing. Hers were depleted. She was running on empty and the one person she had counted on to help her through this babysitting fiasco had been knocked out of commission on the first day of their mission.

She envied Butler. He was now lolling the hours away in the quiet seclusion of his quarters, happily numbed to the situation by a substantial dose of Darvon.

Lord, how the Beauvais children had rendered Butler immobile, she thought with a shudder. The indomitable Alistair Urquhart-Butler, who had run her father's household for four decades. The man who had stood the test of time, who had outlasted Laird Hamilton's five wives, and helped raise six Hamilton children, had finally been brought down by a roller skate. It was unthinkable. It was especially unthinkable because he had helped coerce her into coming to New Orleans in the first place.

"Aye, lass, I'll go with you," he'd said. "I'll lend you a hand. You can count on me."

All the counting she'd done on him so far was to count him out when he'd hit the polished pine floor with a bone-jarring thud.

As the doorbell sounded a second time, she glanced up, ignoring the intricate plaster moldings on the ceiling of the beautifully preserved Garden District home. Her interest was focused on an even higher plane. "Lord," she muttered, "this had better be the nanny or we're going to be looking at serious infractions of some of the major commandments."

I could always plead temporary insanity, Danielle thought. In fact, it had to have been some kind of temporary insanity that had allowed her to agree to stay with Suzannah's children in the first place. She usually made it a point to stay clear of children. She had to have been disoriented and confused or she never would have agreed to this. Suzannah had taken advantage of her jet lag. Her sister had pounced on her practically the minute she'd stepped off the plane that had returned her to the States after her yearlong project in Tibet.

"Oh, Danielle, won't you *please* come stay with the children while Courtland and I go on vacation? They need a 'family influence.'" Danielle mocked her sister's plea as she continued down the hall toward the front door and her salvation. She gave a rude snort. "What they need is a drill sergeant."

In the hall lay an exhausted heap of brown fur that had begun the day as a large enthusiastic dog of indeterminate background. Head on his paws, he was obviously reconsidering the wisdom of moving into the Beauvais house. Danielle was reasonably certain he didn't belong there. The children had assured her he did, yet each called the poor animal by a different name. Suzannah hadn't mentioned a dog.

Suzannah hadn't mentioned a lot of things. In her haste to leave on her Caribbean vacation with her husband, Danielle's half sister had failed to mention that her children were monsters. She had conveniently forgotten to tell Danielle that mere mention of the Beauvais house was enough to strike terror into the heart of nearly every nanny in New Orleans. After two days with her five nieces and nephews, Danielle doubted Mary Poppins would have been willing to take them on. The Beauvais children called for sterner stuff—the Marines, for instance.

She stepped over the dog and paused to take a deep breath and regroup her dwindling resources. It had taken nineteen phone calls to locate an agency willing to send a nanny to the Beauvais house. After being turned down by every place in town, she had resorted to going through the list again, disguising her voice and omitting the family name of the children. She didn't want to do anything to scare this woman off. If she didn't get reinforcements soon, she was going to have to buy a gun—for self-protection.

The ornate gilt-framed mirror that hung above the hall table told no pretty lies. Danielle groaned at her reflection. She hadn't looked this bad after two months in the Amazonian jungle. She looked like thirty-nine had come and gone several times instead of just once. Her ash-blond hair that hung just past her shoulders looked like a rag mop. Two sleepless nights of sitting up with the baby had painted purple smudges beneath her gray eyes. She had inherited her mother's classic bone structure—the world-famous Ingamar cheekbones, the slim straight nose, the sculpted chin. But what was currently arranged over it would have sent her mother, the renowned model Ingrid, into shock. Bags, shadows, and worry lines, a model's nightmare.

Remnants of the lunchtime food fight between Tinks and Jeremy clung to her lavender silk T-shirt. There were two large paw prints on her khaki safari shorts. The Hermès sandals on her feet had been painted fluorescent orange by four-year-old Ambrose while she'd attempted to feed the baby strained beets.

"This woman is going to take one look at you and run," Danielle muttered. Scrunching a handful of hair in her fist, she discovered a dried glob of beets. "No one with an ounce of sense would come near this place."

Heaving a sigh, she pulled open the heavy oak door and her breathing stopped altogether at the sight of the person standing on the other side of the wrought-iron security door.

He was no Mary Poppins.

# two

**WHAT A FACE! DANIELLE'S FIRST INSTINCT** was to grab her camera and capture it on film—even though she had given up taking portraits a year ago.

Twinkling black eyes stared at her from a face that was wide, strong, and utterly masculine. Faint laugh lines fanned out from his eyes as a smile tilted up one side of his black mustache. He had a solid square jaw and bold, aquiline nose. Danielle's toes tingled. She'd always been a sucker for a man with a great jaw. A deep dimple in his left cheek revealed itself as his smile broadened. His even, white teeth flashed against his deeply tanned skin. The effect was enough to make a woman offer her services as a love slave.

His body wasn't going to change her mind on the subject either. He had the build of a heavyweight boxer—broad shoulders and a thick chest. He wore a necktie, but the top button of his shirt was undone, as if he hadn't been able to get the collar closed around his neck. Danielle would have bet her favorite Nikon that under his conservative white shirt and charcoal slacks this man was a veritable sculpture of muscle.

Her gaze drifted back to his face. "Let's run away together."

His dark eyes widened in surprise. "I beg your pardon?"

"Never mind," Danielle said dejectedly as a crashing sounded somewhere in the house behind her and reality returned with a vengeful rush. There were five little reasons she couldn't fulfill her fantasy and one *big* reason. He had to be nearly ten years younger than she was and a hundred years younger than she felt. She couldn't have run off with him: he would have had to push her in a wheelchair.

"I can't leave the house," she said flatly. "I'm waiting for a nanny—or the hardening of my arteries. Whichever comes first."

"You're Mrs. Hamilton?"

"*Miss* Hamilton," she hastened to correct him. No sense in feeling more matronly than she already did in the face of all that youthful virility. "Danielle Hamilton."

"Oh, I'm pleased to meet you. *Miss* Danielle Hamilton," he drawled, his words tumbling out of his mouth lazily, all soft vowels and Cajun French inflection. He said her name as if he already knew her—intimately. His voice was like raw silk, at once rough and smooth. His eyes glittered like polished onyx.

Danielle's toes curled against her fluorescent orange sandals. She wondered vaguely if anyone had ever formulated a theory on the voice as a sex organ. She could feel his every syllable stroking her senses. It was incredible and more than a little disturbing. She was a mature, experienced woman. She couldn't remember the last time a man had turned her bones to marshmallow with nothing more than the sound of his voice.

Holding eye contact, he reached a wide hand through the bars of the security door. Danielle's elegant hand inched forward to meet it tentatively, as if she wasn't sure she could withstand the shock of touching him. Considering what his voice was doing to her internal temperature, she was liable to combust spontaneously if they touched.

"Remy Doucet," he said, curling his fingers around hers. The left corner of his mouth tugged upward and his dimple deepened. "I'm your nanny, *chère*."

Danielle stared at him in stunned disbelief. "I must be delirious," she said at last with a twitter of hysterical laughter. "I thought you said you were my nanny."

A delicious sexy grin spread across his face. "I am."

"You are?"

"Oh, absolutely," he said, his voice low and smoky.

Danielle shook her head, as if trying to come out of a trance. This devastating hunk of masculinity was a *nanny*? *Her* nanny? All she'd done was punch a phone number and someone had sent this piece of prime beef to her doorstep? Dial-A-Stud. What a concept!

She leaned heavily against the door frame as all sorts of illicit ideas sapped the strength from her knees. If he accepted the job, he would be in the house day and night—at Suzannah's expense, Danielle thought, a malicious smile curving her wide mouth. She would be able to look at him whenever she wanted to. The trouble was, looking wasn't the only thing her suddenly crazed hormones had in mind.

She thunked herself on the forehead with the heel of her hand. Lord, she was getting the hots for the family nanny! She was fantasizing about having a handsome young man at her beck and call. What kind of depraved, nearly middle-aged person was she turning into? This was completely unacceptable behavior. She was Danielle Ingamar Hamilton, for heaven's sake! She had dated princes. She had survived jungles and deserts and life in New York City. She was known the world over for her calm, cool demeanor in every circumstance.

"You did call for a nanny, didn't you, *chère*?" Remy asked, his dark brows lifting.

"Sure I called for a nanny," Danielle said, pulling herself together. She gave him a skeptical look. "But you're not exactly what I had in mind, Mr. . . . ?"

*"Doucet,"* he finished for her, his eyes flashing with a quick burst of Gallic temper. And this job wasn't exactly what he had

in mind either, lady. He was a geologist. But there wasn't a lot of work for geologists in South Louisiana these days. Things had tightened up a few years back when the oil economy had gone belly-up. He'd still had a job then. But when Eagle Oil had been absorbed by the foreign corporate octopus Knox Amalgamated, just a year ago, corporate restructuring had left him with two alternatives—relocate to the Outer Hebrides or relocate to a new profession. He had tried the first. Now he was trying the second.

"What'sa matter, *chère*?" he said defensively. "You think a man can't be a good nanny?"

"Well, no, I—"

He planted his hands at his waist and leaned forward aggressively. "You think a man would be a lousy nanny just 'cause he's not a woman?"

"Um—I haven't given the subject a great deal of thought, actually."

He shook a thick finger at her through the bars of the security door. "You think I can't be a nanny just 'cause I don't have breasts?"

Danielle cast an appreciative look at the expanse of solid male pectorals straining the confines of the white dress shirt. "Believe me, Mr. Doucet, I'm *glad* you don't have breasts. I can probably speak for all of womankind on that question."

"There's no rules against men being nannies, you know. A man can do this job just as well as a woman." His words to his sister Annick had been more along the lines of "anyone could do it," but he prudently decided to modify the statement slightly for his future employer.

"I'm sure you're right." At least Danielle wasn't about to argue the point with him. By the look of him, she figured he could probably do anything he darn well wanted to. It was kind of sweet, really, that this incredibly macho-looking guy wanted to take care of children for a living. The idea touched her in a very private, very vulnerable part of her heart.

"So, you gonna let me in, or what, darlin'?" Remy asked with a sudden irrepressible grin. His flare of temper had passed as quickly as a summer cloudburst. He leaned a beefy shoulder beside the door, crossed his ankles and fanned himself with his hand. "It's gettin' hot out here."

Not any hotter out there than it was inside her skin, Danielle thought, but she kept that little observation to herself. Remy Doucet struck her as a man who didn't need a great deal of encouragement to be outrageously flirtatious.

She unlatched the security door and, with a sweep of her hand, stood back and motioned for him to come in. As he stepped past her, her mind searched frantically for a room they could go to that didn't look like the aftermath of a nuclear holocaust. There wasn't one. Since their parents' departure the Beauvais offspring had reduced the showplace home to a shambles. They could have gone into the darkroom for the interview, but considering the man's magnetism, that didn't strike her as the brightest idea—appealing, yes, smart, no.

Remy glanced around the elegant entrance hall. Ivory silk moiré wallpaper, a chandelier of crystal prisms, a curving staircase that was like something out of *Gone With the Wind*. Nice. And despite the fact that the lady standing before him was obviously dead on her feet, there was an air of elegance about her from the top of her tousled blond head to the tips of her—fluorescent orange sandals? He frowned a bit at the footwear.

"We'll go into the salon down the hall," she said. *There's no food on the walls in there.*

Remy followed her down the hall, his appreciative gaze assessing his potential employer. She was tall, no more than a few inches shy of his own six feet, and built with the angular grace of a model. Svelte, but not skinny. Nice behind. *Really* nice behind. The kind of legs that haunted a man's most erotic dreams. He wondered if they were as silky as they looked. He flexed his fingers at the thought of running them down those long limbs.

Hold it back, Remy, he warned himself, the lady's gonna be your boss.

*Well*, said the little devil on his shoulder, *lookin's no sin*.

As usual, he took the devil's advice with a grin.

As they drew even with an archway a blast of rock music hit them with the force of a hurricane wind. Jeremy leaped out of the hall closet directly in front of Danielle, a nylon pulled down over his face, mushing his features grotesquely. Danielle shrieked and flung herself back up against the wall, banging into a narrow Louis XIV table and overturning a cobalt vase of fresh flowers. Tinks dashed out of the family room with a replica Uzi propped on her hip. She executed a neat shoulder roll and came up behind a startled Remy. Using his muscular legs for cover, she took blind aim at her brother and shot a staccato burst of grape Kool-Aid across the hall that left a wet purple trail on the floor.

Before Danielle could do anything more than holler their names, the marauders vanished out the front door. Her heart sank. There was little doubt in her mind Remy Doucet would now take his gorgeous body and his child-rearing skills and head straight back to the nanny agency from whence he had come. He had a rather shell-shocked look about him at the moment. As soon as he came around he would bid her adieu and vamoose like any sane, sensible person.

A sudden sense of panic gripped her. She didn't want him to go. He was the only adult she'd been able to find who was brave enough or foolhardy enough to set foot inside the Beauvais house. What was she going to do if he took off? She would be left alone again with *the children*. Goose bumps raced over her flesh. The children would be left alone with *her*. The combination was toxic.

She leaned in the family room doorway and shouted at the top of her lungs. "Dahlia, turn that stereo down or you won't live long enough to find out what 'I Want Your Sex' means!"

Dahlia flipped a knob on the stereo and sauntered toward

her aunt with a smug look. She flipped her long copper hair back over her shoulder and said, "I already know."

Danielle turned to Remy with a pained smile and gave him one of Suzannah's most famous lines. "They're such spirited children."

Remy ducked his head and cleared his throat.

"Who's the hunk?" Dahlia asked, eyeing him with outrageous audacity.

"I might be your new nanny," Remy said, trying to look stern. He was fairly certain the nanny training manual would take a dim view of being amused by impudence.

Dahlia grinned. "Radical!"

Danielle turned the girl by the shoulders and nudged her back into the family room. "Why don't you go browse the catalogs for training bras, dear?"

"I want the push-up kind. Like Madonna has." Dahlia dropped to her knees and dug through the rubble on the coffee table for a catalog. "Molly Gerard's mother ordered her one just like this." She glanced up out of the corner of her eye to see how well her story was being received.

Danielle gave her a look. "Right. Nice try."

Remy looked over the girl's shoulder, his eyebrows bobbing up at the sight of a red lace bustier. He glanced askance at Danielle. "She's got good taste."

"Small consolation," Danielle muttered dryly. "She may not live to make use of it."

A floor above them a baby began to cry. The sound came in a kind of stereo effect, crackling over the monitor Danielle wore hooked to her beaded belt and wafting down the stairs. To her extreme horror, Danielle's eyes suddenly brimmed with tears. She was exhausted. She was frustrated. She was secretly terrified of babies. Why, oh why had she let Suzannah talk her into this?

Biting her lip, she stepped past Remy with her head down, her hair shielding her face from his curious gaze. She took the stairs two at a time, her hand skimming up a mahogany banister that was dull with sticky fingerprints. She could hear Remy's footsteps right behind her.

"How many are there altogether?"

"Five."

His eyebrows shot up. She didn't look like the mother of five. Nor did she seem particularly well equipped to deal with five children. But then this was a swanky part of town. Danielle Hamilton didn't have to be well equipped for motherhood. All she needed to be able to do was dial the phone so she could hire someone else to handle the task. Anger flared through him. He was of the firm belief that people shouldn't have kids if they didn't know how to love and care for them.

Putting a tight leash on his opinions, he said neutrally, "Raisin' five kids all alone must be some kind of job, eh?"

"Alone?"

"You're divorced, right?"

"Me? I've never been married."

Disappointment settled over Remy like a thick mist. Five kids and she'd never been married? That was a hell of a track record. He whistled between his teeth. "Ah, me, *chère*, you get around."

Danielle wheeled on him at the door of the nursery, her eyes like twin silver moons. "Me? You think these are *my* kids? You've got to be kidding!"

Remy stared at her, confused but relieved. "They're not your kids?" he asked above the wail of the baby.

"No, thank God. I'm only here because I'm a sucker. These little darlings belong to my sister, Suzannah Beauvais. She and her husband are allegedly on vacation. Personally, I think they've skipped town. Who ever heard of rich people going to the Caribbean in the dead of summer?"

Remy shrugged, deciding to treat it as a rhetorical question. He didn't know all that much about rich people.

Danielle shook her head in disgust as she crossed the plush rose-colored carpet to the white crib where little Eudora sat alternately bawling and choking herself with her fist. "She wanted me, of all people, to stay with her children as a family influence while she and Courtland are away. I'm sure if she ever does come back she'll be prosecuted to the full extent of the law."

She stared down forlornly at the sobbing baby, wondering how she was supposed to know what Eudora's problem was. She had absolutely no clue how to go about deciphering the moods of a ten-month-old baby. What a failure she was as a woman, she thought as two big fat tears rolled over Eudora's lashes and down her cheeks.

Remy scooped the baby up, cuddling her close and murmuring to her in Cajun French. She was a cute little thing. Twenty pounds of baby fat with big blue eyes and fuzzy red hair. With one hand Remy found a soft terry-cloth elephant stuck down in one corner of the crib. He handed the toy to Eudora, who promptly began gnawing on the elephant's trunk. The baby's wails immediately died down to whimpers, then segued into contented cooing and intermittent hiccups.

Danielle gave him a wary look, as if she'd just witnessed an act of witchcraft. "How did you do that?"

"It's all done with mirrors," Remy replied. What kind of woman didn't know enough to comfort a teething baby? What kind of mother would leave her children with someone who was so obviously lacking in any maternal instincts? His temper surfaced again and he vented it on Danielle, momentarily forgetting that she was his prospective employer. He was much more used to giving orders than taking them. "She's cuttin' teeth. Don't you know enough to give her something to chew on? What kind of a babysitter are you?"

"I'm no kind of babysitter!" Danielle snapped, frustration pressing against the backs of eyes in the form of hot tears. "I'm just supposed to be the family influence. Butler is the babysitter, dammit, and where is he when I need him? Felled by a roller skate! I don't know anything about babies! How was I supposed to know they don't come with teeth included? That's what I'm hiring you for!"

Remy felt a stab of panic as Danielle turned her back to him and started to cry very quietly. It was just a gentle sniffling, a slight trembling of her shoulders. Exactly the way he had always imagined classy ladies would cry. But it was one thing to quiet a baby. A full-grown woman was something else altogether. He could hardly placate Danielle by sticking a terry-cloth elephant in her mouth.

He set Eudora back in her crib and went to stand behind Danielle, not sure what he should do. It tore him up inside to hear a woman cry. To know he was the cause of those tears was like salt on the wound. He doubted most trained nannies would take their boss in their arms and hold them, but that was what he wanted to do. It was the only thing he could think to do.

"Don't cry, *chère*," he begged in a low, smoky voice, turning Danielle gently by the shoulders. He gathered her up against him, stroking a big hand over her soft mane of angel hair, drawing her head down to his shoulder. She stood as stiff as a rail against him, fighting her tears and the comfort he tried to offer. "I'm sorry, darlin'. I shouldn't have gotten after you like that."

"I'm—doing the—b-best I—c-can!" she said with jerky indignation. "I—c-can't help it—I d-don't know any-thing!"

"Course you can't, sugar," Remy murmured, secretly baffled at the prospect of a woman who was not adept at handling babies.

"I—I'm t-tired and fr-fr-frust-strated."

"Sure you are."

"And I've g-got—beets in my hair!"

It was that final small indignity that made the tears gush forth in a tidal wave. It had been ages since Danielle had cried in front of anybody. She had always found those rare occurrences embarrassing, undignified, and well beneath her powers of self-control. But the horse was out of the barn now. There seemed no point in trying to hold back. Besides, she didn't think she had the strength to stem the flood. She hadn't had a wink of sleep in over two days and it felt so darn good to have someone to lean on, if only for a few minutes.

Remy's eyes misted over as he felt Danielle let go of her pride and sag against him. "Aw, you just put your pretty face on ol' Remy's shoulder and cry it all out, darlin'."

He stroked her back with a slow steady hand, sympathy seeping through him. The poor thing. Why had she taken on this job when she admittedly had no experience with kids? It was a well-known, scientifically documented fact that kids could sense that kind of thing and mercilessly rode roughshod over rookies. Poor Danielle.

Oooh, he liked the way her name sounded in his mind—kind of soft and sexy. It was the kind of name that would roll easily off his tongue during lovemaking, sounding dark and erotic. He liked the way she felt against him too. Their bodies were instinctively curving into one another, finding all the places where they fit perfectly, like two pieces of a puzzle. Desire sluiced through him like a hot lazy river.

"They won't listen to me," she mumbled, her face still squashed against his brawny shoulder.

"I know they won't," he murmured, his lips teasing her silvery hair.

"It's not that I don't like kids. I used to be one once."

"Sure you were, *bébé*." But she wasn't anymore. She was a woman, and a damned appealing one.

"Suzannah never should have asked me to help," she said, her heart filling anew with despair. "She knows I'm terrible at this."

"Oh, no, *chère*, no," he whispered as she hiccuped. "It's gonna be all right, you'll see. I'm here now." Every protective instinct Remy possessed surfaced at the thought that she needed him. He was a man who had always respected and acted on his instincts. "It's gonna be all right," he said again, tilting her face up with a finger crooked beneath her chin.

Danielle looked at him as though he were the only man left on earth and the two of them had been designated by God to perpetuate the species. *Bon Dieu*, but she was pretty, even with beets in her hair.

He brushed a tear from the corner of her mouth with the pad of his thumb. Then he bent his head and kissed another from her cheek. It seemed the most natural thing in the world to lower his head another fraction of an inch and settle his lips against hers.

Danielle felt all her bones melt the exact instant Remy started to kiss her. All thought of nannies and demonic children and her own inadequacies flew right out of her head, leaving behind bright bursts of star dust and gold dust and a soft, hot feeling that oozed through her and settled low in her belly. She pressed herself closer to him as her lips parted, inviting him to deepen the kiss, but Remy moved back a fraction of an inch and raised his head instead, breaking off the delicious contact.

Danielle felt as if she were going to crumble to the floor like so much discarded clothing. "Holy smoke," she muttered, staring at him. Dazed, she lifted her hand to touch her fingertips to her stinging lips and scratch at the spot his mustache had tickled. That kiss had curled her toes. She'd heard bells. Some welcome to the neighborhood. She doubted Mr. Rogers had ever kissed anybody like that.

"I don't think you're old enough to kiss like that," she said, instantly annoyed with herself for raising the subject of age.

"I been outa short pants a long time, sugar," Remy assured her.

"Oh, yeah? I'll bet you don't know who the Shirelles are."

"No," he admitted. "Do you know the Balfa Brothers?"

"No."

He shrugged. "Then we're even."

"Even? Huh," Danielle huffed, crossing her arms over her chest. She scowled at him, her straight dark brows pulling together. "How old are you, anyway?"

"Thirty-one. How old are you?"

"I'm—" She gave him a narrow-eyed glare. "None of your business."

"Oh, come on, sugar, you can't be—what? Thirty-five, thirty-six?"

Danielle couldn't decide whether she should be flattered or offended. It seemed like a good time to change the subject. Age wasn't going to be relevant at any rate, because she most certainly wasn't going to get involved with him.

"Listen, I'm sorry to have wasted your time, Mr. Doucet, but this is a really bad idea. I don't think nannies should kiss like that."

Remy grinned like a pirate. "You wanna show me how nannies should kiss? I'm willing to try again."

Danielle stepped behind a white rocking chair as he took a step toward her. "I appreciate your enthusiasm, Mr. Doucet—"

"Remy," he corrected her with a *tsk-tsk*.

Danielle swallowed hard. "Remy." Just as she had feared, his name sounded sexy even from her own lips. It tasted sexy. Just saying his name recaptured the rich dark flavor of his mouth. "No offense, but doesn't your agency have any stout ladies with ironclad hairdos and support hose?"

"Sorry, *chère*," he said with a devilish sparkle in his dark, dark eyes as he stepped around the rocker and trapped Danielle against it with an arm on either side of her. "We're fresh out of them little blue-haired ladies."

"How about one of those pudgy Aunt Jemima types?"

He shook his head, his inky hair tumbling into his eyes. "All gone."

Danielle thought her heart was going to pound its way right out of her chest. Remy stood close enough for her to see the shadow of his afternoon beard darkening the broad plane of his cheek. How could she hire a nanny who kissed liked a bandit and had to shave twice a day? But there he stood—tall, dark, and Cajun, with three wayward locks of unruly black hair falling across his forehead and the wickedest bedroom eyes she'd ever seen. Just looking at him made her want to rip his shirt open and run her hands through his chest hair.

It occurred to her that this whole scene was preposterous. She wasn't the kind of woman who succumbed to instant attractions. In fact, she had pretty much decided to steer clear of men altogether after her last relationship had fizzled. It had become apparent to her that, like many a Hamilton before her, she was doomed to nothing but failed romances. That was a fact of life better accepted than fought against. Besides, this man was applying for a domestic position. She had been raised to think it was unseemly to chase the hired help.

Of course, she wasn't the one doing the chasing now. She eyed Remy warily as he inched a little closer. He was staring at her mouth as if it were nature's most fascinating phenomenon. Anticipation rippled through her.

"Tell me," she said, sounding breathless instead of droll. "Is this the way you normally interview for a job?"

One side of his mustache hitched up and his dimple cut deep into his cheek. His voice was as smooth and dark as *café noir*. "You oughta see how I ask for a raise."

Danielle felt her stomach drop all the way to her fluorescent feet.

"How many other people you got coming to interview for this job?" Remy asked, forcing himself to take a step back away from her. It was a wonder she hadn't bonked him on the head with something and run to call the cops. He was coming on like a caveman. But then she made him feel a little primitive. The idea of tossing her over his shoulder and carrying her off into the bayou country held an undeniable amount of appeal.

Chemistry. That's what was going on here, he decided. He was a man of science, he knew all about chemistry and the irresistible forces of nature . . . and instincts and biology and birds and bees and beautiful ladies with big pewter-colored eyes . . .

She dodged his gaze and nibbled on her lip, obviously contemplating a fib.

"How many?" he asked again.

"Um . . . a few," Danielle hedged, sucking in a deep breath.

Remy shrugged. "One? Two?"

"Give or take."

"Give or take how many?"

She scowled at him. "One or two."

"See there, angel," he said, wagging a finger at her. "You gotta keep me. I'm all you got."

An interesting thought, Danielle conceded as an ominous thud sounded a floor above them. She'd run out of agencies to call. The next names on her list had been a voodoo priestess and a professional alligator wrestler.

She shot a glance at Remy, who had gone back to the crib to check on Eudora. Like magic, the sexual tension that had hung thick in the air had vanished. She wondered wildly if she had imagined it. Maybe it had been a combination of exhaustion and wishful thinking. Practical though she was, she wasn't above fantasizing about handsome, virile men with more hormones than sense. In fact, as forty loomed on the horizon like a black cloud, she could probably count on a lot of moments of temporary lunacy concerning such things.

"How long are the parents gonna be gone?" Remy asked. He picked the baby up and tucked her under one arm like a football as he began snooping around the well-equipped nursery.

"Three weeks," Danielle said absently, frowning. "Are you sure that's how you're supposed to carry a baby?"

"Oh, absolutely." It seemed the most natural way to tote a baby for a man who had gone to LSU on a football scholarship. He reached his free arm into the small white linen cupboard that was situated in one corner of the blue-walled nursery as he lied smoothly. "It's the first thing they teach us at nanny school."

"Oh. Well . . ."

Eudora squealed in delight, lending credence to Remy's questionable statement. She stuck her arms out like a miniature flying Supergirl and said, "Brrrrph!," spraying drool in all directions.

Danielle grimaced. "They wanted a second honeymoon to celebrate the fact that Suzannah is the only Hamilton in nine generations to have a marriage last more than five years. We're cursed, you see."

Remy shot her a suspicious look. "Cursed? Like black magic?"

"Cursed, like a good old-fashioned Scottish curse," she explained. "I don't ordinarily believe in that kind of thing, but there's plenty of documentation to back it up. A rival clan chieftain put a curse on Ramsay Hamilton in 1516 for stealing his bride. We've basically been failures in marriage ever since. So I guess Suzannah is justified in wanting to celebrate. She and Courtland have made it twelve years.

"Personally, I think three weeks is a little excessive as honeymoons go. I mean, how many different ways can you really . . . ah . . . well . . ." She stammered to a stop and blushed furiously.

Remy turned suddenly and leaned down close to her. "Come on, Danielle," he said in that sandy warm voice. "Where's your sense of romance? Wouldn't you like a three-week-long honeymoon?"

"Sure," she quipped, her head swimming. "Where do you want to go?"

His voice dropped another rough note from satin to black velvet. His gaze caressed her lips. "I'd take you to heaven, angel."

"They'd never let you in," she managed to murmur as shivers washed over her skin.

He chuckled, a deep, masculine sound that rumbled up from his chest. "No, but then it's the gettin' there that's all the fun, eh?"

The man was incorrigible. Here he stood, his future in her hands and a baby in his own, and he had the audacity to flirt with her shamelessly. She might have been offended if she hadn't been so close to having a birthday. The fact of the matter was she liked Remy Doucet a lot. Probably too much.

"Here," he said, flipping off the animal magnetism again as easily as he'd turned it on. "Take the baby."

He thrust Eudora into her arms and Danielle latched on to the poor child with all the awkwardness of inexperience and blind terror. She juggled the baby like an overloaded grocery bag.

"Be careful," Remy added as an afterthought just as Danielle managed to squeeze the baby up against her. "She's soakin' wet."

"Ugh!" Eudora was immediately thrust an arm's length away. She gurgled and kicked her feet merrily in the air. Danielle stared down at the big wet stain on the front of her lavender silk T-shirt and spoke through her teeth. "When Suzannah gets back I'm going to commit unspeakable atrocities on her person. And then I'm going to get *really* mean."

Remy frowned as he took the baby and put her on the changing table. "I take it you're not so happy with any of this business."

"It's not that I don't like kids," Danielle explained. "They're fine as long as they don't throw up or wet on me or have criminally insane minds. Unfortunately, that leaves Suzannah's kids totally disqualified."

Remy clucked as he changed Eudora's diaper. "They can't be that bad."

"Did you ever see *The Omen*?" she asked casually as she

plucked her soggy blouse away from her skin. "I suppose I might be exaggerating. I don't have much experience with kids. My mother divorced my father when I was two. I was raised mostly on fashion shoots. If you need someone to babysit a temperamental model or placate a high-strung photographer, I'm your girl. But when it comes to babies . . . I'm not so good."

Her voice thinned and trailed off, and Remy noted with interest that her gray eyes darkened and a shadow passed over her features like a storm cloud as she glanced away from him. She suddenly looked sad and lost. Her fingers toyed nervously with the fringe on a knitted afghan that lay folded over the back of the rocking chair. He sensed there was more to the story than she was telling, and he knew an intense desire to have her confide in him, though he doubted she would.

"So you've never stayed with your nieces and nephews here before?" he asked, sounding vaguely amazed. It seemed his life was constantly overrun with little relatives.

"No," Danielle admitted, annoyed that she should feel even a pinch of guilt over that. They weren't her children. She wasn't responsible for them. That was a fact that should have made everybody breathe easier. "I travel a lot in my work. I've just returned from a yearlong stay in Tibet."

"Tibet?" Remy echoed, his face the picture of distaste. He plopped the baby down in her crib and handed her elephant back to her. "You got family there?"

"In Tibet? Of course not."

"And you stayed there for a year?"

Not liking the disapproval she thought she saw in his dark eyes, Danielle turned the conversation back in the direction it should have been going all along. "So, how long have you been a nanny?"

"Oh . . . not long . . ." he mumbled, head down as he went to the little white porcelain sink set in the counter beneath the linen cupboard. He devoted what seemed to Danielle to be an inordinate amount of attention to washing his hands.

"I suppose I should ask to see your résumé or references or something."

"Oh . . . darn . . . I guess I forgot my résumé," he said, hoping she might forget about it too. "I've got lots of experience, though, and I did remember to bring the agency agreement along."

He dried his hands on a little pink towel, then dug a folded two-page form out of his hip pocket and handed it to Danielle. She dragged her eyes away from the spot where his fly had snugged up against a very impressive part of his anatomy and took the form, just barely resisting the urge to fan herself with it.

"Actually, I don't think we'll be needing this," she said in a high, breathless voice. She sent Remy a brittle smile and tried frantically to rally her common sense. She really couldn't keep a nanny who unleashed mad desires in her. "You just don't quite fit my needs at the moment."

"Sure I do, sugar," Remy drawled, backing her up against the rocking chair again. "That's the problem, isn't it? Maybe I fit your needs a little too well?"

Danielle tried to talk around the heart that was suddenly lodged in her throat. Her eyes fastened on the masculine curve of his lower lip and her palms started to sweat. "I don't know what you mean."

"You hadn't ought to fib, angel. That's a bad example for the little ones."

He moved back a fraction, giving them both room to breathe. He needed this job. He needed the money, for one thing. But overshadowing that practical reason was a lady with quicksilver eyes and hair like winter moonlight. More than the job, he wanted the chance to explore this volatile chemistry that simmered between himself and Danielle Hamilton. While he was at it he could certainly manage to take care of a few little kids. The first thing, though, was to get the position, and he wasn't exactly doing a great job of that. It didn't take a genius to see Danielle was nervous about the attraction pulling them together. It was the reason she was trying to push him away.

He sighed and ran a hand back through his hair. Putting on his most contrite expression, he said, "Look, *chère*, you need a nanny and I need a job. I promise you, I'm good with kids and I'll be on my best behavior."

"That's probably not saying much, considering what I've seen so far," Danielle said, folding her arms defensively over her chest.

"I'm not gonna lie to you and tell you I'm not attracted, sugar, 'cause I am. But like I told you, I need this job and you need a nanny. Who else you gonna call?"

"Well, Rambo was next on my list."

A small figure wearing a Ronald Reagan mask suddenly appeared at the door of the nursery. Bright orange hair stuck up like a rooster's comb above the mask. Below it was a pair of rumpled Spiderman pajamas. There was a ragged, dirty black and white stuffed dog tucked under the child's right arm. "Auntie Dan-L?"

"Hi, Ambrose." Danielle smiled warmly at the four-year-old. "What's happening?"

"Jeremy's hanging Tinks from the roof by her feet."

# three

**REMY PAUSED OUTSIDE THE FRONT DOOR** of the Savoy Agency to pull himself together. The agency was housed in a narrow three-story red brick building built during the last days of the French rule of New Orleans. Like the others that crowded shoulder to shoulder along the street, it still gave all the appearances of being an elegant town house with its black lacquered front door and shutters and the delicate ironwork balconies that graced the second and third floors. Only the polished brass plate on the door gave any indication that a successful business was conducted behind the quaint façade.

Remy straightened his tie, slicked his hair back with his fingers, and took three slow deep breaths. *Bon Dieu*, those Beauvais kids were monsters! Damned if he was going to admit that to his sisters, though. He pasted on a brilliant smile that lit up his dark face, pushed the door open, and sauntered into the air-conditioned cool as if he'd just come from a refreshing walk through Audubon Park.

The interior of the building was every bit as gracious as the exterior. Burgundy velvet drapes hung over white sheers at the tall window in the reception area. Two camel-backed sofas in the same color invited clients to sit and browse through the magazines scattered over the walnut coffee table. The overall effect was of understated elegance only slightly broken by the pink beanbag chairs and assortment of toys that were nestled into one corner for clients' children.

Remy's younger sister Annick sat behind the delicately carved walnut reception desk with the telephone receiver sandwiched between shoulder and ear. Two thick books lay open on the desk before her. She scribbled in a spiral notebook as she spoke, effectively dividing her attention between the call and her studies in the way only a harried law student can. As she glanced up at Remy, she smiled and brushed her black bangs out of her dark eyes with the eraser end of her pencil.

He spread his arms wide and executed an ambling pirouette as if to say "Here I am, and in one piece yet." Annick bid her caller good-bye and hung up the phone, never taking her eyes off her big brother. Remy perched a hip on the corner of the desk and stuck his hand out, palm up. "Fork it over, *'tite soeur*."

"What?"

"What! The twenty bucks you owe me, that's what."

"I don't know what you're talkin' about. You don't, either, if Giselle asks you. I already got the sharp side of her tongue when I told her you'd gone out. You were supposed to work the desk until four."

"I couldn't very well do that and prove to you what a good nanny I could be at the same time, now could I?"

Unconcerned by her warning, Remy pulled the agency agreement out of his pocket and handed the crumpled papers to Annick. "I am now officially the Beauvais family nanny. Here's your proof, darlin', signed, sealed, and delivered."

Annick unfolded the forms, her pretty mouth turning in a frown of distaste. "This is filthy! What's all this here down at the bottom?"

Remy glanced away, rubbing a hand across his mouth as he grumbled. "Um—that's nothin' much, there. Just a little blood, that's all."

"Blood? Yours, I hope," Annick sassed. "You a nanny. Talk about!"

Her mocking laughter cut off abruptly and she winced as the door behind her flew open and Remy's twin sister Giselle stormed out of her office, blustering like a human hurricane. Her black eyes flashed as she rounded the desk and planted her hands on her nicely rounded hips. She may have been dressed like a businesswoman in her fitted blush-pink suit, but her expression was more that of a tag-team wrestler.

Both Remy and Annick instinctively leaned back away from her as she let loose a string of backwater Cajun expletives that singed Remy's ears. When she switched back to English, her temper thickened her accent and eroded the proper grammar she normally used.

"What'sa matter wit de two of you? You tryin' to ruin my business or somethin'? Me, I got a fine reputation in this town, no thanks to the likes of you! Annick, you coverin' for Remy while he goes out masquerading as one of my nannies. What he knows about babies, that one, you couldn't feed a crawfish!" Giselle wasn't in the least softened by her brother's hurt-offended look. "And you!" She jabbed his sternum with a neatly manicured forefinger. "You oughta know better. You ain't a nanny, but you sure oughta have one!"

"I got the job," Remy said softly.

Pacing back and forth in front of the desk, Giselle ranted on. "Impersonatin' one of my nannies! My nannies are de finest in all of N'Awlins—trained, experienced—" She brought herself up short and stared at him suspiciously. "You what?"

He picked up the agency agreement Danielle had signed and waved it, a smile of smug satisfaction lighting up his handsome face. Giselle snatched it away from him and studied the document with the critical eye of a business-school graduate, grimacing at the ratty state the thing was in. "What did you do to this, *cher*? Run over it with your car?"

Getting run over by his car was about the only indignity the contract had escaped. It had been to the roof of the Beauvais house where he had rescued Tinks from Jeremy's evil clutches and been kicked in the shin for his troubles. Ambrose had tried to feed the form to the dog, who had opted to bury it in the rose garden. Remy had extricated the thing from under a freshly fertilized bush that was mostly thorns, and had bled all over it before he could hand it to Danielle for her to sign.

"The only thing that counts is the bottom line," he grumbled.

"No matter." Giselle shook her head, her fashionably bobbed black hair swinging around her face and falling neatly back into place. "You got no training, you got no experience—"

"I got plenty of experience!" Remy argued. "How many times have I taken care of your kids? Or Alicia's? And how about cousin Emile's boys? I've looked after them plenty."

"Well, yes, but—"

"It's the Beauvais house." Annick said with appropriate awe as she tapped at the agency agreement with the end of her pencil.

Giselle's eyes widened in disbelief. "What?" She jerked the form back up in front of her face and read the line twice. "I told that woman we didn't have anybody to send there."

"She gave the name Hamilton when I talked to her," Annick said.

"Huh! I'll bet," Giselle snorted. "She must have gone through every agency in the book, found out no one was crazy enough to send a nanny to that house, then started all over again with an assumed name. Of all the low—"

"It wasn't exactly a trick." Remy jumped to defend Danielle, then purposely relaxed as his twin's keen eyes fastened on him a little too intently. With studied nonchalance he asked, "So, you got anybody else you'd send there?"

"I wouldn't send the devil himself to that house."

"Remy's the next best thing," Annick said with a giggle. He slanted her a look and pinched her cheek.

Giselle's expression was apprehensive. "You sure you want to do this, Remy?" she asked, as if he were volunteering for a suicide mission.

He gave a lazy shrug that said it didn't matter much to him one way or the other, while visions of Danielle danced in his head. He could still taste her, sweet and warm on his lips. He could still see the look of unabashed wonder in her eyes as she had recognized the electricity that hummed between them. He could still sense the sadness and uncertainty in her when she'd told him she wasn't much good with kids. Was he sure he wanted this job? Was he sure he wanted to spend day and night in the company of Danielle Hamilton? What a question!

"I'm good with kids." Grudgingly he added, "I need the money."

Giselle patted his cheek and gave him the same look of sympathy she would have given one of her own children. "I know you do, *cher*."

She had hired him to help answer the phone while her regular receptionist was on maternity leave, but that wasn't much of a job as far as pay or prestige went. Her brother was a proud man. He didn't like the position he'd been put in by unemployment. He hadn't complained, but Giselle knew. As twins, there was a level of communication between them that needed no words.

She nibbled at her lush lower lip. "Well, it's a sure thing that woman isn't going to find anyone else to help her. And you *are* good with the little ones. I guess the job is yours, if you really want it."

Remy barely managed to keep from leaping up and dancing his sister around the room. He thanked her with his smile.

Giselle picked up the agreement again and studied it more closely. "Who is this Danielle Hamilton? Why didn't Mrs. Beauvais sign this?"

"Mrs. Beauvais is away on a second honeymoon with Mr. Beauvais. Danielle is her half sister. She agreed to stay with the kids, but—"

"*Danielle*, is it?" Annick questioned, brows lifting above wickedly sparkling dark eyes. She leaned over the desk and poked him with her pencil. "Who is this Danielle, Remy? Is she pretty?"

He shrugged and dodged his sister's teasing look, but he couldn't stop the flush that rose up from his shirt collar. *Bon Dieu*, he felt like a teenager caught staring at his secret sweetheart. It was on the tip of his tongue to say that Danielle was a shrew-faced hag. Of course, it was too late for that; his blush had given him away.

Giselle crossed her arms over her chest and tapped a pink pump on the sensible flat gray carpet. She drilled her twin with a look that discouraged prevarication. "Oooh, now we get to the heart of the matter, eh? You want to take this job because of *une belle femme*?"

Remy scowled. "She needs help."

"*Mais non, 'tit frère*, you gonna be the one needs help if you damage the reputation of my business tryin' any cha-cha with one of my clients. You got that?"

His mustache twitched from side to side like the tail of an annoyed cat as he glared down at his dirty wingtips. "Mmmbrl."

"What kind of answer is that?" Giselle demanded. "Mmmbrl? I want you to promise me, Remy Doucet. I want your solemn oath that you will *not* embarrass me."

Remy rubbed a hand across his jaw. The devil on his shoulder told him there was a lot of leeway in the interpretation of that statement. He grinned up at his sister. "I promise."

Annick rolled her dark eyes and laughed in disbelief. "That's like askin' *m'sieu renard* to stay outa the henhouse and believin' him when he says *mais* yeah."

Remy shot her a look. "Who asked you, *gosse*?"

"Nobody. And don't you call me a brat."

"Brat."

She stuck her tongue out at him. Remy grinned and mussed his baby sister's short hair. Annick might have been twenty-three with a promising career in law ahead of her, but he still enjoyed teasing her as much as he had when she'd been thirteen.

Giselle shook her head and sighed a long-suffering sigh. "Ah, me, who would guess by the way you two act you're a future lawyer and a man with a college education?"

"The Amazing Kreskin?" Remy offered with a hopeful look.

Giving in to his boyish charm, Giselle chuckled. "Oh, Remy, what am I gonna do with you?"

"Dance!" He hopped off the desk, grabbed his sister, and swung her into a two-step.

"Oooh, my poor old aching back!" Alistair Urquhart-Butler groaned. His face screwed up in a grimace, he cracked one eye open ever so slightly to see how Danielle was reacting. Oblivious to the performance, Danielle moved around the bed straightening his covers, her lovely mouth frowning, worry lining her forehead. "I'm so sorry I'm of no help to you, lass. How are you getting on with the wee bairns, then? Fine, I trust."

"Oh, just peachy," Danielle drawled. She poured him a glass of ice water and handed him the brown bottle of pills he kept on hand for his bad back. She watched as Butler shook two out and tossed them back, making a great show of swallowing them down.

He sighed and shook his head and looked generally woebegone. "I feel terrible being brought down in the line of duty this way with you trusting me to help you with the children—"

"It wasn't your fault," Danielle said, sitting down on the edge of the bed beside the man who had helped raise her off and on during her formative years.

Butler was as much a father to her and the other Hamilton offspring as Laird Hamilton himself was. Stern, but loving, he had always been there when one of them needed a helping hand or a smack on the fanny. He loved them all like family, she knew, and his feelings were reciprocated.

She studied him now as he leaned back against the carved headboard in his Hamilton tartan pajamas with the clan crest embroidered on the pocket, thinking he never looked any different to her. No matter how long she was away she knew when she came back Butler would be the same man who'd patched up her skinned knees and scolded her for getting sick on her father's cigars. He was past sixty, but he still had his full head of fine red hair, which he had always worn neatly combed and parted on the right, held in place with witch hazel gel. He had the same bold Scottish features as her father—the high, broad forehead, the stubborn chin and substantial nose—and the same undiluted burr even though both of them had lived in the States for more than half their lives.

"Still, I wasna counting on this atall," he said, making another pained face and checking to see that she'd caught it this time.

Danielle pleated the plaid bedspread with her fingers and frowned. "Divide and conquer. That's their strategy. But I don't want you to worry about it. You lie here and rest. I'll manage."

"See there, lass, I told you you could handle this," Butler said with pride. He started to sit up, thought better of it, and leaned gingerly back against the pillows, wincing. "I knew if you but put your fears behind you—"

"I've hired a nanny," Danielle said, as much to stem the flow of Butler's pep talk as to impart the good news. She hadn't put her fears behind her. She didn't think she could stand having him praise her for rising above her past when she doubted she would ever be able to do that. The memory of what she'd done would always be too fresh in her mind, the pain too deep in her heart.

Butler's keen blue eyes widened a fraction. His voice lost all trace of weary suffering. He looked a bit peeved. "You've done what?"

"I've done what every good rich girl does in the face of adversity—I've hired help." She rose and straightened her fresh melon-colored tank top, then double-checked the baby monitor hanging from her belt to make sure it was working. "He seems perfectly competent, if a bit unconventional—"

"He?"

"Remy Doucet. He'll be moving in tonight. I'm sure he'll do fine. Don't you worry about a thing. I'd better go check on the baby now," she said, fussing with the monitor. "Have you got everything you need?"

"Aye," he said absently.

Danielle glanced around the room. It wasn't as large as the one she had commandeered upstairs, but it was certainly comfortable. Besides the carved mahogany double bed there was the marble-topped nightstand, a matching dresser, and a tall armoire that housed a television with a VCR and a stereo. Butler's quarters had all the comforts of home and the added benefit of being off-limits to the Beauvais children. Danielle would gladly have traded places with him—bad back and all.

"Get some rest," she said, moving toward the door.

"Aye, you too now, lass," he mumbled.

If she hadn't been so preoccupied with her own thoughts, Danielle might have noticed that he sounded just a little bit guilty. But she was too tired and too flustered and too determined to do her duty until her replacement arrived. She slipped out the door of Butler's room and headed up the servant's staircase. All she had to do was hang in there until Remy arrived, then she would steer clear of him and the Beauvais darlings. They could keep each other occupied for the next three weeks and Suzannah could take her idea of family influence and choke on it.

Butler held his breath as he listened to Danielle's footsteps fade away. The poor lass. She looked like death warmed over. He'd been so sure she would rise to the occasion, but the purple crescents under her eyes told a different tale. Now she'd gone and hired a nanny. Things were not going according to plan.

Shaking his head, he tossed the covers back and pushed himself out of bed. He put the two pills he had palmed back in their bottle, sure that Danielle was in too dazed a state to notice the supply wasn't dwindling. He stretched both hands toward the high ceiling, then bent and touched his toes. When he had all the kinks out, he reached for the phone on the nightstand and punched out a number.

"It's me," he said in a low voice. "We've got a wee bit of a problem."

# four

**"WHAT'S THAT, AUNTIE DAN-L?" AMBROSE** asked as he peered through his Lone Ranger mask at the casserole.

"Macaroni surprise."

"What's the surprise?"

Jeremy gave a derisive snort as he poked at the noodles with a long-handled spoon. "If we eat it and live, she'll be surprised."

"Not to mention disappointed," Danielle muttered under her breath, leveling a glare at Jeremy.

The children had caught on rather quickly to the fact that she was not a cook. She knew she was not a cook; the news came as no surprise to her. The sense of hurt did, however. She had gone to the effort to make the kids a home-cooked meal, hoping that would in some way make them look at her as a kind of mother figure.

*Face it, Danielle*, she told herself, swallowing down the bitter taste of defeat, *you can't bond successfully through macaroni. You can't bond successfully, period. Who are you trying to fool?*

She had known for some time that she wasn't cut out for this. So why was the idea choking her up now, she wondered, as she stared morosely at the unappetizing casserole. She liked her life the way it was. She was free to travel wherever she wanted, whenever she wanted. If she got the itch to snap a few pictures of the Mayan ruins at Chichen Itza, all she had to do was pack up her cameras and go. If she wanted to spend the entire night working on printing techniques in her darkroom, there was no one to complain to her about being neglected.

Her life was unencumbered by people who needed to know where she was every waking minute or wanted to make demands on her time. Her relationships with men never lasted, so there was minimal distraction there. She was basically free to pour herself completely into her art and that was the way she wanted it.

She would always be an artist first. And as an artist she required a spare, focused life. The muse was a selfish mistress, demanding all the artist's attention, a shameless wanton who pushed away all others vying for the artist's time. It was because of her muse Danielle didn't know how to cook anything more edible than limp macaroni. But an artist was all she had ever wanted to be.

She'd spent less than a week with the Beauvais kids and already she'd had a stomach full of the family scene. The constant tension, the constant distractions were overwhelming her. Danielle Hamilton didn't need a family. No sirree. What she needed right now was a ticket out of this funhouse. She missed her peace and quiet . . . sort of.

"Do we have to eat this?" Tinks asked, staring at the steaming lump of gook on her plate. "It's gross."

Danielle scowled at her and swore to herself that her feelings weren't hurt. Her shoulders slumped as she stared down at the disgusting mess on her plate. They were right. It was gross.

"It looks like cooked brains," Jeremy said with malicious delight as he reached his fork onto Dahlia's plate and stirred her dinner around. "Gooey, slimy cooked possum brains."

Dahlia looked up in horror, her freckles standing out in sharp relief against her white face. "Make him stop it! Make him stop, Aunt Danielle! I'm gonna gag!"

Jeremy chortled maniacally, his pleasure in grossing out his sister such that he could barely keep himself on his chair. "Gooey gator brains! Slippery, slimy snake innards!"

"I'm gonna throw up!" Dahlia cried.

Danielle gave her nephew her sternest look. It didn't faze him. "Jeremy, stop it or you won't get any supper."

He rolled his eyes. "*That's* a threat? Ha!"

"Look, guys," Danielle said, diplomatically taking another tack. "This stuff is good for you. It's loaded with protein."

"So are cockroaches," Jeremy muttered. "We don't eat them."

"It could be arranged." There was just enough menace in Danielle's voice to give credence to her words. Four red-haired heads bent over their plates. Forks clicked against china.

Danielle ignored her own plate on the excuse that she had to feed Eudora, who sat beside her in her yellow high chair. Knowing nothing about baby diets, she had decided it would be potluck night. She had chosen three jars of strained and mushed stuff on the basis of a pleasing color combination. Eudora didn't seem to mind. She ate every other spoonful with the relish of a gourmand and spat alternating helpings at Danielle.

Unaffected, Danielle went on feeding the baby. Getting spat on was nothing. She'd been spat on by a cobra in Africa and still had gotten the shot she wanted. It was one of her most famous wildlife photos and had graced the cover of the *National Geographic*. She could handle getting spat on. It was the least of the abuse she'd taken so far from Suzannah's little ghouls.

Eudora grabbed a handful of peach cobbler and flung it into Danielle's face with an exuberant cry of "Whee!"

Danielle gritted her teeth, wondering how long it was going to take for her to grind the enamel right off them. Lord, she couldn't wait for Remy to relieve her.

Relief? Was that what she called getting kissed until her ears rang? Her toes tingled at the memory. Brother, that man knew how to kiss! But that was irrelevant, she told herself sternly, spooning up another glob of pureed peas on the baby's rubber-covered spoon. Remy's kiss might have been a doozie, but it was in the past, over, finished. From this moment on she was going to endeavor to behave like the mature woman she was. No more losing her head over young, brawny, devastatingly sexy Cajun men. No more sizzler kisses. No more clinches in the nursery. No more fantasizing about his fabulous fanny.

She stared up at a spot of pulverized peas dotting the kitchen wall, fanning her flushed face with her free hand. Well, maybe it wouldn't hurt to fantasize a teensy bit. After all, at her age, fantasizing about a younger man was probably *all* she was ever going to do. And if she were to pick a man's fanny to fantasize about, Remy Doucet's was it. The man had a real power tush.

But no touching, she told herself, frowning. Absolutely, positively *no* touching.

Lord, she groaned, her fingers were itching to touch him! She'd probably go crazy and grope him the minute they were alone in the same room. What lousy timing. She'd never met a man she wanted to grope more than Remy Doucet and he was off-limits. Even if she hadn't just hired him as a nanny, there was the little matter of the fact that he hadn't even been a twinkle in Papa Doucet's eye when she was discovering the wonders of grammar school.

"My luck," she muttered, her arm swinging back and forth as she tried to zero in on Eudora's dodging mouth.

Well, she would just have to leash her lust before he arrived.

"Hey, Danielle," a melodic male voice called cheerfully from the kitchen doorway. "Where you at?"

As all her insides turned into curlicues at the sight of Remy in snug jeans and a black polo shirt, Danielle forced her mind to ponder his typical New Orleans greeting. Why didn't he ask *how* she was? He knew *where* she was. She was sitting right there in front of him with mushed gook all over her. Decidedly unromantic, she thought, glancing down at the front of her blouse, which had been tie-dyed with Gerber's finest.

A little tingle of panic shot through her. She didn't want romantic, couldn't have romantic. Nothing about this arrangement was romantic. He was the kids' nanny. She had to think of him as Mary Poppins with five o'clock shadow.

"Hello, Mr. Doucet," she said, offering him a businesslike smile. "Kids, say hello to Mr. Doucet."

When no sound issued forth except Eudora's happy beet-juicy gurgle, Danielle glanced around the table. The kids had jumped ship. She had been so immersed in her thoughts about Remy's masculine attributes, she hadn't even noticed them leave. Yet another example of what a fine mother she would make.

"They're in watchin' TV," he said, setting down a maroon nylon carryall. He settled his big hands at his waist and grimaced at the congealing lump of macaroni on an abandoned dinner plate, the corners of his mustache tugging down around his mouth.

"Go ahead. Say it," Danielle snapped defensively. "I can take it. It's written all over your face. I'm a lousy cook."

"You're a lousy cook." Cautiously he poked at the mess with a fork, as if he expected it to come to life and attack him. "What is it?"

"Macaroni surprise."

"Did they eat it?"

"No."

"I'm not surprised."

He was a little disappointed, though. He would never have admitted it, but he was a chauvinist through and through. Where he came from, women knew how to cook—actually, most everybody knew how to cook. They also knew how to raise children. Danielle didn't appear to be adept at either of those womanly arts.

She sure was pretty, though. That made up for a lot, he thought, taking in her perfect patrician features as she glared up at him defiantly. Her translucent gray eyes glittered like sterling. Her chin jutted forward aggressively. How she managed to look so dignified while covered with baby food was beyond him. He decided it was the mark of a true lady.

"You see this finger?" she asked, raising her left fist with the forefinger extended. "This is my cooking finger."

"Your cooking finger?"

"This finger can dial the number of every major take-out place in every city in the world. I ask you, what more do I need?"

Remy picked a striped dish towel off the corner of the table and swiped a speck of peach cobbler off the tip of her nose. "A shower."

Danielle blinked. Even through terry cloth his touch was electric. Prince Abdul Rifal of Dakjir had once taken a fingertip tour of her face through a silken veil and it hadn't affected her nearly as profoundly. Forcing the thought away, she looked down at the front of her T-shirt. Sunburst patterns in green, ruby, and peach were splashed across her chest in lumpy, liquidy glory. The same colors dotted her arms like three-dimensional freckles.

"Yuk."

Remy clicked his tongue and shook his dark head. "You're a mess, you are, *chère*. Mebbe we oughta just take you out back and hose you down."

"No thanks. I like the idea of a hot shower much better."

"Me too," he said in that intimate, velvety tone of voice that just reeked of sin. He bent over her, one hand on the table, one on the back of her chair. His eyes captured hers like hot black magnets capturing steel. He waggled his brows. "You need any help with that, *chère*?"

The mere thought made Danielle's insides go as soft as the overcooked macaroni on her plate. The picture of the two of them in the shower stall together, steam rising, soap bubbles sliding over slick skin, darn near made her faint.

"No!" she said suddenly, leaning back in her chair, trying to escape his male aura. "I can manage."

"You sure?" Remy murmured, forgetting what little sense of propriety he had as he stared at Danielle's breasts as they thrust up toward him. They were small but firm and round and unfettered by the bonds of a bra. "I'm real good with my hands."

Danielle's breath soughed through her parted lips. She could imagine the feel of those big hands stroking her, caressing her, cupping her breast and guiding it to his mouth as the shower pounded down on them. Her gaze fastened helplessly on Remy's mouth, so close, so tempting. He leaned a little nearer.

"What happened to your pledge of good behavior?" she asked breathlessly, clinging to the last ragged threads of her sanity.

His eyes sparkled as he gave her his slow piratelike smile. His smoky voice stroked over her like a caress. "This is as good as it gets."

"Oh, my . . ."

Eudora gave a sudden squeal of delight and mushed a handful of peas into Remy's face. "Eii-up, da da da da!" she chortled merrily, clapping her hands together and splashing vegetable matter in all directions, effectively breaking the mood, much to Danielle's relief—or was it dismay?

"Looks like I'm gonna have to join you in that shower now, yes?" Remy said to Danielle with a grin as he scraped the bilious green goo off his face with the dish towel.

"No, I don't think so." Danielle ducked under his arm and rose to her full height, eliminating his advantage. She composed herself admirably just long enough to tell him where to put his things, then she dashed for the door, chanting "no touching, no touching" under her breath like an incantation against evil spirits.

Remy straightened and watched her flee, guilt poking at him as he thought of his promise to his sister.

Eudora squealed and reached her arms up, begging to be taken out of her high chair. She looked like she'd been to a body-painting salon. Her little fingers were dripping baby food. The front of her romper was covered. Peach cobbler had been run through her duck fuzz hair like gel, spiking it up in a punk fashion. Her face was coated with pureed peas. She looked enormously happy, though, in spite of, or maybe because of, her slovenly state.

"Happy as a pig in pink mud, aren't you?" Remy said with a chuckle. Heedless of his shirt, he scooped her up in his arms and headed for the door. "Come on, *pichouette*, looks like you're the only lady I get to bathe tonight."

By the time Danielle emerged from her room, freshly showered and dressed in trendy loose purple cotton slacks and a matching top, Remy had bathed Eudora and dressed her for bed in a snowy white sleeper with a herd of hopping yellow bunnies printed on it. The older children were still firmly entrenched in front of the television, absorbed in the latest escapade of *McGyver*.

"They're actually quiet," Danielle murmured, looking in at them from the hall. Under the chilling spray of the showerhead she had wrestled her rampant hormones into submission and righted her normal calm sense of self. Her unsettled emotions had crawled back under the carpet of wry humor. She felt in control of herself again, and reasonably certain she would stay that way—just as long as she didn't come within kissing distance of Remy again. She checked the distance between them and sent him a sardonic smile. "If I didn't know better, I might mistake them for a normal family."

"Aw, come on, sugar." Remy chuckled, conveniently forgetting the afternoon episode on the roof. He lowered Eudora into the playpen that sat just inside the family room door and handed her a foam ball which she promptly began to chew on. Straightening, he settled his hands at the waistband of his jeans. "This household isn't so different from any other house with kids in it."

"I'd call that one heck of an argument for planned parenthood," Danielle quipped. She took a step back from the domestic scene and nodded toward the back of the house. "If you have a minute, I'll introduce you to Butler now. It's time for his pain medication. Maybe if we're lucky he'll share some with us."

Remy frowned at that, but decided she was joking. He fell into step behind her, admiring the sway of her hips. "Who is this Butler fella? You mentioned him this afternoon, but what with all that cryin' and carryin' on I forgot to ask."

Danielle shot him a look that told him she didn't appreciate the reminder of her disgrace. "Butler is the butler."

Stunned to a standstill, Remy gave a snort of outrage. "Well, call the poor man by his name, at least! The days of the name going with the station are long gone, even down here. And if you think for a minute I'm gonna let you get away with callin' me Nanny, you can just think again," he said, jabbing the air with his forefinger.

Danielle pushed his hand aside and rolled her eyes. "Save your temper for a better day, *Mr. Doucet*. Butler *is* his name—Alistair Urquhart-Butler."

A deep flush seeped under Remy's tan. "Oh."

"Oh." Danielle shook her head. "Jeeze, what do you take me for?"

A rich, spoiled, pampered woman who paid servants to do every job she deemed unpleasant. But he didn't say that in view of the fact that she could fire him just as easily as she had hired him, and he needed—no, *wanted* this job. He wanted the chance to find out what other misconceptions he had about Danielle.

"I guess I'm not all that familiar with the way wealthy people treat their hired help," he admitted.

Danielle stopped at Butler's door and gave Remy a strange look. "I would have thought you'd be well acquainted with the relationship. Mr. and Mrs. Factory Worker don't hire many nannies. Who have you been working for?"

"Oooohhh . . ." Remy's throat constricted around his answer and he was about to choke on it when a wavering voice called out on the other side of the door.

"Danni? Is that you, lass?"

Danielle swung the door open and strode across the room with a concerned look on her face. "You sound terrible! Are you feeling worse?"

Butler shifted positions against the pillows, wincing but putting on a brave face for Danielle. "Oh, dinna fash yourself, lass. The pain is terrible, but I can bear it. 'Tis the worry that's about to do me in."

"I told you not to worry. I've got everything under control. I've brought the new nanny in to meet you."

Butler raised a brow in surprise as Remy stepped forward, his broad shoulders nearly filling the doorway.

"This is Remy Doucet," Danielle said, stepping aside to fuss with Butler's pill bottle as the men regarded one another. "Remy, this is Alistair Urquhart-Butler, devoted retainer of the Hamilton clan for lo these many years."

The men shook hands, Remy raising a brow at the strength of the older man's grip. Butler quickly let go and groaned a little as he settled back against his mountain of pillows. "I'd get up, Mr. Do-sit, but as you can see, I'm incapacitated."

"Much to my dismay," Danielle said. "Butler was going

to look after the children. I was just brought in for window dressing."

"Well, there's no need for you to worry yourself, Mr. Butler," Remy said with a deceptively placid smile. "I'll take real good care of the kids." His voice dropped a husky fraction of a note. "And Miss Danielle too."

He delivered his little addendum with a perfect poker face and still Danielle blushed. Immediately she felt Butler's keen blue eyes dart to her face, homing in like heat-seeking missiles. It was as bad as when she'd been fourteen, spending the summer at her father's home, and Butler had somehow known just by looking at her that she was engaging in nightly necking sessions with Jamey Sheridan from across the lake. He looked at her now and she was certain he could see every hormone she had gravitating toward Remy Doucet.

She thrust his pills at him. "Mr. Doucet comes from one of the best agencies in the city."

"Does he now?" Butler never took his eyes from his mistress's flaming face. Danielle squirmed and looked away, missing completely the act of Butler palming his medication. When he handed the bottle back to her, she gladly took it for something to hang on to. "And just how long have you been a nanny. Mr. Do-sit?"

Remy cleared his throat and handed the supine butler a glass of water from the nightstand. His dark eyes caught Butler's and held them with a meaningful look. "Better wash those big horse pills down. Mr. Butler. We wouldn't want you to choke now. Those painkillers are so big, a man might as well just leave 'em in his fist and swallow that too."

Butler blanched and coughed a bit in genuine distress. Taking a sip from the glass of water, he forced a wan smile. "What a relief it is to know Danielle will have help with the children."

A wry smile twitched up one corner of Remy's mustache. "Isn't it, though?"

"How was your dinner?" Danielle asked, suspiciously eyeing the empty plate on the bed tray.

"Fine, lass." Butler twitched the bedspread to make sure the portion nearest the floor covered the wastebasket full of macaroni surprise. He sat up a little straighter and stretched his arms a bit. "About the meals. You know, I'm fair certain I'll feel up to standing a wee bit tomorrow. Perhaps I could resume my duties in the kitchen."

"Absolutely not!"

"I can handle it, Mr. Butler." Remy grinned. "I'm a good cook . . . for a price."

"Name it," Butler blurted out.

"Hey!" Danielle propped her hands on her hips and scowled at the pair of them.

Butler gave her an apologetic look. "No offense, lass, but Julia Child you're not."

"Oh, fine," she snapped, unreasonably hurt at having her paltry domestic skills criticized. "I'll gladly turn my apron over to the Cookin' Cajun here. Everybody knows I wasn't cut out for kitchen duty or diaper detail."

Remy gave her a curious look, having picked up a little too keenly the bitterness in her tone. He glanced from her to Butler and back, reading a tense mix of emotions on the two faces.

"Now, lass—"

"We ought to let you rest, Butler," Danielle said stiffly, fearing she had already let something slip that she would rather have kept firmly tucked away. She didn't like the way Remy was looking at her and she knew she didn't want to hear what Butler was about to say. She backed toward the door, fighting the need to simply turn and hightail it. "Besides, we really shouldn't cluster ourselves all in one room this way. Jeremy is liable to nail the door shut."

Remy bid Butler a restful night and followed Danielle back out into the hall. "You sure you don't mind me cookin', *chère*?"

"Mind? Why should I mind?" She flapped her arms in an exaggerated shrug and twirled around the kitchen like a demented ballet dancer, gesturing to the stove, the cupboards, the gourmet gadgets lining the countertops. "Cook! Cook away! Cook yourself into a frenzy!"

"You just seem a little upset, is all," he observed, taking a baby bottle from the drainer by the sink. He went to the refrigerator, took out a carton of milk and filled the bottle, keeping one watchful eye on Danielle throughout the entire process.

The lady was rattled about something and he was willing to bet it was something a lot more important than macaroni surprise. There were things going on here he knew nothing about, but he could feel the undercurrents just the same. He could also feel the need to reach out to Danielle, to offer support and comfort. It unnerved him a little bit. She wasn't the kind of woman who normally inspired protective feelings in him, not by a long shot.

Danielle watched him shut the refrigerator with a breath-catching little bump of his hip. He went to the stove and set about warming the baby's bottle, his movements as sure as if he'd done this every day of his life. For the short time she'd been in charge of Eudora she had gone around with a book on child care in one hand until she'd practically had to have the thing surgically removed.

"I seem upset to you?" she asked. All the reminders of her ineptitude ganged up on her at once and lodged like a rock in her chest. The calm she had worked so hard to resurrect had deserted her utterly, leaving her feeling more unsettled than ever. "Well, in addition to being a rotten cook and a lousy babysitter, I'm also a temperamental bitch," she said, her voice hoarse from trying to hold back her true emotions. She tossed her hair back over her shoulder and gave Remy her haughtiest look, though she wouldn't meet his eyes. "Us rich women are often like that, you know. You might as well get used to it."

With that she flounced from the room, leaving nothing behind but the sting of her words and a fragrant trail of Giorgio.

Remy made a face and whistled through his teeth as he stared at the swinging door. "The lady bites like a gator. I wonder why."

# five

**FEELING LIKE A FOOL, DANIELLE WANDERED** barefoot out onto the wide veranda that graced the front of the Beauvais house. Remy had to believe she was a little unhinged after her performance in the kitchen. She was beginning to wonder about it herself.

The time she'd spent in Tibet had been intended as healing time, time to put things in perspective, time to reconcile herself to her future and dull the memory of what had happened in London. She had spent months living in a simple shanty on the edge of the Chang Tang plateau with only a yak and a goat for company. Her days had consisted of work, shooting endless rolls of film of the bleak Tibetan landscape. Her nights had consisted of quiet meditation. She had returned feeling at peace with herself. But that sense of peace had been both false and fragile. Now she felt a fool for ever having believed in it.

As a sense of despair welled up inside her, she hugged a smooth wooden column, pressed her cheek against the white painted wood. She was vaguely aware of the heavy scent of flowers in the thick warm air, sweet and cloying like a bordello madam's perfume on a Saturday night. The sun had set but darkness had yet to wrap its cloak around the Big Easy. The

Garden District was quiet. The French Quarter would just be coming to life.

Out on the street a carriage full of tourists clomped past, drawn by a tired-looking black horse. The tourists craned their necks to get a look at the magnificent homes that lined the block. Cameras swiveled in Danielle's direction and she managed to smile at the irony of her being a subject of a photographer's curiosity.

Remy stepped out onto the veranda with Eudora tucked into the crook of one brawny arm, an unlit cigarette dangling from his lips. Danielle watched from the corner of her eye as he settled himself back in one corner of the porch swing and gave the baby her bottle. His dark eyes drifted her way and studied her openly for a long moment before he spoke.

"Why don't you sit down, *chère*?" he asked, his voice low, his tone not overtly sexual, but inviting and compelling.

Danielle felt as if she were walking through ankle-deep molasses as she crossed the porch. Her instincts were screaming at her to run away, but she blatantly ignored them. She was a grown woman, a woman of the world, a—how she was growing to hate this word—mature woman. She would sit on this swing and have a civil conversation with this man, just as she would get through these next weeks living in the same house with him.

She wedged herself into the opposite corner of the swing, drew her feet up to the seat, and wrapped her arms around her knees. "I'm sorry I snapped at you in the kitchen. I've been a little on edge lately."

Remy continued to study her, unblinking, his expression closed. "Why is that?"

There was a wealth of reasons, none of which she was willing to explain to him. The temptation, however, was strong. She felt a part of herself wanting to tell him, and that kind of wanting was a dangerous thing when having was out of the question.

"I'm not used to being around so many people," she said. It was at least part of the truth. "The part of Tibet I stayed in isn't exactly Times Square."

Remy took his cigarette from his lips and tucked it behind his ear like a pencil. His thick brows drew together as he looked at her with open curiosity. "What were you doing all that time in such a place?"

Hurting, thinking, doing penance, and trying to heal, she thought, but she glanced away from him again before he could see any of those answers in her eyes. "I was taking pictures. I'm a photographer."

"Oh yeah? Like for a magazine or what?"

"I sometimes contribute photographs to magazines. Most of my work ends in galleries and books. My series from Tibet will be a book. *Moonscapes, Landscapes: A Portrait of Tibet*."

Remy looked suitably impressed. There was something else in his expression, too, though, something like concern. He shifted Eudora in his arms, adjusted the angle of her bottle, scooted over on the bench an inch or so. "You travel around a lot doing that?"

"All over the world."

"And it doesn't bother you?"

"Why would it bother me? I grew up living out of suitcases. My mother was an international model. She took me with her everywhere she went."

"But don't you ever get the urge to just stay home, put down roots, raise a family?"

"My home is wherever I hang my camera bag."

"And the rest?"

"Is none of your business, Mr. Doucet," she said coolly, lifting her slim patrician nose a notch.

Remy scowled at her tone of voice. She was trying to make him back off. He didn't for a minute believe she was the kind of society lady who demanded the hired help bob and tug their forelocks in her presence. That was the impression she was trying to give him now, though.

She had unfolded her long legs from the seat of the swing and demurely crossed them in that impossible pretzel-twist taught at finishing schools. She was good at looking cool and unapproachable, but the act was wasted on him. He had held her, had felt the fragile vulnerability that lay beneath her surface; he had tasted the sweetness in her kiss. There was much more to Danielle Hamilton than prim deportment and a taste for the finer things, and he had every intention of uncovering the secrets that lingered in her big eyes.

"You like all that traveling?" he asked, unable to keep the amazement out of his voice. He inched a little closer to her.

Danielle relaxed a degree as he let go of the topics she dreaded most. She settled back into the flowered cushions of the swing again and nodded. "I love discovering different parts of the world, what the people are like, what the food is like, the environment, the history. It's all fascinating to me."

Remy looked down at Eudora, frowning absently. He couldn't understand that kind of wanderlust. It made him vaguely uncomfortable to think of it and to think that Danielle was so different from him. He would have preferred their only major differences to be the fun kind—anatomical.

Danielle studied him as he seemed to lose himself in thought. A sweet pang shot through her chest at the sight of little Eudora snuggling against Remy's chest, her fair lashes fluttering against her chubby cheeks like fairy's wings as she drifted into sleep. She looked completely relaxed, as if she felt absolutely safe and secure, and Remy looked oddly natural with the baby in his arms. It didn't make sense. A big, brawny guy like Remy Doucet, who seemed to exude masculinity from every inch of his brawny body, shouldn't have been so at ease feeding a baby. But he held Eudora with the kind of second-nature casualness that came from long experience.

Danielle caught herself wishing she could trade places with her niece. She had a feeling nuzzling against Remy's chest would be a very cozy place to fall asleep . . . or something. The memory of his arms around her came back with the tempting lure of a siren's call. She had to struggle to remember that the siren's victims always met with disaster—which was what she was headed for fantasizing about Remy's chest.

She cleared her mind of romantic notions and cleared her throat to break the languid mood that had settled over them as tangibly as the Louisiana humidity. "I take it you've been here all your life."

"Pretty much. My family's been living on the Bayou Noir for 'bout two hundred years."

"Gee, you don't look a day over a hundred and three," she said dryly.

Remy smiled like a crocodile, his dark eyes glittering as he leaned a little closer. "Does that mean you don't still think I'm too young for you, sugar?"

Danielle snapped her teeth together and fumed while her cheeks flushed a shade to rival the geraniums that spilled out of stone pots on either side of the front door.

Not wanting to scare her off, Remy changed the subject before she could say anything. "I moved from Lou'siana once. I was working for an oil company and had to transfer to Scotland—the Outer Hebrides." He rolled his eyes and shuddered at the memory.

Danielle had spent a month in the Hebrides one summer. It was a harsh place, but beautiful. She had enjoyed the sounds of the wind and the sea, the rugged treeless landscape, the earthy practicality and hospitality of the islanders. Remy obviously had not.

"I had to come back home," he said. "This is where my family is. How could I live someplace else?"

Danielle shrugged. "My family is scattered all over the globe. That doesn't makes us less of a family."

"How many brothers and sisters do you have?"

"Five. We're all related only through our father, though, except Drew and Tony—they're twins."

"*Bon Dieu!* Your papa, he's really had *five* wives?"

She nodded and shrugged, her angular shoulders lifting and falling gracefully. "The Hamilton curse," she said blandly. "Women fall in love with Laird at first sight. They just can't stand being married to him. Oddly enough, they've all remained friends after the divorces. It's not at all uncommon for one or more of the exes to be in residence at the compound at any given time."

"And you believe in this curse, *chère*?"

Danielle wasn't sure how much credence she put in the curse, but she certainly couldn't dispute the fact that her relationships with men didn't last. When she was feeling practical she admitted she wasn't an easy person to live with. When she was feeling put upon she blamed the curse. "Well, I'm not exactly a missus now, am I?" she said by way of an answer.

"Mrs. Beauvais is."

"Suzannah is the exception to the rule."

Danielle looked past him, through the window into the house. From her position she couldn't see the children, but the television was still glowing and mumbling.

"What did you do to the Wild Bunch?" she asked dryly. "They haven't been this quiet since they were in their mother's womb."

"I told 'em I learned how to be a nanny through a correspondence course while I was in prison."

Danielle's heart froze for one terrifying second, then lurched into overdrive. What had she done now? She should have insisted on checking his references. She had been too enthralled with his fabulous fanny to think that he might have been a psychotic killer or something. For a split second she thought of snatching the baby from his arms and dashing into the house, but she dismissed the idea. She would rather take her chances with an escaped convict than be locked inside the same house with Jeremy Beauvais.

"Relax, darlin'," Remy said on a chuckle. "I'm just exactly what I appear to be."

No great comfort there, Danielle decided. He appeared to be deliciously, intoxicatingly, irresistibly male. He appeared to be the answer to every erotic dream she'd ever had. He appeared to be too young for them to be included in the same demographic group. She swallowed hard and bared her teeth in a parody of a smile. "Wonderful."

"I think you're pretty terrific, too, Danielle."

Danielle felt everything inside her begin to overheat. It was then that she realized Remy was no longer safely tucked back into his own corner of the swing. His muscular thigh was brushing against hers. He had slid his left arm along the back of the bench so that his fingertips were resting just behind her bare shoulder. He leaned a little closer. She gave him a dour look that made him sit up but didn't quell him into retreating to his own side of the swing.

"Can't blame a guy for tryin', now can you?" he said, giving her his innocent altar boy look.

"You're a regular Cajun Casanova, aren't you?" Danielle accused. "And with a baby in your arms. You ought to be ashamed."

He didn't look ashamed, but he did glance down at Eudora dozing contentedly on his arm. A soft, heart-stealing smile lifted the corners of his mustache. "She's a little doll, *oui*?"

"Yes, she is," Danielle murmured, biting her lip as she looked at her little niece. Eudora was unquestionably precious with her pudgy cheeks and duckling fuzz hair. No one would have guessed from looking at her she was going to grow up to be one of the infamous Beauvais clan. She had stolen Danielle's heart immediately and now that heart squeezed a little in her chest as Danielle reached out a slightly trembling hand to brush at the baby's fine red hair. "I think she even likes me some of the time."

The wistfulness in her voice hit Remy square in the chest. He looked at her now when her guard was completely down and a knot of some unidentifiable emotion wedged itself into his throat. The woman who had the ability to look fierce and imperious and as icy as a winter day in the Hebrides now looked haunted and insecure and filled with longing.

"Sure, she likes you," he whispered, brushing back a lock of Danielle's angel hair with his free hand. "You wanna hold her?"

Danielle made a face. "I'm not very good at that."

"Don't say that," he said in that soft seductive tone that never failed to make Danielle's toes curl. "All you need is a little practice."

He scooted closer to her again, until his thigh was solidly pressed to hers. Danielle felt the heat of him and wondered if it was possible for flesh to fuse through a layer of denim and cotton gauze.

"Here," he said, positioning the baby to slide her into Danielle's arms. "All you gotta do is relax, darlin'."

With his dark eyes locked on hers, Danielle completely lost track of the conversation. The moment was suddenly charged with all kinds of possibilities—possibilities that involved a lot less clothing than she was wearing now. As her breath grew painfully short, her nipples hardened beneath the suddenly abrasive fabric of her tank top. Memories of the kiss she'd shared with Remy flooded her foggy head—the brush and tickle of his mustache against her skin, the sensuous fullness of his firm lower lip, the clean earthy scent of him. She was on the verge of begging him to kiss her again when Eudora's weight settled into her arms.

She looked down at the sleeping child and automatically tightened her hold. Eudora squirmed and made a face in her sleep.

"Relax," Remy coaxed gently. "Don't squeeze her; she's not an accordion. That's right. Just relax, *chère*, she won't break."

He slid his arm directly around Danielle's shoulders this time, not bothering with subterfuge. She needed his support now. The sight of her holding the baby, her gray eyes full of uncertainty, stirred feelings deep within him—protective feelings, primitive feelings. There was a tenderness, a sweet, aching kind of tenderness that shamed the mere lust he'd felt for her earlier.

"*Bien*," he murmured, leaning down to brush his lips against her temple. "That's fine. You're doing just fine."

Danielle soaked up his words like a dry sponge absorbing rain. In that instant she didn't feel forty, she felt afraid. And Remy wasn't too young, he was too good, too sweet. She lifted her gaze, intending to dispel the magic with a wry remark, but her heart caught in her throat as she met his earnest, caring look.

Remy stroked his fingertips down her cheek, his thumb brushing the corner of her mouth. Then before the spell could be broken, he leaned down and caught her parted lips with his. It was a sweet kiss, a soft kiss, not threatening or demanding. It was all too brief, and yet it was long enough to send all of Danielle's senses into a frenzy.

She could have put it down to the fact that she hadn't been near a man in a long time. Or she could have put it down to the stress she'd been under recently. But under all the excuses lay the basic truth—she was attracted to this man in a way she couldn't remember ever having been attracted before. It was frightening, particularly now when she had decided she wasn't going to find fireworks or bliss, now when she had finally resigned herself to the fact that some dreams weren't meant to come true.

Looking down at Eudora, she tried to clear some of the huskiness from her voice, but managed only a hoarse whisper when she said, "Maybe you should take her up to bed now."

Remy sat back thinking it was Danielle he wanted to take to bed. He wanted to hold her and love away all the shadows in her pretty gray eyes. He wanted to kiss her and bury himself inside her and tell her how pretty she was and how hot she made him. *Bon Dieu*, he thought, it was a wonder the swing didn't burn away beneath him.

A brief flash of movement at the front door caught his attention and he glanced over expecting to see one of the children, but the figure that quickly ducked back was much too tall to be a Beauvais. He rubbed the back of his neck and narrowed his eyes in thought as he pulled his cigarette out from behind his ear and planted it in the corner of his mouth. There was something very strange going on around here.

"That Butler," he began. "What sort of fella is he?"

"Butler?" Danielle repeated dumbly, her brain still shorting out.

"Yeah. He wouldn't—"

His question was cut short by the resounding *Ka-boom!* of an explosion taking place somewhere inside the house.

Remy bolted to his feet and dashed for the door. Danielle stood and stumbled as the swing hit her in the back of the knees. She snatched Eudora tightly up against her shoulder, waking the baby and scaring her so that she immediately set up an ear-piercing wail.

It wasn't difficult to tell where the blast had taken place. Smoke rolled out of the kitchen under the door. A cloud of it billowed out as the door swung open, and from the cloud emerged little Ambrose, his hair sticking up and a big grin on his face beneath his Lone Ranger mask.

"Ambrose! What happened?" Danielle asked frantically as

she rushed down the hall with Eudora bouncing in her arms, the baby's cry taking on a kind of yodeling quality as she ran.

"Tinks blowed up the macaroni surprise with a firecracker," he said with a giggle. "It was fun."

Bracing herself for the worst, Danielle pushed the kitchen door open and stepped in. Remy was standing near the table with a fire extinguisher in his hands. The table was lost somewhere under a sea of white foam. There was macaroni everywhere. It was stuck on the walls, on the white cupboards. Wiggling worms of macaroni dangled from the ceiling and the light fixture.

It was clear, though, that Tinks had got the worst of it. She stood at the head of the table looking like something from a cheap horror movie. Her face was covered with a slimy layer of cream of mushroom soup, dotted with bits of mushroom and crescents of overcooked pasta. Luckily, it appeared that the only thing seriously wounded was her pride. Her lower lip stuck out through the goo in a threatening pout.

Eudora, on the other hand, had stopped crying. She stared around the room, her blue eyes round with wonder as she took in the sight, as awestruck as if it were Christmas morning.

"Ah, me." Remy groaned, setting down the fire extinguisher. He speared both hands back through his dark hair as he picked his way across the macaroni-strewn floor toward the perpetrator of the crime. "What a mess!"

"Radical!" Jeremy exclaimed, bursting in through the door and bounding past Danielle. "Tinks slimed the kitchen!" He skidded across the slippery linoleum, pretending it was a skating rink.

Dahlia opened the door just enough to stick her head into the kitchen. Taking in the scene, she made a horrified face and squealed, "Gross! I'm gonna gag!"

With Eudora perched on her hip, Danielle tiptoed into the

room, carefully tracing Remy's path to where he stood scraping Tinks off with a spatula.

"It would seem the caution inspired by the tales of your incarceration has worn off."

Remy said nothing, but scowled down at Tinks, his temper simmering.

From the hall on the other side of the kitchen Butler emerged panting, his hair disheveled, cheeks flushed. He looked to Remy as if he might have just run up the front stairs and down the back, but Remy made no comment other than a raised eyebrow at the Scot's shoes—a pair of black wingtips that looked very out of place beneath the legs of his pajamas.

"What the devil is going on here?" Butler demanded breathlessly. He tightened the belt of his robe and started forward into the room, remembering belatedly to stoop and press a hand to his back. "A man canna get a moment's peace in this house!"

"It was nothing, Butler," Danielle said reassuringly. "Just a minor explosion. You can go back to bed." She stopped herself and shook her head, a horrified look coming over her face. "What am I saying? *Just* an explosion? This isn't a household, it's a training facility for midget terrorists!"

Remy turned his attention back to Tinks, his big hands planted at the waist of his jeans, his shoulders looking impossibly huge as he leaned over her. "You're in a whole lotta trouble, *'tite rouge*. I want you upstairs an hour ago. Got it?"

Tinks gave him a mutinous glare. "You can't make me. I don't have to do what you say."

A muscle tightened and kicked in Remy's jaw. "You wanna take bets on that?"

She hauled back and kicked him in the shin a split second before he could grab her. Remy winced, biting his tongue on the string of expletives that threatened. Tinks turned to make a break for it, but Remy caught her around the waist and swung her up, spinning her around and plunking her over his shoulder like a sack of potatoes. Her breath left her on a surprised "Oof!" She tried to kick him once. He stilled her squirming with one hand shackling her ankles and one smacking her smartly on the fanny.

"We'll be upstairs discussing the new house rules regarding explosives," Remy said tightly to Danielle as he passed her, his face dark with fury, black eyes flashing.

Danielle, Eudora, and Jeremy watched them go. Jeremy looked stunned and pale, his freckles stood out in sharp relief against his skin. His eyes bugged out like Bart Simpson's. Butler looked thoughtful. Eudora gave a startled little gasp and pressed a chubby hand to her mouth as the kitchen door swung shut.

"Uh-oh is right, sweetheart," Danielle said, with a smile of smug admiration. "I think Tinks has met her match."

"Do you think he'll kill her?" Jeremy asked in a hushed tone. "Do you think he'll dunk her in chicken broth and feed her to the alligators?"

Danielle gave him a look. "Of course not. Mr. Doucet is a trained professional nanny."

Butler gave a snort at that, but declined to elaborate when Danielle turned toward him. She looked from his face to Jeremy's to Eudora's, her initial pleasure at Remy's actions fading. She might have wanted Tinks to have an attitude adjustment, but she certainly didn't want the little girl hurt, despite the many dire empty threats Danielle herself had made. She turned and stared at the kitchen door as if it were the portal to hell, her ears trained to catch the faintest sound of suffering. The house was ominously silent.

What did she really know about Remy Doucet? As paranoia tried to get a foothold in her mind, she walked calmly across the carpet of macaroni, not wanting everyone to panic.

"I think I'll take Eudora up to bed," she said, putting so much false serenity into her voice she sounded like she'd had a lobotomy. "Why don't you all go back to whatever you were doing?"

After depositing the baby in her crib. Danielle crept down the hall toward the sliver of light that escaped Tinks's room to fall across the darkened hall. The rumble of Remy's husky voice gradually came into focus as she sidled up against the wall beside the partially opened door and peeked in through the crack.

"You coulda been hurt. You coulda hurt one of your brothers or sisters. How would you have felt if Ambrose had got his head blown off?"

"I dunno," Tinks mumbled meekly. She sat perched on the edge of her bed, her head down, her hands folded in the lap of her yellow nightie. She had been efficiently washed down and her red hair combed back behind her ears. Remy stood before her with one leg cocked, his hands on his hips, a solemn, expectant look on his face. Tinks peeked up at him and dropped her head again. "Bad, I guess."

"You guess." Remy gave a snort. He raised neither his hand nor his voice, but he brought Tinks to the brink of tears with his next words, just the same. "He's your little brother and he loves you. You remember that the next time you go to do somethin' stupid."

"Yes, sir."

Danielle's eyes widened at her niece's respectful tone.

"And how do you think your *Tante* Danielle feels, you blowin' up the dinner she made for you?"

"But it was gross!"

Remy's expression quelled her protest. "I don't care if it tasted like dog food right outta the can. You hurt her feelings and you oughta be ashamed."

Danielle bit her lip, her own eyes filling with tears of sympathy for Tinks, pity for herself, and tenderness for Remy for him thinking about her feelings. He really was a sweet man. A sweet *young* man, but that didn't matter so much at the moment.

Tinks hung her head even farther and tried unsuccessfully to sniffle back her tears. Remy relented then and sat down beside her on the bed, gathering the little tomboy to him for a bear hug. Tinks wrapped her arms around his brawny neck and cried on his broad shoulder for a couple of minutes. Remy rocked her and murmured to her, his lips brushing her temple every so often. Finally he whispered something in her ear that made her giggle. She sat back on his lap and rubbed her eyes with her fists.

Remy tweaked her nose and winked at her. "Bedtime for you, *pichoutte*."

"What's that mean?" Tinks asked as she scrambled under the covers and Remy tucked her in.

"Little girl."

"Yuk!"

He chuckled and turned toward the door. Too late, Danielle jumped back from the opening. He had seen her clearly. Their eyes had met unerringly in that split second. She cursed her slowing reflexes. They were the first to go. Next she'd be asking people to talk into her good ear.

She turned to make a token attempt at escape, but Remy caught her from behind when she was no more than three steps from Tinks's door.

"Spyin' on me, boss?" he asked softly, his dark eyes twinkling as he neatly trapped her with her back to the wall. He planted a big hand on either side of her shoulders and leaned toward her, giving her a teasing, questioning look. "You checkin' up on me? Hmm?"

Danielle swallowed hard. The inside of her mouth seemed to have turned to cheesecloth the instant Remy had gotten too close. "I—um—well . . . you looked so angry . . ."

"I *was* angry," he admitted. "I've got a helluva temper, *chère*. But it's like that firecracker—one blast and it's all over."

"It's all over all right," Danielle said, seizing the opportunity to steer the conversation away from dangerous territory. "It's all over the kitchen. We'll be cleaning up macaroni until the Second Coming."

"I take it there's no housekeeper?"

"She ran off the day Suzannah and Courtland left. Said something about preferring to take a job as a tour guide in Beirut."

"Yeah, well, some people got no guts atall," he said dryly. "I'll take care of the kitchen tomorrow."

"Thanks." Danielle gave him a wry little smile of appreciation and apology. "Kids, cooking, cleaning. I guess you got more than you bargained for taking this job."

His expression softened as he gazed at her, his eyes looking like black velvet in the dim light of the hall. "I sure did, sugar," he whispered, stepping closer, gently pinning her to the wall with the weight of his solid, muscular body. "I sure did."

Danielle sighed at the feel of him settling against her. He caught the sigh with his mouth the instant before his lips touched hers. It was a gentle kiss, almost tentative at first. He rubbed his lips over hers, softly, giving her the chance to deny him. When she didn't, he took it a step further, tracing the line of her mouth with the tip of his tongue.

Danielle trembled at the effort to resist temptation, but she lost the battle. It had been too long. She had secretly yearned for this while trying to tell herself she didn't need it, could live without it. She had denied herself before, but she couldn't deny herself now. She couldn't deny Remy. Her mouth opened beneath his like a flower opening to the heat of the sun.

He groaned his satisfaction as he wrapped his arms around her and slid his tongue inside her mouth in a languid caress that sapped the strength from her knees. She sagged against him, an electric current of pleasure zipping along her nerves from the spot where his burgeoning arousal nudged her belly.

It felt so good to be wanted, to be touched. She'd lived the last year in a cocoon of solitude. Now her senses were awakening with a sharpness that nearly took her breath away. When Remy broke the kiss and put an inch of space between them, she nearly cried out.

Remy watched her face as Danielle's sanity returned by degrees. Her look of frustration gave way to surprise then to horror then to forced anger. She scowled at him, her dark eyebrows pulling together in annoyance, her wide mouth turning down at the corners.

"You followed me up here 'cause you were afraid I might actually hurt the little demolition expert, no?" he said, taking the offensive before she could tell him he shouldn't have kissed her. He damn well should have kissed her and he intended to go on kissing her. There was no point in arguing about it. "I think you like these kids more than you let on. I think you like 'em a lot."

He spoke the words like a challenge. Her scowl darkened. She didn't want him to think she cared all that much about the little monsters her sister had saddled her with, but he could sense she did. He had seen it in her eyes as she'd held little Eudora. He'd seen it as he'd hauled Tinks out of the kitchen. It was there even now behind the ferocious glare she was directing at his keen insight.

"Bite your tongue," she said, pretending offense.

Remy waggled his eyebrows at her and backed toward the steps with a devilish grin. "I'd rather bite yours."

"I ought to fire you," Danielle threatened, trying her best to ignore the blast of heat that shot through her at his audacious suggestion. "You're insubordinate."

"Yeah, but I'm a helluva kisser, eh, *chère*?"

On that note of truth he turned and trotted down the grand staircase, whistling.

# six

**DANIELLE AWOKE WITH A START, JACKKNIF**-ing upright in bed and gasping for air. Her nightgown was soaked through with sweat. Shaking violently, she wrapped her arms around herself and held on. The room around her was cast in silvery light as a big New Orleans moon shone through the open drapes at the tall windows. Everything was still. Everything was quiet.

It took a moment for her to realize where she was and why she was there. The nightmare had seemed so real. She couldn't shake the feeling that she was in London, in the flat she'd rented in Kensington, facing the bitter accusations of a woman who had been her best friend. It was her punishment that that night should remain so vivid in her mind. Over a year had passed and still she could feel the chill of the night, the knife-edge of the words. She could still smell the scent of the darkroom chemicals that had hung in the air that night, and for an instant everything in the room took on the red haze of the safelight. She could feel the intensity that enveloped her when she worked, pulling around her like a blackout shade, cutting out all distractions that didn't pertain to her art. And the awful stillness that had later pierced through her like a lance plunged into her heart once more.

She jerked around toward the nightstand, automatically reaching for the monitor she had carried with her since arriving at the Beauvais house. It was gone.

Without trying to bring some measure of sanity into the muddle in her mind, Danielle threw back the covers and launched herself from the bed. She didn't stop to put on her robe or her slippers. The panic drove her directly out into the hall.

The house was quiet. It was past two o'clock in the morning. Everyone was asleep. Even the fiendish Jeremy was snug in his bed, dreaming his diabolical dreams. Danielle hurried down the hall, her heart pounding in her breast, her bare feet scuffing along the soft blue runner that covered the hallway. At the door to the nursery she paused and stood there shaking with dread for a fraction of a moment. Then she reached for the crystal knob with a violently trembling hand and let herself into the room.

On the same side of the house as her own room, the nursery was flooded with moonlight. The white furniture glowed with it. In the crib, Eudora lay on her tummy, her cheek pressed to the sheet, eyes closed peacefully, her little mouth a perfect O. Danielle dropped to her knees and stared at the baby, her fingers grasping the bars of the crib like a prisoner clutching at the cell door. She held her breath tight in her lungs as she stared at the baby. Her eyes burned as she held them open, watching for Eudora's back to rise and fall.

When she was certain the baby was breathing properly, she let out a ragged sigh, the worst of the tension draining from her with the expelled air. The shakes returned full force then as she dragged the rocking chair into position beside the crib and crawled into it. They rattled through her like the aftershocks of an earthquake, each one taking a little more of her strength with it. She pulled her feet up onto the seat of the chair and wrapped her arms around her knees unconsciously trying to hold herself together.

Eudora was fine. Everything was all right. Nothing had happened in the time since Danielle had finally succumbed to the need for sleep. She had broken the vigil, but nothing had happened. This wasn't Kensington. This wasn't Ann Fielding's baby.

Gradually the trembling subsided and a blessed numbness drifted through her. Motionless, she sat and watched her niece sleep.

Remy watched from the doorway, his shoulder braced against the jamb. The light that fell upon her face illuminated a kind of pain he'd never known, had never seen. It was so stark, so bleak it took his breath away. She was curled in the chair in a posture designed to shut the world out, but her expression told him she hadn't been successful. He had the feeling that what was hurting her was coming from within and her defenses couldn't guard her against it.

"Danielle," he said softly.

Danielle pulled herself out of her private hell long enough to glance toward the door. She stared at Remy as if he were a trick of the moonlight. He leaned against the door frame with a masculine grace that was both casual and arrogant. His white oxford shirt hung open, revealing a pelt of dark hair swirling over the sculpted muscle of his chest. He was barefoot. His jeans were zipped but not buttoned. The waistband gaped in a little vee where the line of dark hair that bisected his belly disappeared from view. He was a prime example of the male of the species—handsome, virile, strong, but tender. Too bad he was beyond her reach.

"Danielle," he said again when she turned away from him. He padded across the carpet to kneel down by her chair. "What are you doin' here?"

"Watching the baby," she whispered, never taking her eyes off Eudora.

"She's asleep."

"Hmmm."

"You oughta be too."

"I'm fine. What are you doing here?"

"It's my job. I thought I'd better take a peek to make sure she was resting. I never figured I should be checkin' on you too."

"I'm fine," she said again, but still she didn't look at him.

Remy sighed and combed a hand back through his disheveled hair. It would have been apparent to the densest of people that Danielle was not fine. She looked like she was hanging on by a thread. As exhausted as she had appeared to be, she should have been sleeping like a corpse, but here she sat, staring at Eudora Beauvais almost as if she were afraid to look away from the sleeping infant.

Her ash-blond hair was mussed around her head and shoulders in wild disarray. She made no move to smooth it. There were lines of strain around her mouth and one digging a crevice between her eyebrows. None of that did anything to diminish the fact that she was pretty. As she sat there looking cool and aloof in her lavender silk nightgown, Remy wanted to reach up and touch her. He wanted to pull her down onto the floor with him and make love to her on the plush carpet, but he throttled his desires. There was something wrong here and he was going to have to find out what it was before he could begin to help.

Rising to his feet, he held out a hand to Danielle. She glanced at it, but turned her attention back to the baby.

"I'd rather just stay here, thank you. Feel free to go back to bed."

"'I'd rather just stay here, thank you,'" he said, parroting her prim tone. He didn't withdraw his proffered hand, but nodded toward the cushioned window seat. "Come sit with me, *chère*. Come tell ol' Remy what you're doin' here in the middle of the night when all good boss ladies should be sleepin'."

Danielle considered her predicament. Enough reason had returned that she knew he would think her very strange for insisting on remaining in the chair. Not enough had returned to allow her to leave the room. She had no intention of telling him why she had come in here, but it would only pique his curiosity if she refused to talk at all.

Finally she pushed herself out of the rocker. Taking an anxious look at Eudora, she moved toward the window seat and situated herself on the edge of the rose velvet cushion, her back straight, her gaze on the crib. Remy sat opposite her, his back against the wall, left foot planted on the cushion, right one on the floor. Danielle could feel him watching her, waiting for her to say something.

"I had a bad dream," she admitted, not looking at him because it was far from the whole truth.

"About Eudora?"

"I thought I would feel better if I came in here and sat with her."

Silence reigned for a few minutes. Danielle continued watching the baby. She wondered what Remy was thinking. She wondered if he would accept her explanation at face value or if he would try to dig deeper. And she struggled with the conflict within herself. A part of her wanted to tell him the truth. He seemed like such a caring person, an understanding person. But who would ever be able to understand what had happened that night in London? And who would ever be able to forgive her when she couldn't forgive herself? The risk of condemnation wasn't worth the momentary relief she would receive by unburdening herself.

Remy watched her quietly, thoughtfully. He pulled a cigarette out of his shirt pocket and planted it loosely between his lips, inhaling the faint fragrance of the unlit tobacco. The woman before him was a puzzle. She was wealthy, but with none of the airs he associated with breeding and money. She was independent, but he sensed a longing in her, a loneliness. She was confident, but insecure about what he considered to be the most mundane things—cooking and raising kids. She talked as if she would rather have taken a trip to the dentist than take care of her nieces and nephews, yet here she was keeping watch over Eudora in the dead of night like a guardian angel.

Rolling his cigarette between his fingertips, he said, "How come you don't have any babies of your own?"

Danielle started at the sound of his low, rough voice. Or perhaps it was his question that made her flinch. She ordinarily met that sexist query with a sharp "none of your business," but she supposed it was a valid question considering the circumstances.

"I guess I'm just one of those old-fashioned girls who believes in marriage first."

"And how come you've never married?"

Her smile was wistful. "The men who asked were never right and the right man never asked."

Remy pocketed his cigarette again and frowned. "Who is this right man?" he asked a bit gruffly, all his territorial instincts bristling like the ruff on a guard dog. "He got a name?"

"No," Danielle said, amusement distracting her from her watch. She turned a little and settled herself more comfortably on the bench. "I'm a Hamilton, remember? Mr. Right wouldn't be liable to last any longer than the time it would take to get all my monogrammed towels changed."

"You really believe in that curse business, don't you?"

"Oh, it's not the curse," she admitted. "I'm not an easy person to live with. I suppose I take after my father that way. I don't have a very good track record with men. I imagine it's because I'm an artist," she said, glancing back at the sleeping baby, her wry smile fading. "An artist is always married to her work first. It's an obsession. I haven't run across many men willing to play second fiddle to my muse."

Remy leaned forward slowly, a predatory light in his black eyes. His right hand came up to comb Danielle's hair back from her cheek. Anchoring his fingers in the silvery mass, he tilted her head back so she had to look up at him. "Mebbe you just haven't found one man enough to knock your muse for a loop," he drawled in a voice like liquid smoke.

His threat was implicit. He was man enough. Excitement sizzled through Danielle. It swirled around like a whirlpool low in her belly and burned in her breasts. A latent sense of recklessness awakened within her and urged her to lean into him, to press herself against the broad male chest that was covered with curling black hair. She could feel his body heat; it lured her closer, just as the sensuous curve of his lower lip lured her closer.

Crazy, she thought, fighting the primitive urgings of her body. Somewhere she managed to find a cocky smile as she said, "Men have tried and men have died."

"Oh, yeah?" Remy chuckled. His smile flashed in the dark like the blade of a pirate's knife. "Sounds like a challenge to me."

"Sorry, you don't meet the age requirement."

He made a face as he released her and sat back. "You're like a terrier with a rat on that age thing, aren't you? Must be a birthday loomin' on the horizon."

"The big four-oh, if you must know," she said, squaring her shoulders and lifting her chin. "There, I've said it. Now you can slink off and feel properly foolish for coming on to a woman old enough to be your—"

"Lover." The word was a caress coming from his mouth. He said it with all the heated passion the term implied. He said it with the kind of excitement that brought to mind images of rumpled sheets and sweat-slicked skin. Danielle's breath whistled out of her lungs. "So you got a coupla years on me, *chère*. What difference does it make? What's between us has got nothin' to do with age."

"You can say that now, but what will you say when you see my steel-belted foundation garments?" she quipped, swallowing hard as her head swam.

"Kinky." He grinned when she rolled her eyes at him. "You're really that bent outa shape about turnin' forty? What's the big deal? It's only a number. You're a long way from joinin' the prune juice set."

He was right about that. Any other year she would have said the same thing. Age had never mattered to her. It was just that forty was a more significant peak. She was going to be forty and what did she have to show for it? She had a successful career, but she hadn't pursued her career in search of success; she was an artist for the sake of art, not fame. She was wealthy, but she had been born that way; it was no achievement.

Maybe what was bothering her was the fact that in a matter of days she was technically going to be over the hill and she had nothing of significance to show for the climb. As she looked at Eudora she wondered if maybe she had begun to think that children were a way of gauging a life and she had none; she would never have any. She had her art, but her art would not lament her when she was gone.

"You're a beautiful woman, Danielle," Remy whispered.

"And you're the nanny," she countered, using a tone designed to put servants in their place. The trouble was, this Cajun rogue didn't know his place. His dark eyes flashed with a rebellious light as he continued to stare her down.

"What about you?" she asked. "Why aren't there a passel of little Doucets dogging your heels?"

Remy's expression grew thoughtful. He didn't have a very good answer for her question. The fact of the matter was he had always wanted a family, and he still planned on having one. Even though he enjoyed playing the carefree bachelor, he liked the idea of married life—the constancy, the stability, the comfort of a mate. And the truth was he could have had his pick from a number of lovely ladies. One in particular had made it more than clear that she would marry him in a minute if he would but ask the question. But he hadn't asked her and he wasn't sure why. Marie Broussard was exactly what he wanted in a wife—a pretty Cajun girl who shared his values. Problem was he had never quite been able to fall in love with Marie. He liked her fine, but he didn't love her, and he was too much the romantic to settle for less.

He sighed in reflection then raised his eyebrows and turned up the corners of his lips. "You wanna do somethin' to help that situation, *ma chère*?"

Instead of the witty rejoinder he expected, Danielle's eyes went bleak. She turned away from him. "I'm the last person you should ask."

This wasn't about the curse, he thought as he studied her. This wasn't about her upcoming birthday. They were back to the little matter of why she was sitting there in the dark tearing herself up when she should have been asleep.

"You've seen a small sample of my expertise with children," she said sardonically, the thickening in her voice ruining the effect of the sarcasm. "No one's ever going to nominate me for mother of the year."

She had to know herself better than he did, Remy thought; he'd only met her. But he found himself wanting to refute her statement. Maybe that was for his own benefit. Maybe he wanted Danielle to be more adept at motherhood than she really was. Or maybe he was simply responding to the sadness in her voice. Whatever the reason, he acted on his instincts and pulled her back on the window seat, paying no attention to her struggle to resist. He pulled her back into the vee of his legs and hugged her to his chest.

"Mr. Doucet!" she hissed, fighting in vain to pull away as his arms banded like steel around her midsection, beneath the fullest swell of her breasts. He held her as easily as he would have held little Ambrose.

"Hush," he commanded, giving her a squeeze to still her squirming. "You'll wake the baby."

"That should be the least of your worries."

"That threat's losin' its starch, sugar. You aren't gonna fire me; you need me too much. Now lean back here against ol' Remy and stop thinkin' those dark thoghts that haunt your pretty silver eyes."

His insight effectively took the wind from the sails of her indignation. She'd always believed she was a good enough actress to hide the pain, the self-doubt. He had seen through her shield with ease. And he was going to offer her comfort whether she liked it or not.

Slowly the stiffness melted out of her body and she sank back against him. He was as solid as a rock, as warm as a security blanket. It felt much too good to be in his arms. Nothing about this situation was proper, but nothing had ever felt so achingly right. She was too tired to fight it now. She let her head fall back against his chest, her face turning so that her cheek brushed against the soft mat of hair. She breathed deep of the warm, masculine scent of him, and sighed out the last of her resistance.

Remy pressed a kiss into the tangles of her hair and softly sang a few bars of what sounded to her like a Cajun lullaby. He had a wonderful voice. It was as smooth as good whiskey, as seductive as a kiss. Without even realizing it, she snuggled closer into his warmth and her eyelids slid to half-mast. Her gaze was still on the baby, but all the tension associated with that task had left her. She listened to Remy's voice, her brain idly attempting to sort through the words, but the Cajun dialect was as different from the French she had learned as Elizabethan was from modern English.

"What does that mean?" she asked softly, half waiting to hear words of love. Half hoping as her mind drifted into the shadows of sleep.

He smiled against her hair and whispered. "'Workin's too hard and stealin's not right.'"

A soft laugh left her on a puff of air as her eyes shut. "How unromantic."

*"Demander comme moi je t'aimais, ma jolie fille,"* he sang

softly, changing tunes to suit her. *Ask me how much I love you, my pretty girl.*

His heart skipped curiously and he held his breath a minute, wondering if Danielle had noticed. But she had fallen sound asleep in his arms. She lay against him, as trusting as a child, as beautiful as an angel. She was all wrong for him—an *américaine* lady who roamed the world with a restless heart and a hunger for things he couldn't understand. She was the client his sister had warned him away from.

He tightened his arms around her and sighed into her soft wild hair. She may have been all wrong for him, but she felt so right. According to the rules, he wasn't supposed to want her. *But then*, said the little devil on his shoulder, *you ain't never been much for rules*.

*"Mais non, I haven't,"* he murmured, his grin lighting his face like a crescent moon.

# seven

**DANIELLE AWOKE SLOWLY. DURING THE COURSE** of her career she had gotten up at whatever hour was necessary for her to get the shot she wanted, but she was by nature a night person. When she had her choice the most strenuous morning activity she tackled was peeling her eyelids up far enough to focus on the alarm clock by noon. She hadn't voluntarily seen a sunrise since 1981.

An enormous weight fell across the bed, pinning her legs to the mattress. The antique mahogany four-poster rocked beneath her. Obviously, this was an earthquake and the ceiling had fallen on her, she thought, not moving an inch. She decided she could just as well sleep until a rescue team arrived to dig her out of the rubble.

The bed shook again. The weight on her legs crawled its way up toward her head. A long wet tongue slurped over her cheek.

"Wake up, Auntie Dan-L."

Danielle managed to raise one eyelid just enough to make out Ambrose standing beside the bed wearing Smurf pajamas and a pair of black glasses with a big fake nose, bushy eyebrows and mustache attached. His ragged stuffed dog was tucked under his arm.

"Do you want Puppy Chow to kiss you again?"

She turned her head, coming face to face with the Old English sheepdog that had settled on the other pillow. He was as big as a pony and so shaggy the only feature of his head that stood out was the tip of his wet black nose. He slurped her again, point-blank.

"Ugh!" Pulling her pillow over her face as a shield, she spoke to her nephew through it. "Ambrose, this is not your dog."

"Uh-huh."

"No, it isn't." She forced her legs to drop over the side of the bed and struggled to sit up. "I distinctly remember your dog being brown."

The boy giggled as if she'd just said the silliest thing. He grabbed her limp hand and tugged. With wobbling legs and a fuzzy head, Danielle stood up and wandered around the elegant room like a zombie. She ran a hand over her tangled hair and tried to recall her return to bed the night before. The last thing she remembered was the sound of Remy's voice as he sang to her. Glancing back at the rumpled bed, she wondered if he had carried her to it from the nursery. Had he slipped her beneath the sheets, tucked her in, brushed a kiss to her lips?

Heat suffused her at the thought and she shuddered. She was too attracted to him. He was too tempting. He was too young.

She scowled at the reminder.

While she stood lost in thought, Ambrose went about in a businesslike manner, selecting clothes for her to wear, pulling garments out of the closet his mother used for storage. He trailed the clothes across the wild-plum carpet and handed them to Danielle. Automatically she put the articles on over her nightgown without paying any attention to what they were. Her brain had fallen back into the blissful blankness that hovered just above sleep. When she finished dressing, her nephew took her by the hand again and led her away from the bed where the sheepdog had begun chewing on her pillow. He piloted her through the door and down the hall, jabbering all the while about his plans for the day.

"Coffee," she mumbled like one transfixed. "Coffee."

Remy stood in the kitchen with Eudora tucked under one arm and a spatula in his other hand, tending a pan of scrambled eggs on the stove. He glanced up as the door swung open and Ambrose led Danielle in. The air turned hot in his lungs. He uttered a prayer for mercy as his every male molecule snapped to attention.

She looked like an expensive date from a house of ill repute. She wore the same short lavender nightgown she'd had on when he'd last seen her, but over it was a sheer black pegnoir trimmed in lace and belted at the waist with a wide leather strap. A flowered silk scarf was draped jauntily over one shoulder. Her shapely legs were bare to a breathtaking few inches above mid-thigh. One good deep breath and he'd know whether or not she slept in panties.

He could have peeked the night before when he'd carried her back to her room, but that wouldn't have been fair. He wasn't into ogling unconscious women.

Barely conscious now, she shuffled across the floor, her eyes mere slits in her face, chanting, "Coffee . . . coffee . . ."

Remy dropped his spatula and handed her the cup he'd poured for himself. She wrapped both hands around the ceramic mug and brought it to her lips as if it contained the elixir of life. The strong hot liquid seared a bitter path down her throat, leaving behind an aftertaste of chicory. It hit her stomach sizzling and boiling like a witch's brew. The caffeine went directly to her brain, jolting all the little gray cells to life. Her eyes snapped open looking twice their normal size. She stared down into the cup at coffee that was blacker than a bayou at midnight.

Her words came out on a thin breath. "It's a little s-s-strong."

"Good, yes?" Remy said. He leaned close, bracing a hand on the counter on either side of her. He had put Eudora down on the freshly scrubbed floor. The baby crawled off happily in search of toys. "Like coffee oughta be. You like it?"

Danielle managed a wan smile. "Let's say you're not exactly Mrs. Olson."

"Yeah," he drawled, as he shifted his hips and shuffled a little nearer. "Ain't you glad?"

A giddy twitter was her only answer.

"That's a helluva an outfit you got on, *chère*," he said in his dark velvet voice. His black eyes glittered as his smile cut across his face. "You tryin' to tell me somethin'?"

Danielle glanced down at herself. Her jaw dropped so hard it nearly bruised her chest. She looked like she was ready to interview for a job on Bourbon Street. "Holy smoke!"

"My sentiments exactly," he agreed in a lazy drawl. His mustache tugged upward on the right as he let his gaze slide down over her again.

"Doesn't Auntie Dan-L look pretty?" Ambrose asked proudly. "I picked her clothes out myself."

Remy grinned. "You're a man after my own heart, Ambrose. That's a fabulous outfit."

Ambrose beamed behind his goofy glasses. "You really think so?"

"Oh, yeah . . ." His voice dropped another heart-stopping step. "Absolutely."

Danielle turned burgundy in spite of the fact that she thought she was too old to blush. She carefully removed Remy's arm from her path, her stomach flipping over at the feel of muscle and crisp dark hair under her fingertips. She kept an eye on him as she moved prudently away.

He was dressed again in jeans that accented every masculine inch of his lower body, displaying to blatant perfection the impressive part of his anatomy that made him male. Spanning his mile-wide shoulders was a khaki T-shirt emblazoned with a smirking alligator hawking beer. No one had a right to look so sexy so early in the day, Danielle thought crossly as she headed for the door.

"Oh, Danielle," he called. "Would you please pick up that toy car there on the floor before someone trips on it?"

She started to bend over automatically, but caught herself at the feel of her nightgown climbing up the backs of her thighs. She straightened and leveled a narrow-eyed look over her shoulder. "Not a chance, Doucet."

He shrugged and grinned an irrepressibly boyish grin. "Can't blame a guy for tryin'."

No, she couldn't blame him for trying. She blamed herself for wanting him to try. How was she going to get through the next two and a half weeks, she wondered as she showered.

She needed a distraction even more powerful than Remy's male allure. She pondered over that seemingly impossible quest as she dressed in knee-length navy-blue shorts and a prim white sleeveless cotton blouse with a Peter Pan collar. She picked up the scarf Ambrose had chosen for her and fingered the whisper-soft silk. It wasn't that she was falling for the kid, she told herself as she used the scarf to secure her hair at the nape of her neck. Sure, she wasn't falling for Ambrose any more than she was falling for Remy Doucet.

Brother, was Suzannah ever going to pay for this! But revenge would come later. Now she needed a distraction. She needed . . . work. Work! That was it. Few things had ever been able to cut through the concentration she poured into her work. All she had to do was hang a camera around her neck and it would act as a talisman to ward off virile younger men who had no business coming on to her. Virile younger men who sang to her and held her and kissed like bandits, stealing every scrap of common sense she possessed. Virile younger men with dark Cajun voices and pirates' smiles.

Her knees wobbled and her resolve swayed ominously as she rushed to the darkroom where Courtland Beauvais developed his own black and white prints as a hobby. She unlocked the door with the small key that was always left on top of the door frame and fell to her knees on the cool linoleum floor beside her own battered camera bags.

Work. Blessed, glorious work. She would do a perspective of New Orleans. The architecture of New Orleans. No, she needed something more focused than that. The doorways of New Orleans. Yes, that was it. Doorways. She'd do them by sections—the French Quarter, the Garden District, Bourbon Street and Magazine Street. She sighed with relief as a flood of images washed through her brain. This was the perfect diversion. Work was her life, after all.

Ignoring the pang of emptiness that thought brought on, she slipped the camera bag over her shoulder and headed for the stairs.

Remy sat at the kitchen table lingering over another cup of killer coffee and the business section of the *Times-Picayune*. There wasn't a Beauvais in sight. The only sound was the bouncy zydeco music coming from the radio on the counter. Danielle thought the raucous accordion music very nearly drowned out the pounding of her pulse when Remy glanced up and assessed her new outfit with a slight frown.

"Where are the kids?"

"Gone swimmin'. All except the baby. She's down for a nap."

Great. Danielle groaned inwardly. The children were gone, out of the house, out of the picture. She was essentially all alone with Remy Doucet, Cajun hunk of the year. Terrific, she thought with a sinking feeling as she lowered her camera bag to the floor. Where were those rotten kids when she needed them? Her gaze ran around the room in the attempt to find something to look at besides Remy.

"How did you get this room so clean so fast?" She hadn't noticed on her initial trip into the kitchen, but there wasn't a trace of last night's disaster. She couldn't spot a single worm of macaroni anywhere. No one coming into the room now would have guessed her dinner had been so inedible the children had felt compelled to blow it up.

"I told the kids they had to help me or they couldn't go swimmin' with their friends."

"Extortion." Danielle nodded her approval. "Why didn't I think of that?"

She poured herself half a cup of coffee and filled the mug the rest of the way with tap water. One sip of Cajun coffee had been enough. With a belated look of disbelief she slid down onto a chair kitty-corner from Remy at the table. "The Beauvais kids have friends?"

"Saw them with my own eyes. Hard to believe, isn't it?"

"Oh," she said on a wistful sigh. "I guess they have their moments when they seem almost humanoid."

Remy studied her expression as she gazed off into space. He set his paper aside and leaned his forearms on the table. "They're not so different from regular kids. They just need a little discipline is all."

"You're very good with them," Danielle said, trying to sound like a boss complimenting an employee. Recalling lessons in deportment, she sat straight in her chair as she sipped her watered-down coffee and nibbled on a beignet. "How did you become interested in being a nanny?"

Remy glanced away guiltily. She wasn't likely to be pleased if he told her he'd taken the job on a dare. He didn't like lying to her either. He swallowed hard as the noose he'd made tightened around his throat. The little devil on his shoulder came to the rescue.

*You don't have to lie. Just don't tell the truth.*

"Oh, well," he began, his roguish grin firmly in place once

again. "There's lots of Doucets back on the Bayou Noir. I've been takin' care of nieces and nephews and cousins and all for years. It's sort of a family calling, don'tcha know. My sister Giselle has made a great success of her agency here in N'Awlins." And she will whip my sorry behind if I screw this up, he reminded himself. "I'm countin' this all as good practice for when I have kids of my own, aren't you?"

"Me?" Danielle fidgeted on her chair. "What would I do with kids?"

"Love them," he said simply.

Dodging his steady dark gaze, she tore off a crumb of beignet and ate it, daintily licking powdered sugar from the tip of her index finger. Love them. Didn't he know that love wasn't always enough? Obviously not. He was talented with children. The talented could never quite understand how special their gift was or how rare. Perilously close to falling into melancholy, Danielle fought off the feeling with dry humor. "How could I have kids? I'd need a bigger apartment, more luggage, a man."

"You asking for volunteers?" Remy's eyes lit up. His voice dropped a sexy notch. "Go put that other outfit back on and we'll talk."

"Somehow I don't think that costume would inspire much talk," Danielle said dryly.

"No," he agreed with a predatory smile. "But it sure would inspire a whole lotta action."

Making a supreme effort to bring the conversation back to a nonsexual level, Danielle put on her best business face and said, "I'm normally on the road. My work isn't conducive to home and hearth."

Remy frowned. "It sounds to me like your life isn't conducive to anything but loneliness."

The accuracy of his observation stunned her. And it surprised her. She had never considered her life lonely. She had friends and colleagues all over the world. She loved her work. But what she had lived with over this past year was exactly what Remy had said—loneliness, loneliness that had little to do with the solitary life she'd led in Tibet; it went much deeper than that. His statement also unnerved her, but she wasn't about to let him see that.

"I love my life," she said. "I get restless stuck in one place too long. I love to travel, see the world, meet people."

"So I guess you'll be leavin' N'Awlins once Mrs. Beauvais gets back."

She pushed her chair back from the table and stood. "There's nothing holding me here."

Before she realized what was happening, Remy was out of his chair and she was wrapped in his arms, up to her ears in Cajun charm. His pirate's grin slashed across his dark face and his ink-black hair tumbled across his forehead as he bent her back over his hard-muscled arm. "I'm holding you here, darlin'. Wanna dance?"

"You're a lunatic," Danielle said breathlessly, amazed at his mercurial change of mood. She thought she was going to melt where her thighs pressed to his. He was as solid as an oak tree and as easily moved. Her struggling only resulted in bringing her into even more intimate contact with him, her pelvis arching into his as she pressed her palms against his chest for leverage. She scowled at him. "If I hadn't been so desperate. I would have checked your references."

He quirked a brow. "Desperate for me? I like the sound of that."

"Oh, yeah? Do you like the sound of bones breaking? I'm going to punch you if you don't let me go."

He straightened, flung her out away from him by one arm, twirled her around and pulled her back into his arms so that she landed with a thud against his chest—if anything, even closer than she had been before. He adopted a look much too innocent to be trusted. "You'd punch me out for giving you a dance lesson?"

"Dance lesson, my foot."

Her heart had gone on a rampage, pounding against not only her breast but Remy's as well. She could feel the sharp rise and fall of his chest as he, too, struggled for a good deep breath. Knowledge that he was every bit as aroused as she was only served to heighten the excitement she was trying to fight. She had sworn to herself she was going to stay away from him, but she hadn't been pressed up against his body at the time. If that wasn't enough to make a woman willing to throw caution to the winds, nothing was.

The music coming from the radio had turned sultry. "Yellow Moon," a sexy song by the Neville Brothers, a song that inspired swaying hips, a song designed to ignite forbidden fires—as if her fires needed any additional fuel, Danielle thought. Remy's body picked up the rhythm of the music and he began to move automatically, almost absently, as if dancing were as natural to him as walking.

"Let's go dancin' tonight. Beausoleil's at the Maple Leaf."

"What about the kids?" Danielle asked breathlessly, caught up in the seductive sway of his body and the feel of his big hands on the small of her back.

"We'll get a sitter."

She planted her feet firmly on the linoleum and gave him a look. "*You're* the sitter."

Remy made a face and dipped her. "Such a stickler for details, angel. Loosen up. This is N'Awlins, darlin', the Big Easy. *Laissez les bons temps rouler*—let the good times roll. You gotta go dancin' while you're in N'Awlins. I think it's a city ordinance."

"I'm in trouble then, aren't I?" she said, refusing the call of his senuous movements and resolutely keeping her sneakers rooted to the floor.

"Don't worry. I'll teach you."

"Do you value your feet?"

"Only when I need 'em to walk." His jet eyes gleamed with mischief and his dimple cut deep into his cheek. "If you cripple me too bad, I guess I'll have to spend all my time in bed."

"Think how lonely you'll be," she said, gritting her teeth as her knees began to sway of their own volition.

With his eyes locked on hers, Remy lowered his head and nipped at her lower lip. His voice was as dark and textured as rumpled black satin sheets. "Not if you're there with me, *chère*."

Chemistry is an amazing thing, Danielle reflected dimly as Remy's mouth settled on hers. All Remy had to do was touch her and steam rose. The hot haze of passion clouded her mind, obscuring all thoughts of age and propriety and safety. She forgot she didn't have much luck with men, that she had, for all intents and purposes, given them up. The heat Remy generated against her and within her burned everything else out of her mind.

She melted against him, sighing as he deepened the kiss with masterful strokes of his tongue. Her head swam with the taste and scent of him—warm, dark, utterly masculine, coffee-flavored. Shivers showered down her body as his mustache tickled her upper lip. He laid claim to her mouth with a predatory possessiveness, probing, stroking. His right hand slid from the small of her back up and around her rib cage to claim her swelling breast. He cupped her, kneaded her, groaned into her mouth as his thumb flicked across her nipple. Pressing gently against the tightly knotted flesh, he rubbed in circles, sending shock waves through Danielle that reached clear to her toes.

She found her own hands wandering over the broad expanse of his back, exploring the planes and ridges of hard muscle through the fabric of his T-shirt. It was both exciting and frustrating. She wanted to feel his flesh, bare and warm. She wanted nothing separating her from experiencing the flex and strain of his muscles beneath his smooth skin. His shirt was denying her the privilege and that denial only served to sharpen what was already a rampant hunger.

She discovered the hem and reached beneath it as Remy backed her into the kitchen table. Her hips bumped against the edge of it and she automatically raised up on tiptoe to half sit on the polished pine. Remy nudged her knees apart, stepping in between her legs and pressing himself intimately against her. Danielle raked her short fingernails against his back as he rubbed his erection against her in the same rhythm as he thrust his tongue into her mouth.

The message was unmistakable and irresistible. Still he dragged his mouth to her ear and murmured, "Oh, Danielle, I want you. Let me love you, *chère*. Let me please us both."

Danielle groaned at the raw desire in his voice. It echoed her own. She wanted him more desperately than a five-year-old wants Christmas. Her blood was searing her veins and the heat was pooling into liquid warmth between her thighs. His hips moved against hers insistently. His strong, blunt-tipped fingers massaged her breast. She had no idea how things had gotten so out of control so quickly, but then she was beyond reason.

Remy's hand slid down from her breast to the waistband of her shorts and he deftly popped the button from its mooring.

"No," she whispered, her fingers closing over his before he could lower her zipper. For an instant she almost thought she was going to try to stop him, then her mouth said, "Not here."

Remy turned her hand and brought it against the front of his jeans, cupping her fingers around his sex and groaning as she stroked him through the denim. "We'll go to my room," he growled through his teeth. "It's closer."

"Good day all!" a falsely cheerful voice boomed from the doorway to the back hall.

"Butler!" The name burst from Danielle's lips like a curse.

She leaped away from the table and folded her hands nervously at her waist. "What are you doing out of bed?"

"Stoppin' us from gettin' into it," Remy muttered under his breath. He snatched up the folded newspaper he had left on the table and held it in front of him, trying to look casual. He sent the Scot a fierce scowl.

"I thought it might do me good to move around a wee bit," Butler said. He tightened the sash on his tartan robe and moved gingerly into the kitchen.

"Yeah," Remy agreed, a muscle tightening in his square jaw. "Mebbe you oughta take a *long* walk. Call us when you get to Baton Rouge, we'll come pick you up."

Butler made no comment, but sent him a cool look brimming with smug triumph.

"The children have gone swimming," Danielle said, moving to the counter to pour the butler a cup of Remy's paint-stripping coffee—and to fasten her shorts unobtrusively. "You should have taken advantage of the peace and quiet and rested."

He accepted the mug and raised a pious eyebrow at Remy. "The young charges off swimming and the nanny didna go with them?"

"The nanny stayed here with the baby," Remy said stiffly.

"Indeed," Butler said doubtfully. "With the mistress as well." His gaze dropped to the younger man's hands. "Is that today's paper?"

"Yesterday's," Remy said through his teeth. "Not good for anything but wrappin' fish."

Danielle blushed at the thought of the whopper that paper was presently protecting. Trophy-size. Suitable for mounting. The heat of embarrassment spread out to the tips of her ears. How could she have let Remy get her into such a compromising position? She knew better. Lord, she'd nearly made a fool of herself right smack on her sister's kitchen table! She had to be losing her mind. Senility, that's what it was, the onset of Alzheimer's. She couldn't get involved with a man like Remy Doucet, a man with roots and a yearning for a family.

Her eyes fastened on the camera bag she had abandoned earlier and she fell on it like a drowning woman on a life preserver. Hefting the bag up, she settled the strap on her shoulder and started toward the door. The two men snapped out of their scowling match, their heads swiveling in unison toward her.

"Lass?"

"Hey, where you goin', sugar?"

"To work," she said, steeling herself against the looks of disappointment that were being leveled at her for different reasons. "Where I belong."

# eight

**DANIELLE MANAGED TO ESCAPE REMY AND** the kids all day. After leaving the house in the morning she wandered the City That Care Forgot, doing her darnedest to forget her own cares. It was a fruitless effort. Even though she had cursed Suzannah's grand plan that she be a "family influence," even though she had hired a nanny with every intention of abandoning said nanny with the children, she felt guilty. It was insane, but she sort of missed the sound of death threats and crying.

She walked the few blocks to Magazine Street where she spent the better part of the day photographing the doorways of antique shops. When images of Remy clouded her view, she quickly reminded herself that she was not far from being eligible to join the pricey old merchandise that filled the display windows.

Many of the brick buildings along the street dated back to the seventeen and eighteen hundreds. Their doorways were works of art. They weren't simply the entrances to businesses, they were the faces of buildings that had seen Spanish rule and French, pirates and belles, soldiers and carpetbaggers. They were archways to other eras.

It was a working day, and the shops were open, but the

intensity of the heat and humidity had kept most sane people indoors. That suited Danielle fine; she wasn't feeling a bit sane. She blocked the sultry weather from her mind. So it was ninety-five in the shade and she could have cut the air with a machete. Sweat ran in rivulets between her breasts and down her back. It was nothing compared to the steamy scene she'd shared with Remy in the kitchen. She pulled a battered khaki cap from her camera bag and tugged it on. The subtropical sun couldn't fry her brain any worse than Remy's kisses had.

She was disgusted to find that the concentration she had always been famous for seemed to be eluding her. More often than not she found herself distracted from a shot by thoughts of Remy; mostly choice memories of their near miss on the kitchen table.

It wasn't like her to lose her head that way, she mused as she picked at a scrumptious-looking seafood po'boy sandwich late in the afternoon. She sat at a little wrought-iron table in a sidewalk café in the French Quarter. The bottle of cold mineral water she had ordered went down easily, but she nibbled at the edges of the sandwich like a mouse, not really tasting the freshness of either the bread or the tiny shrimp.

The restlessness within her was a terrible thing. It wasn't the same thing she felt when some faraway place beckoned her muse. This was altogether different. It was almost the same inner turmoil that had driven her from London. She hated this tormenting demon, yet felt almost powerless to resist its command.

Damn Suzannah, she thought, tearing off a bit of bun and tossing it to a pigeon that had come to beg at her feet. If it hadn't been for her half-sister, she would have been off in a place where no one could bother her . . . or depend on her, or expect anything more of her than clicking the hours away with a camera in her hands.

The routine Danielle fell into over the next two days was exhausting, but it effectively kept her away from the Beauvais house. Or, more precisely, away from the inhabitants of the Beauvais house. She rose at the crack of dawn, escaping with camera equipment in tow and returned at the children's bedtime, when Remy was preoccupied. She would bid everyone a good night and then sequester herself in the darkroom past midnight. In the small hours of the morning, she would slip into Eudora's room and watch the baby sleep. She would get precious little sleep herself, dozing off and on, until it was time to start the whole routine over.

The grueling routine kept her away from Butler's too-watchful eye. It kept her away from the children. It kept her away from the temptation of Remy. It was also making her miserable and exhausted. Her nerves were shot. She felt guilty. She felt as if something in her chest were tearing in two. The only way she kept going was by reminding herself it would all be over in two weeks and promising herself she would then crawl off somewhere and sleep for a solid month.

"Or maybe two," she muttered to herself as she hauled her gear up the curving grand staircase and headed down toward the darkroom on the third night of her ordeal.

"Auntie Dan-L!" Ambrose called, scrambling out of his bedroom as she passed. He ran up to her wearing his Smurf pajamas and a Mardi Gras mask made out of blue feathers. His stuffed dog was tucked under his arm. A real dog—a brown and white terrier—scampered along at his feet. The pair skidded to a halt before her. "Where have you been all day?"

"Working. Ambrose, that isn't your dog. What happened to the big shaggy one?"

Ambrose ignored her question in the way only children can. "You work all the time. You missed the fun. Mr. Butler went out to sit in the garden and Tinks bombed him with a water balloon. Splat!" His face lit up with glee as he used his hands to demonstrate the explosion. "Mr. Remy laughed, but I'm the only one that saw him; it's my secret. And then Jeremy put a sock down the toilet and it flooded all over. Dahlia gagged."

Danielle was too weary to fight her smile. She knelt down and ruffled the boy's bright hair. "Sounds like you had quite a day."

"Yup. I missed you, though. I wish you'd stay more."

A lump the size of a Bermuda onion lodged in Danielle's throat at her nephew's candid admission. Ambrose missed her. Sentiment gushed over the dam of her resolve and swamped her. "I missed you too," she whispered.

"Then why do you have to work? Why can't you be with us?"

"It's kind of complicated, Ambrose," she said. It had to do with wanting things she couldn't have and doing something for the greater good of all concerned. She only wished it didn't have to hurt so much.

There was suddenly a thunder of footsteps on the stairs. Danielle turned to see Tinks and Jeremy barreling toward her, looking as if they had just escaped some unnamed terror by the skin of their teeth.

"Hi," Jeremy said between gasps for breath. His eyes fastened on the door behind Danielle, then turned to her. "Can me and Tinks come in the darkroom with you?"

Danielle shook her head, though she was secretly pleased they wanted to spend time with her. Maybe she wasn't as big a flop with kids as she thought. Ambrose missed her. Jeremy and Tinks wanted to be with her. "Nope. Sorry. You know the rules about the darkroom—absolutely no kids allowed. There's too much stuff in there that could hurt you."

Jeremy gave her his best pleading look as Tinks stole a nervous glance over her shoulder. "Aw, come on, Auntie Danielle. Please. It'd be so cool."

Danielle felt herself relenting, but she didn't give in. As

much as she wanted the kids to like her, she had to think of safety first. A darkroom full of chemicals was no place for an insatiably inquisitive nine-year-old and his anything-on-a-dare little sister. "Nope. I can't let you, guys."

They were about to really start begging when heavier footsteps sounded on the stairs. Tinks and Jeremy both went a little pale beneath their freckles. The terrier whined. Ambrose giggled.

Remy appeared on the landing like an avenging Cajun god—big, dark, and brooding. His gaze flicked over Danielle but homed in quickly on Tinks and Jeremy. As he stalked down the hall, his expression ominous, he raised a hand and pointed at the pair.

"You two, back to the kitchen. Don't you be makin' me any more ticked off than I already am or I'll hand you over to my brother Lucky and let him use you for gator bait."

Without a word, Jeremy and Tinks scooted past him and disappeared down the stairs. Danielle swallowed the disappointment she felt at discovering the children had only wanted to use her and the darkroom for a hideout.

"What have they done now?" she asked, pushing herself to her feet.

Remy planted his hands on his hips and gave her a wry look. "You know that oil portrait of the Beauvais who fought beside Andrew Jackson in the Battle of N'Awlins?"

"The one that hangs in Courtland's study?"

"*Oui*, the very one. The Dynamic Duo decided he'd look better with a mustache and a goatee."

Danielle's face dropped. "They didn't."

"They did. In indelible laundry marker. They are now supposed to be pondering the error of their ways as they scrub the kitchen floor with toothbrushes."

"Mr. Butler got *really-eally* mad," Ambrose added, his eyes bugging out behind his mask.

Remy grimaced at the reminder of Butler, the bane of his existence. Checking his watch, he said, "It's past your bedtime, *'tit chaoui*."

"That means little raccoon," Ambrose explained to Danielle with no small amount of pride. He tugged on her hand so she would bend down for a good-night kiss, then trotted back to his room with the day's mystery dog right behind him.

The instant the boy disappeared Danielle became painfully aware of the fact that she was alone with Remy for the first time since their infamous shake-and-bake kitchen scene. She pulled her camera bag into her arms and hugged it to her.

"Well," she said, her mouth cotton-dry, gaze aimed just to the left of Remy's head. "Guess I'd better get to work. I'm glad to know you're handling everything here while I'm out."

"Oh, I'm real good at handlin' things," he said, his dark voice dripping insinuation. He smiled a little to himself as he watched the color bloom across her gorgeous cheekbones. "Can *I* come in the darkroom with you, Danielle? I'm a big boy."

Was he ever, she thought, not quite able to keep her gaze from flicking hungrily over his muscular frame. Heat swept through her, making a mockery of the mansion's central air-conditioning. "I don't think so," she stammered. "I don't like distractions when I'm working."

Attempting to dismiss him, she turned and took the key down from its hiding place and unlocked the door. He wasn't leaving; she could feel him standing right behind her. "Good night," she mumbled, slipping into the darkroom. She tried to pull the door shut behind her, but one big sneakered foot prevented her.

"This once," Remy said with a boyish grin. "I wanna see what you been doin' all day besides avoiding me."

He muscled his way into the narrow room that had at one time been a gentlemen's dressing room. Danielle scowled at him. "Have you ever considered a career in selling door-to-door?"

Ignoring her sardonic question, he set about exploring the darkroom, keeping one eye on Danielle. She didn't like him trespassing on her private territory and stood in the far corner bristling like a cat. Well, that was just too bad, he thought as he poked around, examining the tanks, print trays, the various bottles of mysterious solutions, the enlarger, the print dryer—the tools of the trade she claimed to prize above all else. He had his doubts about that, but he was going to keep them to himself for the moment.

He'd found several books of her work prominently displayed in the Beauvais library and had studied them intently over the past few days. Even his untrained eye could recognize Danielle's brilliance. She had a wonderful talent for capturing the essence of each person she photographed. The life and thoughts of her subjects were there for all to see—joy, sorrow, innocence, pride, even the most complex mix of emotions came through with striking clarity. Her photographs were so vivid, so true-to-life, they seemed almost three-dimensional.

Her book *Americans* had more than once nearly moved him to tears. A World War II veteran holding hands with the son who had lost his legs in Vietnam as a Memorial Day parade passed before them. A Midwestern farmer and his wife dancing joyously in their yard, arms raised to the heavens as rain poured down to end a summer drought. A homeless woman on the streets of San Francisco holding her child on her lap, her pride shattering as she begged a stranger for spare change.

These were not the photographs of a woman who valued art above all else. These had come from the genius of a woman who was perhaps a bit too sensitive, too insightful. She had laid her own soul bare in her work, and Remy had found himself falling a little more in love with her. He even found himself able to forgive her for abandoning him to the wiles of a dour Scot and a gang of kids destined for reform school.

"If you're through snooping," Danielle said sharply. "I have work to do."

"Mmmmm..." he hummed, working his way back to her corner.

If the lady thought he was going to allow her to avoid him indefinitely after their incomplete chemistry experiment in the kitchen, then she would have to think again. He'd never experienced that kind of spontaneous combustion in his life, and he was willing to bet Danielle hadn't either. That was part of the reason she'd run off, he was sure. It had frightened her to lose control that way. It had excited the hell out of him, but then he wasn't terrified about getting involved. He had decided to let her dodge him for a couple of days, hoping she would come around to his way of thinking. But it looked as if she'd go on running forever if he didn't put a stop to it.

"Are these the pictures you've been taking?" he asked, pulling a stack of black and white photographs off a shelf.

"Feel free to look them over," she said, crossing her arms over her chest.

There had to be a hundred, eight-by-tens and five-by-sevens, light, dark, taken from every conceivable angle. Every one of them of a doorway and nothing more. Photo after photo of closed doors. Remy sorted through them, frowning, his brows drawing together and etching a little worry line into his forehead as he pondered their meaning.

"There's no people in these," he said slowly.

"Darn—knew I forgot something," she said. She slapped her forehead with the palm of her hand. "How absentminded of me." Scooting around him, careful not to touch, she set about preparing everything for developing yet another five rolls of uninspired doorway photos.

Remy set the stack of pictures back where he'd found them

and studied Danielle intently as she poured developer into the tank and checked the thermometer to make sure the temperature was within range. "Why no people?"

"Because I didn't feel like taking pictures of people."

"But you always take pictures of people—people in Tibet, Bora Bora, Des Moines. . . ."

She passed the comment off with a shrug, trying not to take any delight in the fact that he'd been studying up on her.

"You ought to have had people in them."

"Everybody's a critic," she mumbled, too aware that in one corner of her mind she knew he was right. More than once a part of her had prodded her to snap the doorway when a happy patron was leaving a shop with a treasure, or when a bored salesgirl had come out for a breath of air, or when the owner's wife had set out a bowl of milk for some sleek stray cat. But she hadn't taken those pictures. She had waited until the door had closed.

She nervously glanced around. The equipment and chemicals were ready, but she couldn't proceed without turning off the ordinary light and flipping on the dim red safelight, which didn't seem like a good idea at all with Remy in the room.

"I'm takin' the kids to the zoo tomorrow," he said. "Seems to me you got enough pictures of empty doorways to last a while. Come along with us."

She gave him a look. "Spend a day at the zoo with the Beauvais kids? What fun. Couldn't I just stay home and hit my thumb with a hammer?"

"What are you afraid of, sugar? That you might actually enjoy it?" he asked, the light of challenge in his eyes.

That was *exactly* what she was afraid of, but there was no way she would admit it to Remy. She would only be in deeper if she confided in him. There was too much room for error, for rejection, for pain. Taking her cue from him, she simply didn't answer, but went to dig her cameras out of her bag. "How was Butler today? Is his back getting any better?"

Remy rolled his eyes and snorted. "That man is a royal pain in the posterior."

"He happens to be very good at what he does."

"Layin' around and complainin'? *Mais* yeah, I don't guess I've ever seen anybody better at it. He's a master, he is."

"Oh, you're just sore because he interrupted us—" She cursed herself for resurrecting the subject and the memory. Heat flashed through her in a quick burst.

"Sore is a good word," Remy said lazily. He trapped her against the counter with an arm on either side of her and very deliberately snuggled his pelvis up against her bottom, drawing an involuntary gasp from Danielle. "I've still got that ache, *chère*," he said on a low groan. "And now that we're alone mebbe you'll help me do somethin' about it."

"I don't think so." Her voice came out much thinner than she had intended, much less resolute.

"Why not?" Remy asked, deftly turning her in his arms so she could no longer hide her face from him. "I'm attracted. You're attracted. We're both mature adults."

"Some of us more mature than others," she muttered.

Annoyed, Remy snagged a hand in her ponytail and tilted her head back so she had to look him in the eye. "Don't give me that age crap, Danielle. If it doesn't matter to me, then it shouldn't matter to you."

"Well, it does matter to me. I don't think we should get involved."

"That's the trouble with you, angel," he said on a growl. "You think too damn much."

His kiss was hot and hungry. He slanted his mouth across Danielle's with a sense of purpose that sent shock waves to her most feminine parts. To her shame, she did nothing to stop him. Her traitorous needs pushed aside the fears and the doubts and the sense of self-preservation, as she greedily took what Remy offered. As if a switch had been flipped, she stopped thinking and let herself feel.

It was a powerful and frightening force, this desire that sprang up inside her. It was like nothing she'd ever known, and that scared her. If she had never felt this way before in nearly forty years, she thought, chances were she would never feel this way again. This one man might be the only man, and he was all wrong for the kind of life she had chosen.

But none of that mattered now when Remy's mouth was on hers, when his tongue urgently sought out hers. Sinking into bliss, Danielle let herself revel in the experience of kissing him. She soaked up every sensation as if it had been years since he'd last touched her. She enjoyed the brush and tickle of his mustache, the coffee-flavored taste of him, the power in his brawny arms as he held her. She curved her body into his to better feel the hard masculine contours of him, to arch against the evidence of the passion she inspired in him.

Without breaking the kiss, she reached an arm behind her and fumbled blindly with the panel of light switches. Soft white gave way to the hazy red of the safelight, and Danielle thought dimly that she would never feel quite the same way about working under that light again. That soft glow of red would ever after bring to mind hot Louisiana nights and the taste of black coffee and the feel of strong arms.

"*Ah, chère, j'aime te faire l'amour avec toi*," Remy murmured, trailing kisses down the column of her throat as his hands swept up her sides to claim her breasts through the soft peach-colored T-shirt she wore.

She didn't have to understand the words to understand their meaning. He wanted her. She wanted him. With common sense suddenly nowhere in sight, Danielle wasn't sure she could come up with a reason to stop from giving in this time.

As it turned out, she didn't have to. Someone on the other

side of the darkroom door did it for her. At the sound of the knock Remy turned and kicked the baseboard, swearing a blue streak in French, in English, then in a combination of the two. He glared at the door with fire in his eyes.

"This had better be one hell of an emergency!"

Scraping her composure back together, Danielle took a deep breath and pushed the door open, her eyes rounding as she looked at the person standing behind Dahlia Beauvais. Dahlia was looking a little stunned herself as she said, "Mr. Remy, your voodoo priestess is here."

"Voodoo priestess?" Danielle said, her disbelieving gaze darting from the strange woman to Remy.

"Mam'selle Annick," the young woman said, giving Danielle a dramatic bow, holding her slender arms out to the sides and shaking the array of primitive rattles she held in her hands. She wore a multicolored caftan, belted at her tiny waist with about twenty strands of beads. Around her neck were enough necklaces to put Mr. T to shame. She had a ring on every finger and long red false nails. Her makeup looked like something from *Cats*—outrageously outlined dark eyes, overdone brows, long false lashes. Her black hair had been teased into a lion's mane that stood out all around her head.

Remy didn't seem surprised in the least. He scowled at his visitor and said, "Your timin' stinks."

Mademoiselle Annick's eyes twinkled. The corners of her purple-painted mouth twitched a bit. Danielle had the very disconcerting feeling that the woman knew exactly what she had interrupted. She forced the thought away and turned to Remy with her hands on her hips.

"What's this all about? I'll tell you right now, I'm not letting her put a curse on Jeremy—"

Remy shook a finger at her. "You're startin' to like those kids."

Danielle's nose lifted a fraction. "Don't try to distract me with insults. I know he probably deserves worse than anything Vampira here can dish out, but—"

"Don't worry, *chère*," Remy said, leading her out of the darkroom by the elbow. His temper evaporated entirely as he speculated on what was about to happen. "The mam'selle is here to cure your Mr. Butler."

Danielle frowned. "He isn't going to like this."

"That's what I'm countin' on," Remy muttered under his breath. He'd had enough of that old fraud skulking around spying on him and clicking his tongue in reproach at the way Remy dealt with the duties of his station. But mostly he wanted revenge for the interruption in the kitchen. If it hadn't been for the Scot's meddling, Remy was certain Danielle wouldn't have spent the last three days hiding behind her Nikon and he wouldn't have spent the last three nights under the spray of a cold shower.

They made their way back to Butler's quarters, an odd parade with Danielle and Remy leading the way, followed by the bizarre Mam'selle Annick, and trailed by the Beauvais children all bursting with curiosity. Remy flung the door back without knocking. Butler jumped then bent over the putter he'd been practicing with and hobbled across the room to his bed, using the golf club like a cane.

"Time for your medicine, old friend," Remy said with a smirk.

"Butler!" Danielle exclaimed, stomping across the room. "What are you doing out of bed? Your back is never going to heal properly unless you rest it."

Butler flushed guiltily and dodged her gaze. "Just changing the telly," he mumbled, settling back against the pillows.

"There's a remote control for that."

He snorted and waved a hand. "I canna work the blasted thing. Too many wee buttons."

Danielle gave him a doubtful look. Her father's house had

more electronic gadgets in it than a James Bond movie. Unless the old man was getting senile? Her heart sank horribly at the thought of her old Butler going dotty.

Remy rolled his eyes and pulled his priestess into the room, closing the door in the face of their would-be audience. "No need for those useless pills anymore, Mr. Butler," he said with a jovial grin as he ushered Annick toward the bed. "I've got just the thing here for you. Mam'selle Annick, practitioner of the ancient ways, doctor of roots and fruits. She'll fix you right up *bon*."

Annick shot her brother a glance and spoke softly through her teeth so only he could hear. "Giselle will skin us alive if she finds out about this."

He gave her a look brimming with menace. "Then she'd better not find out, *'tite soeur*."

Butler took one look at the startling mam'selle and blanched. Annick rushed up to the side of the bed, gave him a wild-eyed stare, and shook her rattles at him. The old butler snatched up his putter and warded her off as if with the sword of righteousness. "Ye'll not lay one heathen hand on me, witch!"

Danielle watched with growing suspicion as Annick danced around in a circle chanting the words to "Iko, Iko," the old Dixie Cups song, shaking her rattles. Then she tossed some brown powder at him that smelled suspiciously like instant hot cocoa. At the foot of the bed Remy stood with his arms crossed over his chest, fighting a furious battle with laughter, his mustache twitching.

His face red with an oncoming attack of apoplexy, Butler took a poke at the priestess with the golf club. "Be off with ye, heathen wench! I'll have none of your dark ways practiced in this house!" He stole a glance at Danielle and suddenly fell back against his pillows with a pained expression. "Ooooh! I've taxed it again! 'Tis all his fault!" he wailed, pointing an accusatory putter at Remy.

Remy started to protest but was cut off by a dark look from Danielle.

"Okay, folks, the floor show's over," she said dryly, catching hold of the dancing priestess by one of her bead belts, nearly toppling her. She escorted the woman to the door and shooed her out, scattering wide-eyed Beauvaises in every direction. "Send your bill in care of Mr. Doucet," Danielle said with a smile. "And if he doesn't pay promptly, feel free to create a likeness of him and stick it full of pins."

Closing the door in the priestess's face, Danielle turned and regarded Remy with a dire look. "You ought to be ashamed of yourself, perpetrating such a hoax."

"Me?" Remy itched to denounce his adversary. He scowled at Butler, who was looking altogether too smug, and ground his teeth. He couldn't expose the Scot or the Scot would expose him. He couldn't tell Danielle her precious old butler was playing her for a sucker without having her find out that he himself had duped her as well.

"I think you have some apologizing to do, Mr. Doucet," Danielle said primly. "I'll leave you to it."

Remy seethed as Danielle let herself out of the room. He whirled around to shake a finger at Butler. "You're a fraud, old man."

"So are you," Butler volleyed, a truculent gleam in his eye and his putter at the ready.

"Your back isn't any worse than mine."

"And you're no more a nanny than my big toe."

"Seems to me what we've got us here is a good old-fashioned Mexican standoff, Scottie," Remy said, deftly plucking away Butler's putter. He nudged a couple of golf balls out from under the bed skirt with his toe, took a practiced stance, and methodically tapped each across the rug. The first missed its mark by a fraction of an inch. The second rolled precisely into the overturned water glass tucked beneath the armoire. Holding his position, he glanced over at Butler and raised a brow. "What are we gonna do about this, *mon ami*?"

Butler narrowed his shrewd blue eyes, taking in both Remy's face and his grip on the golf club. He seemed to consider for a moment. "You're a golfing man, Mr. Do-sit?"

"Had a nine handicap back in my oil company days."

He nodded and his expression softened a bit, as if Remy's impressive handicap automatically qualified him as a decent sort of person. Finally he tugged close the belt of his plaid robe and said, "I'll no have ye hurt the lass."

"I don't plan on hurting her. Seems to me she's been hurting herself enough, yes?"

"Oh, aye, laddie," Butler murmured. He compressed his mouth briefly, as if warding off an inner pain that had nothing to do with his back. "She has that. She has indeed."

Remy pulled a chair up alongside the bed and settled himself in it, propping his feet up on the mattress. Still playing absently with the putter, he gave Butler a long level look and said, "Why don't you tell ol' Remy all about it?"

Butler stared back at him, outwardly impassive, inwardly pleased.

"It's me," he whispered into the receiver after Remy had gone. "Not to worry. Everything is back on track. Better than ever. Oh, aye, we hit a wee bit of a snag there for a day or two, but it's all coming around. It'll all work out in the end, I'm sure of it."

# nine

**SWITCHING OFF THE LIGHTS IN THE DARK-**room, Danielle let herself out into the hall. She had seen neither Remy nor Butler since the Mam'selle Annick freak-show incident earlier in the evening. She wondered if they had settled their differences. Butler had wasted no opportunity to defame Remy's name to her every chance he'd had over the past few days. And Remy's opinion of Butler was not by any means glowing. The whole thing smacked of jealousy. She smiled a little at the thought, but quickly forced the corners of her mouth back down.

The nursery door stood open and she walked toward it automatically, resigned to taking up her nightly vigil. Her own bed would bring nothing but nightmares.

Remy sat in the rocker, moving it slightly to and fro. His hair was tousled, gleaming faintly in the pale light. He wore the same unbuttoned white oxford shirt he had the first night. His unlit cigarette dangled from his lip. Snuggled into the crook of his brawny arm was the baby, sleeping peacefully as Remy sang to her in a whisper-soft voice.

Danielle knew she should turn and run. Her instincts were

telling her to get far away as fast as she could. But she couldn't move. She was rooted to the spot and the scene before her worked its magic with a swiftness that took her breath away.

What could have looked more precious, more loving, than the sight of a big tough macho guy like Remy Doucet holding a baby in fuzzy pajamas? He was the picture of raw virility, yet he held Eudora with such care, such tenderness. And his voice, so low and rough, was as soft as eiderdown as he sang to her in the language he knew first and best.

He looked up at her and she knew it was too late to back out.

"That was lovely," she whispered, taking another hesitant step toward him. "What was it about?"

"A guy who gets steamed at his pal for raidin' his trotlines. They beat each other senseless then go off together to drink and complain about the cruelty of women."

"Charming."

"It's my brother's favorite."

"He must be quite a guy."

Remy thought about it and decided to reserve comment. He loved his brother Etienne, nicknamed Lucky. Lucky's reputation with women was notorious, however, and every girl in Partout Parish had been in love with him at one time or another. Lucky, of course, had never let any woman steal his heart or his freedom, but that had only spurred the feminine instinct to domesticate him. It was a strange phenomenon and not one Remy cared to test with Danielle. He planned to keep her all to himself.

His little heart-to-heart with Butler had been enlightening. He wondered now how much he should let Danielle know he knew. He certainly wouldn't tell her about the little alliance he and the old man had formed. At best she'd have their hides if she found out about that. As for the rest, he decided he should play it by ear.

"I was heading for bed," Danielle said. "Thought I'd take a peek in here first."

"Mmm."

She glanced at the baby. "I can see she's fine, so . . ."

She looked even more hesitant about leaving the room than coming in. Remy's heart twisted with sympathy for her. She would have denied it with her last breath, but she was afraid to leave the baby. Remy had sensed that the first night. He'd sensed it every time he had come to check on the baby and had found Danielle sitting in the very chair he sat in now, keeping a silent vigil over her niece. He hadn't intruded those nights. He had simply watched her from the covering darkness of the hall. Now he knew Danielle's secret. Even if he hadn't known, he had seen the fear in her eyes. He had sensed the conflict within her that tore at her soul every night.

Rising carefully out of the rocker, he leaned over the crib and settled Eudora in among her stuffed toys and teething rings, then covered her with a light blanket. When he turned Danielle's gaze darted from the baby to him and back again.

"Maybe I'll sit here for a while and unwind," she said, her voice nowhere near as confident as she would have liked.

She took a step toward the rocking chair but Remy turned and caught her shoulders gently with his big hands. She looked at him sharply, unable to decide how she should interpret or reply to his actions.

"She's fine, Danielle," he murmured. "She's just asleep."

"I know that," Danielle said defensively. Her gaze belied her words, though, darting to the child, intent upon seeing the baby's chest rise and fall.

Aching for her, Remy pulled her into his embrace. He wrapped his arms around her and rubbed his cheek against her mane of silvery waves. "It wasn't your fault, darlin'," he whispered.

He knew. Danielle didn't bother to pretend ignorance.

Remy knew about London, about Ann Fielding's baby. Apparently he and Butler had more than buried the hatchet, she thought wryly, feeling betrayed and vulnerable.

"It wasn't your fault," he said again.

Danielle disconnected herself from his embrace, shrugging off the comfort he offered because she didn't believe she deserved it. "Tell that to the woman whose baby died while I was supposed to be watching."

"It wouldn't have made a damn bit of difference if you'd been standing right there."

"Well, I wasn't standing right there," she said bitterly, the old recrimination coming easily to the surface. "I was in my darkroom engrossed in the only thing I do very well or care about at all. I was working instead of watching my friend's baby the way I had promised I would. I was so engrossed in printing my latest masterpiece that I completely forgot Ann's daughter was asleep in the next room. By the time Ann came back her baby was dead."

"Sudden infant death," Remy said, nodding. Butler had explained. Remy had some knowledge about the syndrome from reading Giselle's child-rearing periodicals while he'd been tending the phone at the agency. He knew enough not to condemn the woman before him. "You couldn't have prevented it, Danielle. No one could have."

"I could have been there," she whispered, her voice choked with remembered pain and regret.

She would have given anything, anything in the world, to relive that night. She would have given her talent if she could have. Tears spilled down her cheeks now as she realized, not for the first time, that nothing she could do now would make amends. No amount of pain, no amount of self-sacrifice, would bring Ann's baby back.

She brought a fist to her mouth and bit down hard on one knuckle as she thought of the tiny life that had slipped away that night, all alone in the darkness of a strange room, with no familiar voice or touch to say good-bye. And the pain sliced her heart in two as if a year hadn't passed, as if enough years could never pass to dull it.

Her shoulders shook convulsively as the sobs wracked her—silent because she didn't want to share them. Still, when Remy turned her and put his arms around her, she didn't fight him. She didn't have the strength. The pain was hers alone to bear, but God help her, she didn't have the strength to turn away his second offer of comfort. It was just another weakness in her. What was one more?

She let her head fall to the broad width of his shoulder. She let him hold her close and kiss her hair. She let herself cry. In her mind she made herself listen again to Ann's bitter accusations. Danielle was not fit to be around children, she had screamed. Danielle was disgustingly selfish and consumed by her work. Danielle was a woman who never deserved to be a mother. And Danielle cried harder because she knew it was all true.

"Don't cry so, darlin'," Remy whispered around the lump in his throat. "Don't cry so, *chère*, you're breakin' my heart."

He hurt so for her, he nearly couldn't stand it. Strong, independent Danielle. Danielle, who professed to need no ties. She was trembling in his arms as if the very last ounce of her inner strength was being wrung from her.

"Now you see why I don't belong here," she murmured. "She never should have asked."

"No," Remy said, holding her tighter. "Now I see exactly why she asked." He could also see how deeply Suzannah Beauvais cared for her half sister and how that love was returned. That Danielle would put herself through such emotional hell just because Suzannah had asked her told him a lot. "She asked because she trusts you."

"Trusted me to hire you, maybe," Danielle conceded. "More likely I was the only person in the western hemisphere who hadn't heard the legend of the Big Bad Beauvais clan. She probably thinks these kids are tough enough to survive anything—even me."

Her voice tightened painfully on those last two words and Remy winced a bit. The lady was hard on herself; not the mark of someone who was habitually selfish. She was unsure of herself; not the sign of a woman so self-possessed that she needed no one else in her life.

"How long are you gonna go on blamin' yourself for somethin' you didn't do?" he asked quietly. "You're only human, Danielle, not God. That baby dyin' was a sad, sad thing, but you didn't cause it. It's somethin' that happens. We don't know why. We can do our grieving, then get on with our lives."

"How can Ann get on with her life? She lost her child."

"And I can't even imagine her pain. But what good will it be for her to let it go on forever? Then two lives are lost, not one, you see. Where is the sense in that? Don't throw your life away, too, Danielle. It won't bring that baby back. You let the guilt drive you away from your family, away from your art, maybe even from me, yes?"

"No!" she said, realizing too late that she was neatly trapped. If she was denying only the last of the statement, then she was admitting that the first part was true. If she thought she was denying the whole charge, then he would know that she was lying. She had banished herself to Tibet to take pictures of bleakness. She had cut people out of her life, thinking to save them from her selfishness. And nothing she had done had made any difference.

He had her dead to rights. The man was too blasted insightful. Since when had men become insightful? Wasn't that against the rules of machismo? Glancing up at Remy, she almost laughed. There hadn't been a rule made this rogue wouldn't go over, under, or around.

"You're a weasel," she said.

"I'm your friend."

That was true, she thought, a little amazed.

Remy smiled gently. "So you gonna stop taking pictures of closed doors and start livin' again, *chère*? Let some of those doors open?"

"Where did you get to be so smart?" she asked dryly, trying to keep herself from bursting into tears of gratitude. "Nanny school?"

Remy bit back his grimace of guilt. This didn't seem the time for a confession that would brand him a fraud. "Just runs in the family, I guess."

"Well, wherever it comes from," she whispered hoarsely, "thanks."

Remy lowered his head and nuzzled her cheek, coaxing her to turn her lips to meet his. She kissed him, her arms sliding up around his neck, her body still pressed limply to his. He had been her anchor as the storm of her emotions had battered her. Now she clung to him still, too spent to let go of his strength. She allowed him to kiss her deeply and thoroughly, but when the kiss was finished she peeled herself away from him and stepped back.

"We shouldn't."

There wasn't much conviction in her voice, Remy noted. His conscience pointed out to him that only a scoundrel would take advantage of her vulnerability. The little devil on his shoulder rationalized that what Danielle needed was a diversion from her emotional self-flagellation. She needed some fun, some renowned Doucet-brand T.L.C. She needed to get involved again with life and with people. She might as well start by getting involved with him.

"Why shouldn't we?" he said, his gaze full of challenge. "We're both adults. We know what we want. Hell, sugar, let's be honest. We've both wanted it since the minute you opened that front door and found me on the other side."

Danielle felt the undeniable tingle of temptation as she looked at him. He was impossibly sexy. His shirt hung open, draping down from massive shoulders to frame a thick chest. A carpet of black curls over sculptured muscle thinned at his washboard belly and disappeared into the low-riding waistband of his jeans. But more than this breathtaking masculine vision, she was attracted most by his expression—teasing and tender, sweet and mischievous. The look in his dark eyes invited her to run wild with him, to give in to temptation, to indulge the desires she had been trying for days to repress. She felt more alive just looking at him. The sexual energy rolled off him in waves and heightened her awareness both of him and of her own long-neglected needs.

"There are a million reasons we shouldn't," she said, praying he wouldn't ask her to name them.

With a sexy swagger he closed the distance she had put between them. That devilish light was dancing in his eyes. His mustache twitched up at the corners in a smile reminiscent of a cat closing in on a cornered canary. "All of them together don't add up to a flea."

He put his hands on her shoulders then slid them deliberately down her sides and around to the small of her back, his thumbs brushing the sides of her breasts as they went. He drew her lower body close to his and began swaying as if in time to some sensuous music only he could hear. "Come on, *chère*, admit it, this attraction is bigger than both of us. Why fight it? This is N'Awlins, *bébé*, let the good times roll."

Danielle's hips had begun to move in time with Remy's. She couldn't seem to stop them. Did she really want to? With him so close, so sexy, inciting her senses to riot, her reasons for not getting involved with him drifted away like smoke. It was remarkable, really, how swiftly and effortlessly he had altered her mood.

She quirked a brow at him. "I ought to roll you right out to the unemployment line."

"We'd both have a lot more fun if you'd roll me to your

bedroom," he said, bending down to nip at her earlobe. "We can both do some real rollin' then, *oui*?"

Danielle's head swam a little at the images that sprang to mind. He was right. Why was she fighting it? She should have been jumping at the chance to have a fling with an incredibly handsome young stud before she was too old and decrepit to enjoy it. Where was the harm? They would be together for a matter of days. What could possibly go wrong in so short a time?

Somewhere in the dim recesses of her mind she knew the something that could go very wrong. She could fall in love with him. But in her current state of mind she dismissed the possibility. She was a Hamilton; relationships never lasted for her. She knew better than to let her heart get too involved. They would enjoy each other, then go their separate ways with fond memories.

Remy knew the instant she decided in his favor. He felt the wall of her resistance crumble. She stopped dancing and looked up at him, her gray eyes clear and earnest in the pale light of the fading moon. He went still and looked down at her, his heart pounding in his chest, suddenly aware of how much this meant to him. He wanted to take away the tension that had painted dark crescents beneath her eyes. He wanted to show her with his body how desirable she was. He wanted to love all the loneliness out of her restless heart and fill it up with passion.

Without a word he took her hand and led her from the room, stopping only to reassure Danielle that the baby was sleeping peacefully. Sliding an arm around her waist, he guided Danielle down the hall to her room. Her step faltered a bit as he bypassed the bed, but she followed him willingly into the spacious bath where moonlight coming through the window gave the white tile a silver glow.

He didn't turn on a light but went to the long marble vanity and lit the three fat fragrant candles that sat on one end. Their light reflected in the mirror and created a lush pool of amber that extended to the shower stall, which was walled by frosted glass on two sides.

Danielle's knees trembled and her insides turned warm and syrupy at the memory of the day they had met when she had first pictured them together under the hot spray of the shower. The reality was at hand. Remy adjusted the faucets in the stall and by the time he turned toward her steam was already beginning to rise, lending their surroundings an ethereal, mystical quality.

He faced her and slowly shrugged the white shirt from his shoulders, letting it fall to the tile floor. Danielle didn't try to resist the urge to touch him. She raised her hands to his chest and splayed her fingers wide as if to touch as much of him in one stroke as possible. His nostrils flared as she drew her fingertips downward, tracing every ridge and valley of muscle, skimming his rib cage and catching in the waistband of his jeans. He sucked in a breath through his teeth as she teased him, slowly dragging her fingers along just inside his pants to the button. Holding his gaze, she released the metal disk from the buttonhole and traced the newly revealed skin. As she lowered his zipper, he hooked his thumbs in the waist of both jeans and briefs and was out of them in two smooth steps.

He stood back then a little, letting Danielle look her fill. Her mouth went dry at the sight of him magnificently naked in the flickering candlelight. He looked a little primitive and all male, his body a solid block of muscle sculpted by nature into a masterpiece—upper body a powerful wedge, hips trim, thighs sturdy, and at the juncture of those thighs thickening evidence of his desire for her. He grew hard as she watched and the word "magnificent" suddenly took on a whole new meaning for her.

He was easily the most beautiful man she'd ever seen. She made that judgment with the objectivity of an artist. The woman in her agreed wholeheartedly. The woman in her longed to touch, to taste, to experience. She stepped forward. He stepped back, shaking his dark head, a lazy smile carving out the dimple in his cheek.

"Your turn, angel," he murmured. "I like to look too."

Danielle's fingers trembled as she fumbled with the fastening of her shorts. Every insecurity she had about her age came rushing to the surface, but there was no turning back now. She hesitated, glancing up at Remy with a narrow-eyed glare.

"One crack about cellulite and you're a dead man."

Remy's heart melted. If the lady had any idea how much he already loved her, she'd have run like hell. Danielle wasn't ready to hear professions of love. He knew without asking that she thought this would be a short-term affair. He had every intention of proving her wrong, but no intention of tipping his hand at this point.

He moved closer and reached out to cover her hands with his own. Pushing downward, he whispered, "You don't have any idea how beautiful you are, how hot you make me." The shorts dropped to the floor. "How I've dreamed every night about seein' you naked, about touchin' you." He released her right hand and touched her through her panties, sliding his fingers slowly between her legs and rubbing the silk against the tender flesh that was already hot and moist. His voice dropped another rough note. "About havin' you touch me."

Still massaging her with one hand, he drew her hand to his erection and hissed through his teeth as her cool fingers closed around him. His chest rose and fell like bellows as she explored him, stroking the rigid length of him, fingering the velvety tip.

"Oh, Remy," she whispered, her breath shuddering out of her. She felt vaguely faint at the prospect of joining with him. She felt too dizzy to finish undressing herself and decided instead to indulge one of her own fantasies. Looking up at him, her eyes hooded with passion she murmured. "Take off my blouse."

Remy thanked heaven Danielle was wearing a T-shirt and nothing with buttons, because he would have died of frustration getting her out of it. His hands shook violently as he pulled the top up and over her head and flung it aside. All thought of just looking was vaporized as his hungry gaze swept over her body. Her breasts were high and firm, small enough that she could get away without wearing a bra, full enough to make a man's hands itch to touch them—which Remy did not hesitate to do.

He cupped her breasts, one in each hand, and brushed his thumbs over her dark nipples, wringing a gasp from her. The gasp turned to a groan as he quickly bent his head and took first one rigid peak and then the other into his mouth for a hard sucking kiss. His hands swept down over her then, as he returned his mouth hungrily to hers. Tongues dueled and teeth clashed and he hooked his thumbs in the waistband of her panties and jerked them down, pulling her up and against him in his next move, his fingers biting into the soft flesh of her buttocks.

Danielle moaned at the feel of his maleness, hard and hot between them, pressing urgently into the smoothness of her belly as his tongue thrust aggressively into her mouth. She wrapped her arms around the small of his back and slid her hands down over the deliciously rounded swell of his buttocks, squeezing and kneading. Her right knee pulled upward as they kissed and rubbed sensuously against the outer part of his thigh, climbing higher with each stroke of his tongue.

He carried her into the shower, breaking their kiss only long enough to open the glass door to the stall. Danielle wasn't at all sure the steam rising around them wasn't generated by their passion rather than the hot water raining down out of the showerhead. She'd never felt so consumed by the inner flames of desire as she did now. And Remy made his feelings more than clear. He wanted her with an intensity that glittered fiercely in his eyes. All the teasing, the mischief, was gone now, replaced by a rapacious desire that made Danielle's blood sing in her veins.

The water pounded down over them, slicking their skin, adding to the heat. Droplets caught in Remy's chest hair and Danielle collected them with her tongue. He stood for the torture until she flicked a drop off one flat nipple. Then a growl rumbled low in his throat and he hauled her up against him for another kiss.

Backing her into a wall covered in smooth tile, he lifted her with a hand on the back of each thigh, tilting her hips toward him. Pulling her legs around his hips, he moaned as he sank into the tight hot pocket of her womanhood. His breath caught in his throat and he whispered to her, urgent words, words of praise, words of sex in a language she didn't speak. The message was plain enough, and Danielle responded by moving against him.

It was wonderful, primal, perfect, she thought. She rejoiced at the feel of him moving inside her and against her, pinning her to the tile. He made love with earthy honesty, holding nothing back. He made her feel more alive than she'd felt in a long, long time. She wanted to tell him so, but there didn't seem to be enough breath in her lungs. Besides, her mouth seemed perfectly happy fused to his, and her brain had other things to think about—like the incredible sensation that was building and building in the pit of her belly. She concentrated on the feeling of it growing and growing with Remy's every thrust, until it burst and she was caught up in the wild whirlwind of the explosion.

She clung to Remy's broad shoulders as he, too, surrendered to a shuddering climax. In the end they were both gasping for breath. Danielle managed a weary smile and coughed.

"I'm drowning," she mumbled.

"Oh . . . me, too, *chère*. That was incredible."

"No. I mean—" She coughed again. "I'm really drowning."

"Huh?" He raised his head from her shoulder and his eyes widened as he realized the spray of the shower was hitting her full force in the face. "Oh, jeeze. I'm sorry, darlin'."

"It's okay," she said. He slid out of her but held her close still. They leaned against each other as if for support. Danielle wound her arms around his waist. "What a way to go."

Remy picked up the thick bar of imported soap and began running it up and down her back, smiling as she arched against his touch like a cat. His hands brushed the suds down over her hips to her delightfully rounded derriere and he shook his head slightly at her insecurity about her looks. She had a body a lot of younger women would have wanted. A lot of men, too, he thought, a surge of jealousy burning through him. Danielle was a very desirable woman. It was his job to prove that to her tonight.

Stepping back, he brought his hands around to the front of her and began the process all over again, slicking bubbles over her breasts, her belly. He lowered his head and kissed her as he teased her mercilessly with the bar of soap, until she was gasping for mercy. Then she managed to wrest the bar away from him and set off to do a little teasing of her own.

They made love again under the spray, then dried each other with thick towels. Remy put the candles out and ushered Danielle from the room, turning on a small table lamp as they returned to her bedroom.

"Will you stay with me?" she asked quietly, feeling suddenly uncertain again. It had been a long time since she'd shared a bed. It had been forever since she'd wanted to as badly as she did now.

He turned her by her shoulders and looked into her eyes, reading secrets in their pewter depths that she couldn't hide from him now, so close after they had shared the ultimate physical intimacy. Love and protectiveness swelled in his heart. He caught her chin in his hand and gave her a fierce, sexy look. "You try to send me away, sugar."

One corner of her mouth tilted up in a shadow of a familiar, wry smile. "I'd rather do the opposite. Wouldn't you?"

Remy chuckled and tumbled her onto the bed, rolling them over until he was on top and he held Danielle's arms pressed to the mattress above her head. Dark eyes glittering, he leaned down and flicked his tongue across her nipple.

"Oh . . . absolutely, darlin'. Absolutely."

# ten

**"FIVE BEAUVAIS TURNED LOOSE ON AN UN-**suspecting public with only two adults to supervise," Danielle murmured, shuddering involuntarily.

She stood on the side veranda in a black tank top and khaki walking shorts, staring apprehensively at the loaded minivan in the driveway. The older children had already settled into the vehicle after a spirited battle for choice seats. Dahlia was sitting on the far side in the backseat, only her silhouette visible due to the shade of an enormous magnolia tree and the shadow cast by the wide brim of her straw hat. Danielle thought she was being a little too unobtrusive and made a mental note to check for makeup before they pulled out. Ambrose sat at the opposite window wearing a pirate eye patch and a bandana tied around his head. Tinks and Jeremy had commandeered the seats in the far back of the vehicle. At the present moment, however, Jeremy was attempting to lower Tinks to the pavement by her ankles through the opened back window.

"Jeremy, haul your sister back inside and behave yourself!" Remy called calmly, stepping out the door with Eudora on one arm. On the other hung an umbrella stroller, its handles hooked around his forearm. Over his shoulder was slung a blindingly pink diaper bag. The picture he presented was incongruous and adorable.

"I don't know about this, Remy." Danielle shot him a glance. "Are you sure we can do it?"

Remy's gaze immediately turned hotter than the Louisiana summer. "I suppose we could call off this little field trip, lock ourselves in your room, and spend the day findin' out." His eyelashes swept down like black lace fans. His voice was like liquid smoke. "But after last night, I don't know how you can ask."

Danielle blushed to the roots of her hair. "That's not what I meant!"

He clucked his tongue in reproach. "You gotta stop leadin' me on this way, Danielle."

"Leading you on?" Danielle sputtered, briefly considering smacking him with her camera bag. "I ought to lead you to the unemployment line."

"But you need me," he singsonged.

She pretended a scowl. "I refuse to answer that on the grounds that you will turn it into a sexual innuendo."

"Sexual innuendo." He growled and leaned toward her, his eyelids drooping lazily. "I love the way you say that. It sounds so kinky. Will you whisper it in my ear?"

"I'll box your ear." Danielle fought the giggles that threatened and snatched the baby away from him. "You should be ashamed, saying things like that in front of an impressionable child."

She tried to straighten the impossibly crooked yellow bow she had tied in a strand of Eudora's red hair. The baby squealed a protest and sprayed the front of Danielle's blouse with spittle.

"That'll be an interesting defense mechanism when she's old enough to date," Danielle said, unaffected. She was in too good a mood to let a little saliva ruin her day. She snatched a towel out of a pouch on the diaper bag and repaired the damage as best she could.

Butler came to the door to see them off. He stooped over and hung onto the brass doorknob for support, going through his repertoire of pained faces. "I'm sorry I canna go with ye, lass," he said, looking properly contrite.

"Me too." Danielle suspiciously eyed the plaid golf slacks peeking out beneath the hem of his robe. "You know, Butler, the walk might do you good."

"Oh, no," Remy blurted out. "Rest and relaxation." He gave her an annoyed glance and started for the van. "The man oughta know his own back, Danielle."

"Wise, wise," Butler chanted, nodding sagely, gazing off after Remy with approval. "And a braw handsome lad too. Och, a lass could do worse."

Danielle gave him a strange look. "Stay out of the sun, Butler. You're not used to all this heat. I think it's affecting you."

They loaded the baby into her car seat, then settled in themselves, Remy behind the wheel. Dahlia was sent back to the house to remove the half-pound of makeup she had worn. Ambrose waited until they were to the end of the driveway to decide he had to go to the bathroom. They had to pull over when Jeremy and Tinks fell on each other in mortal combat over who could spit the farthest. But eventually they made it to the zoo.

The day was hot and clear, the butter-yellow sunshine filtering down through the haze of humidity to which Danielle was gradually becoming accustomed. It was the heart of summer in the Deep South, hot, sultry, semitropical. If her crisp cotton shorts were wilted before they made it through the entry gate, then everyone else around her was wilted too. Except Remy. He didn't look wilted, she thought as she took in his outfit of cuffed black walking shorts that molded his fabulous fanny and a loose white shirt that accented his dark skin. He looked wonderful... touchable... good enough to eat.

He caught her looking and sent her a secret smile. Danielle felt the now familiar zip of electricity racing through her to curl her toes inside her canvas sneakers. She smiled back, feeling like a giddy teenager with her first big crush on the football captain.

They had made love long into the night, Remy tapping a well of sexuality in her she hadn't known existed. He had slept in her bed till dawn, then crept back to his own room before the children woke. One night in Remy's arms had left her feeling full of life's joy and ready to take on any challenge—even supervising her nieces and nephews at the zoo. The quiet talk she and Remy had shared, both in the nursery and later in bed, had soothed her fears about her abilities to handle and relate to children. He had told her to relax and not worry so much about goofing up on little things, and she had decided to take his advice. He was the expert, after all. Besides, trying a fresh approach was certainly better than being miserable with the status quo.

They strolled the paths together at Remy's stern insistence. Dahlia led the way, staying just enough in front of them so she wouldn't feel embarrassed by being with "kids." Jeremy and Tinks came next. Jeremy in a camouflage cap, Tinks in a plastic pith helmet. Both of them with their eyes peeled for misadventure. Remy pushed Eudora in the stroller. Danielle held hands with Ambrose, who had added a blue Audubon Zoo visor to his pirate getup.

Also there at Remy's insistence was Danielle's trusty Nikon, hanging around her neck like an amulet. He encouraged her to take pictures of everything and, more importantly, every*one*. And for the first time in a year she broke her self-imposed ban on photographing people. She photographed the children, the animals, the zookeepers, men in Bermuda shorts and black socks, women who had attempted to squeeze winter-fat bodies into summer spandex outfits. It was like breaking a fast. She started slowly, then made a glutton of herself. By lunchtime she had gone through five rolls of film.

And as they walked along, browsing at flamingos and sea lions and tigers, Danielle let herself fantasize that they were a family, she and Remy and the Beauvais brood—just to see what it would be like. It wasn't that she had any intention of marrying and having five children. Not at all, she assured herself. She was merely a little curious, that was all.

It felt okay.

It felt nice.

*The day was not without its little incidents.*

*Jeremy, leave those snakes alone... So sorry, sir. We adopted him from a circus. One can only imagine the kind of upbringing a child receives from clowns.*

*Jeremy, where's Tinks? What do you mean she found a hole in the fence?*

*Sorry, ma'am, I'm sure she didn't realize it was an endangered species.*

*Tinks, where's your brother?... What wading pond?... The one by the alliga—!*

"It's too bad we missed your sister today," Danielle said. "I would have liked to meet her. She must have just missed us."

"Yeah," Remy said with a notable lack of remorse. "What a shame."

He cast a glance heavenward and thanked that little angel he so often ignored. He shuddered to think what kind of shape he'd be in now if it had been Giselle at the darkroom door last night rather than Annick. His conscience pricked him at the reminder of the little secret he was still keeping from Danielle, but he ignored it. There was plenty of time to tell her he wasn't exactly a nanny. Besides, everything was going perfectly as far as he could see. He had more important things on his mind tonight.

"Have you really been to all those places you were tellin' the kids about tonight?" Remy asked.

They were comfortably ensconced on the porch swing, Remy leaning back into the corner with his left foot planted on the bench and his right on the floor. Danielle lay against him, her head on his chest, her long legs tucked up on the seat. The children had all been fed, bathed, and put to bed with the array of stuffed animals Danielle had bought for them in the zoo's gift shop. Butler, looking oddly flushed—almost sunburned, Danielle thought—had eaten dinner with them, but had pleaded a headache the instant Danielle had commented on his appearance, and had retired to his quarters.

The Beauvais house was peaceful. The night was full of the sounds of insects, the distant wail of blues from a house down the block. The air was still thick with humidity and the scent of boxwood and roses, sweet olive and dozens of other plants that flourished in the hothouse environment of the Southern summer. Danielle smiled sleepily, comfortable and happy in the oasis of yellow light on the veranda, comfortable leaning against Remy rather than fighting against the attraction she felt for him.

"Sure," she said, around a lazy yawn. "I've been all around the world."

She said it as if it were the most commonplace thing, as if she thought everybody had been to Malta and Taipei and Antarctica. Remy tried to ignore the stirring of nerves in his belly. Of course it was commonplace to Danielle, he told himself. She had traveled from an early age. It was probably old hat, boring stuff to her by now . . . he hoped. Even as he hoped he heard the echo of an earlier conversation when she'd said she loved discovering new places and meeting new people.

A chill chased over his skin despite the fact that the night was hot. He brought a hand up to toy with the wildly curling tendrils of Danielle's hair. So soft, so silvery. A strand coiled naturally around his index finger and he wished it would be so easy to bind her to him. The light glittered off the bracelets that were draped around her delicate wrist like strands of angel's hair and he wished he could somehow use them to chain together their hearts.

He was in love with her. He wasn't precisely certain when it had happened. It might have been when she had turned to him in tears. It might have been when he'd watched her watch the baby sleep. It might have been when she had patiently listened while Ambrose had explained why his stuffed dog needed to sleep with a night-light on. All he knew for certain was he had looked at her today as they had walked along the paths of the zoo and realized that he had finally, really fallen in love.

It scared the hell out of him. All his life he'd just assumed he would fall for a Louisiana girl, if not Marie Broussard, then someone else who shared his background and his beliefs. Never in a million years would he have expected to fall for a long-legged blond Yankee with a wanderlust that put the great explorers to shame. But in love was exactly what he was, he had no doubts. It didn't matter that he'd known Danielle only a matter of days. It didn't matter that she'd fought the attraction between them. He was a man who trusted his instincts and his instincts told him in no uncertain terms that this was the Big L.

The question was, what was he going to do about it? What would Danielle do about it if he told her? She was so cynical about relationships. How many times had she told him hers never lasted?

"Where you gonna go next?" he asked in a tone flat from a complete lack of enthusiasm for the topic.

Danielle hesitated. As eager as she had been to get away from New Orleans two days ago, she had no answer now.

Everything had changed. The situation had changed. Her feelings had changed. *She* had changed. "Uh—I'm not sure." She shifted position so he wouldn't be able to feel her heart pounding and thought, *I'd stay here if you asked me*.

That was silly, of course, she told herself. Why would he ask her to stay? They were having fun together, but they both knew this was only a very temporary arrangement. She was being uncharacteristically fanciful imagining a future with her handsome young lover.

"Ever been to the bayou country?" Remy asked. Hell, what did he have to lose? He was already in over his heart. Maybe if he took Danielle to the muddy banks along the Bayou Noir, she would find a home at last and forget about the allure of all those exotic places her restless heart had taken her.

She turned and looked up at him and his breath caught at the steady searching gaze of her big pewter-colored eyes. "No," she whispered. "Would you take me?"

*"Oui."*

The word was little more than an exhalation of breath as he leaned forward and captured her parted lips with his. Hope welled inside him, pushing out fear for the moment. Then passion swept all of it aside. He wrapped his arms around Danielle and pulled her even tighter against him as he tried to convey his love to her without words.

It was a slow, deep kiss. Danielle drank it in and savored it, thinking it was more intoxicating than the finest wine, more addictive than any drug. She loved the taste of him. She loved the way he kissed. The brush of his mustache against her upper lip sent shivers dancing over her. The feel of him, strong and solid against her, made her feel safe and feminine and cherished. When she was in his arms nothing else mattered.

No sooner had the thought crossed her mind than the baby monitor sitting on the floor crackled. Instantly Danielle stiffened and tried to push herself off Remy, her heart hammering triple time as all manner of horrible scenarios flashed through her mind.

"Hush," he whispered. "Listen."

She tried to swallow her anxiety as Remy reached down and picked up the black box. She watched, her body still tensed and ready to bolt, as he lifted the monitor close to his ear and listened. Slowly a smile curved his mouth and he tipped the monitor to Danielle's ear.

"She's not in trouble," he said, chuckling softly. "She's talkin' in her sleep."

Danielle sagged against him, all strength draining out of her as she listened to the mumbled stream of baby babble. In that instant she thought she'd never heard anything as dear to her ears.

Remy listened some more then set the box back down. "She must have had quite a time today if she's still talkin' about it. What about you, *chère*? What kind of time did you have?"

"I had a wonderful time," Danielle said candidly. She sat up and regarded him with a serious, honest look. "Thank you."

She didn't have to say for what. It was clear to Remy she was thanking him for helping her take the first steps back from her self-imposed sentence of isolation. He had watched her slowly blossom today, filling with glowing energy as she photographed the children discovering the wonders of the zoo, as she made a few discoveries of her own. Having the opportunity to watch that happen was all the thanks he needed.

"You're a beautiful, vital, talented woman, Danielle," he murmured. "The world shouldn't be robbed of you." His mustache quirked up and his dimple dented his cheek. "See, I was the one being selfish, no?"

"No."

Her disagreement elicited nothing more than a Gallic shrug that blithely dismissed the topic. Danielle let the topic slide. There was no point getting maudlin when both of them knew exactly what had happened and why. No matter what the future brought, she would always have a special place in her heart for this man because he had helped her heal a wound that might have ruined her life. She hadn't forgotten what had happened in London. She never would. But it would no longer gnaw at her like a cancer, eating away at her soul, a little bit more each day.

"Well," she said on a sigh, pushing herself off the swing. She stretched like a cat and yawned again. "I guess it's time to call it a day. We should get some rest so we can be ready for whatever diabolical scheme Jeremy has planned for tomorrow."

"You're goin' to bed?"

"I guess," she said, fighting a smile of anticipation. She gave him a long look as electricity crackled in the air between them. "What are you going to do?"

"Me?" Remy got up slowly, making a great show of considering his options. He gave her a bland look that was ruined by the banked fires in his dark eyes. He shuffled a little nearer and a little nearer, until a scant inch of humid air separated them. He traced a finger over the vee of her collarbone. "Me, I thought I might take a *long* shower first."

A feline smile curved Danielle's mouth as she tilted her head and looked at him from under her lashes. "You need any help with that, *cher*?"

# eleven

**"I'M GONNA GO ALL OVER THE WORLD, JUST** like you do, Auntie Danielle," Jeremy said between slurps of cereal. "I'm gonna go all around finding weird animals and catching them like that guy on *Wild Kingdom*."

Danielle beamed. It seemed she'd finally struck a chord with her little relatives by telling them tales of her travels. She felt ridiculously pleased.

Tinks looked up, a milk mustache on her upper lip. "Yeah, and I'm gonna follow him around and take pictures and we'll go all over to places like Africa and Borneo and get shot at by guys with spears like Indiana Jones."

"I'm gonna be a garbage man," Ambrose announced shyly, his cheeks flushed with secret passion.

The other two snorted their derision, Tinks reaching over to push down the brim of Ambrose's black gaucho hat.

"Leave him alone," Remy snapped. "There's nothin' wrong with bein' a garbage man."

Tinks and Jeremy exchanged another glance, deciding by tacit agreement to make their exit before their nanny's temper boiled over. Danielle watched them slink away, followed by Ambrose. The door swung shut and Danielle looked at Remy. He was scowling down at his bowl with a thunderous expression that had apparently scared the snap, crackle, and pop right out of his cereal.

He raised his eyes to her face. "I was a garbage man during the summers when I was in college. You wanna make somethin' of it?"

"No."

"Well, I didn't traipse all over the ever-lovin' world doin' it. I was right here in N'Awlins the whole time." He scraped his chair back from the table and turned to tend Eudora.

So that was what this turn toward churlishness was all about. Danielle raised her eyebrows. Remy had been in a strange mood for two days—ever since their trip to the zoo. In that time Jeremy and Tinks had not stopped pumping her for stories about the exotic places she'd been. She had indulged them enthusiastically, never thinking that Remy might feel left out as she had felt left out many times before. He had managed to shed his temper in time for his midnight visits to her room, but she had to admit his lovemaking had taken on a certain fierceness. Not violence, just a certain edge, as if he were trying to convince her of something.

He had convinced her that he was incredible in bed. She flushed at the thought. He'd taken her places she hadn't dreamed existed. They'd done things she'd only read about in books. It was heady stuff, the intensity of his passion. It made her giddy just thinking about it. It was silly. It was wonderful. It was more than she'd thought she could hope for. It was . . . love.

Oh, no, she thought, pressing a hand to her forehead as if to feel for a fever. It couldn't be love. She was mistaken. She couldn't have fallen in love with him.

She glanced across the room with a kind of desperation, her gaze fastening on Remy as he attempted to hose oatmeal off Eudora with the spray nozzle on the kitchen sink. Her heart rolled over like a trained poodle.

Remy turned, the baby tucked under his arm like a baton.

He draped a dish towel over her head and rubbed at her hair. *"Mon Dieu, chère,"* he said, taking in Danielle's stricken expression. "You look like you got a whiff of the diaper pail. What's wrong?"

"Wrong?" *Oh, nothing. I'm just making a fool of myself, that's all.*

"Look, sugar, I'm sorry I snapped at you. I was worried you might think less of me 'cause I was a garbage man." It was part of the truth, anyway. Remy thought. He was feeling a little too vulnerable to tell her what was really bothering him, namely her attraction to travel. He had tried leaving Louisiana once and had given up his career in order to come back. The thought of leaving again made his heart sink, but the idea of Danielle leaving him behind had much the same effect. Unless he could convince her to stay, it was a no-win situation.

"You were a garbage man in New Orleans in the summer. I think you deserve a medal," she said. "I might have an obscene amount of money in my bank account, but that doesn't make me a snob, you know."

He worked up a wily grin as he took his seat. "How obscene?" He leaned across the corner of the table, staring at her mouth. "Will you whisper it in my ear tonight?"

Danielle rolled her eyes, ignoring the bolt of desire that rammed through her. She watched as Remy perched Eudora on his knee and played peek-a-boo with her with the dish towel. "Are you really supposed to wash babies with the dish sprayer that way?"

"Oh, yeah, absolutely. It's much better than the bathtub."

"Hmm . . . I think you really started something with Jeremy. His sudden interest in zoology is great. Before that trip to the zoo all he ever talked about was living in a secret tunnel in the sewer and robbing banks. You may have gotten him off *America's Most Wanted* and onto *Wild Kingdom*."

"Hard to picture, huh?"

"Yeah. Well, I guess I've pictured him on *Wild Kingdom*, but not in the Jim Fowler role. I can hear Marlin Perkins saying, 'While I repair the tent flap Jim is downstream struggling to subdue Jeremy, the Wild Boy of the Garden District.'"

Remy chuckled. "You're startin' to like that boy."

"I'm sure I'll get over it."

I hope not, sugar, Remy thought, I'm betting my heart on it.

They drove out into the bayou country packed into the minivan like sardines. Going west out of New Orleans they encountered swamps and marshlands as the city faded behind them. The landscape changed to chemical factories with smokestacks thrusting into the sky like rusty exclamation marks. Then came rice paddies and canebrakes and sugarcane processing plants. Miles of elevated highway seemed to float above endless acres of undulating saw grass. Glimpses of bayous spread back into the cypress stands like ink spots. Danielle watched it all roll past with the same kind of wonder she experienced seeing any new place for the first time, her eyes automatically assessing everything she saw for its possible artistic value.

Remy watched her out of the corner of his eye as he drove, taking them off the interstate and into the region of Louisiana known as Acadiana. More than once he realized he was holding his breath, waiting for an adverse reaction. It was terrible how badly he wanted her to like his home country. The potential for disappointment was enormous. He was leaving himself wide open for a broken heart, but then he guessed love wasn't worth much if there wasn't this heightened sense of awareness and fear. It made him feel acutely alive, acutely aware of every nerve ending just under his skin. He kept the Cajun station on the radio turned down to a whisper and still it seemed loud to him as he held his breath and waited for Danielle's verdict.

Suddenly she looked over at him and smiled her wide brilliant smile and said softly, "It's beautiful, Remy." And he felt the dam of tension burst inside him and relief flood through him to the very tips of his fingers and toes.

Luck, Louisiana, ranked just above "wide spot in the road" on Danielle's scale of town sizes. Luck had not one but two traffic lights, although one seemed more than sufficient. The main street boasted the usual small-town businesses. There was a grocery store with a sign in the window advertising a special on crawfish and a butcher shop with a sign in the window saying *"Ici on parle français,"* indicating that French was the language of choice inside.

Luck was shabby and quaint in the way of small towns everywhere, and Danielle fell in love with it on the spot. Her hands itched to pick up her camera and capture it all on film—the restaurant advertising cold Dixie beer and boudin sausage, the thin old men sitting on a bench in front of the hardware store swapping tales of times gone by and watching diligently for strangers, the woman emerging from Yvette's Salon with a fresh permanent.

They drove into a residential area and skipped over a couple of blocks until they found the street that ran parallel to the Bayou Noir, a wide ribbon of sluggish water that was as black as its name promised. The last house along the row of neat bungalows set well back from the bayou belonged to Remy's parents. It was a pretty brick ranch-style house with a screened porch running along the entire front. It was shaded by live oak hung with bunting of gray moss and there was a little flower shrine with a white statue of the Virgin Mary in the middle of the front yard.

Noelle Doucet came out a side door wiping her hands on her apron. She greeted them all with smiles and hugs as if they were relatives who had been too long away from her. She was a small plump woman with sparkling dark eyes. The scent of baking bread clung to her like perfume. She welcomed her son home with a kiss and a rapid stream of French.

"Where's Papa?" he asked.

"Down at Lawrence's gettin' a part for his motor. He'll be back in time for supper. He's never late for a meal, that man." She smiled at Danielle in feminine conspiracy. "Late for his own wedding, yes. Late for supper, *mais non*!"

Remy engulfed her in a big bear hug that had her giggling like a girl of twenty. Danielle looked on, enjoying the sight but feeling a faint twinge at the same time. He looked so young—a grown-up boy teasing his mother, his eyes shining with a distinctive resemblance to Noelle's. "What's for supper, *Maman*?" he asked. "You cookin' my favorites?"

"My gumbo and maquechou and bread puddin' for dessert if you behave yourself, *cher*."

"I guess that means there'll be plenty for the rest of us," Danielle said dryly.

Noelle laughed and disentangled herself from her son's embrace, saying something to him in French that made him blush.

"She's wondering if I've finally brought home a prospective daughter-in-law," Remy whispered to Danielle as his mother busied herself getting acquainted with Butler and the Beauvais children.

Danielle went utterly still, staring up at Remy without the usual snappy rejoinder. Her cheeks grew hot and she cursed her adolescent reaction.

Remy's gaze burned a smoldering shade darker as he studied her. "You're blushin', angel," he murmured, feeling a little flushed himself at the implications of her silence.

"That's not a blush, it's a hot flash," she grumbled. "Early sign of menopause."

Remy chuckled and brushed a kiss to her temple.

"We're going to be a huge imposition on your parents, Remy." The house looked a comfortable size, but it didn't seem big enough to hold them all. Danielle shuddered to think of turning her nieces and nephews loose in someone else's home. God only knew the havoc they would wreak.

"We aren't stayin' here. We'll be at the Hotel Doucet," he said, hooking a thumb in the direction of the bayou.

Danielle squinted against the sun as she looked west. "That looks like a barge."

"You got it in one, *chère*."

They walked over to explore the accommodations, leaving Noelle in her glory serving cookies and lemonade to the children at the picnic table in the backyard. Butler watched Eudora as he sprawled in a chaise on the patio; he waved them off with a placid smile.

"He's certainly changed his tune about you," Danielle said as they crunched down the clamshell path toward the barge.

A secret smile tugged up the corner of Remy's mustache as he thought of the alliance he and the Scot had formed. Once Remy had made it clear he cared deeply for Danielle the irascible old butler had been the picture of cooperation. "Guess he just had to get to know me. To know me is to love me," he said, grinning and batting his thick eyelashes at her.

Wasn't that the truth, Danielle thought, her heart jolting in her chest. She had gotten to know him, had fallen in love with him, and now she was in over her head. It was yet to be determined whether she would sink or swim.

The Hotel Doucet, as Remy called it, was a campboat, a wood-frame house built on the rusting hull of a barge. It had originally belonged to Remy's grandparents, but now served as guest house for visiting relatives when the main house overflowed. The house itself was two stories high and one room wide, the exterior covered in gray cypress shakes. Big sections of the first-floor walls were hinged, raised and propped up on railroad ties, creating a gallery of sorts and revealing huge screens that would let the evening breeze through but keep the insects out.

Much of the deck of the barge had been covered in vibrant green AstroTurf. Halved whiskey barrels squatted in strategic spots, overflowing with geraniums and petunias. A concrete turtle peeked out from under a huge hairy fern. A cherub balanced a bird-bath on one pudgy shoulder. The overall effect was a little like a miniature golf course, but homey and welcoming.

Danielle was delighted. "The kids will love staying here!"

"Yeah, I don't know about you and me, though. It's kinda small." He gave her a long, somber, meaningful look. "We aren't gonna have any . . . privacy."

"Oh."

Her look of disappointment warmed him. He slung an arm around her shoulders and walked her to the bow of the barge. "I know you're sad, sugar, but don't pout. You can live without me for a couple of nights."

Danielle ducked away from him, shooting him a look. "Yeah, I've lived thirty-nine years, three hundred and sixty some nights without you. I think I can manage a couple more."

Remy snatched hold of her hands, pulled her to him, and danced her around the deck, grinning like a pirate. "That wasn't what you were sayin' last night, *chère*."

"Oh! Not fair! The words of a woman on the brink of orgasm cannot be held against her."

"No? Can I be held against her?"

Without waiting for an answer he pulled her into his arms and kissed her soundly. They had danced around to the far side of the house and were out of sight from the road. For the moment it was just the two of them with only a spindle-legged heron watching them from the far side of the bayou. Remy pressed his palms against her back, splaying his fingers wide. His mouth slanted against Danielle's temptingly, insistently, his tongue seeking and gaining entrance to the honeyed warmth beyond her lips.

Gulping air, he changed angles and kissed her again. His right hand strayed down the curve of her hip then up again to find her breast and fondle her budding nipple, and he smiled and caught her sigh of pleasure with his mouth.

"I've arranged for us to have a little time alone tomorrow," he murmured against her lips. "I want to give you a tour... among other things."

Danielle lifted her sleepy lids and tried to clear her head of the sensual haze Remy had so easily stirred up. "What about the kids?"

"Nanny's day off. My folks have agreed to look after them."

She gave him a dubious look then shrugged. "Well, I guess if they survived raising you, they can survive the Beauvais."

"Very funny." He pinched her bottom through her shorts then smoothed his hand lovingly over the fullness, squeezing gently the way he might test a peach for ripeness. "How about you, *chère*?" he asked, his voice a low purr that lulled and excited her at once. "You gonna survive me?"

I don't know, Danielle thought as his mouth settled down on hers once more. And as she gave herself over to the magic of kissing him she wasn't sure she cared. When she was in his arms nothing else mattered, nothing intruded on her happiness. When he kissed her this way it didn't matter that he was younger and it was all right that she had foolishly fallen in love with him.

"You're sure this is okay?" Danielle asked, casting a worried look back at the dwindling sight of the Doucet house. "I feel guilty about it."

"Jeeze, Danielle, will you give yourself a break?" Remy fiddled with the throttle arm on the outboard motor, revving up the little engine and making the blunt-nosed *bâteau* spurt ahead in the inky water of the bayou. "My parents love havin' kids around," he yelled above the noise. "Papa will take charge of Tinks and Jeremy, Mama and Butler can handle the other three. Sit back and enjoy the ride, darlin'. Or maybe it's the idea of the swamp you don't like, *oui*?"

He held his breath as he waited for her answer. *Dieu*, was he out of his mind? Expecting a sophisticated woman like Danielle to like putting around a swamp in a little boat that reeked of fish. He was just asking to have her hand him his heart on a platter.

"Absolutely not!" Danielle insisted, offended. "After all the places I've been, I'm hardly afraid of this swamp. I've got nine rolls of film with me, and if I don't get a close-up of an alligator, I'm going to hold you personally accountable."

His grin broke across his stormy expression like the sun coming out from behind a thunderhead, and Danielle felt her heart give a little leap. The cynic in her, the sensible star-crossed Hamilton in her, told her she was being a world-class idiot, but the tender spot Remy had touched in her soul turned a deaf ear. She smiled at him and on they went, away from Luck and the campboat, up the Bayou Noir and into the primeval world of the cypress swamp.

When they were deep in the heart of it Remy cut the engine and the mechanical buzz of the motor died off into stillness that was gradually filled by the sounds of nature. The screech of an eagle, the beating of an egret's wings, a splash, a slithering in the duckweed along the bank, the distant hoarse bellow of an alligator. He watched Danielle's face as she looked and listened, and adrenaline pumped through him at the brightness of excitement that shone in her eyes.

"It's wonderful," she whispered, loath to disturb nature with the sound of her voice. "Like the Amazon. Like the Ituri in Zaire. It's fabulous."

There was a flush on her high, perfect cheekbones. Beneath the fragile covering of her tan camisole blouse her breasts rose and fell with her shallow breaths. Her excitement was telegraphed to Remy like electric currents through the heavy air. It simmered in his blood and settled low in his belly.

With the agility of one raised on the water, he moved from his position at the back of the *bâteau* to settle on the plank seat beside Danielle, his hip brushing her hip, his shoulder nudging hers. She looked up at him and the faintest of breezes stirred a curling tendril of silvery-blond hair against her cheek. She had pulled her wild mane back and secured it with a heavy gold barrette, but almost immediately strands had escaped. Now Remy reached up with gentle fingers and brushed the curl back.

Danielle stared at him, at the smoldering passion in his jet eyes, realizing only when her lungs started to burn that she had forgotten to breathe. She shivered a little at the thought of how powerful the pull of desire was between them. They were in the middle of a swamp, for heaven's sake, and all she could think about was having him make hot wild love with her.

He drew a bit of his lower lip between his teeth and nibbled at it as he leaned a little closer. "I love that perfume you're wearing," he murmured in a voice as dark as the bayou.

"Deep Woods Skeeter Stop," she whispered, staring at his mouth.

He sniffed and hummed appreciatively. "My favorite."

"I feel like we're the only people on earth."

"We're the only people here."

She glanced around at the lush jungle. There was something incredibly sensual, incredibly sexual about it—the wild fertile smell, the heat. "Remy . . ."

"Why not, *chère*?" he whispered, his rough voice a caress. "I missed you like hell last night." He stared at her from beneath the fringe of black lashes, his gaze as hot and relentless as the sun that lifted steam off the stagnant water. His smile was so frankly carnal it took her breath away. *"Laissez les bons temps rouler."*

"Yeah, right," Danielle muttered. "We'll let the good times roll us right into the swamp where we will be promptly devoured by alligators."

"Don't you trust me, angel?" he asked, sliding to his knees on the floor of the boat, sliding the strap of her blouse down off her left shoulder.

"About as far as I could throw an elephant," she said, then Remy lifted her breast out of its lacy confines and took the tip of it in his mouth and all reservations were canceled by the instant rush of passion.

Danielle moaned softly and let her head fall back as she brought her hands up to thread her fingers through his shining dark hair. Oh, how she loved the way he made her feel. Each tug of his mouth dragged a little more of her sanity away, stripped away another layer of civilized veneer.

His hand slid up under her loose cotton shirt, pushing aside the soft, sand-colored fabric to brush his fingertips against the satin skin of her inner thigh. She scooted closer to the edge of the bench, tilting her hips forward, inviting him to touch her intimately, and when he tugged aside the leg of her panties and stroked her moist heated flesh, she gasped and moaned a little bit louder.

His fingers moved slowly, rhythmically, savoring her honeyed heat. With his thumb he rubbed the tender bud of her desire as he tested the depth of her readiness, wringing another, louder moan from her. With his free hand he jerked open the front of his jeans, his manhood springing free, swollen and eager.

A sliding sensation dipped through Danielle's stomach and she realized belatedly she was slipping off the bench. Remy gathered her skirt up in fistfuls, anchoring his hands at her waist as he pulled her toward him. She curled her fingers around the back side of the seat for support and eased herself down, her knees brushing his hips as she settled on him. They both groaned as she took him deep into the hot wet silk between her legs.

Remy fastened his mouth on her nipple again and sucked strongly. Danielle panted as a raw jolt of electricity shot directly from her breast to the pit of her stomach and tightened her convulsively around his throbbing shaft, then it was Remy's turn to pant.

They made love slowly, thoroughly. With the rich wildness of nature all around them they did the most natural thing in the world, the most basic of acts between male and female, made beautiful by what was in their hearts. The passion consumed them both, building like a storm on the horizon, hotter and hotter, and when the storm broke and the passion crested, their cries of completion split the air, mingling easily with the sounds of the swamp.

They collapsed against each other, sweating and spent, gasping, lungs in search of oxygen in the sultry air. Eons passed. Danielle mustered a smattering of strength and brushed a mosquito the size of an aircraft carrier off a vital-looking vein on the back of her hand.

"I'll be eaten alive," she mumbled, her love-bruised lips brushing the shell of Remy's ear.

"Mmmm," he groaned, not stirring. "Is that a request?"

She was beyond innuendo. Her brain felt like Yorkshire pudding in her head, blitzed by the onslaught of a zillion sex-starved hormones. "There are mosquitoes out here large enough to qualify as blood-mobiles."

"Wait till you see the snakes." He lifted her back onto the bench, fastened his jeans, then dug into the cooler they'd brought along for an icy can of beer while Danielle straightened her clothes.

"I can't believe we just made love in the middle of a swamp," Danielle said, wonder in her voice and in her eyes as she took in their surroundings all over again before settling her gaze on Remy. He looked rugged and handsome sitting on the plank seat across from her, his dark face flushed. "And it felt so right," she murmured.

Remy's heart pounded against his breastbone like a fist. This was it. This was perfect.

# twelve

**RENARD'S WAS A COMBINATION RESTAURANT,** bar, and dance joint situated along the bank of the bayou, just down the road from the Doucets' house. Set at the edge of the woods, it was a large, unpretentious clapboard structure perched some feet off the ground on cypress stilts. The parking lot was filling up as the dinner crowd arrived.

Remy rolled his eyes and raised his arms toward heaven. "*Mon Dieu*, Danielle, come on in."

Danielle took a step backward. She felt like a fool. She'd dressed to come here, putting on a purple silk tank top and a skirt she had picked up in India that was two flowing layers of vibrant blue gauze with batik designs in soft yellow, dark blue, and fuchsia. But her enthusiasm for the night out had dwindled with every article she put on her freshly showered body. By the time she had fastened on the gold hoop earrings with the painted wooden beads, she had pretty much convinced herself she would rather just crawl under a bed and hide.

This very day the calendar page had flipped, the old body odometer had turned over. She was forty. The sun had pinkened her face, emphasizing those tiny lines and wrinkles miracle skin cream commercials are always lamenting. She had gone over her body with the too critical eye of an artist, sure that the early signs of sagging were there. Her breasts had started to slip. In her hysterical imagination she thought she could actually see gravity dragging them down, and her butt right along with them. She'd turned and given her fanny a smack, watching in the mirror with horror, waiting for it to jiggle like an unleashed Jell-O mold.

She was a forty-year-old woman dressing up for a date with a man who thought the Supremes were soda crackers. Who was she trying to kid?

"Danielle," Remy said in his most cajoling tone. He hooked a finger through the two fine gold necklaces she wore and gently drew her close. "Come on, *chère*. I finally get a chance to take you somewhere, show you somethin', have a nice meal with no baby food involved. Come on." He gave her a lost-puppy look, tilting his head for effect.

Danielle snarled a little through her teeth as her resolve melted and her knees went weak. The blasted man knew exactly how to use all that Cajun charm to his advantage. "Oh, all right."

Remy heaved a sigh of relief, took her by the arm and led her up the steps to the door of the restaurant. The instant the screen door banged shut behind her, she knew something was terribly wrong. All the fine hairs on her arms stood on end. Remy turned her left and propelled her toward a long row of tables against the far wall and she gasped in shock and horror.

"Happy birthday, Auntie Dan-L!" Ambrose shouted, leaping in the air and flinging a fistful of confetti at her.

Tinks and Jeremy and a passel of children she'd never seen before blew on party horns until their faces turned purple, garnering the attention of everyone in the place who might by some miracle have missed the shout.

Also seated at the tables were Butler, Mama and Papa Doucet, and half a dozen other adults Danielle didn't know. All there to celebrate a birthday she would rather have skipped.

She turned around and stared up at Remy, holding herself perfectly still lest she explode into a million furious fragments. "You told these people it was my *birthday*?" She said the word with incredulous emphasis, as if he had told them her bra size.

Remy was wearing that dumbfounded-male look. "I didn't tell them which one!"

She glanced back at her party guests and gave them a wide, brittle smile, speaking right through it. "We'll be right with you, folks." Turning back to Remy, she said, "It's a shame you have to die so young."

"Oh, come on, sugar," he said with a chuckle. "All these folks want to party with you. They're all glad you were born today. I sure am glad you were born today. What difference does it make how many candles are on the cake?"

"There's a cake with *candles*?" she hissed, horrified.

"Naw." Remy winked at her. "Fire marshal wouldn't allow it."

She managed a weak laugh at that, then glanced back at the expectant faces of their dinner party. It was awfully sweet of them all to come—whoever they were. And the children looked so excited. With a little lump in her throat she thought of her last birthday, spent in Tibet with a yak and a goat.

"How old are you, Auntie Dan-L?" Ambrose asked, coming to take her hand and lead her toward the place of honor.

"Thirty-nine," she lied smoothly, murmuring under her breath, "Again."

She was promptly introduced to everyone at the table. There was Remy's oldest sister, Alicia, her husband and three children; youngest sister, Annick, who bore a striking resemblance to Remy's voodoo priestess; a couple in their sixties introduced as Tante Fanchon and Uncle Sos. Sitting to Remy's left was his twin sister, Giselle, her husband, and their twin five-year-old daughters. Absent from the Doucet brood were youngest brother, Andre, and eldest, Etienne, better known as Lucky.

With introductions out of the way everyone fell into animated conversation. Much to Danielle's relief, she discovered the Doucets pounced on the slightest reason to get together and have fun, so there was no embarrassing fuss made over her. Beyond the initial announcement and heraldry, little mention was made of the occasion, which suited her just fine.

She listened to the chatter around her, slightly distracted, her emotions in a turmoil. She studied Remy's sisters, all of them fussing happily over children. Annick, who had none of her own, had adopted Eudora for the night, much to Eudora's delight. As they waited for dinner to be served, Remy entertained two of his nieces with the G-rated version of his excursion into the swamp with Danielle.

"Auntie Danielle," Jeremy said, appearing at her side to tug at her arm. "You'll never guess what me and Tinks saw today."

"Hmm? What was that?" she asked absently, lost in her own uncertainty.

"We went into the woods with Papa Doucet and he showed us all kinds of animals and—"

"Oh, that's neat, Jeremy." She gave him a vacant smile. "But you'd better go sit down now. I think our food is coming."

"Yeah, but I want to show you—"

"Maybe later, okay?"

The boy sighed and stomped back to his seat as a pair of waitresses brought out their dinner.

Renard's was a comfortable place with natural wood paneling and big screened windows. The tablecloths were red and white checked plastic. Statues and pictures of foxes abounded. The place was doing a booming business. If the waitresses' figures were anything to go by, the meal promised to be as delicious as it smelled. Both were on the plump side with cheeks rosy from the heat in the kitchen. All the Doucets were familiar with the young women, calling them by name, asking after their families. They chatted as they served, their musically accented voices rising above the general din of plates and silverware and talk from other tables. The array of dishes was served family-style at the table.

The dish that caught Danielle's interest was the steaming platter piled high with boiled crawfish. Remy instructed her on the fine art of eating the small dark red crustaceans that looked like miniature lobsters, showing her how to break off the tail, crack the shell with thumb and forefinger, and dig out the rich white meat inside.

"And then," he said with a wicked gleam in his eyes. "If you're a real Cajun, you suck the fat out of the head."

"Whoa, forget it!"

"Ah, me, how we ever gonna make a Cajun outa you, *chère*?"

"You aren't if it involves sucking fat out of the head of a decapod," Danielle said dryly. "I've eaten a lot of weird stuff in a lot of weird places, but even I draw the line somewhere."

That won her a round of good-natured laughter from everyone but Remy, who merely forced a smile and sat back in his chair. He hadn't needed the reminder of her footloose lifestyle, not tonight when his heart was so set on asking her to stay forever. His stomach churned a little and it had nothing to do with the generous amounts of spicy food being served at the table. It did a barrel roll as Alicia's husband asked Danielle to tell them about some of the exotic places she'd been.

"I forgive you, *cher*," Giselle said, leaning close.

Remy looked at her as if she had just sprung up out of the ground.

His sister's eyes sparkled with the wisdom of a twin. "You're in love with her, yes?"

There was no point in denying it. Giselle was too in tune with his feelings, as he was with hers. "*Oui*," he whispered, swallowing hard.

"Then I forgive you for taking the name of my agency in vain."

"Hey," he huffed indignantly. "I'll have you know I'm a damn good nanny. I may just keep this job."

Giselle sniffed and rolled her eyes, then glanced around him at Danielle. "She's very pretty. She loves you too, yes?"

He forced a grin. "I hope so."

His twin was hardly fooled. She leaned up and kissed his cheek, her dark eyes full of understanding. For just an instant they shared an aching, uncertain heart, then Giselle smiled and said, "Poor Danielle, she's got no chance against all that charm of yours, *cher*. She'll be a Doucet before she knows it, she will."

"I hope you're right," he murmured. But as his gaze turned toward Danielle and he watched her tell a story about photographing the Efe tribe of the African Congo, all his hopes twisted into a knot of apprehension. She looked so vibrant when she spoke of those faraway places. Could he really expect her to give all that up and put down roots along the bayou when her heart had been so restless for so long?

At length the dinner plates and empty platters were cleared away by the same plump smiling waitresses. A band took the stage on the other side of the big open room and began to tune up, plucking and sawing at fiddle strings, strumming a chord on a guitar, checking the keys of the small Evangeline accordion. The level of excitement started to rise, hitting a crescendo of clapping and whistling at the opening bars of "Allons à Lafayette."

Half the tables emptied, their occupants spilling onto the dance floor in a flood of humanity. Smiles flashed, heads bobbed, feet shuffled as they made their way around the floor in variations of the two-step. The music Danielle was beginning to love was loud and happy-sounding, the little accordion huffing and puffing between its master's hands, the triangle player bouncing with the beat, the fiddle player wailing out the French lyrics with gusto.

Danielle smiled as she listened. It was almost impossible not to move in time with the beat. As she watched the patrons of Renard's dance and laugh and chug down cold beer, she felt herself getting caught up in the atmosphere. She had been many places and seen many things, but she had fallen head over heals in love with Louisiana, with the people and the culture, the music and the land. For the first time in a long time she had begun to fantasize about staying put. It scared the hell out of her.

The raucous two-step eventually gave way to a graceful waltz. Remy rose and held a hand out to her. "How about it, sugar?"

Danielle had waltzed with princes and playboys, but their memories paled into oblivion as Remy took her in his arms. His dark eyes never left hers as he swept her around the floor, moving with a fluid natural grace no dance instructor could have taught him. Danielle found her heart fluttering and shook her head a little in amazement. The waltz was hardly a sexy dance. It was old-fashioned and formal, straight-backed and straitlaced. But she couldn't have felt more aware of Remy had they been writhing out the Lambada. And her heart swelled with love for him and her uncertainties and reservations swelled right along with it.

Like a knucklehead she'd gone and fallen in love with a younger man, a man who had pursued her with the motto of "let the good times roll." They'd had a good time. He hadn't asked for more and she would have had to have been completely obtuse to think he might ask. He was a family man, domestic for all his wily wicked charm. What would he want with her—an aging photographer with a curse on her head? She might have made an interesting diversion for the summer, but he wasn't liable to think of her as making much of a wife. No, Remy would want to look for a sweet young thing adept at cooking and cuddling babies. Cuddling a Nikon wasn't going to rank high on his list of priorities. It would probably be just below "in need of a face-lift."

Really, she thought, mentally tearing little bits off her heart, he should be looking for someone like the dark-haired little gal who was presently dancing in the corner with his twin nieces. She looked about twenty-five. Her cheeks were still slightly pudgy with the bloom of youth. Her long hair hung in a single braid down her back like a length of silken rope. The little girls she was indulging looked completely enamored of her—and she of them; as the music ended she wrapped them both in an exuberant hug. Then she looked up and caught Danielle staring and her dark eyes flashed with unmistakable dislike. Danielle frowned, unable to pull her gaze away from the acrimonious look even as Remy steered her out of the flow of traffic to the very edge of the dance floor.

"Danielle," Remy started, then choked a little as his heart leaped into his throat. He was going to do it—right here, right now—he was going to tell her. So they'd only know each other a short time, that didn't make a damn bit of difference. He was dead certain of his feelings. "Danielle," he started again. "I lo—"

"Hey, Remy!"

He squeezed his eyes shut just briefly, as if a sudden knifing pain had gone through his head. Marie. The tireless Marie. Marie the Undaunted. Marie "I Want Us to Get Married" Broussard. She couldn't have chosen a worse moment to show up if someone had given her a list of ten ways to ruin his evening.

"How about a dance, *cher*?" she said, blatantly ignoring the fact that he was holding another woman's hand.

He started to scowl at her and was about to tell her no when Danielle suddenly backed away. He looked at her, surprised and annoyed and confused. She gave him a smile as phony as a three-dollar bill and said, "Go ahead, Remy. My arthritis is acting up anyway."

Marie latched on to him with all the tenacity of a snapping turtle, her small hand clenching his in a fierce grip. She jerked him out into the throng of dancers, as purposeful as a tugboat hauling a barge up the Mississippi. He gave Danielle one last befuddled look before she disappeared from view.

Danielle stood at the edge of the crowd watching even though it was torture for her. The dark-haired young woman fit perfectly with Remy. She was petite and feminine, looking virginal and bridelike in her white sundress. She stared up at him with affection and determination.

"Auntie Danielle," Jeremy said, tugging at the leather cord of her belt. "Will you come and see now? It's so neat and I know the way and I'll bet you've never seen anything like it even in Africa."

She looked down at her nephew, perversely annoyed that he had distracted her from wallowing in self-pity. "What, Jeremy?"

"Will you come now?"

"Come where?"

"Out to see our secret."

"Jeremy, it's dark out. I'll come see it tomorrow. Why don't you go see if Tinks will dance with you?"

He regarded her with utter disgust, turned and stormed away. Danielle sighed. Another strike against her in the child-rearing category. She looked back out at the dancers, wincing as she caught sight of Remy and his little partner.

"I could look that young again," she muttered to herself. "With the aid of a belt sander and a tube of caulk."

"Oh, that Marie Broussard," Giselle said, shaking her head with disapproval as she took up the spot Jeremy had vacated. "She's been chasin' him so long you'd think her legs woulda give out by now."

Danielle's head snapped around and she had to strain to sound nonchalant. "They've known each other a long time?"

"Always. They went to school together." Giselle rolled her dark eyes and tilted her head to the angle of conspiracy and said, "You think she might have taken the hint by now. *Mais non*, she still thinks he's playin' hard to get. Some folks just need to be hit over the head with a thing, you know?"

"Yeah," Danielle whispered. "Some folks do. If you'll excuse me, Giselle, I think I'm going to step outside for a breath of fresh air."

She didn't wait for a response. She didn't even chance a look at Remy's sister for fear she might see pity in her eyes. She mowed a path to the front door and nearly stumbled down the steps in her haste to get away from the people and the music. Her sandals scuffed over the crushed shell of the parking lot as she walked out toward the bayou.

As she stared out at the black water she gave an involuntary little moan. Her feelings felt like they'd been run through a blender on puree. In the course of a matter of days they'd been jerked out of the compartment she had relegated them to, turned inside out and upside down. This was all Suzannah's fault. If it hadn't been for her half-sister, she would have right now been happily holed up in some remote corner of the world in a photographic frenzy, wearing out her Nikon shooting pictures of boulder formations and window casings. Well, "happily" might not have been the right word to use, she reflected, but at least she would have felt calm and in control. She wouldn't have been doing something stupid like falling in love with younger men.

"Hey, Danielle, where you at?"

Remy's low, rough voice came to her with all the beckoning warmth of a flannel blanket on a chill night. She wanted to wrap herself in it and shut the world out. The cynic in her sneered.

"I'm right here," she said, not turning around.

He shuffled up behind her and slid his arms around her waist, dropping his chin down on her shoulder. "Don't be ticked off at me 'cause I danced with Marie. She's like a pit bull, that one. Once she latches on it's hard to shake her."

"I'm not mad," she said flatly. "You're my nanny not my personal slave. Dance with whoever you like."

"I like you." He twirled her around to face him and pulled

her into his arms for a slow dance to music he provided himself, his voice rising softly above the hum of insects and the far distant bellow of an alligator. *"Demander comme moi je t'aimais, ma jolie fille."*

"What's that one about?" Danielle asked dryly. "Cooking muskrats on an open fire and the treachery of women?"

He tilted his head back and gave her a sober look as he translated. " 'Ask how much I love you, my pretty girl.' "

"Maybe you should sing that one to the long-suffering Marie."

"I don't love Marie. I love you."

Danielle was certain her heart had stopped. Catastrophic full cardiac arrest. She swayed a little on her feet as she stared at him. He'd said it. Heaven help her. The fool in her had wanted to hear those words so desperately and now he'd said them. Now what was she supposed to do? Be selfish and grasp what he was offering or be noble and give him up for his own good?

She stared at him and considered as her emotions wrestled inside her. He was so handsome and so sweet. He made her feel things she had only read about in *Cosmo*. Did she really want to give all that up? No. She was by nature a selfish person. Hadn't she been told as much? Hadn't she drummed that idea into her own psyche over the last year? Why should she change at this late date? Why shouldn't she just throw caution and good sense to the wind and indulge herself? Why shouldn't she tell Remy she loved him?

"Remy, I—"

"Auntie Danielle!"

Danielle looked past Remy's broad shoulder to see Tinks barreling across the parking lot as fast as her little feet could fly. Her face was stark-white in the dark.

"Auntie Danielle! Come quick! Jeremy's hurt real bad!"

The emergency room of the community hospital in Luck was painted a shade of green guaranteed to make a person sick if he weren't already ill to begin with. The chairs in the waiting room were molded plastic, the floor covered with a hard gray linoleum that amplified the sound of pacing footsteps.

Danielle could not sit, unable to contain her worries to a chair. Back and forth the length of the reception desk, her arms wrapped tightly around her as if she were trying to physically hold herself together. Remy had tried to console her, but she had shrugged him off. He had finally relegated himself to a chair, pulled his cigarette out of his pocket and lit it, drawing owlish stares from his family. The entire herd of Doucets had followed the ambulance, with the exception of Giselle and her husband, who had taken all the children to Remy's parents' house to wait for word of Jeremy's condition.

*This is all my fault*, Danielle thought for the millionth time. If only she had paid more attention to Jeremy when he tried to get her to go outside with him. If only she had let him tell her the story of what he and Tinks had discovered on their nature hike with Papa Doucet. If only she hadn't been so wrapped up in her own worries, wallowing in self-pity because it was her fortieth birthday. Now, for all she knew, Jeremy might not live to see his tenth.

They had found him in the dense forest behind Renard's, unconscious, a gash in his forehead and a snake bite on the back of his small hand. He and Tinks had snuck away from the dance, bent on bringing their find to Danielle if they couldn't get Danielle to their find—an abandoned quail's nest with eggs still in it. According to Tinks, they had swiped a flashlight out of the minivan and stolen off to the woods to get the nest. Unfortunately, a copperhead had chosen the same time to make his dinner of the abandoned eggs. Jeremy had been bitten just as he'd reached for the nest. Terrified, the two children had turned and run back in the direction of Renard's, but Jeremy, possibly already feeling the effects of the snake's venom, had stumbled and fallen, striking his head.

Every time she closed her eyes Danielle could see the terrible image of her nephew, the mischief maker, the human tornado, lying so unnaturally still on the ground. And it was all her fault. Her stomach turned as she wondered how she would ever again be able to face Suzannah.

As if her thoughts had conjured up her sister, the waiting room doors slid open and Suzannah burst in with Courtland right behind her. Danielle stopped her pacing, stunned into motionlessness, and stared, thinking somewhere in the back of her mind that the pair didn't look as if they'd just come from the Caribbean. There were no signs of recent fun in the sun. They were dressed casually, as if they had just been called from a quiet evening at home. Courtland's pale hair was sticking up in back as if he might have fallen asleep on the couch while reading the newspaper. Suzannah's patrician features were scrubbed clean of cosmetics.

Suzannah rushed toward her, her flame-red hair flying behind her, her big gray eyes shadowed with worry. "Danielle! How is he? Have you heard anything?"

Danielle stared at her sister, dumbfounded. "Suzannah? Courtland? How did you get here?"

There was a flash of guilt in Suzannah's eyes as she exchanged a look with Butler, but the explanation was put on hold. The doors to the emergency room swung open and the doctor came out asking for Jeremy's parents. The trio disappeared into the nether regions of the hospital, leaving the rest of the group wondering if the news was good or bad.

Danielle wheeled on Butler, feeling she had somehow been played for a fool. "What exactly is going on here, Butler? There's no way in hell Suzannah and Courtland could have gotten here from Paradise Island in the ten minutes since you called them."

The old retainer shifted uncomfortably on his chair, his

cheeks flushing to a color that nearly matched his hair. "Och, well now, lass, they werna exactly that far away."

"How far away were they *exactly*?"

Butler stared down at his shoes. "Ar—um—the Grande Belle Inn. Here in Luck since yesterday. At the Pontchartrain Hotel before that."

"There was never any trip to the islands, was there?" Danielle asked quietly.

He looked up at her and sighed, his eyes so full of pity Danielle almost couldn't bear it. "No lass. Your sister was worried. Aye, we all were worried about you. You hie yourself off to godforsaken Tibet. We see not hide nor hair of you for a year. We had to do something to get you back amongst the living. Suzannah came up with the notion of having you stay with the bairns to prove to yourself you could do it."

"To prove that I could do it," Danielle whispered, appalled and humiliated. "You made a royal fool of me. Thank you very much. And look what happened." She swung an arm in the direction of the doors to the ER. "I said from the first I was the last person Suzannah should have called on to stay with her children and I was right."

"This wasn't your fault, Danielle," Remy said, pushing himself to his feet.

"Wasn't it?" she asked, turning tortured eyes toward him.

"He'd been told not to go into the woods alone."

"He wouldn't have been alone if I had listened to him, if I had been paying attention to him instead of worrying about myself. Hell, he only wanted to impress me and I couldn't bother to pay enough attention to him to realize that."

"He wouldn't have gone out there at all if I hadn't taken him there first, *chère*," Remy's father said, his dark eyes solemn, the line of his mouth grim above his square jaw.

"You don't understand," she mumbled, tears rising up in her throat to choke her.

Remy started to put an arm around her, but she shrugged him off again. She was responsible, she should have to bear the pain alone. She'd been right to leave after the tragedy in London. She wasn't fit for the role of parent, surrogate or otherwise. In London it had been her art that had distracted her from her duty. Here it had been her love life. Either way the proof was there: she was simply too self-absorbed to be reliable in a parental situation. She belonged alone. Like many a Hamilton before her, it seemed she was destined to be alone.

She had known that for some time now, had accepted it. Then Suzannah had lured her to New Orleans and she had been given a glimpse of the life she would never have. It seemed fate had an exceedingly cruel sense of humor, she thought as she leaned a shoulder against the plate-glass window and stared out at the parking lot. During this time with the children and Remy she had been forced to dig up every emotion she had. She'd banished demons she had never wanted to face and fallen in love with a dark-haired Cajun devil who was wrong for her from the word go.

Now she would have to cram all those feelings back into their compartment like springy trick snakes in a can. For the first time ever her restless heart had longed for a home, but she was going to have to tear up the fragile roots that had already begun to grow and move on. She was going to end up playing it noble after all, she thought, her mouth twisting at the irony. She would leave the children to their parents, leave Butler to meddle in someone else's life. And she would leave Remy to that young, sweet-faced, wonderful-with-children Marie. And she would go back to the one thing she did very well or cared enough about. It was just too bad for her that her muse suddenly seemed lacking as a companion.

"Danielle, don't do this to yourself, sugar," Remy whispered.

His reflection loomed up directly behind hers in the glass,

broad and strong, young and handsome. And her heart squeezed unmercifully at the thought of losing him. Oh, why couldn't they just have left her to her nomadic, solitary life? It was so much easier to live without something when you didn't know what you were missing. Now she would know and the sense of loss would be with her always.

A nurse came through the double doors to tell them that Jeremy would have to remain in the hospital for a day or two, but that he would be all right. Murmurs and sighs of relief cut through the tension in the waiting room like a sudden cooling breeze on an unbearably sultry day. Remy lifted his hands to Danielle's shoulders and rubbed at the knotted muscles.

"See?" he whispered. "He's gonna be fine."

"No thanks to me," Danielle murmured. She ducked out from under his touch and walked out of the hospital into the warm Louisiana night.

Remy started after her, but Butler called him back.

"Let her go, laddie. Give her a wee moment to herself."

Remy stopped himself at the door, not altogether convinced of Butler's wisdom, but not wanting to push Danielle too hard either.

And in that wee moment Danielle slipped around to the front of the building, got into the only taxi in town, handed the driver two hundred-dollar bills, and settled in for the ride to New Orleans, leaving Luck and Remy and her heart behind.

# thirteen

**DANIELLE THREW OPEN THE WOODEN SHUT**ters and stepped out onto her balcony. The scents of goats and car exhaust fumes, human sweat and cooking meat, all combined into one hot blast of air that made her think of a monkey cage at a zoo on a steamy rainy day. She staggered back into the suite and collapsed on the rattan sofa, feeling as green as new grass.

Maybe Madagascar had been a bad choice.

She had first gone to New York, but Manhattan had been too loud, the sounds too discordant. The smell of garbage smoldering on the curbs had been an affront after sweet olive and roses. Off she had flown to Paris, but the sound of Parisian French had somehow pained her heart. It lacked the warmth of its Cajun relative. And every time she turned and caught a glimpse of a man with wicked dark eyes and a black mustache her heart went into a dangerous irregular kind of rhythm. So much for France. After wandering aimlessly around Switzerland, Italy, and Greece, she had found her way to Bangkok. But the tinny sound of gongs and high-pitched oriental melodies had clashed with her idea of what a sultry night should sound like—New Orleans jazz and the basso blast of a barge horn on the river—and Bangkok had been left behind.

She had settled on Madagascar—Antananarivo, a place she couldn't even pronounce the name of—largely because she hadn't thought she could stomach a longer flight. And before she could change her mind, she had called her agent and told him she was going to do a photographic essay on lemurs. She'd been there a week and had yet to open her camera case, let alone make the necessary arrangements to go into the forest. Merrick would be peeved that no photos of lemurs were forthcoming, but Danielle couldn't work up the energy to care.

It had been two months since she'd picked up her trusty Nikon. Not since that day in the cypress swamp with Remy had she had the urge to take any photographs. All she'd really had the energy for lately was crying and throwing up. For the first time in her life her art held no appeal, offered no comfort or distraction. Her muse had been completely overwhelmed by her misery. She felt abandoned.

Never in her life had she been homesick. She had never consciously called anyplace home. But she missed Louisiana with an ache that went soul-deep. She longed for the sights, the smells, the sounds, the people. Most of all she, the perpetual loner, the independent woman of the world, missed the people she had left behind.

She had called Suzannah after her hasty departure to check on Jeremy and to apologize. Suzannah had done some apologizing of her own for duping Danielle in the first place. Danielle didn't harbor a grudge. Suzannah's heart had been in the right place. She had entrusted her children to Danielle's care to involve her with life again and to show her nothing bad would happen. Danielle was only sorry her sister's trust had been so misplaced.

Suzannah had asked her to come back, but Danielle had declined. It was better for everybody that she stay away.

News of Remy had been painfully sparse. When he had realized she'd left without so much as a good-bye, he had pulled a vanishing act of his own. Butler, having undergone a miraculous recovery from his back injury, had stayed on to help Suzannah with the children.

The children. Heaven help her, she even missed the little monsters.

Feeling the need to get really depressed, Danielle reached for the box of photographs she had been dragging around the world with her. On her flight from Luck she had stopped at the campboat just long enough to grab her camera bag, which had been loaded with memories condensed into little canisters of film. Ambrose in his Mardi Gras mask and a blue cape, sweetly innocent and strangely noble, a mysterious dog in the background. Jeremy and Tinks, eyes glowing as they contemplated a way to get into a pen full of monkeys at the zoo. Dahlia stealing a glance at her own reflection in a window, looking a little uncertain about leaving childhood behind. Little Eudora, duck fuzz hair sticking up, grinning after taking a bite out of Remy's Sno-Kone, her lips outlined in blue like a clown's makeup; Remy laughing at her, his dark face bright with the joy in his eyes. Remy pointing out a heron to Jeremy as they sat on the deck of the campboat. Remy in a rocking chair, holding the baby in his brawny arms, her head pillowed on his broad shoulder, both of them sound asleep. Remy squinting off across the bayou. Remy . . .

The tears squeezed themselves out, clinging to her lashes then rolling down her cheeks to drip onto the oversized gray T-shirt she wore. She'd never missed anybody the way she missed him. She was too old for him, too wrong in all the ways that mattered most. But her heart hadn't heeded those logical reasons. It seemed her heart was set on him being the one great love of her life and she had had to leave him behind.

"Dammit," she swore, smacking the end table with the flat of her hand in an eruption of frustration. Her soul wrung out a few more tears. She hated being noble and unselfish, giving up the only man who had ever stilled the restlessness in her. Why couldn't she have run true to form and hung on to him for her own selfish reasons?

Maybe this was the Hamilton curse resurrecting itself, making her behave out of character just to fulfill itself. Or maybe it was love. She loved Remy Doucet till she hurt right down to her toenails. Could she really have saddled him with an aging, domestically inept, career-obsessed artist when she loved him so much? No. So here she sat in the middle of Madagascar, alone.

Of course, she wasn't completely alone, technically speaking. A tiny person had taken up residence inside her. She wasn't much for conversation, but she certainly made her presence known, Danielle thought as another wave of nausea rose in her throat. A doctor had pronounced her pregnant, just shrugging when Danielle had argued the impossibility of it, as if to say "so much for the reliability of birth control."

She was carrying Remy's baby. The miracle of it awed her. The reality of it scared her spitless. Fresh tears flooded her eyes as a fresh batch of self-doubt swelled inside her like rising bread dough. She was the absolute last woman on earth who deserved to be a mother. She had proved that fact tragically.

But if she couldn't have Remy, maybe she could have this small part of him, this little person she had created with him during a night of sweet loving. She pictured the baby having his dark hair and eyes, a dimple in her plump cheek as she grinned, and Danielle thought her heart would burst with longing. Her little part of Remy, her reminder of a love that had healed her soul and brightened her life.

But who would that be fair to? She wasn't fit to raise a child on her own, and Remy, who had many times expressed his desire to be a father, would be denied the experience of knowing his own child. Her spirits plummeted again. She picked up another saltine and munched it morosely, staring unseeing at the splash of antique-gold light the morning sun spilled on the rough plaster wall across the room.

Her hand strayed to her belly and she had a sudden vision of herself rounded and heavy with child. She would have to tell Remy, of course, but she would burn to a crisp in perdition before she would give her baby to the doe-eyed Marie Broussard or any other young, incredibly pretty woman Remy chose for a wife.

Her lifestyle didn't leave room for a baby? She would change her lifestyle, she declared resolutely. Heaven knew she had lost her taste for exotic places, anyway. She would settle. Her career distracted her from other duties? She would try to cut back on the amount of work she did. She would do her best to domesticate her muse and she would hire a full-time nurse. She would be a single mother, but there was no reason she had to handle the job alone, especially when she was so afraid she would botch it. She knew her own limitations. That gave her an advantage, didn't it? She would do what every good rich girl did in the face of adversity—hire help.

Her burst of enthusiasm fizzled at the thought that there would probably be no dark-eyed Cajun rascals coming to interview for the job. Her emotions rode the roller coaster back to the bottom.

For a time after she'd fled Louisiana she had fantasized about Remy coming after her, but he hadn't. He had no doubt come to his senses, going weak with relief over his narrow escape from her. She recalled his endearing confession in the swamp after they had made love, that he was a geologist. Perhaps he'd found a job at last with an oil company.

Danielle struggled up from the low sofa, grabbed her purse off the coffee table, and headed for the door. There was no point in sitting here brooding. She could brood while she was sightseeing. Maybe Remy was gone from her life, but the rest of the world was still out there. Her stomach had settled and there was an open-air market just down the street. She'd go for a walk, find something to eat, and when she came back she would call the airlines and book a seat on the next flight headed in the general direction of the United States. She had a life to get on with, broken heart or no broken heart.

Remy barely spared a glance for the ancient sights of Antananarivo. He was dimly aware of the putty-colored houses piled up and down the steep hillsides, looking like an elaborate sandcastle city. He was acutely aware of the congestion of the traffic and he cursed under his breath as the cab slowed again. He'd been two steps behind Danielle everywhere she'd gone. He couldn't escape the urgent feeling that if he didn't get to her in the next second, he would be too late again.

He kicked himself mentally for not going after her that night at the hospital. He would have been saved a great deal of emotional turmoil and pain had he caught her there and demanded she marry him. Instead, he had let her go and then spent the next month feeling sorry for himself because she had taken off. He had wasted all kinds of time telling himself it was probably for the best because Danielle loved to travel and he couldn't bear to leave home. But home had seemed an empty, lonely place without her, and he had finally admitted he didn't want to live without her, even if it meant living in Antarctica.

The cab had stopped altogether and the cabbie was casually rolling a cigarette. This had all the earmarks of third world gridlock. Remy swore again and stuck his head out his window, trying to get a gander at the source of the problem, when a flash of silver-blond caught his eye and his heart began to race. Up ahead, half a block away, an unruly ponytail was bobbing down the street. He caught a glimpse of long legs and a camera bag and he leapt from the cab, throwing a wad of money through the window at the startled driver.

"Danielle! Hey, Danielle!"

Danielle slowed her step and shook her head, certain she was hallucinating. But the shout came again, whiskey-hoarse and masculine. The throng on the sidewalk flowed around her like a river around a boulder as she turned slowly and looked back.

"Remy," she whispered, as if saying his name louder would somehow break the spell and make him vanish.

He stopped a full six feet away from her and stood there looking rumpled and road-weary and uncertain. His eyes were bloodshot and the shadow of his beard looked blue against cheeks that were thinner than she remembered. He wore jeans and sneakers and a pale pink oxford shirt creased with the marks of sleeping in a plane seat. She had never seen anything more wonderful.

He dropped his duffle bag and said, "I don't know if I oughta kiss you or turn you over my knee for all the heartache you've caused me, *chère*."

Danielle solved the issue by swaying unsteadily on her feet and keeling over unceremoniously. His heart in his throat, Remy jumped to catch her.

"Danielle? Sweetheart? Are you all right?"

"What are you doing here?" she mumbled, trying to bring him into focus.

"Holdin' you," he murmured, his lips just above hers, his dark eyes intense. "And it feels pretty damn good."

"I mean, how did you find me?" The strength came back to her knees and she straightened, but Remy made no move to release her. They stood thigh to thigh, breast to chest, in the middle of the sidewalk.

"Butler tracked you down through your agent," he explained. "*Mon Dieu, chère*, you get around. It's gonna take me a while to get used to this pace."

"What do you mean?"

"I mean I love you," he murmured. "I was plenty ticked off when you split that night at the hospital without even sayin' good-bye. I went out to the swamp and stayed with my brother Lucky for a while. But the more I listened to his grumbling about how rotten women are, the more I missed you."

Danielle stared at him, bemused, not sure whether she should thank him or slap his face.

"It took me a while to get used to the idea of leavin' Lou'siana," he went on. "Leavin' my family. But the more I thought about it the more I realized how much I want *you* to be my family." He paused, screwing up his courage, giving Danielle warning that what he was about to say was momentous. "I want to marry you, Danielle."

Her head swam at the idea and for an instant Danielle was certain she was going to go down for the count, but she locked her knees and managed to remain upright. Lord, what a delicious fantasy. To marry Remy and live happily ever after. But it was just that—a fantasy.

"No, Remy," she murmured, backing out of his embrace, shaking her head sadly. "I can't let you do that."

"Let me?" he said, incredulous, jamming his hands at his waist. He looked like a man at the frayed end of his temper. "I been chasin' you all over the ever-lovin' world! I've borrowed enough money to fly so much I've got enough Frequent Flier miles for a free trip to the moon! I finally run you to ground and you tell me you can't *let* me marry you?"

"You don't want to marry me," she said, shaking her head as she began shuffling backward toward her hotel. "I'm old and I have a curse on me. You could do lots better, Remy. Marry Marie Broussard. She seemed like a nice girl."

"Mebbe I don't want a girl. Mebbe I want a woman," he said, advancing aggressively. His hand shot out and he caught her by the wrist and hauled her up against him again. "Mebbe I don't give a fat rat's rump about some moldy old Scottish curse. I want you, angel, and I don't care if I have to go to the ends of the earth to get you. Now what do you think?"

Danielle stared up at him as all her blood drained into her feet. "I think I'm going to throw up."

"Really, Remy," Danielle said, coming out of the bathroom, her bare feet slapping on the cool tile floor. Her head was a little clearer now that she had brushed her teeth and splashed some cold water on her cheeks. She felt much more capable of talking him out of ruining his life. "I'm impossible to live with. I'm selfish and self-absorbed. I'm set in my ways, and I'm pretty sure my fanny has started to fall. Why would you want to get stuck with all that?"

Remy lounged on top of the hunter-green bedspread, his back against the rattan headboard, a suspiciously wise gleam in his dark eyes. He gave her a lopsided smile, his dimple cutting into his cheek as he pushed himself up off the bed and sauntered toward her. "Because I love you and you love me and if your fanny's gonna fall I wanna be the one to catch it."

He wrapped his arms around her, his hands sliding down over her hips to cup her bottom through her shorts. He waggled his eyebrows. "Feels pretty good to me. What is this really all about?"

"I don't understand," Danielle whispered, suddenly serious, suddenly overcome by the emotions that had pushed her to run away in the first place. She looked up at him, her gray eyes somber and uncertain. "I don't understand why you would still want me after what happened."

"Danielle, what happened was an accident. It wasn't your

fault—not what happened to Jeremy or what happened to your friend's baby. Bad things happen, sugar. Mebbe Jeremy wouldn't have gotten hurt if you'd gone with him, mebbe you would have gotten hurt instead. That would have been Jeremy's fault then, yes?"

"Well, no, of course not—"

"You're not infallible, Danielle. Everybody makes mistakes."

"I just don't want me to be one of yours," she murmured, fear and misery crowding the words in her throat and pushing at the tears behind her eyes. She loved him so much, wanted him so badly, but she wanted his happiness above her own. "I want you to be happy, Remy."

His heart gave a big thump and he felt moisture rise in his own eyes. Some selfish, self-absorbed woman she was—putting his needs first. He'd been terrified that when he finally caught up with her, he would discover that she didn't really need him, didn't really love him, that she'd been glad to get away from Louisiana and the threat of a family. But while she'd been in the bathroom tossing her cookies, he had made a quick reconnaissance of her apartment, finding the most telling evidence he could have hoped for—the photographs. Danielle unmasked her own feelings in her art, whether the picture depicted the loneliness of a closed door or her tender love for a child. What he'd seen had been emotions unfurling, longing revealed, love. So much love in that restless heart of hers just waiting for him to claim it.

He brushed a wild strand of angel's hair back from her perfect cheekbone and said. "I'll only be happy with you. Can't you see that, angel? I love you more than Lou'siana. I missed you so much I thought I'd die of it. I don't care if we have to live in Manhattan or Madagascar. Home is where the heart is, and my heart is with you, Danielle."

Two fat teardrops spilled over the dam and down her cheeks. Her soft mouth trembled. "Oh, Remy, I'd live anywhere with you if I thought it could work, but there's my muse to consider—"

"Tell your muse to move over, baby," he said on a sexy growl. " 'Cause I'm not givin' you up."

"But you're so young and—"

Remy cut her off, stepping back and holding up a hand. "We're gonna settle this age thing right here and now. You got a pen?"

"A pen?"

He nodded impatiently, spying one himself and snatching it off the night stand. He dug two fingers into the hip pocket of his jeans and produced a folded piece of paper which he opened and spread out on the small round table by the window. Danielle watched, bemused, as he pulled a small bottle of White-Out from the breast pocket of his shirt. "What is that?"

"Your birth certificate, courtesy of Butler, God bless him."

"My—?" She peered over his shoulder as he pulled the little brush out of the White-Out and stroked it with an artistic flourish over the year of her birth. "You can't do that!"

Remy grinned like a pirate. "Why not? Loosen up, *chère*. Let the good times roll!"

Danielle laughed, caught between hysteria and bliss, as Remy took up the pen and carefully inked in 1960.

"There you go, darlin'. We are now officially the same age." He rose and handed her the document, his dark eyes sparkling with wicked merriment.

Danielle looked down at the paper in her hand and smiled. "Gee, I feel younger already."

Remy slid his arms around her waist and started a slow dance to some secret music in his head. "Do you feel like gettin' married?"

She looked at him, amazed and in love. The man was determined; who was she to argue? He was handsome and sexy and wicked and wise beyond his years. She would have had to have been an idiot to give all that up. "Yeah, I do," she murmured, swaying in time with him.

Remy pulled her closer and kissed her, savoring the taste of her as if she were his first and last sip of a life-giving elixir. Danielle wound her arms around his neck and basked in the joy of touching him again. She felt renewed. The glow of love filled her with golden warmth. Her heart swelled in her breast as she thought of telling him about the baby . . . later . . . after they'd given each other a proper lover's welcome.

"You know," Remy said, lifting his head just enough to speak. "I suddenly feel in need of a long, long shower."

Danielle gave him a sultry, sexy look. "You need any help with that, *cher*?"

"Oh, yeah," he drawled, his dark eyes dancing. "Absolutely."

# about the author

TAMI HOAG'S novels have appeared regularly on national bestseller lists since the publication of her first book in 1988. She lives in Los Angeles.